TIME LOTTERY

NANCY MOSER

ISBN 1-58660-587-9

Acquisitions & Editorial Director: Mike Nappa
Editorial Consultant: Liz Duckworth
Project Editor: Jeff Gerke
Art Director: Robyn Martins
Cover: Lookout Design

Published by Barbour Publishing, Inc., P.O. Box 719, Uhrichsville, OH 44683, www.barbourbooks.com

Our mission is to publish and distribute inspirational products offering exceptional value and biblical encouragement to the masses.

Printed in the United States of America
5 4 3 2

DEDICATION

To my family. I am incredibly blessed.
Given a second chance,
I wouldn't change a thing.

PROLOGUE

There is a time for everything,
and a season for every activity under heaven.

ECCLESIASTES 3:1

The front door was open.

Alexander MacMillan shook his head, peeved that Holly would be so careless. They'd made an agreement: When Holly was home alone with Andrew, the front door would remain locked. You did not live in a five-thousand-square-foot home without taking some precautions, especially with the amount of travel Mac's job required. Marketing everything from corporations to movie stars was out-of-town work. Their agreement was a way for him to feel at ease leaving his family behind.

He walked in. "Holly? Why is the front door—?"

A vase lay on the floor, broken.

Mac noted the silence for the first time. "Holly? Andrew?"

No answer.

His eyes were drawn to the foyer table. A family photo was face down, and the table itself was a few inches cockeyed from the wall.

"Holly?"

He looked to the left. The living room was pristine. An elegant room for entertaining CEOs and Hollywood bigshots. Nothing was wrong there.

It's fine. They're out in the pool taking a dip until I get home. Maybe Holly went out the patio door, but then Andrew wanted to drag his wagon back there so he went out the front, leaving the door open. It was the wind that knocked the vase over.

He remembered her words just an hour before: "Hurry home. Hot dogs, lime Jell-O, and grape Kool-Aid await."

Andrew's favorite meal. For his fourth birthday.

A sound came from the kitchen. Mac held his breath. It was the pop and sizzle of boiling water hopping over the top of a pan onto a hot burner. *Holly wouldn't leave water boiling.*

His insides quivered. Something made him not want to look in the kitchen.

He took a deep breath, then headed toward the sound. Maybe if he acted normal, everything would be—

He saw them.

Things would never be normal again.

CHAPTER 1

"He redeemed my soul from going down to the pit,
and I will live to enjoy the light."

Job 33:28

Mac's eyes shot open. The silence of the darkened living room covered him like a shroud. He wiped the sweat from his forehead.

If only.

It was a familiar mantra. It had no object, no verb, no adjective to soften or enhance.

He sat up on the couch and rubbed his face, forcing reality into his pores. It had been nine months since he'd come home to a house full of death and pain. Still, grief and guilt were all-consuming. Debilitating. He found himself daydreaming a lot these days. It was an escape, a way to snatch moments of time where he could try to change what had happened, make it all go away.

Over the last weeks, the daydreams had grown stronger. Clearer. Frantically real. Colors, shapes, sounds—he tapped into all of them, desperately trying to change what was into what could have been.

Mac forced himself to his feet and stumbled through the shadows.

Help me, God. I don't want to hurt anymore. Show me how to move on.

He tripped over a pile of books and fell to his knees. *But I can't move on. Can't move. Can't.*

Oh, to lie there forever and never get up. Never see the light. Expire in the darkness of death, strangled in the smell of dust and fibers.

"Daddy?"

Mac saw Andrew standing in the foyer. He forced the tears away. "What is it, buddy?"

"Are you thinking about Mommy again?"

Mac cleared his throat. "Yes."

Andrew padded across the carpet, the feet of his pajamas making a scruff-scruff sound. He wrapped his arms around his father's neck, and Mac pulled his son's head close. He stroked the tousled hair, careful to avoid the scars. The physical ones, at least.

"I wish we could go back, Daddy."

"Go back where?"

"To before Mommy went to heaven."

Mac was shocked that his little boy's wish mirrored his own. Yet why should he be? Mac had come upon the aftermath of the violence. His son had lived it.

This little four year old had seen the stranger appear at the door, demanding money, ranting about some slight he'd endured during one of Mac's publicity campaigns. Andrew had looked to his mother to explain. Her fear had sparked his own. *He'd* seen his mother fight. Heard her scream. *He'd* tried to save her, only to be flung across the room to hit his head on the edge of the counter. *He'd* lain unconscious in a pool of blood. *He'd* had surgery. *He'd* finally opened his eyes to discover his mother was gone. Forever.

Mac had merely found them. The guilt was overwhelming: guilt for not being home, guilt for believing that such evil would never dare touch his world, guilt for living on without her.

Mac began to rock back and forth. He synchronized his breathing to that of his boy, needing the give and take as much as Andrew did.

If only. . .

The call came the next day while Mac was making tacos for dinner. It was Bob Craven, his cousin.

"You working much, Macky? I haven't seen your handsome mug on TV for ages. You'd better watch it—you don't want to lose your Image-Maker title now, do you?"

"Whatever."

"Whatever nothing. You're important. You're a hot property. You can't throw all that away. Surely you've been getting calls from your VIP friends, begging for your services?"

Mac glanced at the kitchen desk, piled high with

requests and offers—most unopened. "Not really."

"Well then, let my voice be the sound of opportunity knocking."

"What are you talking about?"

"Remember I told you about my new job at TTC?"

Mac remembered that Bob had moved to Kansas City for this new job and that it had something to do with scientific research. He couldn't remember what the letters stood for. "Vaguely. I'm sorry I don't remember more. My mind's been—"

"You're forgiven. But here's where the knocking comes in. And here's where it gets hard because I can't tell you as much as I'd like to tell you."

Mac added salt to the meat. "Is the point to this conversation looming anywhere close?"

"Hey, I'm trying to tell you about a huge opportunity here."

There was only one way to get rid of him. Mac turned off the burner. "Okay. You got my interest."

"Good. Because what I'm about to tell you could change your life."

Mac took a seat at the kitchen table. He glanced toward the sound of TV cartoons in the next room. Andrew lay on his stomach on the floor, his ever-moving legs visible through the doorway. "I'm all right, Bob. I don't want any more changes right now. We're good. I'm—"

"Fine. I've heard it before. But you're not fine. You've barely left the house since Holly died. Last time I saw you, you looked like an unmade bed. And Andrew. . . Spending extra time with your son may seem like a good idea, but what good does it do him if his father is quiet and mopey all the time? You've got to hear me out, Macky. For your own good."

"Fine."

"First off, I don't know the details, they're strictly hush-hush—"

"So why are you even calling me?"

"You're a pain, you know that?"

"Sorry. Go ahead."

"Macky, the scientists here are developing time travel."

Mac stifled a laugh. "Yeah, right."

"I'm serious. But it's not the kind of time travel you see in movies where people go visit Elizabethan England or the twenty-eighth century. It's something different. And here's the clincher: They want you to work for them."

"What? Why? I've never done anything with the scientific community."

"So let this be the first. Come on, if you can make Lose-It-Now the hottest weight loss program in America, you can promote anything. That state-by-state drawing to get a makeover and a walk-on part in their favorite TV show was a stroke of genius."

"That doesn't—"

"And didn't you make Melanie Malloy a country singing star by weaving your PR magic?"

"She's a great singer."

"With a marketing genius behind her."

"But I'm—"

"And didn't you take Jeremy Briggs from the brink of career suicide because of his drug problem and make him the recipient of an Oscar? Face it, Macky, if people can afford your services, you can make their dreams become reality."

"So TTC has dreams?"

"Oh, yeah. And they can afford you. *They* came to *me* about getting you to work for them."

"How did they know we were cousins?"

"Give me a break. You can't blame us no-name relatives for bragging on our famous kin, can you?"

"Do they know about Holly?"

"Well. . .sure. Everybody knows. It was on CNN, remember? And they feel real bad about it. Macky, will you talk with them? See what they have to offer?"

Mac rubbed his forehead. Time travel was science fiction. He had tacos to make. Chutes and Ladders to play with his son. Laundry to fold. Blank air to stare at. "I'll think about it. Thanks for calling."

"That's it? Thanks for calling? You're not going to talk to them?"

"I have to think, Bob. I have to think things through carefully—for Andrew's sake. I just don't know if I'm ready."

A moment of silence. "Just don't discount it, okay? Who knows? It might be perfect for you."

Mac hung up and moved to the stove. Tacos. He could deal with tacos.

The next day TTC's chief administrator, John Wriggens, called Mac at home.

"Mr. MacMillan," Wriggens said, after offering a few lines of flattery, "TTC would like to engage your services."

"I'm really not interested in any job offers at the moment, Mr. Wriggens."

"But this is more than the offer of a job."

"How so?"

There was a moment's hesitation. "Let's just say we are prepared to offer you a perk—a signing bonus, as it were—if you will agree to come to our little company and work your magic."

"I don't need money, Mr. Wriggens. In fact, I've found that money has pretty much lost its appeal since—"

"Your wife's horrible murder. That was tragic. So tragic. And we offer our sincere condolences."

Mac shut his eyes. "If it's not money you're offering, then what?"

"I'm afraid I can't say."

"Good-bye, Mr. Wriggens. Thanks for your offer, but no thanks."

He unplugged the phone.

Wriggens called seventeen times in the next few weeks—calls Mac did not take or return. Wriggens also sent restaurant gift certificates for Mac and toys for Andrew. Mac gave the gift certificates away at church but let Andrew keep the toys.

A part of him was genuinely curious to hear more of what TTC was offering, but now it had become a matter of honor to ignore them.

A month after the initial phone call, while sitting in his study, Mac read a newspaper headline: TIME TRAVEL POSSIBLE.

The article was all about TTC—the Time Travel Corporation.

He read over the scientific jargon, trying to make sense of

it. As far as he could determine, the article said that scientists had discovered a way to tap into a portion of the brain—they called it the Loop—where memories were stored, and somehow fix it so people could go back into their own pasts.

Mac felt a stirring of interest. Was he reading correctly? Time travel. The ability to go back and change something. . . . Might he actually be able to go—?

He reread the closing quote by Wriggens: "Although tests are ongoing, initial findings show conclusively that time travel is indeed possible. We anticipate that, in the near future, this fantasy that has pursued man throughout all history will become a reality."

Mac filtered out the PR jargon to find the real truth. They had tested it on humans. And it worked.

Tests are ongoing.

Three very special words. He thought of the job—and the special perk they were offering. Could it be? With Holly's death he'd be the perfect candidate. Mac crumpled the newspaper in his lap.

"Andrew?"

His son flew an airplane into the room. "Hi, Daddy."

Mac pulled him close as he flew by. "Let's get you dressed, buddy. We're going on a trip."

Andrew landed the plane on Mac's arm. "Where are we going?"

"Kansas City."

And, God willing, far beyond.

Chief Administrator John Wriggens rocked in his executive

chair. His body took up every available inch. "We appreciate you finally coming to talk with us, Mr. MacMillan. We're excited about the possibil—"

"I haven't taken the job yet. I'm just here to talk. To learn more."

"I'd be very happy to oblige."

Mac heard Andrew playing with the secretary in the outer office. "I saw the article on time travel. You've done it? You can send a person back?"

Wriggens's smile was full of self-satisfaction. "I see we finally have your interest."

"You have the world's interest."

"Ah, but there's the rub. We have their interest, but we need the expertise of someone like you to take us the next step."

"Which is?"

Wriggens adjusted his body in his chair. "I'm sure you'll understand my dilemma, Mr. MacMillan. Although we have no doubts about your abilities, we cannot reveal the details of our discovery until we have your commitment. As you know, proper timing, preparation, *and* secrecy are everything in launching a new product."

"Product? What product are you developing?"

Wriggens resumed his rocking.

So it was up to him. Mac walked to the window. His sudden chill had little to do with the weather in K.C. *If* time travel worked, and *if* he could go back ten months. . .

"We'd let you try it."

Mac spun around at the words. "What did you say?"

"We'd let you go back."

Mac moved closer. "But how can you—?"

"So you *will* take the job?"

How could he refuse? *God, be with me.* "I'll take the job."

"Excellent."

He returned to his seat, and Wriggens stood and shook his hand.

"Congratulations, Mr. MacMillan, you are now an integral part of a project that will change mankind."

"What project?"

"The Time Lottery."

CHAPTER 2

The race is not to the swift or the battle to the strong,
nor does food come to the wise or wealth
to the brilliant or favor to the learned;
but time and chance happen to them all.

ECCLESIASTES 9:11

Alexander MacMillan looked at his watch. Two minutes to go. He would walk through the doors at exactly noon. He hoped that the reporters would take note that Alexander MacMillan and the company he represented were masters at controlling time.

In the months leading up to the moment when they had announced that TTC *had* perfected a way to travel back in time, Mac and his marketing staff had labored to fine-tune how they would present the news to the world. Being laughed at was not an option. Nor was being doubted. This was science, and proper presentation was essential.

Their diligence had paid off. The press and the public had pounced on the idea as if the reality of time travel was, well, only a matter of time. Then, when Mac's crew had presented the *pièce de résistance*, a national Time Lottery, the response had been everything TTC could've hoped. People were used to fantasizing about what they could do with monetary lottery winnings, but getting a chance to go back into their own lives—and then to be given the option of staying there. . . The idea had been irresistible.

Of course, Mac's position in the organization had made its own waves. The world knew Alexander MacMillan as an image maker, but also as a famously tragic celebrity. The inevitable question had arisen: Was he going to go back to save his wife?

He and Wriggens had discussed the best answer. If he said no, the media would ask, "Why not?" And yet Mac had not wanted to bring Holly's death into the forefront again. His contract with TTC stipulated that he would get his chance, but only *after* the first lottery was successfully completed.

After weighing the pros and cons, he and Wriggens had decided to say that Mac *was* going back. Later. But for now, he was needed here.

There were those who had objected to the Time Lottery, arguing that people shouldn't mess with the life God had allowed them to live—and that corporations certainly shouldn't give people the chance to change it. What possible purpose could God have in wanting people to do this?

As a man of faith, Mac understood their concerns and even shared some of them. But their question could easily be countered with another: What purpose did God have in letting us land on the moon? Or climb to the top of Mt. Everest? Or discover something as convenient as microwaves or as mysterious as DNA? The answer was basic and played into God's awesome power: Why would God create the infinite possibilities of the universe and not show them off?

Scientifically speaking, time travel *was* possible. Einstein and others had proven it, at least in theory. If God truly had created all things and was in ultimate control, then it followed that time travel was something He planned to let man discover.

As it had been explained to Mac, reality existed in the place where the mind was conscious. It was very much like sleeping. When a person was awake, *that* was his reality. When he was asleep, his dreams seemed 100 percent real. But which "real" *was* real? *Merrily, merrily, merrily, merrily, life is but a dream.*

The bottom line was that time meant little to an Almighty God who always *was.* In Mac's mind, time was an instrument God had created for man's understanding and need for order. He Himself could do whatever He wanted with it.

So why might God have created the ability for people to travel back into their own lives? Mac's view was simple: So they could have another opportunity to get it right. The Time Lottery would provide a chosen few with the chance to find peace and a better understanding of themselves and their places in the infinite universe. Mac believed in a God of second chances, and third, and fourth.

But that was the future. Right now, there was other business to attend to. The moment to pick the winners was at hand.

Mac squared his shoulders, flipped the lavaliere mike on, took a deep breath, and walked into the auditorium. The TV lights caressed his face. Heads turned and voices shushed. He walked slowly to the stage, nodding slightly to the VIPs in the front row. Let them feel confident and important in their priority seats. It wouldn't help them win. If Wriggens got his way, time travel would be offered as a service for only the wealthiest clients. But for now at least, everybody had the same chance of winning. For the moment, TTC was an equal opportunity time travel provider.

Mac moved to the center of the stage where a huge Plexiglas globe rotated, mixing up the names of all who had bought a ticket. If he had his way, TTC would award time travel through a kind of Make-A-Wish program. But he had a lot of convincing to do to get that going. For now, a time *lottery* was how it was going to happen.

The globe revolved slowly, like the earth turning on its axis. Inside, millions of slips of paper rotated. *Choose me! Choose me!* Although it would have been far easier to let a computer spit out the names of the three winners, Mac had insisted on the creation of this monster globe because it mimicked the Sphere building where the time travel would take place. A computer-generated list was anticlimactic. Drawing three names out of a world-shaped sphere was exciting. Showmanship reigned.

Mac found himself touching the sphere's side, letting the

smooth surface slide beneath his hand, watching the names of the hopeful spin and fall.

If only. . .

Applause swept the room. Mac dropped his hand, blinked twice, and turned toward his audience. He scanned the crowd as they quieted, smiling with embarrassment that he'd been caught thinking private thoughts. He took a step forward and spread his arms in an invitation. "The time has come."

All fidgeting stopped and whispers quieted.

"Welcome, ladies and gentlemen. The Time Lottery is the culmination of twenty-two years of scientific research spurred by the ageless question of 'What if?' Before the inception of the Time Lottery, humankind traveled through life, making mistakes, having regrets, leaving hopes unrealized. But then a miracle. The discovery of the Loop and a way to tap into an Alternate Reality—the Alternity."

He let the word resonate. "You've all experienced it. Those memories and dreams that seem real enough to grasp and hold onto. Moments. Fleeting instants visited, but then lost when the sights and sounds of the present push them away."

I've wallowed in those moments.

He took a breath.

"In just a minute, three lucky people will be chosen to embark on a new adventure, to receive the gift of a second chance. Three explorers will travel back into their pasts, confronting the what-if questions that plague us all, discovering the possibilities of chances not taken and choices ignored. They will visit what could have been, their minds fresh and unburdened by what has happened since that moment, each one free to explore a new choice."

Mac raised a finger. "Think back. Remember that job you turned down because you didn't want to move? Remember your college sweetheart? You've often wondered what could have happened, haven't you?"

He lowered his voice, drawing them in. "How would your life have been different if at one critical juncture you would have said *Yes?* Or *No?* Now is your chance to find out."

He looked across the room. The people in the audience stared back at him, eyes intent. Their foreheads furrowed. *Make them want it. Need it. Ache for it.*

"Now let me share with you, in layman's terms, how this opportunity to travel to the past has come to be. First off, we must ask the question: What is reality? All I know of my world is what I experience from my own point of view, my own perceptions. We each perceive this moment, in this room, in a unique way. And within that part of the brain we've termed the Loop, all the moments of your life—real and perceived—are interwoven into a unique perception of what was, and what could be.

"When you are asleep, your dreams are your reality. You know nothing of your waking life; you *care* nothing about your waking life. Likewise, when you concentrate on a memory, *that* seems to take on a reality, just for a moment. The interweaving of dreams and memories is what the science of time travel taps into.

"Despite what you've been taught by science fiction movies, the past is an *individual* phenomenon, and there are as many timelines as there are people. A new timeline branches off every time you make a decision. Each of us spins off thousands of alternate streams of time every day. Quantum physics has taught us that those timelines have real existence.

"What the technology behind the Time Lottery does is allow the traveler to hop over to one of those other time streams, the timeline of his or her choice. The body stays here, acting like a kind of tether to the traveler in the other reality. If he decides to stay in the new timeline, eventually his consciousness makes the switch permanently. The tether is severed, and this body dies. But in the other timeline, he has a real body and can live out a normal lifespan.

"When we send a person back in time, we place his or her body into a carefully monitored, medically induced coma. Once we've done so, the mind—which went to sleep concentrating on the time and choice it wants to explore—will be free to choose the new timeline extracted from the Loop, that place where the memories of a lifetime are stored."

He walked to the edge of the stage. The TV cameras panned with him.

"After a person has experienced his or her Alternity for seven days—a measure of seven days in the present, but an undetermined number of days in the past—TTC doctors will introduce a gentle electric burst to the Loop, and a strange phenomenon we call Dual Consciousness will kick in. At this point, our time traveler can finally see both lives—the past and the present. It's like waking up from a dream and remembering it with total clarity, seeing both realities at the same time. At that point he or she will make a decision. Stay? Or come back?

"The choice, my friends, will be theirs. Those who

choose to stay in the past will continue on with their lives in their Alternity. That will become their new reality. After they make their choice, the Dual Consciousness will quickly fade. Within a day, their bodies here in the present will die."

He scanned their faces. All of a sudden a few people looked like they hoped they *wouldn't* win.

"However, during the state of Dual Consciousness, the traveler can easily choose to leave the past behind and come back to this present time. The traveler merely has to focus his or her thoughts on something unique in this life in the future, and the power of the mind will draw the soul back here, into his or her own sleeping body. But unlike a person emerging from a normal coma, our Time Lottery winners will be able to remember what happened, and anything they've learned will come back with them.

"One more thing before we draw names. You need to know that nothing the person does in the past will affect things in our present. If someone goes back and decides not to have children in her Alternity, her children in the here and now will not suddenly disappear. So don't worry. The bad news is that those of you hoping to go back and invest in Microsoft and come back to find yourself ridiculously wealthy are out of luck. Each Alternity is separate and distinct, a world within itself."

Mac surveyed the room. They were ready. "And so. . .the time *has* come."

He walked to the globe. There was a communal intake of breath. A tinny drum roll came through the loudspeakers.

He pushed a button and the sphere stopped its roll causing the paper snowstorm inside it to wind down. A small door stopped at Mac's eye level, the pieces of paper plastered to its side. He opened it only enough to extract three slips.

He walked to the edge of the stage and cleared his throat.

"The winners are. . ." The audience leaned forward, as if trying to touch the words as he read the names and numbers: "Phoebe Thurgood, #38294722; Cheryl Nickolby, #28495730; and Roosevelt Hazen, #83920187." The audience rose to its feet in a standing ovation. When it began to diminish, Mac raised his hands and spoke a benediction.

"May the God who transcends time and space be with us all on this great new adventure."

CHAPTER 3

Hope deferred makes the heart sick,
but a longing fulfilled is a tree of life.

PROVERBS 13:12

Phoebe, you're not being reasonable."

Phoebe sat on the loveseat by the fireplace and watched her husband close in for the attack. She walked across the room, the red silk of her lounging pajamas billowing.

"I'm not being reasonable? Listen to yourself, Colin. The first time I see you in three days, you come home and inform me I don't *deserve* to win the Time Lottery? I'm one of three winners in the entire country, and yet I don't deserve it? What kind of statement is that?"

"A logical one." He jingled the coins in his pocket, and Phoebe tensed. "Face it, you'd waste this kind of chance."

Phoebe flicked a stray piece of dust from a lampshade and looked out at the San Francisco skyline in the distance. "Maybe I was unreasonable expecting you to come home and congratulate me. I should have known better."

It wasn't fair how handsome Colin still was. The gray at his temples had only added to his sophistication. According to the world, when men aged, they became distinguished. Women merely got old. Only his eyes had gotten less attractive. They had grown smaller from years of squinting in conspiratorial thought. Though he was fifty-eight, the skin around his eyes was amazingly free of lines. Maybe not so amazingly. You needed to smile to have wrinkles sprout around your eyes. And Colin didn't smile. Gloat, yes; smile, no.

"Let me go in your place."

The words had been expected, but they still surprised her. Her hand flipped the comment away.

"Let me go," he repeated. "I've got big plans, Phoebe. I can do great things if given another chance."

She crossed to the window. "*Great* things, Colin? For whom?" She could practically hear the cogs of his mind juggling for an answer. They both knew the truth. Phoebe closed the drapery and faced him. "There are a lot of wonderful 'G' words, Colin: gallantry, generosity, gratitude. Unfortunately, the only 'G' word you are familiar with is the big one: greed."

He turned his back on her. "I suggest you look around this house and on the fingers of your hands if you want proof you've enjoyed the spoils as much as me."

Phoebe raised one hand as if swearing to tell the truth, the whole truth, and nothing but the truth, so help her God. "Guilty, as charged. I have enjoyed it. I'd have been a fool not to. But there comes a time when material possessions aren't enough." She stepped toward him. "I want to be worth more than money, Colin. You live your life, and the kids live theirs. I don't have much to show for my life except my name on committee rosters, a house full of furniture, and a Caribbean tan."

He looked at her, his eyes reflecting the sparks from the fire. "So the charitable Phoebe wants to go back and give it all to the poor?"

She straightened her shoulders. "I'm no saint. But I would like to see what I could do with *my* life instead of living what you have done with yours."

He turned once again to the fire. "It sounds as if you want to go back to before we were married."

Was that regret she heard in his voice? A hint of fear? Certainly not. Not from the omnipotent Colin Thurgood.

What year *would* she return to? To her childhood to watch her parents' ambitions fizzle all over again? To her senior year in high school when college had suddenly become an impossible dream? To her time as a secretary for Colin when—

The truth was, she missed being needed—by anybody, but mostly by her family. Thomas was a senior at Harvard. He would be a high-profile lawyer someday and do good in the world. Suzanne was a sophomore at Berkeley. She had a bit of the gypsy in her, a trait her father deplored and Phoebe admired. But Suzanne hadn't needed her mother since the sixth grade when Phoebe had tried to explain the facts of life, and Suzanne had corrected her mother's terminology.

Colin had not noticed Phoebe's turmoil. She was not entirely certain he had noticed the children were no longer living at home. His life had not changed. It never changed. He was not a part or a cause of her new aloneness. His life was separate, as it had been since he had discovered that employees could give him the advice and help he needed without the annoyance and back talk of a concerned wife.

And yet, Colin needed her now. She possessed something he longed for.

He turned toward her, his eyes pleading. The look was almost convincing. But then she saw the familiar selfish glint, and her moment of weakness passed like a wave of indigestion.

She took his face in her hands, finding a fiendish relish in what she was about to do. "I understand your position, my dear—and I even agree with some of it."

His smile was full of hope. She kissed him on the lips.

"However. . .at the moment, I have to go."

He blinked. "Go? Go where?"

She walked toward the door. "To the phone of course. I have a prize to claim."

Cheryl Nickolby was asleep in the middle of the afternoon. A sleep mask blocked the reflection off the snow that blanketed her front yard. Although the thermometer outside hovered around freezing, she was cozy beneath the weight of the faded pink quilt that lived on her bed during the Colorado winters.

Cheryl would have been content to sleep until doomsday if the phone hadn't jangled its way into her consciousness. She tried to ignore it, pretending it was just a part of her dream, but it was persistent.

"Cheryl, get the phone!"

She had forgotten she was not alone. A common mistake. After working through the night sewing up two victims of a nasty crash near Lyons, Dr. Cheryl Nickolby had been too wound up to sleep. So she had grabbed Harry Barker, her anesthetist and sometimes lover, and plowed under the covers for a little nootsy-tootsy. They'd only been asleep two hours.

She groped for the phone and fell back into the pillows, pushing the sleep mask onto her forehead. The sunshine was disgustingly rude. "Hello!"

"Cheryl?" The person on the other end was obviously not used to being spoken to in such a tone.

"Hi, Mom."

Harry got up, grabbed his clothes, and waved good-bye, leaving her alone with her mother.

"How are things, Mom? How's Ted?"

"Ted?"

"Husband number six? The latest man you promised to love, honor, and beat at canasta?"

There was silence on the line. Cheryl snuggled deeper into the covers, preparing herself for a lengthy, noneventful conversation. The wax of last night's coffee coated her tongue with a bitter taste.

"You don't know, do you, dear?"

"Know what?"

"Sweetie, I can't believe it! Here I am calling to congratulate you, and I end up telling you!"

Cheryl sighed. It was not unusual for her mother to take a side road. "Mom. . ."

"They just announced it. You're one of the three Time

Lottery winners!"

Cheryl swallowed. "Huh?"

"Ted and I were watching television—you know how he likes to watch the old *Marcus Welby* reruns on channel nine—when his program was interrupted by a special announcement of the winners. Now at first, Ted was upset about the interruption, and I offered to get him a brownie—you know the kind I make with the chocolate mint frosting you both like so much? I had just finished a batch, and they were still warm from the oven, and I thought a big piece with a glass of milk would get rid of his grumpies. But when we heard your name, he forgot all about the brownies *and* Marcus Welby. You were the second person they named."

Cheryl sat up. "Me?"

"Cheryl Nickolby. That's you, dear. That's you!"

She pulled the sleep mask off her head. "Mom, are you sure?"

"You'll have to check the number, but how many Cheryl Nickolbys can there be? So, tell me: What part of your life would you like to relive? Have you thought about it? No, of course you haven't because you didn't know. But I have. Ever since we heard about the Time Lottery and bought our tickets, Ted and I have talked about it many times, just dreaming you know, but we decided if we had the chance we would go back to the time after we moved. . ."

Cheryl stopped listening. Her mother and Ted had been married only three years. What could they want to relive? She fell against the pillows, cradled the phone against her ear, and mechanically answered "um hmm" at regular intervals. She put the sleep mask back on.

Since sleep would not come, Cheryl dug out her lottery ticket and called the Time Lottery people. They made her read off her number: #28495730. It was a match. Her prize was confirmed. Only then did it start to sink in. She'd won the Time Lottery. But what exactly did that mean?

She needed time to think. She dialed the hospital to call in sick.

"Hi, Brenda, put me through to Dr. Crat—"

"Dr. Nickolby, you won. You won!"

So maybe calling in sick wouldn't work. . . . Before she spoke with the chief of staff, Cheryl ended up talking to three other people who offered her congratulations and asked the same questions she was asking herself. The chief was kind enough to let her take two days off to sort things through, as long as Cheryl worked through the coming weekend. What a deal.

The phone wouldn't stop ringing. Well-wishers. Curiosity-seekers. In the end Cheryl decided to drive up the mountain to her cabin near the village of Allenspark. It was either that or perform a phone-ectomy.

She drove up the mountain roads, cracking the window to let the cold air and the pine scent work their wonders to clear out the mental cobwebs—nature's Pine Sol. The snow piled along the road glowed against the wilderness.

At the cabin, Cheryl had to work to make it through the high snow to even reach the door. Once inside, she was faced with the reality of no running water—she had to turn it off in the winter—and no food. She began to question her sanity for coming here. But considering the cabin also lacked a phone, she forgave herself—and left her cell phone in the car.

She said hello to the mice and congratulated her supreme foresight in stocking up on firewood. She got a fire going, poured herself some hot chocolate from a thermos, and inhaled an Oreo cookie. She wrapped herself in three blankets and curled up in the Morris chair in front of the fire. To think.

Cheryl knew that winning the Time Lottery was a wonderful opportunity; she was getting a second chance. That was exactly why she found it so hard: she couldn't think of anything in her life she would change. She was a successful surgeon, she lived in a nice home, she could afford a few luxuries such as the cabin. What needed changing? Still, certainly she wasn't pompous enough to think her life was perfect. Was she?

The moonlight made the snow glow blue as two deer wandered by the window, their noses to the snow. They perked their ears and looked at her through the glass. They must have sensed no danger from a papoose who was too cold to pour herself a cup of cocoa, because they regally walked together into the forest.

"Did you see that?" As if in response, tiny mice feet skittered across the wooden floor. How dare they run away when she was talking to them! Cheryl sat upright in the chair. "I asked you a question, mice. Did you see that?"

The mice wisely stayed away from the crazy woman who was trying to have a conversation with them. Certainly she was delirious from lack of sleep or gone wacko from a chocolate overdose.

What was she doing talking to a bunch of mice? She had just witnessed a scene out of *Bambi,* and the only living things to share it with had been furry brown rodents.

That's when it hit her—*wham bam alakazam.* There was her answer: Cheryl wanted someone to share her life with. Someone to sit beside her, hold her hand, and whisper about the deer, the mountains, and the moonlight. Children were out. At forty-seven, her biological clock was all but broken. But what about a husband?

Not Harry—or Jason, or Rick, or Chuck. Lovers all but husbands none. There were a few men Cheryl liked and even some she might have loved, but there was nobody Cheryl wanted hanging around all the time, dropping his dirty clothes on the floor, and eating her Oreos. Commitment was not for her. It wasn't in her genes. Wasn't her mother on husband number six? The only way not to play marriage tag was not to get married at all.

She had come close to marriage a few times. But something had always stopped her from going through with it: intelligence, maturity, wisdom beyond her years. Fear? Anyway, Cheryl found most men couldn't handle a woman who had a body *and* brains.

Long ago, she had accepted her singleness as a positive thing. She'd even considered adopting a child as a single parent but had never gotten around to it. Maybe she was subconsciously avoiding it. Maybe she was too set in her ways to commit her life to anyone. She didn't even have a cat. Maybe she realized she wouldn't be that great a mother.

Still. . .the idea of giving a past relationship another try was intriguing. The close calls to matrimony weren't worth an encore, but there had been one guy, back in high school. Jake Carlisle.

Jake had been one of the few boys who had been out of

her realm of influence. Popular. A basketball star. King of the in-crowd. The perfect boy. He was always going steady with someone—cheerleaders mostly.

Meanwhile, Cheryl had been interested in relationships that were pointedly *not* steady. Lure them in, try them out, then leave them alone. It was a power thing, with no commitments allowed. Now, as a mature woman who was somewhat versed in psychobabble, Cheryl realized she had probably been seeking physical attention to compensate for the absence of her biological father and her mother's penchant for trading in old models for new stepdaddies who weren't too interested in having an instant daughter in their lives. But back in high school, love had been the last thing on her mind. Cheryl had exercised her sexual experiments with great ferocity and determination. No strings attached. Those were *her* rules. She had been in control.

Considering the fact that Jake had been a good boy, and Cheryl had been a bad girl, they had tread water in opposite ends of the pool.

But now, given this second chance. . . Jake was the kind of guy who was open to commitment. What if Cheryl dove in his end?

She *was* a very good swimmer.

"Cheryl?" Pam sounded half asleep. "Are you crazy? It's six in the morning."

"It's only 4 A.M. here, friend. You're lucky it's this late. I've been waiting for the sun to rise out there in New Jersey. I need to talk to you."

"You won. . .the thing."

"You heard."

"I tried to call you."

"I was at the cabin."

"Oh. Were you hiding out?"

"Absolutely."

"Are you scared?"

Leave it to Pam to get to the point. "Let's just say that I hope they know what they're doing. I wouldn't want to be left floating in limbo-land for all eternity, or for my Alternity, ha ha."

"What year are you going to visit?"

Cheryl wasn't sure how detailed she should get. "1973."

"High school?"

Cheryl chanted their class motto. "The best to be is seventy-three."

"I can't believe you remember that stuff."

"Want me to sing the fight song?"

"I'll pass."

"Good, because I never knew it."

She heard Pam yawn. "What are you going to change?"

"It's a secret."

"Uh-uh. Does not compute. We've been best friends since time began. We have no secrets. Besides, you wouldn't call me at this early hour so you could *not* tell me."

"I might. Everybody has secrets."

"Care to elaborate?"

"Nope."

"Tell me *something*. If you don't, I'll have Julie call and pester you. She'll shame you out of it."

"She was always good at that," Cheryl said. "If you must know, I'm going to check out Jake Carlisle."

"Mr. Basketball Star?"

"Mr. Gorgeous."

"He was out of our league. He never looked at you."

"Only because I didn't let him know I was interested."

"Oh mighty Nickolby, Queen of Sexiness, able to conquer all males at will."

"I am woman, hear me roar."

"I hate that song."

"You liked it at the time."

"At the time I liked hip huggers and going braless."

"Times change," Cheryl said.

"Luckily." A pause. "When do you leave?"

"I called the lottery people. I leave in one week."

"Can Julie and I come see you off?"

"No." She was surprised by her answer.

"Why not?"

"Because if you see me off it's like I'm not coming back."

"That *is* a possibility, isn't it? That's what makes the whole thing so exciting."

"I'm not staying in 1973."

"How do you know?"

"I like my life now."

"But. . ."

"I'm not staying." But this time, there was less conviction in her voice.

Leon Burke heard Roosevelt Hazen's name on his headphones.

His eyes shot open, and he sat up in bed.

Roosevelt's won the Time Lottery?

Leon looked to the bed next to him. Roosevelt Hazen slept on his back, his mouth open, snores grating Leon's nerves. Leon hated snoring. That's one reason he usually stayed away from shelters in church basements like this one. Too many men sleeping in one room. Too many sounds. Too many smells, none of them good. But it was January. The cold had forced Leon inside, and fate had set him on a cot next to Roosevelt Hazen—a man with whom Leon had history.

He doesn't know. Leon swung his legs over the side of the cot and reached to wake Roosevelt.

His hand stopped short. *He doesn't know. And maybe he doesn't need to know. . . .*

"I'll go in his place."

Leon put a hand to his mouth. He hadn't meant to say that out loud. It was just a thought. A hope. An edgy what-if that had no truth to it. There was no way Leon could go in Roosevelt's place. It was just talk.

Wasn't it?

Leon couldn't sleep. Those five little words—*I'll go in his place*—grew big, like they were plastered on a billboard twenty feet high.

When the sun found its way through the room's small window, Leon gave up on sleep. He grabbed the blanket from the bed, zipped up his coat, and left the shelter. He had some mighty thinking to do.

As he came around the corner, he spotted a kid curled up

on a smashed box by a dumpster. Men being on the street was one thing, but kids? Leon couldn't get used to that. This one couldn't be much more than twelve. He let the blanket fall off his shoulders and laid it over the boy, trying not to wake him. The boy's eyes shot open, and his body shifted, instantly wary and defensive. Leon took a step back, raising his hands. "It's just a blanket, kid." He pointed. "Just a blanket. Thought you could use it."

The boy's eyes became a kid's again, and he gathered the blanket close, like a shroud.

"There's a bed available at the shelter," Leon said. "I just left it. I know."

The boy pulled the blanket under his nose and shook his head.

Leon shrugged. "Suit yourself." He must have his reasons. Sleeping in a dorm room with dozens of grown men probably offered its own dangers. Leon started to walk away but then felt a Snickers bar in his pocket. He turned back. "Hey, kid."

The boy opened his eyes, and Leon tossed the candy bar at him. "Chow down."

A smile. An actual smile.

Leon walked away with a spring to his step. Kids were great. One of the big regrets in his life was never having one of his own.

One of his regrets. One of many. Things had gone wrong so many times. He'd tried to do better, but something always pulled him back to doing wrong. He'd had second chances. And third. And twenty-third. He supposed a fellow ran out of chances.

And yet, maybe he had one more. . .

He found a cigarette stub in the gutter and sat on the curb to enjoy a drag. It made him cough. His lungs didn't take to smoke anymore. Not since the cancer had moved in. *Cancer, Mr. Burke. Not much longer, Mr. Burke. Lay off the smokes and booze, Mr. Burke.*

Forget doctors and clinics. What was life without smokes and booze? Leon was a free man. He didn't have a house or family or job, but he was free to do as he pleased, and if he pleased to smoke and drink 'til his body shriveled to nothing, that was his choice. And if he pleased to grab himself another chance. . .

Leon shivered, wishing the sun would hurry and hit the place where he sat. The streets of Memphis were quiet; the red light on the corner turned green, but there was no one to see it. Except Leon. He looked at the light. Red. Green. Red. Green. Stop. Go. Stop—

Go. *I'll go.*

Leon walked the streets, his headphones blaring, his hands in his pockets. It was hard planning a con, especially when he was out of practice. What would get Roosevelt to hand over his prize? It's not like Leon had a lot to offer. *Here, Preach, I'll give you all the money in my pocket, all five dollars and twenty-six cents.*

Leon shook his head. It was hopeless.

A fit of coughing bent him in half. It couldn't be hopeless. He wouldn't let it be. There had to be a way. His life depended on it. He had to get the ticket, one way or another.

Leon saw a torn playing card under a pop can by the side

of a building. What if he got Roosevelt in a poker game and got him to bet his ticket? *I'll bet my ticket if you bet yours, Preach.* It had been a long time since Leon had played poker, but he *could* win. He'd cheat if necessary. And he doubted that Roosevelt—an ex-preacher—would know much about the game.

Leon nodded and smiled to himself. Yes, that would work.

His smile left him. It would only work if poker were an option. But it wasn't. You needed four people to play poker, and Leon didn't want others involved. Besides, men who had nothing to bet didn't play poker. There was no fun in it without something to risk, something to gain. Or lose.

I could steal the ticket from him.

This idea had potential. Leon would wait until Roosevelt was sleeping—or passed out—and go through his pockets. As easy as stealing candy from a baby. Then he could take the ticket to those Time Lottery people and—

The Time Lottery people. They were the real problem. Even if Leon had the ticket, they'd never let him use it without first checking with the real recipient. "Are you sure Mr. Hazen gave this to you willingly?"

If only I could become Roosevelt Hazen.

With that thought, Leon stopped walking. *If I showed up with the ticket, and said I was Roosevelt, who would know?*

The Time Lottery people were waiting for Roosevelt's call. There was nothing on the ticket that would tell them how to get hold of the winners, no ID information. Yet maybe there were all sorts of ways to track down the winners.

Except if they were homeless. And except if they didn't go by their real names. Lots of people on the streets went by nicknames. And Roosevelt was no exception. Everybody called him Preacher or Preach. The only reason Leon knew his real name was that he'd known him before. As far as the population roaming the streets of Memphis was concerned, there *was* no Roosevelt Hazen. Never heard of him.

That was the key. Roosevelt's identity was their little secret, so if Leon showed up with that name, who'd confront him? Roosevelt's family? Surely they'd hear about him winning. But Leon didn't think there was any family—or if there was, they'd probably been out of touch for years and years. A person didn't generally go homeless if there was family to fall back on.

As for looking different, there was more danger people might recognize Leon as Leon than Roosevelt as Roosevelt. Leon ran a hand over his beard. His hair hung well below his collar. He'd been a handsome man once. Could be again if he got himself cleaned up. And his gray hair was like Roosevelt's gray hair. He'd have to risk it.

He'd have to have a long talk with Preach to find out if he knew he was a winner—and more importantly, if he'd already called in. If he didn't know, Leon would steal the ticket and take his place. Piece of cake.

Leon had a headache. The decibel level of the music didn't help. But he didn't turn it down. Its noise was his security blanket, blocking out the world, filling his brain so he wouldn't have to think too much. Silence was scary. He remembered what his grandma used to tell him, "Be still now, Leon. You can't hear God talking to you if you're making noise all the time."

That was the point. Leon didn't want to hear the Lord. Especially now. God wouldn't like what he was planning.

Not one little bit. So Leon covered up the voice of God.

The music in his headphones stopped. *"Now for the news. . ."* As his hand touched the dial to turn to another station, he heard the words, *"Roosevelt Hazen, one of the Time Lottery winners, is the only winner who has not contacted TTC."*

Leon stood in the middle of the sidewalk, staring at nothing, all his concentration focused on the radio. *"TTC representative Alexander MacMillan said their sources can find no valid address for Mr. Hazen."* A distinguished voice took over, delivering an 800-number for TTC and saying, *"Mr. Hazen, if you're out there, please call the TTC offices within the next twenty-four hours to claim your prize. If Mr. Hazen does not contact us within that time frame, we will draw another name from the lottery entries. Anyone knowing the whereabouts of Roosevelt Hazen is urged to contact him or the TTC offices on his behalf."*

Time was running out. If Leon was going to do this, he had to do it fast.

Leon sat on a concrete block, alternating drags on his cigarette with swigs of Thunderbird. The wine was warm going down, coating his innards with a glow he longed for. Once it hit bottom, he felt a twitch, as his stomach or liver—or whatever it was down there that didn't abide by his drinking anymore—squeezed and jabbed. He didn't even taste it. It's what it did for him that mattered. It warmed him and made the days pass.

Leon wiped his mouth on the sleeve of his jacket, one more stain to add to the rest. His eyes locked on Roosevelt "Preacher" Hazen.

Roosevelt sat across the alley, talking to Jimmy and Fatsy, telling them one of his stories. Old Roosevelt was full of stories. They were laughing and smiling like they were having a bad teeth contest. Leon smiled, too. Soon he'd have the last laugh.

But the key thing was, there were *no* stories about winning the Time Lottery. Roosevelt didn't know. Didn't know about that, or the fact that his old friend Leon was going to take his place.

When Roosevelt and Leon had met—actually re-met, six months before—Leon had recognized the older man on the spot. Though Roosevelt was a lot more weathered than he'd been when Leon had last seen him, his eyes were the same—like two black olives. Leon hadn't given his own name right off, not knowing if Roosevelt would be holding a grudge all these years, wanting revenge and all that. But it hadn't taken Leon long to see that Roosevelt was still the same trusting fool he had been in the fall of '62.

It brought Leon up a peg to see that the holy preacher had been brought down a peg. Or two. Leon had been itching to ask him what had happened to his church and to his girl, Sarah, but he couldn't ask specific questions without taking the risk that Roosevelt would remember him. And for all the stories Roosevelt told, not one explained away Leon's questions. Something mighty must have happened to bring down such a good man. Leon almost felt bad doing what he had to do.

But it was a good plan. Fate had placed Roosevelt Hazen back in Leon's life—his life that cancer was going to end too soon. He'd have been a fool not to take advantage of it.

Especially since Leon's life was already mixed with Roosevelt's. Considering that the Time Lottery travel was based on a person's own memories, all Leon had to do was pretend he was Roosevelt until he got in the Time Lottery gizmo. Then he'd get his own memories in gear. After all, he *was* a con man.

Actually, going back to 1962 when their lives were woven together wasn't a bad choice. Though back in 1970 Leon *had* done some real nasties in Mississippi it might be nice to undo, or go back to spend some more time with his mama before she died, '62 had been a turning point in his life, for it had been the start of his jail days. Maybe this time Leon could do things right. Really change his ways.

He laughed. Who was conning whom? He'd been on the far side of the law and good living for longer than this side of forever. He'd skirted the normal life most people lived like a man looking at pretties through a store window. Look, but don't touch.

Could he touch *normal?* Could he be a part of it instead of snatching bits and pieces before running away—thereby getting nothing that lasted? Could he really change himself in the process of changing a few choices here and there?

He sat up straighter. Could taking advantage of this chance be more than running away from his worthless life in the present? Could it really be something to run *to?* Something fresh and good?

But I'm a con man. I've always been a con man.

Only because I had to be.

He shook his head against the lie. He didn't have to do anything. It had been his choice. True, one choice leading to another had made it hard to break away, but more than once there had been times when a window had opened for his escape. If only he'd jumped out, run toward the good instead of hanging back with the bad. But he'd chosen to be around bad people doing bad things. He'd laughed at good people. Used them. Hurt them.

Sarah Hudson, for instance. A good woman. She'd worked with Roosevelt at the church. Doe eyes and a waist so small he could put his hands around it—or at least that's what he'd imagined. He'd never done it. Sarah had been interested in Leon—he'd seen it in her eyes. What wasn't to like? Leon had looked like Chuck Berry back then and was as smooth talking as the wrap-around strains of "Blueberry Hill." Laying a line of flattery for a pretty lady had come as easily to Leon as buttering a piece of toast. And if Sarah had been a normal kind of woman, Leon would have pursued her shy smiles and lowered eyes. He would have made her say yes.

But Sarah had been different from the other women he'd met on the road. She was a *good* woman, and as such, he'd avoided her as if she'd carried some awful disease. In a way, she had. Sarah carried with her the plague of decency and righteous living, two conditions Leon needed to be without if he was going to make a living the way he did.

Truth was, she'd scared him, conjuring up unfamiliar feelings he could do without. Yet since then, Leon had not found anyone like her. She'd been the one good woman in his life who'd ever shown any interest, and he had ignored her as if she were a fly on the back side of a screen, looking in at him, hoping to come close. He'd shooed her away—leaving himself alone. A lifetime of alone.

He'd had women. Many women. Even a wife once. But

he'd never had a partner.

What if he went back among the good people like Roosevelt Hazen and Sarah Hudson and this time let them draw him into their good world? What if he jumped out that window and chose to join them, instead of deceive them? How would his life have been different?

Leon looked across the alley at Roosevelt. What good had being a good man done him? The good man and the bad man had both turned into bums. With smokes and booze Leon could plot the path of his own destruction. But Roosevelt. . . What had happened to bring him down so?

Leon shivered and looked away. The Time Lottery was the doorway to his second chance. He turned up the volume on the music. It seemed like the only way to find the good in his past was to do some bad in the present.

Across the alley, Jimmy and Fatsy stood. Leon dropped the headphones around his neck and walked over to Roosevelt. He wiped the end of the bottle. "Want a sip, Preach?"

The older man chuckled. "Goodness." He took a deep swig from the bottle. "Ahh. Nice." He stroked the white stubble that circled his mouth.

Leon sat next to him, using a concrete block as a chair. "You know, Preach, I've heard you tell some stories. I know you're from Tennessee, but was you born here in Memphis?"

"Nope, over in Hendersonville. Nice place, nice place." His head shook like one of those doggy heads bobbing in the back window of a car.

"So you're fifty. . .three?"

"Now, that's ripe!" Roosevelt laughed. "I haven't been fifty-three for sixteen years. Fifty-three?"

"You? Sixty-nine? I don't believe it."

"I can prove it." Roosevelt groaned as he lifted himself off the ground to reach into his back pocket. "See here, here's my driver's license—an old one, mind you—but you'll see I'm sixty-nine, be seventy in March."

Leon took the billfold and looked at the license. It was full of stuff the Time Lottery people might ask for. There was a birthday and a social security number. With those he would even be able to get a copy of Roosevelt's birth certificate if they asked for it. And Roosevelt was only five years older than Leon. It was doable.

Leon had an idea. He pulled his own lottery ticket out of his coat pocket. "You get yourself one of these lottery things, Preach?"

Roosevelt dug into his front pocket this time. "Yup. Here's mine." He held it between his hands and looked at it. Then an eyebrow raised. "It says here that they picked the winners yesterday."

Uh-oh. . . . Leon laughed nervously. "So much for us winning, huh?" He held out his hand. "Why don't you give me yours, and I'll put it with mine? I like to collect such things." Lame. Very lame.

Roosevelt eyed Leon over the top of the ticket. "No thanks. I think I'll keep it. For awhile at least."

Watch it, Leon! You almost blew it. "Whatever you say."

Leon waited till Roosevelt finished the bottle of wine and fell asleep, snoring loud enough to keep the rats away.

He checked the alley and the windows for prying eyes.

The entrance to the alley shone like a light at the end of a trash-encrusted tunnel. Those who walked by kept their eyes straight ahead.

Leon took a deep breath. It was time. He put on his headphones, turned up the music, and turned off his conscience.

He covered the space to Roosevelt slowly. Roosevelt stirred, but it was only to get more comfortable on the box that kept the cold at bay. Leon saw a problem: Roosevelt was curled up, making it hard to get into his front pocket.

Roosevelt's jacket was pulled up, and Leon could see the outline of his laminated driver's license in his back pocket. He really needed that, too.

Leon rubbed his palms against his pants and sent his hand toward the pocket. If only he were a pickpocket by trade. He formed a claw with his thumb and forefinger, deciding it was best to go for the side edges of the license rather than risk sliding a finger between it and Roosevelt's body.

He held his breath and slid his fingers in. Roosevelt moaned but did not open his eyes. Leon clamped onto the edges of the license and pulled his hand out slowly. *Just a few more inches. . .*

The license dropped to the ground but made no sound. Leon snatched it up and stuck it in his pocket.

One down. . .one to go.

He *had* to get Roosevelt to straighten out. Maybe if he touched his shoulder he'd move toward it, open up. He had to try.

Leon pressed gently on Roosevelt's upper shoulder, pushing him backward ever so slightly. Roosevelt obliged. He rolled onto his back, his upper arm falling to the cold ground with a thud. Leon's heart raced. Everything was working out perfectly. His eyes locked on the front pants pocket. Unfortunately, the ticket had no sharp edges to give away its location. It could be near the top, or way down deep.

Maybe if I do it quick, I can get the ticket and step away. Even if Roosevelt wakes up I can say he's been dreaming.

Leon stooped beside the sleeping man and, with one last moment of hesitation, dug his hand in his pocket. He couldn't feel the ticket! Where was it?

Roosevelt's eyes opened. He looked at Leon. Leon looked at him. Leon's heart decided not to beat for a good three seconds.

Then Roosevelt shoved Leon away with a strength that was totally unexpected. "You can't have it! You can't!"

Leon shoved his hands in his pockets. "What are you talking about?"

Roosevelt was on his feet—unsteady though they were—and shook a finger at Leon. "Don't give me that lie. You were after my lottery ticket. I thought it was strange when you asked to have it. Why do you want it? Did I win? Are you trying to steal my prize?"

Instinct took over. Leon picked up the concrete block and hurled it at Roosevelt. The older man raised his hands but caught the brunt of it in his face. He fell to the ground, hitting the back of his head on the pavement.

Leon froze and sucked in a breath. *What did I just do?*

Roosevelt didn't move. The blood on his face was awful. Leon knelt beside him, his hands fluttering around the wound, not knowing what to do—or if he should do it.

He forced himself to take Roosevelt's pulse. There was

nothing. His chest did not rise and fall.

Roosevelt Hazen was dead.

Leon looked around the alley. It was still except for the sound of his own raspy breathing.

It's done. Get out of here.

Leon reached into Roosevelt's pocket and found the ticket immediately. *Why couldn't I have found it that fast the first time? None of this would have happened.* He stood on trembling legs. His body shook like his heart was the center of an earthquake. He cringed at the sight of his victim, wanting only to be gone. Now. But calm thoughts entered. He rifled through the pockets of Roosevelt's coat. He took a couple bucks but put a pocket Bible back where he found it. His hands were bloody. Last, he took Roosevelt's wallet. Now nobody would be able to say who the dead man was—just a John Doe who'd had a fight with another bum over a few bucks. No ID, no next of kin. A loner.

Leon pulled the body next to a dumpster and covered it with trash. Pickup wasn't for nearly a week. He had that much head start.

As Leon stood over the body, he felt bad. Not just I'm-going-to-throw-up bad, but down deep bad. Although he'd committed more than his share of crime in his life, he'd never murdered. He sensed God pointing a glowing finger at him. But didn't God understand it was a shame to waste the Time Lottery on Roosevelt? He'd had a good chance at life. Leon knew, because for a time Leon had been there with him. Leon had never had a chance like Roosevelt had. He'd gotten off wrong from day one. Jail. Loneliness. Cancer. Didn't Leon deserve this second chance?

He scrambled down the alley but had to stop and lean against a building. He stuffed his bloodied hands in his pockets, not wanting to see.

You couldn't live on the streets and not see blood, but Leon had never had blood stain him or had the smell make his stomach grab and turn. He wanted to plug his nose, but he couldn't without smearing the stuff on his face. He snatched a newspaper and wiped and wiped. Then he threw up.

A car horn down the street brought Leon out of it. He had to get away. He ran out of the alley but then forced himself to slow down so he wouldn't draw any eyes. He felt God's finger on his spine, jabbing him, telling him he had done wrong.

He ducked into the restroom of a gas station. *God won't look for me in no toilet.* Leon shucked off his jacket and dipped the sleeves in the sink. The pink water made his stomach roll. He wrung out the jacket and hung it over the stall to dry. He scrubbed his skin till it tingled. Scoops of water did nothing to take the sour taste from his mouth. Only booze would trade one sour for another.

But then, as Leon looked at the reflection of his eyes, he knew he'd never drink again. Those eyes weren't his. They were dull as pebbles beside a river, rounded and grown hard in the sun. He blinked and blinked again, trying to ease life into them. But the life was gone. Gone away with Roosevelt Hazen.

"Anybody in there?"

Leon sucked in a breath. "Go away! I'm busy."

Fists pounded on the door. "Hurry up. I needs to go."

Leon thought about telling the guy to go in his pants, but he didn't need anyone making a ruckus loud enough that people might come running. Leon ran the water one last time, swishing out the last of the pink. Then he grabbed his jacket, opened the door, and brushed past the man, his head down.

Leon slipped behind the station and walked a good mile before the thumping of his heart toned down. He found a phone and dialed the 800-number for the Time Lottery. They answered after the first ring.

Leon took a deep breath and began to live the lie. "This is Roosevelt Hazen, and I'm a winner."

Funny. He didn't feel like one.

CHAPTER 4

Therefore do not worry about tomorrow,
for tomorrow will worry about itself.
Each day has enough trouble of its own.

MATTHEW 6:34

Leon put the key in the door to his motel room. His own private, paid-for motel room. Thanks to TTC.

From their first phone conversation, Leon could tell that the Time Lottery people weren't sure how to handle a homeless winner. He took advantage of their confusion like it was an engraved invitation to lie. With little effort—and only a few embellishments past the truth—he gave them a sob story so touching they agreed to put him up in a motel. After all, it wouldn't look right having a Time Lottery winner staying in a shelter for the week until showtime. He'd even shamed them into giving him some spending money so he wouldn't starve. Oh, and by the way, how about a little extra to get some decent clothes? It wasn't any of their business if he wanted to use a good portion of their charity on booze and smokes.

Leon liked going to the motel's café and ordering whatever he wanted. He liked the looks he got from other diners and had even given the waitress his autograph—nearly, but not forgetting to write *Roosevelt Hazen.* He liked the attention. Even so, he was hugely relieved that TTC had declared the winners off limits to the press for this short time, explaining how important it was for them to have time to reflect and plan. The media's compensation would be a press conference right before the winners accepted their prizes.

He realized TTC must be pretty powerful to muzzle the news. Or maybe it was just because the press people wanted to earn brownie points, thinking that someday they'd get a chance to go back in time. Either way, it was a relief. No way would Leon have been able to keep his secret with people probing at him day and night.

He went into his room and tossed the key on the dresser. He fell onto the bed and belched loudly, full from his steak dinner with cherry pie à la mode. He hadn't been this stuffed since he'd latched onto a lady friend who'd known cooking like he knew conning. But that had been six years ago. He reached for the remote and zapped the television to life. Yes, indeed. Middle-class living was mighty fine.

The news was on. "A transient was found dead today in the downtown area, his body stuffed behind a dumpster. The man had no identification but has been described as a black male, age seventy to seventy-five. Police are investigating."

Leon shook his head no. He pulled a pillow to his chest then hid his face in it. *Don't see me. Don't find me.*

Two more days to freedom. If only he could hold on 'til then.

The image of Roosevelt's bloodied body flashed into his mind. He shook his head against the pillow, trying to suffocate the memory, but it wouldn't leave. Would it ever leave?

He threw the pillow across the room and hurried to the bathroom.

Where he lost his fine steak dinner.

"Welcome to Kansas City, Mr. Hazen." A white man with blond hair opened the door of the limousine that had brought Leon from the Kansas City airport to the hotel. "My name is Alexander MacMillan. I will be your contact for the Time Lottery."

Leon shook his hand and met MacMillan's eyes. He thought he recognized him, like maybe from TV, but he quickly looked away.

MacMillan took Leon's bag and guided him toward the most beautiful fairyland of a hotel he'd ever seen. Regency Center, it was called. They entered a vast space, open two stories or more. Fountains and grass and little lights all around. Leon tried not to let on how impressed he was. He took a deep breath and yawned, all the while taking it in.

Mr. MacMillan handed him a plastic card.

"What's this?"

"It's the key to your room. Slip it in the door until the

green light comes on. Then push your door open."

"Oh." His room back in Memphis had been nice enough, but it'd had the old-fashioned kind of key on a bulky plastic bobble. A room with a pop machine by the office, next to the owner's red pickup. A motel whose lobby furniture consisted of two plastic chairs sitting in front of Venetian blinds that needed dusting. Not like this place at all.

MacMillan pointed to a grouping of brass doors. "The elevators are over here. Feel free to use the restaurants at our expense—or room service, if you prefer." He put a hand on Leon's arm. "We want you to have a restful, worry-free afternoon, Mr. Hazen, so you'll be fresh when the limousine picks you up at five."

"Five? I don't leave till tomorrow, do I?"

"That's correct. But this evening, there will be a short press conference. Just a few questions. Painless, I assure you."

Leon turned on his most charming smile. "Can't I take a bye on this one, Mr. MacMillan? I've been kind of out of it for awhile. I don't want those people prying into my downward spiral." *Downward spiral. . .that sounded good. Real good.*

"No one wants to embarrass you, Mr. Hazen, and you'll be free to refuse to answer any question you feel is inappropriate. But I'm afraid Mr. Wriggens, our chief administrator, insists the press conference goes on as scheduled." He smiled. "The press has been very cooperative, leaving you alone this week. But they *are* important to our program. I'm sure you can understand that."

"Yes, but—"

MacMillan shook Leon's hand. "I'll do my best to make the experience as easy as possible."

Leon had to accept defeat. He'd make it through somehow. "Don't get me wrong, Mr. MacMillan. Though I'm wary of the attention, that doesn't mean I'm not grateful. You can't know how much winning this Time Lottery means to me."

"Oh, I think I can."

Leon's stomach constricted. *He knows!*

But no. If he knew the truth he wouldn't let him go on with it. If TTC knew, MacMillan would be yanking him off to jail instead of settling him into a swanky hotel.

The elevator doors opened. Leon said his good-byes and escaped upstairs.

Mac's cell phone rang. He moved to a quiet corner of the hotel lobby.

"We have a problem."

As if in direct response to his boss's voice, Mac felt the start of a headache. "What is it?"

"Colin Thurgood, the husband of our winner Phoebe Thurgood, has filed a protest."

"A protest of what?"

"A protest against his wife accepting her prize."

Mac sank into a chair by a potted fern. "He's protesting against his own wife?"

"He wants to go in her place."

Mac wondered why the Thurgoods hadn't mentioned any of this when he'd met their limo at the hotel. First impressions had told Mac that Colin Thurgood was a proud man, even arrogant, but this? "His audacity is amazing."

"And badly timed."

"What does Mrs. Thurgood think about this?"

"That's for you to find out."

Mac checked his watch. "But I've got last-minute preparations for the press—"

"I'll handle that. Make the problem go away. Now. Get it straightened out. The press will have questions."

"The press knows about the protest?"

"Who do you think Thurgood called first?"

Phoebe Thurgood met Mac at the door of their hotel room. She avoided his gaze, but Mac noticed that her eyes were puffy.

She stood to the side. "Come in, Mr. MacMillan. My husband is waiting for you."

Colin Thurgood did not rise when Mac came in. He pointed to a chair. "Sit down, Mac. Let's come to terms."

Mac thought of mentioning that only his friends called him Mac but decided against it. He continued to stand, offering the chair to the lady, instead.

"I'm afraid there's nothing to work out, Mr. Thurgood. The Time Lottery has rules that—"

"Blast the rules. There isn't a rule in this world that can't be changed. It's all a matter of doing the right thing."

"I hardly think claiming your wife's Time Lottery prize is doing the right thing."

Phoebe sat with her hands in her lap, tracing the outline of the camellias that dotted her silk dress.

"It's not my wife's place to use such an opportunity. She has agreed, Mac. Just this morning she agreed to let me go."

Phoebe's hands paused on the stem of a flower.

Mac didn't ask Phoebe if it was true. Within her husband's presence, he was positive Phoebe Thurgood would nod in the affirmative. Mac kept his voice even. "It doesn't matter whether she agrees or not. All winners must go."

Colin scowled. "If she won a million dollars in a lottery, she could give her winnings to whomever she wanted, couldn't she?"

"Yes, I suppose she could," Mac said.

"So why is this different? Instead of money, her winnings are the chance to experience an alternate reality, that Alternity you advertise with such annoying regularity. She should have the same freedom to give it away if she wants to."

Phoebe's hands were busy again. Her eyes were on Mac. Pleading.

"Mr. Thurgood, for whatever reason, or due to whatever force of destiny you wish to credit, your wife has been chosen to win this prize. It is not up to us to analyze or try to understand such things. But my personal philosophy is that the three winners were chosen for a reason."

"Whose reason?"

Mac hesitated. "Mr. and Mrs. Thurgood, I hope you will forgive me for getting a little spiritual on you. TTC is not a Christian company, so what I'm going to say is my own personal belief and should not be construed as the company's official position. But Mr. Thurgood, I believe it was for God's purposes that these three winners were chosen."

"Oh, please."

Mac shrugged. "Believe what you choose. For reasons unfathomable to us, your wife has been given a chance to reassess one of her choices—and to perhaps change it permanently. I see this as a gift that cannot be taken lightly."

"Agreed. That's why I want it."

The gall of this man. "But you can't have it."

Colin stood and pointed his finger at Mac. "Now you listen to me. I've worked too hard, come too far not to get this—"

"Colin!"

The two men turned toward Phoebe's voice. She flinched at their sudden attention and swallowed slowly. "The prize is mine, Colin. I'm going."

"But, you can't. You said yes."

Phoebe's shoulders straightened. She lifted her chin. "Now I'm saying no."

Colin clenched a fist. "The press won't like this. I'll let them know how you agreed—"

Mac smiled. "The press will love this. The press will devour the story of the greedy husband wanting to steal his wife's chance at the Time Lottery. *If* you were invited to the press conference—which you are not—they'd have you for lunch. And I'd say *bon appetit.*"

With that, Mac turned and let himself out.

Mac was surprised to get her call. "What can I do for you, Mrs. Thurgood?"

Phoebe spoke in a whisper. "I just wanted to thank you, Mr. MacMillan."

"You're welcome. I'm glad I could be of some help."

"I have a favor to ask you."

"Yes?"

"Is there any way we can skip the press conference this evening? I don't feel up to it, and, well. . .the truth is that my husband. . . You said he wasn't invited, but I'm afraid he'll find a way to be there. Do you think it's possible to skip it?"

It was almost too bad that Colin wasn't invited. Mac even considered inviting him, just for the fun of watching the press devour him. The fact that he wanted his meek wife's winnings was something the public could relate to. But the fact she had stood up to him was something the public needed to celebrate.

"I'm afraid it can't be cancelled, Mrs. Thurgood. It's important the world sees you, gets to meet you."

"But what about Colin?"

Lock him in the hotel room. Throw away the key.

"I'm sure—I hope—your husband realizes it would be to his advantage to cooperate. To cause problems would cast him in a unfavorable light."

"That's never stopped him before." Phoebe took a deep breath.

"This is your moment of glory, Mrs. Thurgood. Of all the people in the world, you are one of the chosen. Be proud of it."

"But I'm scared. I can't imagine why I was chosen. I haven't done anything monumental with my life—good or bad. I've just been. . .just been. . ."

"Just been you."

"That's not much."

"It's plenty. You've been born for a unique purpose, Mrs. Thurgood. Many people think they've missed God's best for their lives. Maybe the Time Lottery will help you figure out what you're here for."

Her voice softened. "A purpose? For me? It's been so long since I've thought my life was worth anything."

"Then maybe this truly is your second chance."

There was a pause on the line. "Yes, I guess it is." Her voice gained strength. "It's *my* second chance. All right, Mr. MacMillan. I'll be at that press conference."

Mac hung up. He made himself a mental note to try to persuade Wriggens not to pursue the idea of selling time travel trips to the highest bidders. If Colin Thurgood was any indication of the rich, arrogant people they'd attract, Mac didn't want any part of it.

Dr. Cheryl Nickolby put her hand on the window of her hotel room. It was cold. There was no warmth in her touch. There was no warmth from anybody's touch. She was alone.

It was pathetic that tomorrow she was leaving on the journey of a lifetime, and no one had come to say good-bye. Of course, she'd told her friends to leave her alone, so whose fault was it? Still, it would've been nice to have someone at her side. That was why she was traveling back in time, wasn't it—to find a companion?

Yet, if she found a companion in the past—someone she could commit to—she would have to *stay* in the past. Live the majority of her life over again. If she had married the first time around, would she have gone on to medical school? Would she be a successful doctor? Or would she be a mom, sitting at home with a dozen ankle-biters?

She shook her head at the thought. She was not and had never been domestic. But she did like kids. One or two would have been nice. Her mom would have liked that. Grandchildren.

Her mom and Ted had offered to come see her off. She'd declined. But now, with a press conference looming and her departure less than twenty-four hours away, she wanted her mommy—and her father of the month. Even Ted was better than nothing.

The phone rang.

"Hello, dear. Guess what?"

Cheryl sat on the side of the bed. "Hi, Mom."

"Ted and I have decided to come see you off. Don't you dare say no. We shouldn't have listened to you the first time. You need family with you, and we're it. So don't say another word, or I'll get Ted on the phone and he'll give you what for."

"Okay."

There was a pause on the line. "Okay?"

"I'd love to have you here with me."

"Oh. Well. . .that's it, then. We'll be there tomorrow. Ted says we can make a vacation of it and continue on down to Florida. Do you think my gray dress would be okay? I could make a quick stop at the mall and find something new. Ted said I could buy something, and there *was* this mauve dress I've had my eye on over at. . ."

For the first—and maybe last—time in her life, Cheryl leaned against the headboard and relished every word her mother said.

When Mac entered the waiting room, he noticed the three winners were gathered close, talking, like football players before a big play.

But there was a fourth player present: Colin Thurgood. Mac was disappointed to see him. Which part of "You're not invited" didn't he understand? Colin eyed Mac arrogantly, but Phoebe avoided eye contact.

Mr. Hazen removed himself from the huddle and sprawled in his chair, looking like he owned the place. Dr. Nickolby seemed the most at ease. She sat back in her chair, her legs crossed comfortably. She waved at him. "Hey, Mr. MacMillan." She seemed to radiate a passion for life. It also didn't hurt that she was stunning, even if she was ten years his senior.

Mac shook hands all around. "The press conference will begin in a few minutes." He flashed them a reassuring smile. "Don't worry, you're all going to do fine. I'll take you out one at a time, introduce you, and then you will have a chance to make a statement. We will allow a few questions, most of which will probably pertain to which time you have chosen to visit and what choice you're thinking of making differently."

"We have to tell them?" Roosevelt said.

"Well, Mr. Hazen, that *is* the purpose of the press conference. Is there a problem?"

Roosevelt hesitated. "It's just that I don't want the world butting into my business."

Mac nodded. "I understand. But what you need to also understand is that if a winner doesn't come back, TTC needs to be able to relate at least this portion of his or her story. The world will want to know." He shrugged. "Who knows? Maybe the public can even learn something about their own lives by knowing about the choice you make. Letting us in on a bit of your experience is not too much to ask for this opportunity, is it?"

Dr. Nickolby rubbed her hands together. "Nope, no sir. My life is an open book. The pages are a bit coffee-stained and dog-eared, but I have nothing to hide."

"Who said I was hiding something?" Roosevelt said.

"All right, then," Mac said. "So there's no problem, correct?"

Roosevelt shook his head.

Mac took a deep breath. "Okay, back to the press conference. Just be yourselves." He gave Colin a stern glance. "Mr. Thurgood, please help yourself to coffee and snacks while you wait for your wife."

Colin met Mac's gaze and did not look away.

"Now," Mac said, "moving on to tomorrow and your actual journey. Although you will be embarking on a bit of scientific magic, you must remember that we're not controlling anything about what happens in your Alternity. We cannot make the judges choose you as Miss America or make your boss give you a raise—unless *you* do something that would make them legitimately take that action. As you sit here now, you know what you want to change. Perhaps you've grieved over it for years. Now is your chance to make things right or to be the person you always wanted to be."

Everyone nodded. Roosevelt moved to the edge of his chair. He seemed ready to be launched from a catapult.

"After you enter the Sphere," Mac said, "you will lie down in a nice, comfortable bed. We will attach some life support monitors, IVs, a catheter—"

"Oh, goodie," Dr. Nickolby said. "I've always wanted one of those."

Mac smiled. "Once you are all set up medically, we will position a device around your head, pinpoint your Loop, and our medical staff will give you a dose of a serum."

"I assume you have it in bubblegum flavor?" Dr. Nickolby asked.

Mac chuckled. "It's in the form of a shot, I'm afraid."

Roosevelt huffed. "*You're* afraid? I hate shots."

"We'll try to make it as painless as possible. Next you will be asked to think of the time you wish to visit and the choice you'd like to make differently. You will fall into a deep sleep, similar to being put under anesthesia except your mind will be wonderfully awake as you discover this wonderful new—old—world that seems realer than real."

"And bingo, you're there, right?" Roosevelt said.

"Something like that. Your consciousness will quickly adjust, and you will begin your journey through your alternate timeline."

Phoebe laughed nervously. "It sounds simple enough."

"Please note that you will be as innocent of the future as you were the first time around," Mac said. "Will you make the same choices you made before? No. As you're transitioning into your Alternity, you'll be concentrating on the choice you want to make differently. The serum acts as a magnifier for your thoughts. When the moment of choice comes, you will feel strongly urged to take one path over another. In all our tests, it hasn't failed yet. You will be quite free to live the consequences of your new choices."

Cheryl raised a hand. "I prefer to call them the *fruits* of my choices rather than consequences." She winked at him. "Or do you know me better than I think you do, Mr. MacMillan?"

Mac felt himself blush and cleared his throat. "After seven days in your Alternity, we will initiate an electrical charge to the Loop. It will give you the ability to regain your 'real' memories. We call it Dual Consciousness. It only lasts about an hour, but it is plenty of time for you to choose to stay in your Alternity or return to us here.

"If you stay in the past, all memory of your life in the future will fade and seem to you like a dream. As your body here dies a peaceful death in the Sphere, any family you have in this time—or charity of your choice—will receive the benefits of the $250,000 insurance policy provided by TTC."

Roosevelt raised his hand. "We can't get killed in the past, can we?"

Mac nodded. "You certainly can. There will be no magic hands pulling you out of danger. You are totally on your own. Your fate is in your own hands. And God's, if you believe as I do."

"How about getting hurt *while* we're going back?" Phoebe said. "Is the whole thing safe?"

Mac gave her a reassuring smile. "Perfectly. You are going back in time based on the power of your own mind, not some man-made machine. We merely enhance and direct the process."

Mac looked at their faces. "All right, if there are no more questions, I'll leave you a few moments while I check the final arrangements for the press conference."

Leon stared at Dr. Cheryl Nickolby, and it wasn't just because she was pretty.

Dr. Cheryl. . .Dr. Cheryl. . . He'd met her somewhere before. But where? He hadn't been in a hospital since the day he was born. Didn't go to doctors much either—especially lady doctors. He'd been at the clinic, but that was recent and his memory of Dr. Cheryl was old.

He listened to her talk to the other winner—a classy lady and her idiot husband. Their name was Thurgood. An uppity name that matched the man's way of sneering even when he smiled.

"Actually, I've lived all over," the doctor told Mrs. Thurgood. "My mother is the marrying kind. Unfortunately, she's also the divorcing kind. So we moved wherever her husbands' jobs took us. I live in Boulder now."

"Oh, I love Colorado," Mrs. Thurgood said. "Especially Aspen. But we've been in San Francisco for years."

"Really?" the doctor said. "I lived in Oakland for awhile."

Mrs. Thurgood perked up. "When?"

The pretty doctor looked to the ceiling as if there were a calendar there. "Late sixties. Something like that."

"Small world."

"Not so small. . .for me, anyway. I've lived in Oakland, Tulsa, Boulder, Lincoln, Nebraska. . ."

Lincoln! Leon had been to Lincoln. He looked away, trying to zero in on his own memories. What had happened there? It was after he'd gotten out of jail, 1970-something—

Dr. Cheryl! He looked at her close. Blond, thirty years older. . .

She noticed his stare. "Is something wrong, Mr. Hazen?"

He laughed. Too loud. "No, ma'am. Not a single thing. I was just thinking."

"We've all done a bit of that lately." She laughed.

The laugh. The laugh confirmed it. Leon opened his mouth to say something, wanting to share this link with his fellow travelers. But he stopped himself cold.

Leon Burke had met Dr. Cheryl. Roosevelt Hazen hadn't.

Phoebe saw Colin look at his watch and throw his hands in the air the way she'd seen him do a thousand times.

"Well. We're having some fun now, aren't we?" he said.

Cheryl raised an eyebrow. "Actually, I think we are. We're bonding."

Colin stood and began to pace. "Why? You're total strangers. After this press conference is over, you probably won't even see each other again. It's not like you are going to meet up with each other in the past."

Phoebe turned on him. "Stop being such a *nudzh*, Colin. Let us be excited, all right? We're going to visit our Alternity. Like Mr. MacMillan said, I think there's some kind of purpose to it all. Like it was meant to be."

"Oh, please."

Cheryl nodded. "Our purpose. . .hmm. I like that idea. We're the first to go. We're like pioneers—which puts a lot of pressure on us to do good—or at least to do better. But the possibilities are—"

Colin let out a laugh. "Phoebe? Do better? She couldn't possibly get a better life than the one she has right now."

"You take a cocky pill this morning, Thurgood?" Cheryl said. "Or are you always this charming?"

The other winner—Roosevelt Hazen—clapped. "Hear,

hear, little lady! Don't let him talk to you like that."

Phoebe tried not to smile. These two strangers were a balm to her soul.

Colin shrugged. "I'm always this charming."

He was something else. Phoebe turned to Roosevelt. "How about you, Mr. Hazen? Do you feel as though there's a greater purpose behind you being chosen? Do you wonder, 'Why me?' "

"Actually, I've been thinking, 'Why not me?' "

He was right. Why not him? Why not any of them?

Phoebe stood. "Have you wondered why they call it our Alternity? I mean, that's pretty close to the word 'eternity,' right?"

"They say Alternity stands for Alternate Reality," Cheryl said.

"I know, but I was thinking that maybe the Alternity *does* have something to do with eternity. It sounds like a place where we work things out—things we've done wrong."

"A time travel purgatory?" Cheryl said.

Roosevelt fidgeted in his chair. "I don't like the sound of that."

Phoebe shrugged. "It was just a thought."

Colin snorted. "A dumb one."

"Hey," Cheryl said. "Back off, or I'll suture your lips shut."

Phoebe stifled a giggle. She looked at the door Mac had gone through. Meeting dozens of reporters was markedly more appealing than sitting next to her husband for one more minute.

Cheryl stood and stretched. "Whatever this Alternity thing is, I wish we were going today. The waiting is killing me."

Mac came through the door. "Mrs. Thurgood, we'll start with you."

Mac said a silent prayer and opened the auditorium door to begin the press conference. He led Phoebe Thurgood to a table on a raised dais and sat beside her. He noticed Wriggens standing in the back of the room. So much was riding on the next twenty-four hours going smoothly.

As they were settling in, Colin came through the door, strode across the front of the room, grabbed a chair, and joined them at the table.

Mac leaned toward him. "You'll have to leave."

"Make me." Colin flashed a smile to the press.

Mac looked to Phoebe. She shook her head slightly, surrendering the fight. Poor woman.

Mac had instructed the hotel to provide two microphones, one for the winner and one for himself. Colin adjusted Phoebe's microphone.

Mac pulled his own mike close. "Good day, ladies and gentlemen. Thank you for coming out today. At this time I would like to introduce you to the first of our three winners of the Time Lottery. She is from San Francisco, where she is the mother of two grown children. She is active in many charitable organizations and was the chairperson of the Mother's Aid food drive this past year, a campaign which brought in $25,000 in cash donations, as well as thousands of pounds of nonperishable food items. She is an accomplished tennis player and has traveled extensively. May I present to you Phoebe Thurgood."

While Phoebe was nodding to the applause and saying how happy she was to be there, Colin leaned toward the mike, forcing her to move away. "And I'm her husband, Colin Thurgood, a managing partner of Century Enterprises."

Mac spoke up. "Mrs. Thurgood, would you like to make a statement?" She shook her head. Mac addressed the press. "Then you may ask your questions."

A man in the front row raised a hand. "What year are you going to visit, and what is its significance?"

Phoebe leaned into the microphone. "1969." She glanced at her husband. He raised an eyebrow, daring her. She turned back to the questioner. "As far as the significance, it was a time when I was a secretary, when I was single, when my career was just beginning."

"So, you regret not pursuing your career?"

"Not exactly." Phoebe reddened. "I regret some of the decisions I made, some of the attitudes that were born in that time of my life."

"What does your husband think about you going back before you two were married?"

Colin slid the microphone away from her. "He thinks it's a bunch of garbage. The most noteworthy thing that's ever happened to my wife was marrying me."

There was a round of groans. Snickers. Mac watched Wriggens take a step forward.

"It's true," Colin continued. "I'll give her credit, she's a good wife and a good mother. But as far as any earth-shattering accomplishment in her life, I'm it."

"Sir," a woman reporter said, "are you saying that your own wife's life is nothing without you?"

"Absolutely. That's why I want to go in her place."

There was a general intake of breath. A reporter near Wriggens stood. "We heard about that, Mr. Thurgood. But we also assumed, since your wife is obviously still going, that you had dropped the notion."

"I haven't dropped it."

"Why not?"

"Because I deserve to go." Colin turned to Mac and pointed. "But he won't let me."

Colin sat back in his chair and grinned through the ruckus. One question rose above the rest. "What makes you think you deserve to go instead of your wife?"

"Do you want me to make a list?"

The reporters shouted over each other. Mac would have enjoyed watching Colin dig his own grave, but the pained look on Phoebe's face made him jump in. "If you'll all quiet down, we can settle this." He waited until the room stilled. "No matter what opinions Mr. Thurgood may hold, the Time Lottery is nontransferable. Period."

"Mr. MacMillan?" Phoebe said. "May I say something?"

Mac waved an arm, gladly giving her the floor.

Phoebe cautiously slid the microphone away from Colin. "I don't completely understand how this Time Lottery works, but it's a marvelous thing. It's already given me a second chance. I'm starting to feel different about things. Hopeful. Like maybe I don't have to be stuck doing the same things I've always done, feeling the same feelings, saying the same words. Maybe I can change. For the better. Maybe it's never too late."

She looked to her husband, who glared at her. Mac tried to encourage her with a smile. He liked the glow that had come to her cheeks.

"If it was within the rules," she said, "and if I felt my husband should go in my place, I'd let him—with my blessings."

Colin leaned forward expectantly.

"But I don't feel that way. And though most of us will never have the experience of knowing such things for certain, I feel, with as much certainty as I can feel, that I am supposed to accept this prize. I am going to do something good with it. Something to better myself, my family. . ." She looked at her hands gripping the microphone. The image seemed to surprise her. She let go. "I've made mistakes—mostly mistakes of omission. I didn't stand up for the right things. I let people get by with—" She glanced at her husband. "If we turn our heads and refuse to see. . .people need to be held accountable."

"To whom?" a reporter asked.

She hesitated only a moment. "To what's right. To ethics and honesty." She took a deep breath. "I guess that's it."

Perfect. Mac stood. "You heard the lady. That's it. In just a moment I'll bring in the next winner."

Once they had exited the room, Thurgood spun toward his wife. "How could you be so selfish?"

She walked away, her chin held high. "It's easy. I learned it from you."

"Don't be nervous, Dr. Nickolby," Mac said. "Just be yourself."

Cheryl took a deep breath. "*Myself* does not usually speak before the press. Myself is aware of the way the press exaggerates and embellishes." Her hands danced in the air.

"I prefer to exaggerate and embellish my life in private, if you don't mind."

"I'll agree with that one," Roosevelt said.

Mac smiled. After dealing with Colin Thurgood, Dr. Nickolby's charm was a tonic. "Shall we go?"

"Isn't it customary for the victim to get a blindfold?"

"Close your eyes. I'll guide you."

"If only you would."

As Mac led the way into the auditorium and to the table at the front, he was startled by applause. He looked back and saw Dr. Nickolby with her arms lifted like an Olympic champion receiving a medal. She was going to do just fine.

They sat. "At this time, I would like to introduce to you our second winner of the Time Lottery. She is a distinguished surgeon at Mount Mercy Hospital in Boulder, Colorado. But I'll let her tell you about herself. I am honored to present to you Dr. Cheryl Nickolby."

Mac joined the applause.

"Thank you," Cheryl said. "Keep this up and I'll run for president."

They laughed.

She crossed her forearms on the table and leaned forward. The pink of her cheeks complemented her burgundy suit and blond hair.

"Mr. MacMillan didn't know what he was in for, letting me talk about myself. I'm not the shy sort."

"Are you married?" yelled a reporter from midroom.

"Is that a proposal?"

Laughter again.

She raised a finger, scolding them. "You'll get your

chance in a minute. Right now, let me give my spiel, and then you can pounce." She took a breath. "All right, here goes. My name is Cheryl Renee Nickolby. I was born in Tulsa, bred and brainwashed in various other cities of choice. At the present, Boulder, Colorado, is my home. I am old enough to remember hot pants with embarrassment and young enough to look good in them. I am unmarried—never married, if you need to be nosy." She looked in the direction of the first questioner. "But I'm always open to suggestions."

Hoots and whistles. Mac leaned back, enjoying the show.

"As Mr. MacMillan said, I am a surgeon—a great surgeon, last time I checked. Which means I can dissect any one of you ladies and gentlemen who choose to get out of line and then send you the bill." She raised her shoulders. "That's about it. Fire away."

"What year are you visiting?"

"I am returning to 1973, to high school."

"Why?"

She batted her lashes. "Guess."

"Does it have to do with romance?"

"You'd like to think so, wouldn't you?"

"Can I go, too?"

"Maybe next trip."

"Are you planning to stay in your Alternity?"

"I'll answer that with my own question." She smiled wickedly. "How many of you would like to relive your teen years?"

There was a communal groan.

"Exactly. To be truthful, I'm content with my life as it is. I am returning to 1973 for the fun of it. However, if events prove to be irresistible, Mount Mercy might soon be in need of a new surgeon."

A woman raised her hand. "Question for Mr. MacMillan."

Mac pulled his microphone close. "Shoot."

"You've explained about the alternate dimensions or timelines, but I'm still confused about one thing. What happens to the person's 'Alternity' if she decides to come back to us here? You've talked about it being like a dream. Does that mean that that whole other reality ceases to exist if the traveler decides not to stay with it?"

"Oh, good question," Mac said. "Of course we have no real way of knowing, because the only one who could visit that timeline and tell us what's going on there has returned to our time and can't see it anymore. But TTC scientists, backed by the theories of probability studies and quantum physics, believe that the time streams continue as they were. It's like going on vacation. Does Florida cease to exist when we come home?" He smiled. "Or the old conundrum: If a tree falls in the forest, and there's no one around, does it make any sound?"

There was soft laughter.

"The timelines are separate realities. And you and I really *do* exist there. If you were to hop over to another one of those time streams, you would be visiting something already in progress. Before the *you* from this timeline had ever gotten there, the *you* of that timeline would've been born and grown up and everything else. It stands to reason, then, that if you decide to leave it, that timeline will continue on, even though the *you* of this timeline is not involved or aware of it anymore. The *you* of that timeline will go right along on the path you have set while you were there."

The woman shook her head slightly. "It really does baffle the mind, doesn't it?"

"Absolutely," Mac said. He pointed to a reporter on his left. "Go ahead."

"This is a question for Dr. Nickolby. Doc, please tell me if you make house calls."

"Leave your number, and I'll call you when I get back."

"*If* you get back."

"Touché."

The waiting was driving Leon crazy. Why couldn't he have been first?

Maybe there wasn't a press conference at all. Maybe MacMillan had called the others away in order to get Leon alone so he could call in the law. *We're sorry, Mr. Burke, but you will have to come with us.*

Leon jerked when MacMillan came in the door. "Are you ready, Mr. Hazen?"

Leon stood but immediately fell back into the chair.

"Are you all right?"

Leon put a hand to his forehead. He felt green. "It's this press conference. I don't think I can do it." Forget acting sure of himself. He felt as if he were going before a firing squad.

"There's nothing to be worried about, Mr. Hazen."

Leon's stomach churned. His whole life was converging on this moment, and he didn't like it.

MacMillan sat beside him. "Perhaps we should pray?"

"I'm not good at praying." Then he remembered that

Roosevelt had been a preacher. "At least not anymore."

"Then I'll do it for the both of us." MacMillan bowed his head. "Thy will be done."

Leon looked up. "That's it?"

"It's enough, don't you think?" MacMillan stood and extended a hand to help him up. "Let's go."

Leon sat next to MacMillan at a table at the front of the room. Cameras were everywhere. To Leon the press people seemed like wolves waiting for the kill.

MacMillan raised a hand, making them quiet. "I would like to introduce you to our final winner, Roosevelt Hazen. Mr. Hazen isn't feeling very well this evening, so we are going to keep this brief so he can have a chance to rest before his big day tomorrow."

A man in an outdated suit stood up in the front row. "What year are you going to visit, Mr. Hazen?"

That one he could handle. "1962."

"What was happening in 1962?"

Leon looked at MacMillan. "Let's just say that love and money are involved." *Why did I mention money?*

A reporter in the back stood. "This is for Mr. MacMillan. Can any of these winners travel into the future or go back to before they were born?"

Mac leaned toward the mike. "No, they cannot. Since each timeline is reached through the Loop in the individual's brain—that place where memories are stored—they can only access points in time that they have lived. Therefore Mr. Hazen could not go back before. . ." He turned to Leon.

"What year were you born?"

Leon thought fast. Roosevelt was five years older than himself. "1932."

"Mr. Hazen could not go back before 1932—or into the future, to a year he hasn't experienced yet."

Another reporter raised his hand. "Where are you from, Mr. Hazen?"

"Around."

"Is it true you're homeless?"

"If you let me move in with you, I wouldn't be."

The reporters' laughs relaxed him.

"What was your profession in 1962?"

A king of the con men. A master of misdeeds. "I was a preacher."

"Quote us something from the Bible, Mr. Hazen."

Leon tried to laugh. "I don't—"

MacMillan broke in. "Mr. Hazen is nervous enough without you making him—"

Leon wagged a finger in the air. "Wait. How's this one? 'If any one of you is without sin, let him be the first to throw a stone.' " Leon sat back. He had no idea where that had come from. Maybe it was Grammy talking through him. But the words iced the cake quite nicely. The reporters stopped talking.

MacMillan stood. He was smiling. "I think that takes care of it."

Leon let MacMillan lead him from the room. "That wasn't so bad."

"You continue to surprise me, Mr. Hazen," MacMillan said when they were through the door. "First you're about to be sick, and then you handle the reporters like a pro. It's like you're two men in one."

Leon tried to laugh.

CHAPTER 5

Life will be brighter than noonday,
and darkness will become like morning.
You will be secure, because there is hope;
you will look about you and take your rest in safety.

Job 11:17–18

John Wriggens tapped a pencil against his thigh. "Everything had better go smoothly, Mac."

Mac put on his most confident look. "It will."

"The entire future of TTC is at stake," Wriggens said. "The press is hovering. One glitch, one screw-up, and this will be the last Time Lottery. And we will then have no further need of your services."

There it was again. The bottom line. People did not exist for him, only numbers. "Perhaps we should be more concerned with the winners' lives than a budget?"

"Why? Their lives are not in danger."

Mac put a hand on his arm. "Don't worry, John. Everything will be fine. I've got it under control."

Wriggens's eyes flashed. *"You've* got it under control?"

Mac heard voices in the hallway. The winners were arriving to begin their journey.

Mac greeted each of the winners and their families and escorted them to their private waiting rooms. A dressing area was provided where the winners could change into their travel clothes—a pair of drawstring pants and a pullover shirt, hospital-issue garments that should provide them comfort in their comalike state as they whizzed into their past.

Mac knew that the waiting was the hardest part. Once the people stepped through the door into the Sphere, they would be fine.

At least Phoebe had Colin—such as he was—and Cheryl had her parents with her. But Roosevelt Hazen was alone. It was sad. Obviously years living on the street had severed the ties that bind. If Roosevelt had any living relatives, they were far enough estranged not to be drawn to his celebrity. He led him into his dressing room.

"Here we are, Mr. Hazen. Please change into these clothes."

Roosevelt eyed the clothing warily. "I guess I should be glad it's not a gown open up the back." He nudged the pants with a finger. "Actually, I prefer my duds a bit more flashy." Roosevelt started talking fast. "I mean, *I* didn't dress flashy, but this friend of mine did. Leon was a real fancy dresser, yes sir."

"Who's Leon?"

Roosevelt wobbled on his feet. "What?"

"Leon. You just mentioned his name, and I was looking over your TTC entrance interview a minute ago where you also mentioned a Leon. You said that the choice you wanted to change in the past had something to do with him."

Roosevelt's shoulders dropped an inch. "Oh. . .yeah. Leon was a man who came to our church. A handyman. There are a few things that should be cleared up between us." He looked to the floor. "You've had times like that, haven't you, Mr. MacMillan? Things left undone between friends?"

"Certainly. That's the whole purpose of the Time Lottery, to give you a chance to redeem yourself, make things right."

Roosevelt started to unbutton his shirt.

"All right, Mr. Hazen," Mac said, "your turn should be coming pretty soon. We'll get the ladies going, and then I'll be back to get you."

Roosevelt drew in a breath and started coughing. "I'm last? Can't I go first? I was last yesterday. This waiting is murder. I mean, it's hard."

"It won't be long, Mr. Hazen, I promise. We are sending you back in the order you were picked."

Roosevelt fell into a fit of coughing. He made a visible effort to calm his hacking. "How long?"

"Less than an hour and you'll be off." Mac noticed there was sweat on Roosevelt's brow though the room was cool.

Cheryl toyed with the idea of shoving her stepfather's argyle socks in her mother's mouth.

Since they'd arrived, her mother hadn't stopped talking about her favorite recipes. As she launched into the punch recipe used for their wedding—three years previous—Cheryl turned to check her stepfather's reaction. Ted was leafing through a *National Geographic.* Was he mentally traveling to Kamchatka for a bit of peace and quiet?

Cheryl tried to slip into la-la land, a place she had seen her patients explore when too many visitors crowded into their hospital rooms after surgery. She let her eyes glaze over as she tried to figure out why her parents had traveled 250 miles to do whatever it was they were doing.

She was on the verge of screaming when Mac slipped through the door. Her mother stopped her explanation of how to make the best chocolate-covered cherries in the entire world, and Ted closed the pages on New South Wales.

Mac walked toward her, his hands behind his back like a tour guide. "Shall we proceed?"

She stood up. "Yes. Please."

Mac nodded toward her parents. Cheryl took the cue, stood before her mother and Ted, and said her good-byes.

"We love you, sweetie," her mother said. "We'll be waiting to hear all about it when you come back."

Cheryl opened her mouth to remind her she might not be coming back but thought better of it. She kissed her and followed Mac out the door.

The Sphere was not what Cheryl expected. The room was cavernous. The inside of it was painted sky blue. A balcony encircled the room. It was a viewing gallery. Right now it was packed with dignitary types and a plethora of cameras. Cheryl waved and received a few waves back. Even so, thousands of cubic feet remained unused.

"So. . .this is it?"

Mac swept a hand. "This is it."

"I'd fire your architect, Mac. He seemed to misjudge the spatial requirements of the functional space."

"There is reason behind the Sphere's size."

"A big budget?"

He laughed. "Marketing. From the exterior the Sphere stands out on the skyline. Its geodesic nature is associated with science and precision and implies that the Time Lottery is a viable program."

"Marketing baloney. I see why they hired you."

"Thank you."

On the floor at the center of the Sphere there was a team of employees in lab coats seated before a bank of computers and other machines. An authoritative-looking man in a suit stood behind them. His stern expression and the way he held his arms behind his back made Cheryl guess that he was not a man many crossed on purpose.

A doctor and nurse hovered near one of the hospital beds that took up positions at twelve, three, and nine o'clock. In addition to the normal life-sustaining equipment of IVs and monitors, at the head of each bed was a machine that looked very much like a small MRI. Cheryl took a step toward the one to her left, eyeing it. "Is that what I think it is?"

Mac motioned to the doctor standing nearby. "I'll defer to Dr. Rodriguez to answer that."

The doctor moved to the machine with pride, like a game show model exhibiting a new washer-dryer.

"If you mean an MRI, you are correct, Dr. Nickolby," he said. "The roots of this machine are in the fMRI—the Functional Magnetic Resonance Imaging—that is used to map the body. Since we are only interested in the brain, we have minimized the size. To be even more specific, we have perfected a technique for pinpointing the Loop—that part of the brain that's activated by the stimulus of memory. Through this machine we will continuously monitor the brainwave signature of the patient as the Loop uncoils."

He patted the machine. "It works the same as a traditional MRI, through the use of nonionizing radiation, with the signal coming from the exit of protons—" He looked up, met Mac's eyes, and cut it short.

"We tap into the Loop through the use of the MRI's magnetic and radio waves and then go a step further and map your unique brainwave signature. Although we don't have the technology as yet, someday we hope to design a set of sensors that would allow us to make an actual recording of what you are experiencing. Imagine being able to see and hear everything in someone else's—"

"But you can't watch us now?" Cheryl asked. "Big Brother hasn't progressed that far?"

The doctor smiled. "Not yet."

"Yes, yes. Enough of the science lesson." They all turned to see the man in the suit stepping toward them. Cheryl noticed that even though he was overweight, his suit fit him perfectly, and his red tie appeared to be silk. He thrust his hand toward her. "Chief Administrator John Wriggens."

"Dr. Cheryl Nickolby."

Mac stepped forward. "Forgive me. Let me make the proper introductions." He turned to the doctor first. "Dr. Carl Rodriguez, Dr. Nickolby."

They shook hands. Then Cheryl turned to the nurse. "Hi, nice to meet you, Nurse. . . ?"

"Doris Conner. Nice to meet you, too, Dr. Nickolby."

Cheryl looked beyond Wriggens to the people by the computer consoles. She waved. They all smiled, and a few waved back.

Wriggens flipped a hand, dismissing them as peons. "Yes, yes. Hello–hello." He looked at his watch, then at Mac. "Let's get going. We have others waiting, you know."

Cheryl interpreted Mac's look as a silent apology.

"If you'll just lie down, Dr. Nickolby," the nurse said, "we'll begin."

"Absolutely."

Wriggens and Mac stepped away, pulling a privacy curtain to allow Dr. Rodriguez and the nurse to attach the life support tubes, a catheter, and sensors at her vital points. Once she was prepped, they pulled back the curtain and moved the MRI machine into place, surrounding her head. Cheryl was relieved that it did not cover her eyes. Not that she would be awake, but she didn't need claustrophobia to kick in.

As they finished, Mac moved to her side. "Any parting words?"

"This is cool."

Mac laughed. "I see you've already revived the seventies' vernacular."

"*Cool* is ageless."

"Agreed. This is indeed cool." He put a hand on her arm. "If you're ready, we'll inject the serum and let the power of your own mind take over."

"I never thought I'd say this, but I'm ready to go back to high school. Let's do this thing."

Mac squeezed her arm. "God bless you on your journey, Dr. Nickolby." He took a step back, and Dr. Rodriguez moved into his position with a shot ready.

"All you have to do is relax and think of the time you want to visit and the new choice you'd like to make. Don't worry if nothing happens right away. The serum will take effect within minutes and help you hold on to the memories."

Sitting on the edge of her departure, Cheryl wanted to say something witty or profound, but she found herself beyond words. She had a mental image of her mother driving some poor skycap mad with her recipe for ratatouille while Ted tipped him a whole quarter for handling four pieces of luggage.

Cheryl thought of the mice in the cabin, lying on the Morris chair, toasting her departure with a feast of Oreo crumbs.

She thought of the people at the hospital and hoped Nurse Ratchins would remember to watch Mabel Graham's sutures closely. And Nurse Williams—did he remember to put a piece of her good-bye cake in the freezer so she could have it when she got back?

She thought of Pam and Julie. If only they could go with her.

"You'll feel a little prick now."

With the shot, Cheryl's stomach grabbed with nerves and excitement. *Keep me safe, God.*

She closed her eyes. *I live in Lincoln, Nebraska, I'm a senior in high school. My best friends are Pam and Julie, and I'd really like to become the girlfriend of Jake Carlisle.*

Cheryl felt herself relax. Her memories found their own energy and grew stronger as if she were seeing them in the moment, rather than after the fact.

Her body felt weightless. Then suddenly she became heavier, as if she had eaten one of her mother's pound cakes with eight glasses of milk. She found she could move. She could open her eyes.

She needed to go to the bathroom.

"Stop!"

Pam slammed on the brakes, nearly sending Cheryl through the windshield. Julie, who was sitting between them in the front seat, massaged the wrist she had jammed against the dashboard.

"I didn't mean stop in the middle of the street, doofus. I meant pull over."

"Criminy, Cheryl," Pam said. "Don't say stop unless you mean it."

She opened her door. "I mean it."

"Where are you going?"

Cheryl was out and running. "There's a man."

She didn't catch their response but heard Pam's car pull onto the gravel shoulder ahead of her. The brake lights lit the night, then blinked out. Two car doors slammed, and her friends ran back to her.

Where is he? Cheryl had seen the headlights fall on a man's legs, inches from the side of the highway. But it was so dark on these country roads she was afraid the only way she would find him would be to trip over him.

Two legs appeared in her path. The black man lay on his side as if sleeping. But there was blood on his head. Cheryl put her ear to his mouth. She felt faint breath.

Pam and Julie arrived. "Oh my. . .it's a man!"

"I told you."

"I'll get a flashlight and a first-aid kit." Pam ran back to the car.

The man's jacket was an old suit coat that puddled on the ground around his skinny frame. His belt was pulled past its tightest notch, and his pants were gathered. One shoelace was a knotted piece of string. His black hair was long and dirty, but his brown face was handsome.

"He's a bum."

Cheryl looked up at Julie. "What happened to Julie, the Jesus-freak? Love your neighbor and all that?"

Pam returned. She handed Cheryl the first-aid kit and held the flashlight on the man. He looked better in the dark.

"Is he dead?"

"He's breathing. But he's scraped his head pretty bad." Cheryl tore open the antiseptic cloth and began wiping the man's forehead and hairline.

"Ahhhhhhh."

Julie and Pam stepped back. Cheryl stopped dabbing at the blood. The man opened his eyes, blinked, then repeated the process.

"Who are you?"

"You're on the side of the road," Cheryl said. "Your head is cut. What happened?"

The man tried to sit but crumpled back to the ground. He put a hand to his forehead and winced. "Hitchhiking."

"Somebody picked you up?"

Cheryl helped him sit up. "Picked me up and threw me out."

"Who would do that?"

He eyed each of them. "Kids. Drunk kids."

Julie put her hands on her hips. "I can't believe anybody from around here would do such a thing."

The man managed to get to his feet. Cheryl and Pam gave him support. "Maybe you should lie still awhile longer?"

"Can't. It's cold." He staggered a step. "Gotta find a place to sleep."

The girls looked at each other. Christian charity was one thing, but bringing home a bum was quite another. He'd taken three steps before they responded.

"We'll give you a ride into town."

He turned to face them. "No, no, no. Fool me once, shame on you. Fool me twice, shame on me."

"We're not like *them*," Julie said.

Two headlights appeared on the road, coming toward them. The car slowed then pulled onto the opposite shoulder. Two guys got out. Cheryl recognized them at once. Jocks. The in-crowd. The Perfect People.

"Hey, girls? Trying to pick up a date?"

"Lay off, Randy," Cheryl said. "The guy was hurt."

The two crossed the highway, giving the black man a

good stare. Cheryl ignored Randy, but the other guy, Jake Carlisle. . .she'd always found him interesting in a Big Man on Campus sort of way. Interesting—and inaccessible. A challenge she hadn't taken.

"Hi, Jake."

"Hi, Cheryl. Julie. What's-your-name."

Pam huffed. "Thanks a lot."

Cheryl helped the man to Pam's car where he leaned against the trunk. Blood ran down his forehead. "Let me get that cut bandaged before you get blood all over your coat."

Randy laughed. "As if it would hurt it."

The man looked at him. "Sorry, hotshot, my tux is at the cleaners."

"Somebody tossed him out of their car," Pam said.

Randy laughed. "A bum toss. Maybe they should make it an Olympic event."

"That's sick."

"Shut up, Randy." Jake came to her side and held the gauze while Cheryl ripped off tape with her teeth. "You're good at this."

"Thanks."

"You should be a doctor."

She smiled. "I've thought about it, but my mom doesn't seem to think women can do such a thing."

"Baloney. Women are the ones with the power."

Cheryl looked at his face, trying to get his meaning. He grinned, leaving her imagination to run wild. Her insides fluttered. "Maybe I'll have to test the extent of my power sometime."

"You do that."

The bum watched. "Hold the hormones, you two." The man put a hand on her arm and leaned forward to whisper. "Watch the good-looking ones, girlie-girl."

She smiled at him. "You speak from experience?"

His back straightened. "I've had my share."

"Good for you." She applied the last piece of tape.

"You have a soft touch." He held out a hand for her to shake. "Thanks for the help, Dr. Cheryl. My name's Leon." His hand was sandpaper rough. He touched his bandage. "Now, if you don't mind, I'll take you up on that ride to town. I'm sure there's a shelter somewhere."

Jake spoke up. "There's the City Mission."

"I'm thinking we should take you to a hospital," Cheryl said.

Leon moved to the back door of Pam's car. "No thanks. Since I'm temporarily without employment, I don't have insurance. And I'm not hurt that bad." She could see his smile by the car's interior light. "Anyways, you fixed me up good as any doctor."

"Oh. . .your knee. . ." Cheryl pointed to the tear in his pants. Scraped skin showed through. "I didn't notice it before."

"If I moaned over every scraped knee I ever had, I'd never get a word out."

The car door opened across the road, and a woman's voice called out. "Jake? You coming?"

Cheryl looked up. *Andrea Simpson.* She was constantly being voted homecoming queen, head cheerleader, or duchess of the restroom. She had most people wrapped around her spunky little finger—but Cheryl didn't like being wrapped. Besides, ever since Andrea had falsely accused Cheryl of stealing Susan Burger's earrings, Cheryl suspected there were two faces under Andrea's layer of Cover Girl makeup. At least she hoped so. Nobody could be that perfect.

And now. . .Andrea and Jake? Were they going steady? Poster children for apple-pie America? *Gag me with a spoon.*

"Ja-ake!"

"Hold on!" Jake said. He turned back to Cheryl. "I suppose we'd better go."

"It seems Andrea's executing her womanly power? On you?"

He laughed. "I don't think so. I've got control of *her.* I don't give in to just anyone."

"You don't?"

"Nope."

"Sounds like a challenge."

He raised an eyebrow. "Do you like challenges?"

"Absolutely."

"Hi, Jake." Julie appeared beside them.

"Yeah. Hi, Julie. How you doing?"

"Fine. I saw you in the game against—"

Pam clapped Julie on the back. "Let's get going, okay? This goodwill mission is getting old. This is not how I like to go cruising on Friday night. Besides, we need to get the bum to bed."

"Pam," Cheryl said, "don't call him that."

"Fine. The gentleman with no formal abode or taste in clothes needs a place to retire for the night. Is that better?"

Cheryl shrugged. What did she care what Pam called Leon? He *was* a bum. She'd done her duty. Besides, her mind was on other things.

Jake tooted his horn as he pulled away. Cheryl waved.

"Looks like he's taken."

Cheryl blinked at Pam's words. "Maybe."

Julie stared after Jake's car. "You don't have to go out with *every* boy in school, Cheryl."

"I don't *have* to do anything. And remember, blondes have more fun."

"That's good for you and Julie but leaves me out," Pam said. She slapped Cheryl on the back. "But face it, we're nobody, dearie. Accept it. Julie and I don't have whatever it takes to belong to the in-group. And you hardly meet their white glove test."

"I know." Suddenly an image flashed in Cheryl's mind. *Jake standing with a blond, talking in a foyer. He kisses her.*

The image was so vivid. *Me and Jake?*

Her mind cleared. She took a breath as if erasing what she was going to say and replacing it with something new. "Maybe I used to think I wasn't good enough for Jake Carlisle, but now. . . He's not so unapproachable. He's nice."

"Egads, the girl is smitten!"

Julie raised a finger. "But you don't want a boyfriend. You've always said that. You want boys, but not a boyfriend. And certainly not one of *them.*"

Julie was right. Why the sudden change in focus? Cheryl wasn't sure what, but something had happened in the few minutes she'd talked to Jake. Options had presented themselves. Possibilities had screamed to be explored. She shuffled her shoulders. "Why couldn't I be his girlfriend?"

Pam knocked on Cheryl's head. "Are you sure it wasn't you who got tossed on your head? What makes you think

Jake would want you for a girlfriend? And since when do you want a long-term relationship with any guy? What happened to love 'em and leave 'em Cheryl? Purveyor of passion? Commander of control?"

"Maybe I want what they have. Maybe. . ." She sighed. "Isn't a girl allowed to change her mind?"

"Colin, don't pout."

Colin Thurgood crossed his arms. "I have every right."

Phoebe couldn't believe she was spending her last moments with Colin, arguing. Yet, in a way it was appropriate. Colin was an arguer. She was not. She and Colin had remained married for so many years because she always gave in. Kept the peace. Avoided the confrontation. Did what Colin wanted.

Until now.

Colin raised an eyebrow. "What are you grinning about?"

"There's a certain satisfaction, Colin."

"In what?"

"In getting *my* way."

"That's childish."

"From the lips of a child. . ."

"What's that supposed to mean?"

She felt a sudden wave of sorrow. "I wish the kids would have come."

"They have school. They were home last weekend. We had a farewell dinner for you."

"Yes, but—"

"They'll be fine, Phoebe. It's only a week. They moved

out of the house years ago. As it is now, we only see them a few times a year."

But this is different. She took a deep breath. She was running out of time.

Colin looked at his watch. Why did he always give the impression she was keeping him from something more important?

She stood and extended a hand to him.

He looked up at her, failing in his attempt to look ignorant. "What?"

"Take my hand, you fool. Stand up with me. Give me a hug. I'm leaving for a week. Maybe forever."

He stood and allowed her to hug him. She took his face in her hands and kissed him. "I love you, Colin." *In spite of everything.*

"I love you, too, Phoebe. And I. . ."

She felt a flicker of hope. Was he going to say something nice? "Yes?"

"I'll see you when you get back."

Mr. MacMillan came through the door. Phoebe did not hesitate. She went to his side. "I'm ready."

He glanced at her husband. "Is everything all right?"

"Fine, fine. Let's do it."

He waved a hand toward the door. "Right this way."

The enormity of the Sphere was a surprise. She'd always associated science with clutter and tight rooms. Machines, electrical cords, buttons, screens. She liked the blue-sky interior. It reminded her of the skies over Nassau. She saw the people in the viewing gallery but looked away. She didn't want to even think about people watching her. Finally, she noticed Cheryl in a bed to her left. There was a white machine curled around her head. She appeared to be sleeping.

Oh, dear. This is it.

Mr. MacMillan led her past a center console of machines to a bed straight across the room from the door. A doctor and nurse hovered close. A man in a suit joined them. Introductions were made, but as soon as Phoebe heard the names, they left her mind.

The doctor put a hand on her arm. "Would you like to lie down, Mrs. Thurgood?"

She'd love to. Had to. Her legs were turning to Jell-O. She sank onto the bed and lifted her legs onto the mattress.

The nurse pulled a curtain around the bed and smiled down at her, talking softly, telling her what they were doing with sensors and such.

When they were done hooking her up, the curtain was opened, and Mr. MacMillan came close. "Do you have any questions?"

A few. But she didn't feel up to the answers. "Just tell me what to do, and I'll be fine." She realized her statement could have been a life-mantra. Wasn't that what she'd always done? *Don't ask questions. Don't make waves. Go along to get along.* Those traits were exactly why she wanted to go back. Maybe she could gain some backbone this second time around.

The nurse wheeled a machine close and positioned it around Phoebe's head.

The doctor held up a syringe. "All you have to do is concentrate on your memories, Mrs. Thurgood, and the choice you want to make differently."

She nodded. "Mr. MacMillan?"

He took a step closer. "Yes?"

"Thank you. Thanks for everything."

"You're very welcome. Enjoy your trip, and God bless you."

Phoebe received the shot, then relaxed, and the ease of it surprised her. She'd never thought of herself as a pioneer, eager to do new things, and yet. . .

She focused on the thought of her old apartment in San Francisco. An attic apartment with gingerbread accents. *My name is Phoebe Winston. I am twenty-two years old. The year is 1969. I am a secretary at Hopner, Wagner, and Greenfield. This time around I want to be strong and not let Colin pull me into his schemes.*

She felt a surge of energy course through her body from her feet to the top of her head. Each cell seemed to be vibrating ever so slightly. It felt better than her Tuesday morning massage. She tried to open her eyes but found them leaden.

She floated in her memories. Flew. The images of an office building were on the other side of her eyes. She felt herself being drawn to the ground. Gravity had her once again. She felt earth beneath her feet. She opened her eyes.

Phoebe stood in the back of the elevator and watched the numbers light up. *Twenty-one, twenty-two. . .* A sterilized rendition of the Fifth Dimension's "Up, Up, and Away" entertained its captive audience. The door opened and shut, over and over, spitting out its cargo in the morning rush.

Twenty-three. She unbuttoned her coat as she walked to

Mr. Edwards's office where she would meet her new boss. She'd heard he was a real up and comer. Her secret hope was that he would be so impressed with her skills that he'd sponsor her in the associate intern program. That's where she could earn some decent money. Of course, the added prestige wouldn't hurt either. Mr. Edward's secretary, Bonnie, smiled at her. "Good timing, Phoebe. He just arrived." Bonnie leaned across her desk. "You are so lucky, he's a real looker." She buzzed her boss on the intercom. "Miss Winston is here, sir."

Mr. Edwards opened the door to his office and came out to meet her. The new associate followed close behind. "Good to see you this morning, Miss Winston. Are you ready to get started?"

"Yes, sir."

"Then let me make the introductions. Colin, this is Miss Winston, your new secretary. Miss Winston, this is Colin Thurgood, your new boss."

Phoebe put on her best secretary's smile and shook Mr. Thurgood's hand. For a fleeting moment, she felt herself blush. Colin Thurgood was certainly the most handsome of all the associates she'd worked for at Hopner, Wagner, and Greenfield. His dark hair, his brown eyes. Delectable. "Nice to meet you, Mr. Thurgood. I look forward to working with you."

"Thank you, Miss Winston, I'm glad you're here to help me through the rough spots."

Mr. Edwards smiled like a proud father. He clapped both of them on the back. "There. You make a great team. Now, go get moved in. There are some proposals for the Atchison merger on your desk, Colin. I've jotted down the statistics you'll need to research for the Tuesday meeting.

Carry on." He went back into his office.

"If you'll come with me, Mr. Thurgood, I'll show you to your office," Phoebe said. They walked.

"The name's Colin, honey. And you are?"

"Phoebe."

He followed her down the corridor to one of the many offices that ran along the perimeter of the building. She had the distinct feeling he was sizing her up—using her rear view as a guide. She was sincerely glad she had worn one of her more conservative dresses. Unfortunately, the styles were getting so short that sitting and leaning over were dangerous activities.

Colin's office had a large window with a built-in credenza sitting beneath it, a teak desk, and two orange vinyl chairs. He listened while Phoebe explained the layout of the twenty-third floor, though, from the glint in his eye and the smirk, you would have thought she was explaining the finer points of belly-dancing. Then she left him alone, shutting the door quietly behind her.

As Phoebe typed up a new phone list for him, she happened to glance through the glassed-in wall of his office and saw him leaning back in his chair, his feet up on the desk, talking on the phone.

She caught sight of Mr. Edwards heading her way with some papers.

Colin was still on the phone, annoyingly at ease. He would be caught slacking off, and it would not be good for his career. *Should I intercept Mr. Edwards?* She pushed herself out of her chair.

An image flashed into her mind, and she stopped. She saw herself making excuses to an authority figure while

Colin stood in the background grooming his nails.

She sat back down. *No. Hold off. Let it happen.* She saw Colin toss a glass paperweight of the world in the air and catch it over and over. *Sit up, Colin. Or your world might come crashing down.*

Mr. Edwards stopped at her desk. "Here are those papers you offered to type, Miss Winston. I really appre—"

She heard Colin's laughter. Mr. Edwards turned his head. She saw his eyes take it all in. He set the papers on Phoebe's desk. "Excuse me a moment."

He went into Colin's office without knocking. Colin's feet hit the ground. Mr. Edwards closed the door. She couldn't hear what was said, but Mr. Edwards's pointing finger and Colin's nodding head told the story. She looked down at her work. She felt like a mother watching a father yell at their child.

It's for his own good.

Between doing her own work and trying to get Colin to do his, Phoebe Winston was exhausted. She should have followed her mother's advice and become a kindergarten teacher. A room full of five-year-olds would have been easier to deal with than one Colin Thurgood.

The Atchison merger file had made some progress—from the middle of Colin's desk to his top drawer, back to the middle again, only to be put in the upper left-hand corner.

Phoebe had spent all day trying to build up enough nerve to talk to him about it. Now she stood in the doorway to his office and knocked on the doorjamb.

He leaned back in his chair. "Uh-oh. I'm getting that

disapproving look again. What have I done wrong this time?"

Phoebe closed the door and took a seat. Her stomach tightened. Never in her four years of experience had she been put in the position of admonishing her boss.

"Colin, you've only been in the position of associate one day. I'm thinking that maybe you're having trouble understanding your duties."

His brow dipped.

Phoebe looked at her hands. "I've had the privilege of working for two other associates over the years. I have a pretty good idea of what is expected of someone in your position in order to move up the next step."

He clasped his hands across his stomach. "Hmm."

Just say it. She pushed the Atchison file in front of him. "This file has to be attended to. Immediately." She looked him in the eye. "They are having a preliminary meeting Tuesday morning at eight that will require the statistics Mr. Edwards has outlined for you."

"Oh, right." He shuffled through the papers on his desk. "He mentioned that."

Phoebe nodded. "Exactly. It's important. Now, I know you're just getting settled, but it needs to be done this week—along with the rest of your work."

He thought a moment, drumming a pencil on his knee. "You're quite the taskmaster, aren't you?"

"I just know what needs to be done."

"And you're going to make me do it."

Phoebe hesitated a moment. "I won't *make* you do anything. But I am here to help."

"If I look good, you look good?"

She stood.

"I'll let you get back—"

"Thanks, Phoebe. I need a secretary like you."

On the way home that night, Phoebe felt as if she had parted the Red Sea singlehandedly. Things were obviously going to get better.

It was the longest hour in Leon's life, sitting in that room all alone. He started to pray but stopped himself. It wouldn't do any good to draw on the powers of a God who probably wanted to smudge him out for killing one of the Almighty's better ones.

He was glad his body wasn't going to 1962, because these clothes would never do. The first time through 1962 Leon had been a snappy dresser, wearing white shirts, a dark suit, and a skinny tie. His shoes had always been polished. Respectable. He'd found you couldn't come into Small Town, USA, and earn the citizens' trust wearing blue jeans and a T-shirt like a black James Dean.

Back then he'd sold himself as a master handyman. Sometimes he'd even followed through with some of the easy work. Biding his time for the kill. Fix a few leaky faucets, hang a few crooked shingles, then *happen* to discover that the roof leaked or the furnace was making funny sounds. Of course, these items had been working just fine until Leon had done a little tampering, but people never seemed to catch on. "Oh, Leon, can you fix this, too?" Why, sure. It would be his pleasure. Then he'd scratch his chin and act all reluctant about asking for some money up front—for supplies. But they'd give it to him. Then he would skip town. Piece of cake.

Leon looked in a mirror. His wrinkles were as deep as the Grand Canyon. He couldn't wait to be twenty-three again. What an asset his looks had been back then. In his prime he could walk into a room and have every eye turn. The men would be thinking, "He looks like a good guy," while the women. . .they were thinking what he might be good *at.*

He flipped through a magazine, but the smiling faces seemed to be making fun of him. He was there alone. No one to say good-bye to. No one to miss him. And there was the danger, too. Things weren't over yet. Not until the Time Lottery people flipped the switch would he feel truly safe.

The door opened, making him drop the magazine on the floor. MacMillan stood before him with his hands clasped like a mortician getting ready to give the family his condolences. *Uh-oh. . .bad news.*

"Mr. Hazen, are you ready to go?"

Leon let his breath out. "Yes, sir. I want to get it done with."

"That's understandable. Do you have any final questions?"

"Well, I was wondering about timing."

MacMillan smiled, like Leon had told a joke. "That's why we're here, Mr. Hazen."

"I was talking about the time when I'm doing the Alternity thing. I was wondering about the week we get in the past. Are we guaranteed to get the full week? I mean, you won't get us there and then rip us back, will you? You'll give us time to work through our choice, won't you?"

MacMillan didn't answer right away. Had Leon said too

much, somehow given himself away? He stared at the floor.

"Your body, here in the present, will experience seven days," MacMillan said. "But the amount of time you feel like you're living in the past is variable. Like in a dream. Time is relative. Why do you ask?"

Leon shook his head fast. Too fast. "No reason."

"We don't appreciate surprises, Mr. Hazen. Is there something you're not telling me?"

" 'Course not," Leon said. Then he clamped his lips together. *Don't say another word. For once in your life, be quiet.*

MacMillan eyed him a good ten seconds. "Don't worry about anything, Mr. Hazen. The serum doesn't start to wear off until seven days. It does no good to give your Loop a burst before that time. The Dual Consciousness only works at the end of the serum's effectiveness." He tilted his head. "Is there anything else?"

A sudden fear caught in Leon's throat like a fish bone. This was Roosevelt's prize, and he had stolen it in the harshest, foulest way possible. *I'm sorry, I'm sorry. . .I'll make it right. I'll give myself up and—*

He started to cough. It was as if his insides were trying to get out. That cinched it. If he stayed behind, he'd die of the cancer. If he went ahead and they knew the truth, they might kill him in some strange, sci-fi way. But maybe, just maybe, they didn't know. Maybe he was scaring himself for nothing.

It looked like the sky had been shoved inside a huge ball and pressed against the edges. Instead of reaching out ever-after to the horizons, the blue curved round him. At least outside he got a feeling of space, of the sky going on forever. Inside the Sphere, there was no way out—especially with all those people looking down on him.

"Let's go over here where you can lie down," MacMillan said.

Leon noticed the empty bed to his right—and the two other beds along the edge of the room, holding the bodies of the two women.

Bodies? He shook his head. *They're not dead, they're sleeping.*

Leon tried to calm his breathing. Each breath required a thought to make it work. In. Out. There wasn't enough air. In a minute everyone would leave him, and Leon would be all alone. Then they'd flip a switch, and that would be it for him.

"Don't be afraid, Mr. Hazen," MacMillan said.

Mr. Hazen? Why didn't he call me Mr. Burke? Then it hit him. *They don't know! They really don't know!*

Suddenly there was plenty of air. He took a deep breath and straightened his shoulders. "I'm ready now." He walked toward the empty bed.

The nurse eased him in, smiling like he was a mental patient who needed extra care. She and a doctor started explaining about the machine they were going to wrap around his head, about the IVs, about the catheter. . .

Fine. Do it. Do whatever it takes. I just want it to be done.

"Godspeed, Mr. Hazen," MacMillan said. "I'll be praying for you."

Leon commenced with his own round of prayers. *Please, God, I'm sorry. So sorry. Keep me safe. I'll try to do better.*

After all the patches, tubes, and machines were hooked up, it was finally time. The doctor held the needle and Leon looked away; he looked at the blue of the ceiling. It throbbed and pulsed, pulling him in. *Take me. I don't care anymore. . .just take me.*

"Think back, Mr. Hazen. Think back to 1962, to Hendersonville, Tennessee. Think back to what you would like to do differently."

He felt the prick of the shot and tried to do as he was told. And with each passing second, it became easier and easier, as if a scroll with his life's story was being pulled flat so he could read it.

Yes, there it is! I see it. I'm in Tennessee again. I'm driving down the road in my pickup, heading to Hendersonville. The trees are flaming orange and red. It's fall. The air coming through the window is cool on my face. . . .

Leon felt a tingling in his head, and within a few moments he started seeing from the inside, not the outside, as if a movie were being played within his brain. The pictures were clear and vivid, like the brightest dream. Then it was as if he floated and flew down a tunnel. It was cool and warm at the same time, like spring before the humidity took over. Forget the past, forget what might happen in the future.

Then something grabbed hold and yanked him through the end of the tunnel into a bright light. He couldn't fly anymore.

He was home.

Leon shook his head, feeling like somebody had smacked him hard. He parked his pickup, got out, and stood on a sidewalk in the middle of a business district. He turned around, trying to get his bearings. He heard the clatter of glasses and turned toward the building behind his shoulder. Red lettering on a window said "Harvey's Bar." Perfect. He could use a drink and a smoke.

Harvey's was nearly empty. Leon looked at the clock: 3:15. No wonder. Most people were at work.

He couldn't seem to remember what scam he was working on. It was not a good feeling. A con man had to stay in control at all times, be one step ahead. And he couldn't even remember where he was.

He took a seat at the bar. Before he could do more than get the bartender's attention, a lone woman moved onto the stool next to him. She kept one toe on the floor and balanced the other on the footrest. He saw what she was advertising. It was all topped off by a pair of willing eyes.

"Hiya," she said.

"Hiya yourself." Leon raised a finger to the bartender, who nodded.

The woman traced her finger across his shoulder. "My name is Carla. What's yours?"

"Leon."

"Want to go somewhere? Private?"

Leon looked at her, incredulous. Every town had its easy women. He knew many of them by name. But most were a tad more subtle. "You don't waste time, do you?"

She shrugged and waved one knee in-out, in-out, drawing attention. "It's been a slow day. Besides, you look like Chuck Berry. I've always wanted to. . .you know. With Chuck Berry."

Leon looked to the bartender, but he just gave Leon his beer.

As Leon took a sip, Carla draped a hand behind his neck, pulling him close. Her breath smelled like beer. She whispered in his ear. He felt himself blush. She leaned back and smiled, waiting for his answer.

Leon chugged a large portion of his beer and stood. "Okay. Come on, let's—"

Something flashed in Leon's brain, like an idea popping into his head. He saw a lady with black hair wearing a pink sweater. It couldn't be Carla, because she was a brunette, wearing blue. Without quite knowing why, he sat back down. "Not today, chickie."

She stuck out a pouty lip. "Why not?"

"I got business to attend to."

She let go of his arm with an extra shove. "So do I."

The bartender came close. "Sorry 'bout that. I didn't know if you were willing, so I thought I'd let Carla take her shot."

"I *was* tempted."

He glanced at Carla. "Who isn't?" He refilled Leon's glass. "Where you from?"

"Around."

"Well, you're in Hendersonville now."

The world flooded back to him. Hendersonville, Tennessee. It had a little church on the edge of town. He'd scoped it out. He'd seen a couple puttering outside. The man had been trying to mend a fence but appeared to have absolutely no fix-it abilities. The perfect mark.

"Whatcha selling?"

Leon looked up. "Selling?"

"You said you were from 'around.' You're a stranger. One plus one. . ."

Leon reached toward his shirt pocket for a business card. "LB Repairs, Leon T. Burke, proprietor."

"Milt Taylor." They shook hands, then the bartender lowered his chin. "You're a fix-it man, huh?" He didn't sound impressed.

Leon lit a cigarette. "A jack-of-all-trades. A handyman. A wizard with hammer and wrench. You got anything needs fixing?"

Milt shrugged. "My marriage."

"Can't help you there. I haven't succumbed. As yet."

"You looking?" They both glanced at Carla, who was working on a lone man at the other end of the bar.

Leon ran a finger along the edge of the glass. "A fella's always looking. But a life on the road don't sit well with most women."

"Then settle down."

"Can't."

"Why not?"

Because I'm a shyster. He gave Milt a smile that spoke of devilish things. "Because I'm too young and feisty."

Milt shook his head. "Those were the days."

"Those *are* the days."

Milt squinted at him. "Do me a favor. Stay away from my sister while you're in town, okay?"

"I'll do my best." Leon exhaled a lung full of smoke. It was time to get down to business. "I saw a nice church on the edge of town. Looked in need of repairs."

"You must mean Hillside Baptist." Milt wiped the counter. "Oh yeah, it needs repairing all right. 'Twas closed for ten years till Roosevelt Hazen took it over six months ago. Local boy, gone for awhile to seminary. Came home to save our souls. It's his first church. Got the building cheap, but still got rooked."

"I think I saw him fixing the fence."

Milt laughed. "Roosevelt couldn't fix a hole in the ground. Never seen a man more bumbling with his hands. 'Course he never had a daddy 'round to show him."

"That's too bad. Maybe I could be of some help to him."

"They could sure use some."

"They?"

Milt dunked his cloth in a sink of sudsy water. "Sarah Hudson. She's new in town. She helps the preacher."

"Hudson and Hazen. They're not married?"

"Nope."

"She pretty?"

Milt looked up as if to read Leon's intentions. Leon gave him a mischievous smile. Milt returned it. "Looks like Rita Moreno, if you really want to know." The grin faded. "But I'd keep to fixing fences if I were you."

"Why?"

Milt placed one forearm on the counter and leaned on it. " 'Cause Roosevelt likes her, that's why. If anyone has a chance with Miss Sarah, it should be him." He leveled Leon with a look. "You get my meaning, traveling man?"

Leon raised his glass and nodded. "Completely."

But Leon was never one to let understanding put a damper on fun.

CHAPTER 6

You did not choose me, but I chose you
and appointed you to go and bear fruit—
fruit that will last.
Then the Father will give you
whatever you ask in my name.

JOHN 15:16

Creature Feature was on. Pam, Julie, and Cheryl lay on their stomachs in front of Julie's TV. Remnants of popcorn, root beer, and Oreos littered the floor. The flickering light from the television made their complexions glow green. Glowing zits, just what every girl needs.

They'd dropped Leon off at the City Mission and had come over to Julie's to sleep. The Friday night slumber party was a weekly tradition. Saturday was date night.

Cheryl wasn't watching the movie. Her thoughts wandered over the elements of her life, trying to find direction. She hated feeling uncertain about anything. She wanted control—over as much, and as many people, in her life as possible. Perhaps it was because she *had* so little control that she pursued what she could like a Crusader searching for the lost Grail.

Her home life was the core to her need for control. Cheryl's mother was on her fourth husband. Cheryl's biological father—husband number one—was only a vague memory kept alive by two black and white photos Cheryl kept in her underwear drawer. Stepdads were tolerable. Barely. They were nice men who saw something in Cheryl's mother that Cheryl couldn't fathom, and who tolerated the fact that Dorothy Crandell Nickolby Oxner Smith Phieffer had a child. One girl. Cheryl Renee. *Don't mind my daughter, she's always been independent. She can take care of herself.*

It was a true statement. Ready or not, her mother had deemed her independent at age six. Cheryl had learned how to sort laundry, balance a checkbook, and change fuses in the basement. Her mother's contribution to the household was to cook, but not out of love or concern for her daughter, but as a means to an end. The way to a man's heart. . . *Take a number please, Dorothy will be with you in a moment.*

Dorothy spent her life focused on snagging a new husband, or getting over the loss of the previous one, two modes of emotion she usually carried out simultaneously. Being a mother during this exhausting process was not a priority. And so Cheryl did what she had to do. . . .

And went where she had to go to get love.

She turned her head away from the TV, hugging the pillow. She had yet to find love—at least in a man. Pam and Julie loved her with the honest tolerance of best friends. But so far none of the male species had been able to brush the chip off Cheryl's shoulder so they could get that close. At least not emotionally.

Physically was another matter. At age thirteen Cheryl had discovered there was power in sex. By giving it away or keeping it just out of reach, Cheryl found the control the rest of her life lacked. Yet Cheryl *was* known for something besides her sexual prowess.

Brains.

Pam was always warning her to ease up on the smarts. But Cheryl resisted. If a guy wanted to know her, he was going to know all of her, brains to bunions. Besides, from what Cheryl had seen in high school, she wasn't scaring away any Michael Yorks *or* Jonas Salks.

Cheryl didn't have a steady boyfriend, and she didn't want one. Commitment equaled a surrender of power. Jake was right: Women had the power in the world—if they knew how to use it.

Julie screamed, pointing at the TV. "Ueew, bug guts! Gross."

Cheryl realized she still didn't know the plot of the movie—if there was one. Something about giant insects coming to earth and hypnotizing people with their multiple eyes.

Enough. She rose up in front of the TV, blocking the view of the killer bugs.

Pam threw a pillow at her. "Move!"

Cheryl turned down the volume. "Conference time."

"Can't you wait until the good guys squish all the bugs?"

"No."

With a moan, Pam crawled into an orange bean bag chair and pulled her legs beneath her.

Julie busied herself picking up pieces of popcorn from the carpet. "Don't be so rude, Pam. If Cheryl wants to talk, we need to listen."

"If it's juicy, we'll listen. Otherwise, I want to watch the bugs."

Cheryl slapped the TV to silence. "It's about S-E-X."

Even Julie sat down.

"Who's the latest conquest of Cheryl the Magnificent?"

"Pam, it's not polite to ask." Julie always pretended not to be interested. But she *had* stopped picking up the popcorn.

Cheryl grabbed a pillow and sprawled on the floor. "Actually, maybe the sex statement was a bit premature. Who votes for me and Jake? Boyfriend-girlfriend. The real McCoy."

Julie looked away. "You barely know him, and he's. . .he's not your type."

"Who is my type?"

Pam laughed. "Male and breathing."

Julie grabbed the nearest glass, wiping the water ring beneath it. "I've always hated that you're so free with yourself."

"Hey, my mom has messed up the mating process three times and counting. Maybe with a little research I'll get it right. Besides, helping that Leon-guy made me think about pursuing the doctor route. I liked the feeling I got helping him." *And Jake noticed.*

"You *are* good at that sort of thing," Pam said. "But what does that have to do with Jake?"

"Nothing specifically." She wasn't talking about sex when she was talking about Jake. Didn't they realize that? But how could they? Her reputation was too deeply ingrained. She suffered an inward sigh and decided to play along. "As a doctor-in-training, I need to study anatomy wherever and whenever I can." A pillow smashed into her face.

"Does Jake Carlisle count as extra credit?"

"Fifty points. At least."

Pam rolled onto the floor and joined Cheryl in a pillow fight. Julie took refuge out of range, looking worried about the bubble lamp and the bluebird figurine on the end table. When her hands reached her hips, she was a perfect copy of a mother. She only needed an apron to wring in her hands. "Come on, guys. . .stop it."

A pillow landed at her feet. "Is there a problem, Mom?"

"But, Mom. We don't want to go to bed!"

"Actually, that's what I'm trying to do. Go to bed!" Cheryl laughed hysterically, falling backward, scattering popcorn across the floor.

"Stop!"

Pam and Cheryl sat up and stared, amazed at the power in Julie's voice.

"Just kidding, Jules."

"No, you weren't kidding. That's what makes me mad. I know you're not a virgin, Cheryl, but I hate it when you act like a tramp."

Cheryl tried to meet Julie's look but couldn't. She busied herself picking up popcorn. "I like sex."

"So do I," Julie said.

"You?"

Pam narrowed her eyes. "Who with?"

"I. . .I imagine I'll like it." Julie walked closer and sank to her knees, helping with the popcorn. "It's not polite to tell—or ask."

Cheryl shrugged. "It's no big deal."

Julie stared at the floor. Why was she acting so weird? Cheryl wished the TV was on so the scream of hungry bugs would break through the silence.

Pam did the breaking. "It's so pitiful that Jake's running around with rah-rah, pooh-bah Andrea. If she ever got a pimple, her perfect world would be destroyed."

Cheryl jumped in. "Nobody deserves Andrea."

Julie stuck a piece of stray popcorn in her mouth. "She's nice."

"Nice and sickening."

"Boys like nice girls," Julie said.

Pam and Cheryl looked at each other and giggled.

Julie opened her mouth and closed it again. She took a breath. "Sex outside of marriage is a sin."

Pam rolled her eyes. "That's an old rule. The sixties changed all that. This is 1973. The new rule is: Anything goes."

Julie shook her head and looked so stricken that Cheryl went to her side. They all knew how Julie felt about God and sin. She was their conscience, whether they liked it or not. "God's not going to strike you dead if you have sex, Julie."

She looked hopeful. "Love has to be involved. I know that."

Cheryl laughed. "No, it doesn't."

Julie hesitated. "But if they say they love you. . ."

Cheryl and Pam tried not to laugh. Julie could be so

naïve. "They *always* say that."

Julie raised her chin. "I'm not like you, Cheryl. I'm a one-man woman. I *want* a commitment."

Cheryl patted her heart and put on the exaggerated face of sincerity. "Oh, me, too. Me, too. Just get me a ring for my finger and a noose around my neck."

"How can you make fun of commitment and then say you want to be Jake's girlfriend? Or is all that just talk? Maybe you can't handle commitment."

Cheryl knew what Julie was doing. A challenge to Cheryl Nickolby could not be left unanswered. She hesitated a moment, feeling as if something that had been born earlier that night on the side of the road was beginning to grow. She could let it die and continue as she always had, or she could do things differently. With a flash of certainty, she knew which way she had to go. "I can handle commitment. A real relationship. In fact, I *will* handle it. With Jake." She raised a hand, taking an oath. "I am determined."

Pam snickered. "Great Gatsby, the poor boy won't know what hit him."

Julie's forehead tightened. "Since when are you interested in Jake anyway?"

"Since the highway."

"What happened on the highway?"

A flash of insight. . .a vision about a kiss. . .and a conversation about power. . . Cheryl lowered her voice to its serious mode. "Don't you ever want what they have?"

"Perkiness beyond all tolerance?"

"No. The one-on-one thing. The going steady. The class ring worn on a chain around your neck. Jake, Andrea, all their kind. . .they are just so. . .so. . ."

"Disgustingly normal?"

Cheryl shrugged.

Julie ran a finger across the top of the television as if checking for dust. "But you can't have Jake just because you want him. You can't have everyone."

Pam laughed. "Cheryl has already *had* everyone."

"Except Jake."

"But you don't care for those boys you. . .date. You just intimidate them."

"So?"

"You use them."

The truth hurt. Cheryl stood. "Better that than the other way around, Julie." She turned to Pam. "So, I guess it's up to you, Pammy dear. The vote is tied, one-one. Should I go after Jake? Give commitment with Mr. Basketball Star a shot?"

Pam turned the TV back on. "Actually, I vote for Tommy tomorrow and Jake on Sunday."

The killer bugs appeared on the screen. Fire flashes of white light shot from their eyes onto a sheriff's car, burning a hole in the windshield.

"That's right. Tommy. . .I vote for Tommy." Julie's voice was small. "Don't you have a date with him tomorrow night?"

Cheryl grabbed Julie's hands and looked into her eyes. "Not everyone can be as good as you, Julie."

"I'm not. . .it's. . .it's just not polite to be greedy, Cheryl."

It was barely five o'clock when Colin left his second day as an associate. Phoebe was still working on the papers for Mr.

Edwards when Colin walked out of his office, suit coat slung over his shoulder, the epitome of unconcerned elegance.

" 'Night, Phoebe. I'm going to do a little celebrating with a friend of mine. Care to join us?" His eyes were full of mischief.

Phoebe made a show of glancing at her watch: 4:58. "No, thank you. I still have work to do."

He leaned forward on her desk, his arms sturdy posts. "Ah, come on. I'm going across the street to Ollie's. Join me."

"Maybe I'll stop by after I finish my work." She tried to emphasize the last word, hoping he'd get the connection.

He flipped a hand in the air. "Your loss. Maybe I'll see you later."

Phoebe watched with total fascination as he disappeared down the corridor. This was not done. Quitting time for the entry-level positions may have been five o'clock, but the higher you climbed, the longer hours you put in. You stayed until the work was done. And as the secretary of an associate, Phoebe was also prepared to stay as late as necessary.

When she got up to turn out the light in Colin's office, she noticed the mess he'd left strewn across his desk. Coffee cups, waxed paper from his morning Danish, doodles. However, the pile of papers for the Atchison merger lay neatly in a pile—untouched.

What had he done all day? She hadn't a clue. From her vantage point, he'd been on the phone most of the time, though he had received only two calls through her. He had taken an hour and a half for lunch with no explanation or apology for being late. Because of him, Phoebe had not been able to eat her bologna sandwich and apple until nearly 2:30.

She was just finishing some typing when she looked up and found Mr. Edwards standing in front of her desk. He was staring into Colin's darkened office.

"Where is Mr. Thurgood?"

She thought fast. She'd let Colin get caught once already. Twice would be deadly. "I believe he had a meeting."

"Hmm." Mr. Edwards walked away, shaking his head.

Phoebe decided she could splurge on one drink at Ollie's. Besides, maybe if she saw Colin and casually mentioned that Mr. Edwards had come by, Colin would choose to go back to work and get something done; stave off a showdown in the morning.

The voice of Steppenwolf greeted Phoebe as she walked into the bar. "Born to Be Wild" added to the noise of clinking glasses and after-work conversations.

Colin's voice rose above the racket. "Hey, gorgeous. Get me another beer."

He was seated to Phoebe's left, a few tables from the door, talking with a man she didn't recognize. She saw a waitress nod at his request, move to the bar, and mutter something about the egotistical cretin. . . .

As Phoebe took a step toward him, she was stopped by the sound of Colin's hand slapping the table, rattling the four empty glasses already there. He didn't notice her as he leaned forward toward his friend.

"Look at this, Darryl. I bought it over lunch. A genuine diamond tie tack. It's my good luck piece."

Phoebe retreated a step into the anonymity of the darkened entry.

"Aren't you rushing things, Colin? This was only your second day."

"I know, I know. But you simply would not believe the setup I've got."

"You've told me. You've called me a dozen times. What do you want me to do, kiss your feet?"

Colin laughed and swung a foot onto the table, sending the beer glasses crashing to the floor. Phoebe watched as the bartender jerked around with a start, giving Colin a dirty look as he went to fetch a broom.

"Hey, barkeep, don't look so glum. Put it on my tab."

Darryl looked chastened. "Take it down a notch. You're going to get us kicked out of here."

Colin crooked a finger. Then he put his arm around Darryl's shoulders, pulling him close until their foreheads nearly touched. He spoke in a beer-whisper, his voice slithering through the space between them. "Don't sweat it, I'm on the top of the heap, and the world's my oyster. I'm due, and I'm going to take what I deserve."

Like graffiti, his words slashed across the wall of beliefs that Phoebe's parents had so carefully built brick by brick. Honesty, working hard, trying to do your best. Her disapproval pulled her out of the shadows and propelled her to his table. She stood behind him, waiting to be noticed—and heard.

Darryl noticed her first. He nipped Colin's arm with the back of his hand. "We've got company."

Words of contempt flew through Phoebe's mind. But when Colin turned around and met her eyes, her angry words broke apart in a tumble of meaningless letters, an alphabet soup—soggy and meaningless.

"Hey, Phoebe, glad you could join us."

He reached back and wove his arm behind her waist, pulling her close. "Darryl, I want you to meet Phoebe Winston, the secretary who's going to help me climb to the top. Right, Phoebe?" He gave her a squeeze.

With a sudden clarity, she sensed how easy it would be to let twenty-two years of propriety and lessons-learned fall to the floor to be swept away with the shards of broken glass. She could sit beside this handsome, powerful man who had shown interest in her, drink the drinks he bought her, devour the looks he gave her, and soak up the touches and innuendos that were sure to punctuate the rest of the evening.

Or not.

In the two days Phoebe had known Colin Thurgood, she had been introduced to a different kind of boss. One who was at ease and brusque, who knew what he wanted and took it, one who advertised the potential for success and intimate secrets.

They were secrets Phoebe both wanted—and feared—to be told. If she let herself be drawn into Colin's world, would she ever find her way out? She wanted a boss who was honest, intelligent, and forthright, traits Colin seemed to dismiss with every word and deed.

But what she wanted at work was not the only issue. . . there was her personal life, there were her grandmother and parents to consider. They needed her financial help. Soon, Grandma would have to be moved into a home, and there was no one else to help pay the bills. She needed this job.

She needed an internship—and her boss's sponsorship. Toward those ends, it was to her advantage to have Colin need her. But at what ethical cost? If only there were two Phoebes. One who could make choices based on need and self-interest, and one who had the luxury to chose according to right and wrong.

It would be so easy to give in, go along, be on the winning team. In the end, Grandma would profit from it. She'd get in a good nursing home. That was the final goal, wasn't it? Grandma didn't need to know what standards Phoebe bent along the way.

Colin ran a hand along the curve of Phoebe's hip, talking to Darryl as if she wasn't even there. Suddenly she remembered a saying Grandma Winston had repeated many times. *Don't cooperate with the world, Phoebe. Change it.*

Colin Thurgood represented the worst the world of business had to offer.

She took a step away from him, forcing his hand to fall away. He looked up, surprised. She adjusted her purse on her shoulder. "I'd better be going. Some other time, gentlemen."

Phoebe captured the sidewalk with her stride. With her eyes down, her hands dug deep in her pockets, she looked up for no one. The people of the night parted to make a path for the woman who walked with such determination.

She turned a corner and—

"Oomph!"

Phoebe stumbled back, but the other person tumbled to the sidewalk. It was a teenage girl.

"Ouch!"

Phoebe knelt by her. "Are you all right?"

The girl rubbed her bottom. "Serves me right. I wasn't looking."

"And I was walking too fast."

She extended a hand, wanting help up. "Two speeding trains in search of a wreck, huh?"

"Something like that." Phoebe spotted a bench. She led the girl over to it. "You tore your dress."

The girl didn't even look at the hem of her long, ruffled granny dress. "Tear it in two, I don't care."

Phoebe took a moment to look at her. She was thirteen or fourteen, with long blond hair. Her face was confident and pretty. Her dress was pink dotted Swiss, with a lacy bodice and edging on the sleeves.

The girl pushed the sleeves up. "Don't look at me that way. This monstrosity is not my choice."

"It's a very pretty dress. But kind of fancy for walking the streets. At night. Alone." Phoebe looked around. She hadn't been paying attention to where she'd been walking. They were in Haight-Ashbury. Hippie heaven. Groups of kids stood next to buildings and under streetlights, dancing as Janis Joplin music poured out of upper apartments. Peace signs, tie-dyed T-shirts, and money changing hands. Phoebe's conservative clothes branded her an outsider. And two females walking alone. . .

"I am alone by choice, running from the disgusting reality of this lovely evening."

"What happened?" Phoebe asked

"I was forced to witness my mother marrying Don Juan."

"You don't like Mr. Juan?"

The girl looked up to see if Phoebe was that dense. Phoebe smiled.

"I rarely like my mother's husbands."

"How many has she had?"

The girl hesitated. "You don't want to hear all this."

"Sure I do. You have something better to do? I don't."

The girl shrugged. "Oscar is number three. I am the fruit of husband number one, though he hasn't been around since I was six." She sighed deeply and pulled the dress to her knees. She got a wolf whistle from a passerby but left it raised. "My mother is a very insecure woman, always searching for love, always settling."

"Settling?"

"Settling for mediocrity."

Phoebe felt a bit uncomfortable. "But surely having somebody is better than having nobody."

The girl looked right at her but didn't comment.

"At least your mom is committing to someone."

"If you call an average of five years a commitment."

"Hasn't your mother loved these men?"

The girl did not answer right away. "What's love anyway?" She looked at Phoebe and sighed. "So. What's your story?"

"I just got a new boss, and he's driving me crazy."

She laughed. "Bosses and mothers."

Phoebe saw a couple necking. The man's hand ventured where it shouldn't go. She remembered Colin's hand. . . "Life can get so complicated."

The girl swung her legs. "Nah. It's simple. Anything goes." She spread her arms to the teeming street around them.

"Peace, flower power, love, baby."

Phoebe shook her head. She wasn't too keen on what was happening in the world. Bobby Kennedy and King getting shot, drugs, free love. . . She remembered something. "My grandma says we shouldn't cooperate with the world."

"What's that supposed to mean?"

"The world isn't necessarily right, but we need to *do* right."

The girl's legs stopped and she grounded them, toes against sidewalk. "Sounds good to me." She tossed her skirt over her legs and stood. "I'd better get back. Time to eat cake and throw rice or something."

"What's your name?" Phoebe asked.

"Cheryl."

"And I'm Phoebe. Good luck with your new father, Cheryl. Thanks for the talk."

Leon got in his pickup. It was coming back to him now. He'd come into town to find a place to stay. But after his talk with Milt in the bar. . .he'd hold off on paying money for a hotel room. He'd just take himself over to the Hillside Baptist Church and see if his charm could finagle himself a free room.

He hadn't driven a quarter mile when he heard a pop. The right side pulled. A flat tire. He cursed his luck and pulled onto the shoulder. He got out, saw the flat, and kicked it.

He unlocked the back of the makeshift box he'd built over the bed of the truck to house his tools. He had a spare somewhere. . . .

He heard a car coming and was pleased when it pulled

onto the shoulder behind him. Maybe if he worked it right he could get some other schmuck to change the tire for him.

A man stepped out. Tall and skinny, with an oh-shucks smile like Rochester in the old Jack Benny program. He looked slightly familiar. He stuffed his hands in his pockets. "Need some help?"

Leon pulled the spare from the back and bounced it to the ground. "Don't need it but will always take it when offered." He stuck out his hand. "Leon Burke." He pulled out a business card. "LB Repairs."

The man shook his hand, looked at the card, then looked at Leon as if he'd seen a ghost. *Oh no, somehow he knows me. I'd better get this tire fixed and get outta—*

"I prayed for you to come."

Leon felt his jaw drop. "You what?"

The man laughed. "I'm in need of some help of my own—some handyman help. I couldn't hammer a nail straight if my life depended on it, and I have a lot of chores that could use a hammer. So just this morning I asked God to send me some help. And here you are."

It was then that Leon recognized him. He nodded and pointed a finger. "I saw you at the church on the outskirts of town. Fixing a fence."

The man reddened. "I was fixing to fix a fence but didn't get very far. Like I said, I'm in need of a handyman."

Leon grinned. "Then since I'm handy, I'm your man, right?"

"Right."

"And your name is?"

The man stepped forward to shake Leon's hand a second

time. "Sorry. Where are my manners? The name's Roosevelt. Roosevelt Hazen."

Changing the tire got Leon's suit dusty, giving him one more reason to follow Roosevelt to his church—to get cleaned up.

They pulled into the dirt parking lot, the engine of Roosevelt's Packard knocking even after he turned off the engine. "Here we are. My church." He stopped on the walk leading to the front door and looked up at the clapboard building as if it were the gates of heaven itself.

At first, Leon thought Roosevelt was being sarcastic, but when he looked at his face, he knew the pride—right or wrong—was real. The man's eyes were like shiny black marbles, and his skin seemed to glow from the inside out, like a lightbulb was turned on behind his smile. Leon looked at the building again. Maybe he was missing something.

Nope, not a thing. The small window above the door was cracked, the concrete stoop chipped, and the gutters hanging. The crosspiece of the cross on the peak of the roof was off-kilter.

"Come on in, Leon, I want to show you around."

The front door said howdy-do with ribbons of peeling blue paint. Leon followed Roosevelt inside the sanctuary. The wood of the pews was dark with old varnish. At the altar end were two pews for a choir, a piano, a pulpit, and a table with a mismatched set of legs acting as the altar. A wooden cross sat on a white tablecloth that had lace edging hanging loose from one side. If Leon had been an altar and looked like that, he would've been ashamed. The side windows alternated between stained glass and plain, but not in any order, telling Leon the plain glass was filling in for what used to be.

Roosevelt held his arms wide like he was Jesus calling his flock close. He grinned, showing teeth right off a piano. "What do you think?"

Leon grabbed onto the edge of a pew, feeling the warmth of the sun coming in from the west windows. "It's fine, just fine."

Roosevelt's face crumpled like a used paper bag. He nodded as if he didn't like accepting the truth but would if he had to. "It may not be fancy, but it's serving our congregation well. We have fifty-five members—good people, all of them."

Poor people, all of them. "What do you want me to do?"

"Oh, yes. My need for a handyman." He lowered his head and looked up through dark lashes. "I could use you full time for awhile. If you have the time. And if. . .if we can come to terms with the pay." The preacher's face clouded a bit. He stooped to pick an invisible speck off the floor. "I can't offer much—don't want to dip into my savings if I don't have to. Say, twenty-five dollars a week, plus free room and board?"

Savings? Leon rubbed his face, trying to hide his excitement. The twenty-five dollars was barely smokes and booze money. But savings? He looked at Roosevelt and saw a face as innocent as a child's. A dupe. An easy mark. All he had to do was play it slow and easy, and Roosevelt's savings would be his. "That'd be fine."

Leon felt good when Roosevelt's face lost its clouds and smiled again. "There's a room in the back by the fellowship hall. Through there." He pointed to a door at the far left by the altar. "We got a kitchen. A bathroom, too. And I've got a room. . . It's not much, but it's clean. And Sarah comes and cooks for me some. She's a great cook. She lives in a little house out back. Pastor's quarters they were."

Leon remembered the bartender mentioning Sarah Hudson. "If you're the pastor, why don't you live there?"

Roosevelt nudged the floor with a toe. "Oh, I don't need a whole house. I do fine with the room. Sarah deserves. . ." He shrugged. "She comes over often enough and keeps me from starving to death."

"Why don't you go over there and eat?"

He shook his head vigorously. "It wouldn't look right."

Leon couldn't help but smile. "Is Sarah your woman?"

"No, no. . .nothing like that. She's just a good friend. She's helped get the church going. She's a woman of deep faith, full of goodness and virtue and—"

"Did I hear my name used in vain?"

Right off, Leon was taken with the woman who came through the door leading to the fellowship hall. She was as tall as Leon, though three inches shorter than Roosevelt. The bartender had been right. She looked like Rita Moreno's sister. Her eyes were deep and told secrets, and her lips were definitely meant for— And she was wearing a pink sweater, just like the girl in his vision.

She came up the aisle toward the men.

Roosevelt put his hand out, like he wanted to touch her arm, but took it back before he did. "Sarah, I would like to introduce you to Leon Burke, of LB Repairs. He's going to work for us awhile. Get things whipped into shape. Leon, this is Sarah Hudson."

Sarah looked Leon over. Not just a little once-over, but

a real slow look-see of him. He hoped his zipper was shut. She must have found him halfway to her liking because she held out her hand and smiled, just enough to make him melt. He knew the drill—or at least he knew the drill with an ordinary woman. *But she's a woman of deep faith, full of goodness and virtue and—*

No, you don't. Not this one. Leon had the feeling that Sarah Hudson would be wanting more than a flip through the sheets, and he didn't have time to make lovey-eyes with anyone wanting roots. Especially not when he'd have to be heading out quick after getting a hold of Roosevelt's savings. . .

"Nice to meet you, Mr. Burke."

Suddenly, Leon saw another flash behind his eyes, like his mind had decided to turn up the lights. He saw a vision of him and Sarah sitting on a picnic blanket. *She reached over to touch his hand.*

"You're smiling, Mr. Burke. Are we stopping you from a wonderful daydream?"

He blinked and the vision left him. But the warm, cozy feeling of the picnic with Sarah remained. Maybe it wouldn't hurt to play the man-woman game with this good woman. See where it went.

"Call me Leon, ma'am. Nice to meet you, too."

"The lock on the front door's been sticking." She pushed between them, moving toward it. "Can you fix it?"

Roosevelt laughed. "Let the man take a breath, Sarah."

"And let me change out of this suit, too."

She leaned against the end of a pew. "Sorry. I'm just relieved to have a man around—" She glanced at Roosevelt. "I mean a professional handyman." She bit her lip. "Sorry,

Roosevelt. No offense."

"None taken. I agree with you."

She stood and motioned toward the fellowship hall. "Come with me, Leon, and I'll show you where you can change."

"He's going to be staying in the storeroom, Sarah. We can set up a cot."

She hesitated, but only a moment. "Very good then."

She walked down the aisle toward the altar. Leon couldn't help but admire the gentle swaying of her hips.

Oh dear. . .

Roosevelt had told the truth: Sarah was a great cook. After eating a dinner of meat loaf and mashed potatoes at Sarah's house—Leon guessed *two* men and one woman was somehow *not* scandalous—Leon was full and satisfied. He lit a cigarette. The smoke curled toward the ceiling. They sat and drank coffee around a table with metal legs and an aqua top. It wobbled.

Sarah's hair was pulled into a high ponytail. It made her look like a teenager, though he guessed her to be in her twenties. With Roosevelt present, Leon only dared to sneak looks at her, but he could see her face was sculptured and fine. Once, she caught him looking, and he risked a wink. She looked away. This was going to be fun.

"So, Miss Hudson, how did you and Roosevelt meet? I hear you're not from around here."

"Where did you hear that?"

Leon wanted to lock his lips together. He couldn't very

well tell them that he'd scoped them out, plying a bartender for information. "Roosevelt must have told me."

Roosevelt looked confused but let it go. "I don't know what I'd do without—"

She put a hand on his. Sarah lowered her eyes, her strong-woman number crumbling a bit. "Roosevelt took me in. Roosevelt takes everyone in."

Roosevelt turned his coffee cup in circles. "No, I don't, Sarah. I just help the ones who need it most."

"The ones who take the most, you mean." Her voice was strong again. "Roosevelt has a habit of giving away everything he's got. If he finds a five-dollar bill, he gives it away. If we have a good Sunday offering, it's gone by the next Wednesday helping this drifter or that mother. It slips through his fingers, right into someone else's."

Roosevelt sat up straighter in his chair. He tried to look her in the eyes, but missed. "I keep some of it."

"Sure you do. You keep it to put back into this ramshackle church. You fix the lights, and the pipes break; you fix the pipes, and the ceiling leaks. It never ends."

Leon could tell they'd had this conversation before.

"But, Sarah, you know I have my savings to fall back on. There's three hundred dollars there when we need it."

She grabbed his arm. "Hush! You shouldn't blab that around to just anyone."

Roosevelt looked like a wounded puppy.

She touched his arm. "I'm sorry. I'm not being very Christian. I apologize, Roosevelt, but you know I'm right." She turned to Leon. "I don't begrudge him hiring you. If he says you're an answer to his prayers, I believe him. I don't want to believe in any God who won't listen to the prayers of Roosevelt Hazen. And I'm sure your help will save us money in the long run, but people *can* take advantage."

Like me. I have "taking advantage" down to an art. Leon looked at his cup, feeling a foreign guilt as dark as the cold coffee inside. He didn't like it. He was who he was, he did what he did. No one in this entire world had the right to make him feel bad about it. And no one *had* until this woman—this woman he'd just met. He tried to shake the feeling away. "I'll do my best to be of service—to both of you."

Roosevelt slapped the table. "I know you will, Leon. I know it."

Sarah stood to clear the table. "We'd better get to bed if we plan on painting the sanctuary tomorrow."

Roosevelt took the men's cups to the sink. "Can we help you clean up, Sarah?"

"No, thank you. A woman likes having the run of her own kitchen. You two go on. I'll see you in the morning."

Leon snubbed his cigarette and pushed his chair in. He didn't want to leave. He wanted to sit right here and watch her. But at that realization, he was suddenly ripe to go. He was love 'em and leave 'em Leon. Going goo-goo over some church lady was not his style.

The men said their thanks and walked across the yard to the back door of the church. The moon made long shadows as it hung over their shoulders. Roosevelt paused in the fellowship hall until Leon got the light on in the storeroom—his residence for. . .how long? For as long as it took.

" 'Night, Leon. Glad to have you with us. You're a real godsend."

Godsend. The word hung heavy. "No, I'm not, Roosevelt. I'm just a guy passing through."

Roosevelt shook his head and put a finger on Leon's chest. "Face it. You're a godsend, and I'll thank Him in my prayers tonight, you can bet on that."

Leon didn't want to be mentioned in any prayers to a God who might not approve of his plans. "Don't go to any trouble."

"It's the least I can do. 'Night, Leon." Roosevelt walked to his own room at the other end of the fellowship hall.

Leon closed the door, wishing that somehow it could keep out Roosevelt's prayers and high opinions. Leon wanted people to believe him; he just wasn't used to them believing *in* him.

He got out of his clothes, turned out the light, and stood at the tiny window that looked out back toward Sarah's house. The kitchen was dark. The grass glowed with the light from a window. Her bedroom?

Stop it, Leon. You're a godsend, remember?

He lay on the cot, but couldn't sleep. He felt odd sleeping in such a Christian place knowing that his thoughts of Sarah—and his thoughts of Roosevelt's three hundred dollars—weren't entirely wholesome.

It had been a long day, and Mac nearly fell asleep at the wheel on the way home from work. The minds of three winners had been successfully transplanted into their Alternitys. Wriggens was satisfied—for a change.

The three winners were quite a trio. Marketingwise, TTC could not have asked for a better cross-section of America.

Next time it would be nice to add to the demographics. Maybe get a hard-edged trucker, a nerdy professor, and a white-haired grandmother. *I wonder if we could rig the thing. . . .*

But forget about the next lottery winners, *he* was next.

Mac changed lanes. When it was his turn, he'd go back to the day of Holly's murder. He wouldn't be out of town, dealing with the acting career of some Hollywood hopeful. He'd be home, spending time with his family. He'd be there when the bad man—his name was Sidney Graves—came calling, and he'd protect his family.

That was one alternative, to meet the guy face-to-face and take care of the problem right then and there. But another scenario was to not be home at all. To take his family on a fun day of shopping, eating out, and going to the park. Sidney would come calling, and he wouldn't be there. End of story.

But maybe Sidney wouldn't have given up. Maybe he would have come back another day. Stalkers were persistent animals. Maybe he should go back to the event Sidney was upset about and this time be sure he went away a happy customer.

Mac shoved the fantasies away. He didn't have to decide yet. But soon. Soon it would be his turn.

CHAPTER 7

No temptation has seized you except
what is common to man. And God is faithful;
he will not let you be tempted beyond what you can bear.
But when you are tempted,
he will also provide a way out so that
you can stand up under it.

1 CORINTHIANS 10:13

When Cheryl woke up Saturday morning with a crick in her neck and her right arm tingling, her first thoughts were of her dream: Jake Carlisle. His boy-next-door smile. His confidence. His. . .possibilities. It was like starting out on a new adventure.

" 'Morning."

With Pam's greeting, the possibilities disintegrated—the

dream floating from real to oblivion in a few ticks of the clock.

Although Cheryl wanted to laugh away her newborn determination regarding Jake, her gut told her there was more to it than mere infatuation or the challenge of grabbing herself a part of the in-group. It was as if she and Jake were two runners racing around the track side by side, each staying within their assigned lane, knowing neither one could win without crossing over, mingling their space together in a final rush to the finish line.

Why Jake and not somebody else? Cheryl had no idea. It just was.

Pam held a bowl of Cheerios between her knees as she watched Scooby-Doo cartoons. "You've got a strange look on your face, Cher."

"Just tired."

"You getting old? Can't handle the late nights anymore?"

Old. It wasn't that far off. Cheryl was feeling older than her years. Not physically, but mentally. It was as if her brain had added an extra lobe, an extra storage bin of knowledge that complicated what she previously knew.

Julie put a placemat under her bowl as she sat on the floor behind the coffee table. "You feeling all right?"

Julie had provided an escape. Cheryl pulled her hip huggers under her nightgown, turned to the wall, and finished getting dressed. "I need to go."

Pam pointed her spoon, dripping milk. "The Jake patrol needs to start early, huh?"

Cheryl didn't answer. She rolled up her sleeping bag and tucked it under her arm. "Talk to you later." She left the house, leaving them alone to discuss the foibles of her character.

They didn't know the half of them.

Walking the few blocks home did not magically solve Cheryl's dilemma. She wanted a date with Jake. Jake was dating Andrea. Cheryl had a date with Tommy. A soap opera in the making.

Her ability to find dates had never been a problem. She was willing, boys sensed it, and *voilà*. Welcome to mating season. The fact she didn't want a commitment was an added draw. But to attract someone in hopes of a more permanent arrangement. . .how exactly was that done? It's an interesting ques—

Cheryl stopped walking as the idea adjusted itself. *Interesting. . .interest. . .show interest in him.* She clapped her hands, making the Bakers' dog jump away from the tree he was sniffing. It was so simple. Yet so hard. She'd never been *interested* in any of the boys she'd dated. It had been much more primitive: Physical Attraction 101. No homework, no studying. Just one big test, quick, before the bell rang. Cheryl in control, handing out the grades, determining the curriculum. *Next student please.*

But committing to Jake was an entirely different class. She was ignorant, unsure of herself. What if she actually had something to learn? Or horror of horrors: What if she flunked out?

Show interest in him.

It was Saturday. No school. She wouldn't be seeing Jake today.

She clapped her hands a second time, sending the dog to the porch. Jake had a game tonight. Although she abhorred sports, she would go watch him. She would *make* him take note of her interest.

Tommy. . .what about Tommy?

She began to walk again. That was simple. She'd use one man to get another. Her mother did it all the time.

Cheryl called Tommy after lunch. Although he wasn't into sports either, he didn't seem to mind the suggestion. It was a good place for a first date. Loud, public, cheap.

She was ready by seven, all freshly bathed, perfumed, and dressed to perfection. The inside of Tommy's car was a surprise. Although the exterior needed a paint job, the inside was immaculate, as if no human beings had dared defile the interior with their presence. Cheryl thought of pairing him with Julie. Together, they'd make a great mother. Cheryl wasn't sure she knew what to do in a car that didn't smell like French fries or old socks. Or one that wasn't full of last year's history notes, car magazines—or worse.

The basketball game had already started when they arrived. They climbed the bleachers and found a place off to the side, away from the band and the annoying chants of the pep club.

Jake was gorgeous. For being so tall, he had amazing coordination. He would run, pivot, stop, and shoot as if the two points were as inevitable as water falling down a mountainside. And though Cheryl never cared who won any sports event, watching an athlete who was especially good at a chosen sport was like enjoying a work of art, or appreciating a dance for the sheer culmination of the feat.

Jake made another basket. The crowd roared. Cheryl

found herself clapping with an enthusiasm she generally kept for other things. "Yay, Jake!"

Her voice carried past the crowd and sounded alone. She felt herself go red but was thrilled when Jake looked in her direction. She waved. She sat down, remembering Tommy.

"He's good, isn't he?" he said.

"Not bad."

"Wish I could play sports, but I have a bad knee."

Cheryl took his arm, pulling it next to her chest. "Brains are more important than brawn." It was a truth the world often disputed.

"Two bits, four bits, six bits a dollar," yelled the cheerleaders. "All for Southside, stand up and holler!"

As the crowd mindlessly followed the cheerleader's command, Cheryl laid a deep one directly on Tommy's mouth. She caught him—and herself—by surprise. His head jerked back. He quickly recovered and pushed against her, showing promise.

"I want to be alone with you," he said.

Before she could answer, he stood, grabbed his coat, and pulled her down the bleacher steps, brushing by anyone in his path.

If her commitment to Jake had a detour, so be it.

Tommy earned a B+.

He drove directly to Kolben Lake and parked on the north side, down by the end of the parking lot where the street light had been handily broken. Repeatedly.

On the drive over Cheryl noticed his voice lower a

notch, with his words coming out in short bursts as if that was all his increased respiration would allow. His lips were locked to hers before the engine died.

For the first time since beginning her exploration of the male species, Cheryl wanted to stop. She wanted to backtrack to the gym and find herself sitting safely in the bleachers, inwardly complaining about the irritating noise of the pep club and band. There, she would watch Jake from a distance, eat some popcorn, give Tommy a handshake good-night, and find herself safe in her own bed with the pink and yellow quilt.

She bolted upright, sending Tommy into the steering wheel with an *oomph.*

"No, Tommy." The words sounded odd coming from her mouth.

"What?" His eyes weren't focused on the here and now. His right hand crossed the space between them, heading for the buttons of her blouse.

"I said no." Cheryl wanted to say she wasn't that kind of girl, but she didn't want to lie to him.

He ran a hand through his hair and looked out the windshield, coming back to the present one step at a time. "I'm sorry. I was out of line."

Cheryl touched his knee. "I led you on. I'm sorry." And for the first time in her life, she was.

He took her home where she tunneled under her quilt and hugged a pillow close. She didn't quite know what to do with this odd change that had come over her. She wasn't acting like the old Cheryl at all.

The question was whether that was a good thing or a bad thing.

"Mr. Thurgood's office." Phoebe held the phone in the crook of her neck and continued to type. Within a few moments, her fingers stopped in midair as their energy was deferred. "Yes, sir. I'll come right away."

She glanced around the office, surprised to find that not a single pair of eyes had noticed, nor a single pair of ears overheard her summons to Mr. Greenfield's office—*the* Mr. Greenfield of Hopner, Wagner, and Greenfield. She attempted to remove the letter from the typewriter only to discover her hands were shaking.

Phoebe looked into Colin's office. He was still out—which was fine with her. She really didn't want to deal with the sex maniac this morning. She wrote him a quick note and set it on his desk.

On the way to the twenty-fifth floor, she ducked into the restroom. A dose of cold water helped. Why would one of the founding partners want to see her? A promotion? An internship *was* the next step.

A deep breath. In, out. She tried a smile. No, too frenzied. She tried again. Better.

Standing outside Mr. Greenfield's office, she took one final breath. It was cut short by the sound of Colin's voice. Was Colin sponsoring her internship? So soon?

She knocked and opened the door.

"Miss Winston." Mr. Greenfield stood to greet her. "I'm glad you could come so quickly. Please have a seat."

Phoebe took the chair next to Colin, momentarily enjoying the merging of the two male colognes. She smiled, but his smile was perfunctory. Her stomach tightened. She looked to Mr. Greenfield. His face explained nothing. It was an administrative face: concise, courteous, and powerful—especially around the eyes. The expanse of walnut desk separated their stations.

"Now, Miss Winston. Let me get right to the point."

At that moment, Phoebe knew this was not going to be a promotional speech—again, something about his eyes. She forced her mind back to his words.

"It has come to our attention that there have been some unauthorized long distance phone calls. Mr. Edwards and I have had a talk with Mr. Thurgood, and he has informed us that the calls in question were to your family, that your mother is ill, and you have been concerned about her."

She felt her jaw drop. Consciously, she raised it.

Mr. Greenfield continued. "We are very sorry to hear about your mother's illness, but on the other hand, we cannot allow long distance personal calls to be charged on the company account. The amount in the past three days has been over fifty dollars."

Phoebe glanced at Colin. He studied his manicure. She turned back to Mr. Greenfield, her hands digging into the leather of her chair.

"The other concern is that these phone calls were not listed on your long distance phone log. As you have worked for other associates, I know you are aware of this procedure. I must say, we are rather disappointed by this breach."

She pursed her lips together, locking in the explosive anger that craved to escape. She let her mind catch up with her emotions. Mr. Greenfield was waiting for her response.

Colin's eyes darted to hers, then away. Did she catch just a hint of begging in that look?

Phoebe locked her hands together, forbidding them to betray her temper. She knew she shouldn't save him, and if she confronted him in front of their superior, she would be calling him an out-and-out liar.

And yet, her own career was at stake, too. She needed that promotion. Something like this on her record could be professional suicide.

"Miss Winston?"

Phoebe spoke directly to Mr. Greenfield, deciding to go along with half of Colin's lie. "I want to thank you for your concern about my mother." There was the slightest expulsion of air from Colin. "It's very kind, and I want to assure you that her condition is improving. However, I'm afraid I don't understand the long distance expenses. I have not been using the company phone to call home, and I'm sure Mr. Thurgood has been blameless as well. I'm sorry I don't have an explanation, but I'm glad you've brought it to our attention."

"Hmm." Mr. Greenfield looked at her, then at Colin. "You have no explanation?"

"None."

He sighed deeply. "I'm sorry this couldn't be cleared up. I had hoped. . . But I assume this won't happen again?"

"No, sir," Phoebe said.

"No, sir. I can guarantee it," Colin said.

Mr. Greenfield stood. "I appreciate you coming in, Miss Winston. Now, I'll let you get back to work." He sat down and pulled out some papers.

Phoebe left the office. Behind her, she saw Colin standing

in front of Mr. Greenfield's desk. The older man glared at him. "Didn't you hear me, Thurgood? Get back to work."

Phoebe beat Colin to the elevator. He came up behind her and whispered in her ear, "Thanks for nothing."

She decided to take the stairs.

After not taking the blame for the phone charges, Phoebe had tried to lie low and avoid all eye contact with Colin. It wasn't easy, considering his office was directly in her sight line. She felt bad for the tension between them but refused to feel guilty.

At midafternoon he buzzed her into his office. "Close the door and sit down," he said.

She braced herself for the worst. He was going to fire her. They weren't a good match, and other than the sullying of her résumé with the question-raising listing of her short employment as his secretary, she actually wouldn't mind being rid of the stress.

"I owe you an apology." She must have looked shocked because he laughed. "I'm not a total heel, Phoebe. I can admit when I'm wrong."

"Glad to hear it."

He shrugged. "Greenfield blindsided me. I gave him the first answer that came to mind."

"Which didn't happen to be the truth."

"Maybe next time. Anyway, to make amends, I was wondering if you'd let me take you out to dinner this evening."

What would it prove? That he could apologize with class? But as her head shook no, her mouth said, "That would be fine."

He stood, the apology over. "Leave me your address, and I'll pick you up at seven." He followed her to the doorway. "And dress fancy. We're going to do it up right."

Buttoning the last of the pearl buttons on her blue minidress, Phoebe had to remind herself for the four hundredth time that Colin was not interested in her romantically—and she was not interested in him. This was not a date; it was simply an apology dinner.

She rummaged through her jewelry box, looking for her pearl choker. Her cat, Lucy, sat on the sofa bed watching, her front paws primly crossed.

"We have a good working relationship," she told the cat. "He needs me—at work. I'm good for him. I tell him where to go, when; what to bring, where; and who to call, why." She smiled in the mirror. "That was pretty good, eh, Luce?"

The doorbell rang. Colin was on the other side, panting. "Third floor?"

She showed him in. "Have a seat. I'll be ready in a minute."

He fell onto the sofa, making Lucy flee. Phoebe stood at the dresser mirror to apply her lipstick. She saw him scanning her apartment.

His head began to shake. "Not good."

"What's not good?"

"This apartment. It's minuscule. Less than tiny."

"I like it."

He began to roam, pacing off the distance between the kitchenette and the one separate room—the bathroom. "I'll bet you can vacuum this place using one plug."

"The essence of efficiency."

He opened the freezer compartment. "I was going to say you'd have to choose between meat and ice cream, but you have neither."

Meat is expensive and ice cream's a luxury. "It's amazing what you can do with a few ice cubes and some meat tenderizer."

He lifted the corner of the crocheted afghan that stretched across the back of the sofa bed. "Nieman-Marcus, no doubt?"

She went to the afghan's rescue, smoothing it against the cushion. "A Grandma Winston original. Handmade."

He stopped his inspection. "How long have you worked for Hopner, Wagner, and Greenfield?"

"Four years."

His hands swung wide. "And this is all you can afford?"

Phoebe thought of her previous apartment. It had been twice as big, with a balcony. "They pay me fine—though if you want to lobby for a raise on my behalf, or an internship, I'll take it." She slid her arm into her coat. "I happen to have other expenses. Other obligations."

"Sounds mysterious."

"It's not. My grandmother is going to need to move into a nursing home. It's expensive."

"That's not your responsibility."

"But it is."

"What about your parents?"

"It comes down to me."

Colin's index finger found his diamond tie pin. "Too bad."

Phoebe picked up her purse—which contained exactly $12.22. "Shall we go?"

"Absolutely. I've always wanted to feed the poor."

Rigallo's was a ten-minute drive from her apartment. The tablecloths were white, the crystal real, and the aroma heavy with oregano and cheese.

It had been nearly five years since Phoebe had been in a restaurant with wine stewards and more than two forks. The last time had been during the celebration of her father's success at selling an invention to a big corporation—a new kind of flash attachment for cameras. Phoebe had never seen him happier. They had toasted their new prosperity with the *ching* of crystal glasses while they made grandiose plans to eat out once a week. For that one evening, her parents' dreams had come true: they were rich. They had made it. But then the corporation backed out. Tuna casserole and jelly jar glasses took their rightful place as Phoebe's dad wallowed in his disappointment before trying again. And again.

Soft music wove its way into her consciousness. Candles flickered. The linen napkins were starched just right. As she savored each new sensation, Colin draped himself on the chair, resting one arm casually atop the walnut armrest.

"You act as though you come here often," she said.

"I like the best. Don't you?" He took a sip of wine, the ruby liquid catching the light.

"I could get used to it."

He adjusted the napkin on his lap before removing an offending piece of lint from the sleeve of his suit. "So, tell me about yourself. Phoebe—the woman of many obligations. Are you from the Bay Area?"

"I've lived around. My dad's jobs took us all over. But from this point on, I plan to be a lifer right here."

"You could do worse."

She shrugged. "Though I *would* like to see more of the world."

"Then go."

He really did live in his own little world. "It takes a lot of money to travel."

"Marry a rich man."

And he was quick with the easy answers. "It's not that simple."

"Sure it is. You're an attractive woman; you're smart and capable. Find a rich man and go after him. Live in luxury the rest of your life and never have to work another day."

"I like to work. Maybe not as a secretary forever, but I need to do something productive. I want people to remember me. I want to contribute something."

He looked wary. "You're not one of those save-the-world types, are you?"

She hesitated. "I want my life to count."

He leaned forward on the table. "You don't get it, do you? You can accomplish all that *and* have money. Money makes everything easier." He sat back, fingering his tie. "By the way, you've never complimented me on my tie tack."

The "world's my oyster" tie tack. A marquise cut at least one carat.

"It's beautiful."

He nodded. "It's my lucky piece. Go ahead, touch it for luck." He took her hand and pulled it close until her finger touched the jewel. "The best. That's what my future holds.

It can for you, too, Phoebe."

Colin climbed the stairs to Phoebe's apartment a second time. Using her key, he unlocked the door. Lucy was there to meet them, and Phoebe scooped her up. "You really didn't need to walk me all the way up—"

He slid past her, through the door. "I'd love some coffee."

Phoebe took off her coat. He'd just spent a bundle on a nice dinner. She couldn't be rude. "I'll make a pot."

While she did her work, Colin took off his tie and unfastened the top button of his shirt. He sat on a kitchen chair and removed his shoes. "Ah, freedom."

Phoebe raised her eyebrows. If he noticed, he didn't seem to care. He was making himself too comfortable. She turned her back to him and busied herself getting the cups and wiping off the counter.

She jumped when he wrapped his tie around her waist and pulled her back against his body.

"I've got you now."

Her ear tingled from his breath.

Phoebe tried to push herself away. "Colin. . ."

He dropped the tie and spun her around to face him. His hands pressed against the small of her back. His eyes were far too close.

"We make a great team, Phoebe." He smiled as her movements brought her closer. His breath smelled of wine and garlic. "We complement each other. I know the road to the top. I know how to talk to the big boys. I know when to brown-nose and just how much fast talk it takes. And you, my dear Phoebe, know the rest."

He didn't wait for her response. He covered her mouth with his, showing her what else he knew.

With a burst of adrenaline she pushed him away. "Stop it!" He stumbled back, his face a mask of surprise. Had no one ever told Colin Thurgood no?

Phoebe was proud to be the first.

He regained his footing and ran a hand over his hair. "Well, then."

She stepped around him and opened the door. "Thank you for dinner, Colin."

She locked the door behind him.

The next morning, after working an hour on painting the sanctuary of the Hillside Baptist Church, they ran low on paint. Leon offered to go for more, hoping to buy some cheap and charge Roosevelt a higher price—every little bit helped—but Roosevelt had insisted on going himself, saying he hoped to get some paint donated from the five and dime. Knowing that, Leon was glad to let him go. There was no profit to be made in charity.

Besides, with Roosevelt gone, Leon and Sarah were left alone.

Leon filled a hole in the wall with spackling while Sarah climbed a ladder to paint the trim around the ceiling. They were painting the room white—angel white, Roosevelt called it.

After ten minutes of being alone with her, Leon's thoughts were mixed like a potluck stew. With other women, he had no problem keeping up a line, but with Sarah it was different.

She was different. Even in a pair of Roosevelt's overalls and an old white T-shirt, she looked fine. He'd seen women like her before, though there weren't a whole lot around. She was the type who oozed sexiness and made a man think of physical desires while all the time acting—and truly believing, too, if Leon understood them right—like they didn't know a hoot about their power. When a man made a move on such women, they acted surprised, like their appeal was news to them. That was Sarah.

Leon watched her pull the brush across the wall, her forehead getting tight like she was thinking hard. He couldn't help but notice the nice shape of her bosom under her lifted-up arm. Soft. Curvy.

"Leon?"

His heart hit the side of his chest for getting caught snooping where he shouldn't. But she wasn't even looking down when she talked.

"Would you hand me that towel over there? I'm dripping on my hand."

He gave it to her. Then it was just like in the movies when their fingers touched and stayed put a few seconds. Leon saw something in her eyes that made his heart pump faster. It worried him and made him excited at the same time. She turned back to her work, kinda fast, like she felt it, too.

"I wonder what's taking Roosevelt so long?" She talked too loud. "I suppose Mr. Granger won't donate any more paint, so Roosevelt's trying somewhere else. I hope he doesn't go all the way to Nashville." She laughed, but it came out false. "That Roosevelt, he is such a good man. A really good man."

Leon got the message. He looked up, trying to catch her

eyes again, but she ignored him. "I'm done filling these holes, Miss Sarah. Do you want me to trim for awhile?"

She looked down at him like she was figuring his angle. But there was something else in her look. The look of a person coming up to the top of a roller coaster. Fear of the fall. And fear about how much they'd like it.

She took a breath and let it out as if settling some decision. "My arm *does* get tired." She balanced the paintbrush across the top of the paint can and started to back down the ladder.

Leon knew he shouldn't go through with what his body was telling him to do. . .yet it was nearly instinctive. He'd taken advantage of such situations since he'd first discovered that men and women being different could be a good thing. He positioned himself near the bottom of the ladder, holding the sides as if steadying it. Sarah couldn't help but touch him as she came down.

She must have sensed something. Had second thoughts herself. She stopped. She looked down at him, her face unreadable. Leon felt all the lust drain out of him. He couldn't do it.

He moved to the side and held out a hand.

She let out a breath and her face washed with relief—and he liked to think, just a hint of regret? "Thank you, Leon. You're quite the gentleman."

If she only knew.

With the four gallons of paint Roosevelt had talked the five and dime into donating, and with all three of them working, it still took them all day to finish painting the sanctuary.

Once they were done with the painting, Sarah begged off to go to bed early. The two men were left to clean up. Roosevelt fell onto a pew. "Found myself some new muscles today. I must be getting old."

Leon sat down beside him. "Then I'm getting old, too. I'm used up."

He chuckled. "It's a good feeling, ain't it?"

"Yeah. Yeah, it is." Although he never admitted it to anyone, Leon enjoyed manual labor as much as he enjoyed the con. Always thinking two steps ahead taxed his brain. Working his body eased the strain. He stretched his arms above his head, making his muscles scream and sigh at the same time.

"It sure looks nice, Leon. I want to thank you for helping out. Sarah and I could never have got it done without you."

"Sure you could've. But you're welcome anyway." Leon took a chance. "Roosevelt? I know you said Miss Sarah isn't your woman, but are you sweet on her?"

Roosevelt took it in stride, brushing dust off his pant leg. "She's a sweet lady."

"That she is, but are you serious about her—as a woman?"

He looked at the floor. "Like to be. But I don't know if I'm enough for her. There's a fire in that woman, and I'm not a fiery type of guy. Besides, her fire isn't for the flesh."

"It isn't?"

"No, sir." He stretched his legs in front of him. "Sarah's passion is for the Lord."

Leon was relieved. "Oh. . .*that.*"

Roosevelt squinted an eye at him. "Don't 'oh that' as if I just told you she had a passion for green beans. Jesus comes first and foremost in Sarah's life, and I don't think it would be right for a man—any man—to try to come betwixt and between that kind of love."

Leon had heard people say they loved Jesus. His grandma used to call out, "Love You, Jesus!" for everything. When her stomach didn't act up after eating fried chicken; when Grandpa got a job that paid the rent; and even when they'd gotten kicked out of the rat-hole they'd lived in for *not* paying the rent. *Love You, Jesus!*

"But that's just talk. Praise the Lord stuff."

Roosevelt shook his head. "There's more to it than that—"

There was a knock on the church door, and Roosevelt got up to answer it. Leon looked at his watch—it was after ten; late for callers.

He heard a woman's voice speak low from outside. She came into the church, holding the hand of a little boy with huge brown eyes and a pouty lip.

Roosevelt led them over. "Leon, this is Addie Whitney and her son, Marco. They're having some problems with Mr. Whitney, so they're going to spend the night here. Could you set up a couple cots in the fellowship hall for them? And make sure they have some extra blankets. The furnace is being ornery again."

Addie Whitney looked at the floor, but even so Leon could see her right eye was red and blue. Marco watched Leon watch his mama.

"Daddy hit her." No carrying on, just fact.

Addie Whitney shushed him and pulled him close.

Once they were settled, Leon went back to the sanctuary. Roosevelt was sitting where he'd been. "They all fixed up?"

Leon nodded and took his spot. "You have many like them?"

Roosevelt shrugged and yawned, covering his mouth. "Off and on. It goes in streaks. I won't have anybody for a week, and then other times we get full up. Must have to do with the full moon."

"Why do they come here? Why don't they go to the cops if they're being beat up?"

"What's the woman gonna do? Tell them to arrest her husband? Not likely."

The idea of men beating their wives and kids made Leon want to curl up like he used to behind the brown couch. *Sounds of screaming and slapped skin, the smell of beer and sweat. His little sister covering her ears.* He shook the memories away.

"How long do they stay?"

"A night or two. Then they go home, and it starts over again."

"Do you take them all in?"

"I can't turn them away. Could you?"

Leon could. He didn't like being around people who made him remember things.

Roosevelt stood and arched his back. "I'm going to bed. I'll see you in the morning."

"I'm going to sit here awhile."

"Suit yourself." Roosevelt turned out all the lights except the one shining on the altar. The shadow of the wooden cross was crisp against the clean, angel-white walls.

It was a long time before Leon's memories let him go to bed.

CHAPTER 8

Shall we accept good from God,
and not trouble?
Job 2:10

John Wriggens barged into Alexander MacMillan's office without knocking, giving the impression of a battering ram bursting through a barricade. Mac looked up. "May I help you?"

Wriggens tossed some newspapers on the desk. "Some of Dr. Nickolby's past *acquaintances* have decided to cash in on her notoriety. They've sold their stories to the tabloids."

"What kind of stories?"

Wriggens began pacing, his hands flailing. "It seems everyone and his brother has slept with our lovely Dr. Nickolby."

Mac felt a wave of disappointment as if she were a big sister gone astray. "This is unfortunate, but it is her business, not ours."

"It's our business now. The board is demanding some action." Wriggens removed his glasses and rubbed the bridge of his nose. "If only we'd known she was so undesirable." He laughed. "Or rather *too* desirable."

This was too much. "That's what happens with a lottery, John. It's not like we're screening the winners. Besides, the Time Lottery board has no right to condemn a winner without proof—"

"Not the Time Lottery board, Mac. The board of Mount Mercy Hospital in Boulder where Dr. Nickolby works. They're spooked by the bad press. The paper says they're threatening to fire her."

"She's not even here. Why the rush? Can't they wait a week?"

"Perhaps they like the attention. Deal with it, Mac. Work your marketing baloney. Handle the scandal. You've done it for movie stars, now it's our turn." He bit a thumbnail. "Do you think the reports are true?"

"She is a vivacious woman," Mac said. "I imagine she has plenty of admirers."

"Admirers or lovers?"

"I wouldn't know."

"She screws up two lifetimes at the same time. Quite a feat."

Mac glanced at the tabloids. He could read only the headline of the top paper. It was enough: *Doctor Sex Travels Through Time*. How could a noted surgeon have such a reputation? How could she belittle herself by giving herself away so carelessly? And if it *was* an issue to the hospital, how come they hadn't dealt with it before? Dr. Nickolby hardly seemed the type to lurk in the shadows.

"What galls me is, if Dr. Nickolby had never won the Time Lottery, these weasels would never have crept out of their holes." Mac rubbed his face. "Sometimes I get weary of people's insatiable need to dish dirt."

"Ah, but you thrive on it. Dirt is your business, Mac."

"Dirt is *not* my business. Marketing is my business. Image-making is my business."

"Then do your business and save the image of the Time Lottery."

Colin Thurgood slammed down the phone, turned to his laptop, slapped the keys to check his stocks on the Internet, and cursed. Only then did he remember he was not alone. He looked through the glass of his office and saw his secretary looking at him. He turned his chair toward the window.

Two months previous, Colin had overextended himself on a few luxuries for himself and Phoebe such as a cabin in Tahoe and a new Lexus. Then, feeling the surge of confidence he always got when he acquired new things, he got the urge to earn more money so he could buy more cabins and more cars.

He'd heard about a sure thing on the stock market. All he had to do was put a little down, do some fast trading for a few weeks, and he would have more money to play with. But things hadn't gone as planned.

Even before Phoebe had left to go back to 1969, he'd known it was a hopeless situation. If only she would have let him go in her place. . .he wouldn't make the same mistakes again. He'd keep better tabs on his spending. And he certainly wouldn't buy that stupid Internet stock that had made promises it couldn't keep.

But now Phoebe was gone, running around in *their* past, leaving him alone to face disaster. The brokerage house had just told him to pay the $102,857 or—

My brother has that kind of money.

Colin flipped open his address book and found the phone number of Dr. Anthony Thurgood, his rich plastic surgeon brother. Anthony was single and dripping in the dough. Surely he'd give Colin a loan.

He flipped the address book shut. Surely he wouldn't. Not after the names Colin had called him a few months ago. Not that baby brother didn't deserve it. But calling someone an arrogant, egotistical pig did not bode well toward the asking of a favor. A $102,857 favor. Colin would have to think of something else.

"Call on line two, Mr. Thurgood."

"Take a message!"

His secretary gave him another look through the glass, this one less forgiving.

He had to get out of there.

Colin grabbed his coat and briefcase and rushed out. "Got a meeting at the club, Terry. I'll see you tomorrow."

"But Mr. Dresden called about the—"

"Tomorrow."

Colin took the stairs. He didn't want to risk the elevator where he might run into his colleagues and have to explain his early exit. Not that he didn't make his own hours or lie with great efficiency. But he knew when his mind was flustered—as it was now—it was easy to make a mistake. And that he couldn't afford. He'd spent over thirty years creating a persona of power, confidence, and control. He couldn't risk damaging it because of a lapse of financial fortune.

Colin burst onto the street and pulled his coat collar around his neck. If only he could curl up somewhere and make it all go away like he used to do as a kid. When his father had died, his mother had spent some of the insurance money to buy him a tent that he put up in the backyard. It had been a good place to—

Insurance money!

"I need to speak to someone involved with the Time Lottery."

"What is this regarding, sir?"

"I'm a relative of one of the lottery winners."

"I'll connect you with Mr. MacMillan. He'll be able to—"

"No!" Colin toned down. "Isn't there someone else? I don't want to bother Mac—Mr. MacMillan. I just have a few questions about procedure."

"Well. . .I suppose I could give you to Bob Craven. He's one of the Time-Techs who handles the Sphere."

"Bob. That's fine. Let me talk to Bob."

"Please hold."

While he was waiting, Colin moved into an alley, searching for quiet from the street noise. He leaned against a building and tried to calm his breathing. It was imperative he didn't sound desperate.

"Bob here. What can I do you for?"

Perfect. An ignorant comedian. Easily manipulated. A peon in search of power. Give him a little respect, make him feel important, and then ply him for details.

"Mr. Craven, this is Colin Thurgood. I'm the husband of—"

"Phoebe Thurgood. Nice lady. I was one of the people who saw her off in the Sphere. What's up, Mr. Thurgood?"

"It's about the insurance."

"The winners' insurance?"

"That's the stuff." *Careful here.* "I was wondering if it was valid."

"Sure it is. And you don't even have to pay for it. A paid policy is one of the perks of being a winner."

"I'm not worried about the premium."

"Oh. Right."

"Actually, I was concerned about the logistics of the payoff."

"The $250,000?"

"Yes."

"You don't have to worry about that, Mr. Thurgood. The insurance is only there in case your wife decides to stay in the past, and I can't imagine her wanting to do that. I mean, look at your life. You're wealthy, you have everything anyone would ever want. A quarter of a million dollars must be pocket change to you."

Not anymore. He concentrated on his first option. "Actually, my concerns are a little different. I was wondering what would happen if my wife had to wake up before her week was up."

"Why would she do that?"

"Malfunction. Human error. This is the first Time Lottery, isn't it? It's understandable that something could go wrong, and my wife would be cheated out of her full time in her past. And if she was, then there would have to be some compensa—"

"No. . .that won't happen. It can't happen."

"Why not?"

"Because the serum doesn't start to fade until seven days. That's when we give a burst to the Loop and—"

"Excuse me?"

"The winners are given a dose of the serum that is computed down to the minutest measurement for their weight and size. It lasts eight days, but starts its fade at seven. That's when an electrical burst to their Loop starts up their total clarity."

"Yeah, yeah. . .that Dual Consciousness thing."

"Right. That's when they see the outcome of both choices. That's when they get to make their final decision."

Colin turned his attention to Plan B. "The decision about staying behind or coming back."

"She'll be back soon, Mr. Thurgood. Probably. I mean, maybe. . ." He hesitated. "Hey. You wanted to go in her place, didn't you?"

"A lapse of judgment."

"Don't apologize to me. You were only acting like any guy would act."

Don't pull me down to your level, Bobby-boy. "But if my wife *doesn't* come back. . ."

"Well. . .that is a possibility. But don't worry, Mr. Thurgood."

I'm not worried. Not like you think. "Is there any way to contact her now?"

"Like how?"

"Oh, I don't know. . .like get a message to her somehow." *Try to convince her to stay behind for my sake.*

"No."

"You sound so certain."

"Why would you want to get in touch with her anyway? She's going to be back soon."

Colin sighed so Bob could hear. He made his voice quiver. "I. . .I miss her. I miss talking to her."

"That's understandable—and also impressive after all your years of marriage. I hope I meet someone I can love that much. I do have this girlfriend. I think I love her. We've been together for six months now, but—"

"So you can't help me?"

"Contact your wife? No. I'm afraid not. But if there's anything else I can do for—"

Colin heaved his phone into the building across the alley. It splintered into a hundred pieces.

Which was just what his life would do if Phoebe came home.

"He what?" Mac fell back in his chair.

Bob shifted his weight to the other foot. "Thurgood wanted to get in touch with his wife."

"Why?"

"He seemed concerned about what decision she was going to make—to come back or not."

"She's only going to be gone a week. Can't he wait?"

"That's what I wondered."

"Nobody can wait a week around here." Mac tapped a finger against his lower lip. What was Thurgood up to? He certainly wasn't pursuing taking his wife's place anymore. And why had he talked to Bob instead of himself? Then it came to him.

Because I know his game.

Bob continued. "He really got my radar going. First thing he did was ask about the insurance policy."

Mac sat forward. "What about it?"

"He wanted to know the logistics of the payoff—those were his words: 'the logistics of the payoff.' "

"How to cash in?" Mac said.

"He went off on some tangent about what would happen if his wife came back early."

"Hmm."

"It didn't make much sense. He hinted at wanting compensation for her not getting her money's worth."

It sounded like a diversion. "Did Thurgood act as if he needed the insurance money?"

"Need it? He's rich."

"Rich people need money, too. Sometimes more money than the rest of us."

"He didn't mention anything. But once I said I couldn't get to his wife ahead of time, he shut down the conversation."

Curiouser and curiouser.

"Are you going to call him?"

"No, no. You handled it fine, Bob. Let me know if he calls again."

Bob left, and Mac rubbed his hands over his face. He'd felt so good about everything. Three winners, off without a hitch.

Who knew the hitch would come from those they left behind?

The phone rang. "Go away." The phone kept ringing. He picked it up.

"Alexander MacMillan?"

"Yes."

"This is Officer Kranz from the Memphis police department."

Memphis? Who did he know in Memphis?

"We have a Roosevelt Hazen here. We found him in an alley with—"

Mac blinked at the name. "You have who?"

"Roosevelt Hazen. We have his body here, found bludgeoned in an alley."

"His body?"

"Correct. We understand there might be some mix-up. Some of us have been watching your Time Lottery doings, and we noticed that you had a Roosevelt Hazen going back to his past and—"

"He's gone. He's already in his past."

"Well. . .that's the odd thing. According to our computers, there is only one Roosevelt Hazen in the whole U.S. of A., and if we've got him, then you don't."

No no no no no no. "Or if we have him, then *you* don't."

"Well, sir, we've got a Bible," Kranz said.

"A Bible?"

"Long story, but he had a Bible on him that had his name in it. 'Course that didn't prove anything in itself, so we tried the fingerprint route. Found an arrest for vagrancy, back in 1964. It's him."

Mac's mind crowded with new thoughts. "Then who did

we just send back into 1962?"

"I have no idea."

"Can we keep this quiet, Officer? At least for awhile. I don't want the press—"

"Yeah, I get you. I saw the feeding frenzy about that lady doctor's love life."

"Exactly. I don't want that to happen in Roosevelt's case. At least not until we find out the truth. Is that possible?"

"Absolutely. If I had my way, the press would starve."

Mac stared at the scribbled notes in front of him. Memphis. *Roosevelt Hazen. Bludgeoned. Alley.*

Murder.

Mac had felt there was something fishy about Roosevelt —or whatever the imposter's name was. He must have known about Roosevelt's death. But did he cause it? Or did he just come upon the body and decide to take advantage of the situation? Either way the man must have known Roosevelt's body would be found. It was only a matter of time.

Ha. A matter of time. Now the imposter was safely *back* in time. Reliving his life. Taking Roosevelt's chance.

But who was he?

They could run a DNA test since they had the culprit's body right here. But for it to tell them anything, they'd need another sample to compare it to, and few people had their DNA on file. But fingerprints, they *could* match fingerprints. . . .

Catching a killer was not in his job description.

"Yank him back! Get that conniving imposter back here this minute!" Wriggens popped out of his chair and jammed his finger on his desk as if he wanted the man to appear on that exact spot.

Mac took a seat and crossed his hands on top of Hazen's file.

"Mac! Say something!"

"We need to stay calm."

"Calm?" The flush of Wriggens's cheeks spread to his forehead. "We've got a criminal taking advantage of our time technology, disgracing our good intentions by his deceit, and you want me to be calm?"

"The deed is done. It's our job to deal with the situation in a professional manner."

Wriggens sat down heavily. His forehead regained its normal pasty color. "What are the facts as we know them?"

Mac filled him in.

Wriggens tapped his pencil on the desk. "So. What do you have to say for yourself?"

Mac raised his eyebrows. "Excuse me?"

"You *were* the only one who spent any time with the man. You had conversations with him. You answered his questions. You should've—"

Mac sucked in a breath as a memory flooded back.

"What?"

"He did ask some odd questions. He asked if we could bring him back early. He was concerned that we wouldn't give him time to work through his choice."

"Ha! You should have known."

Mac shook his head. "There's no way I could have known. None. It's simply an unfortunate mistake."

"That's it? We're in the midst of a public relations nightmare, and you call it an unfortunate mistake?"

Mac raked his hands through his hair. If this imposter really had killed the real Roosevelt Hazen, then they had just sent a murderer back in time.

Mac cradled the mug of coffee between his hands. He sat on the couch in his darkened den and repeated the verse that had gotten him through the past year. *Hasten, O God, to save me; O Lord, come quickly to help me. Hasten, O God, to save me; O Lord, come quick—*

The phone rang. He did not move to answer it. Whether it was Wriggens or the press, he didn't want to talk with them. Any of them. He'd done his duty.

Or had he?

There was an imposter floating around in the past—perhaps a murderer, Colin Thurgood was asking questions no loving husband would ask, and Dr. Nickolby's reputation was being destroyed in her absence.

Mac used to believe that people were virtuous, that left alone they would naturally gravitate toward good. But with Holly's death, he'd begun to think otherwise. Holly's killer was living a life—albeit in jail—while his beloved Holly was dead. Loneliness was a yoke that crushed him with every breath, every movement. Every memory.

He stared out the window at the woods behind their

house. The branches of the trees jutted into the gray sky like dark fingers. A swing swayed in the wind. The remnants of the garden poked through the snow, reminding him of his neglect. But how could he clear away the garden? Holly's garden. It was her time and energy that had brought it to life. If Mac scraped away the brittle plants and tended the soil, it would be like burying her again. There was so little of her left in the house, as if every time he opened a door or window a bit of Holly escaped in the breeze and was lost forever.

Smells were all he had left. There was no soft skin to touch. No lips to taste. No laughter to hear. And no smile from Holly as Andrew crawled into bed with them on Sunday mornings and cuddled between their pillows, proof that one plus one equaled a miracle.

He needed her. Suddenly, the ache sprang into his body, racing to every cell until all that he was needed Holly.

He stumbled to her closet and ripped open the door. He lunged toward her clothes, burying his face in their folds, searching for her smell.

He couldn't find it! He moved along her blouses and skirts, so neatly hung in their color-coordinated rows. Where? Where? It had to be here!

"No! Don't take this from me, too!"

Blouses fell to the floor. He pressed sweaters to his face, searching, searching. . .

There. There! On her robe. Holly's scent of lavender and sweat and. . .what was that other smell?

He held the robe at arm's length to study it as if it were a DaVinci or Monet. It was as familiar to Mac as his own face. Pink, quilted. Missing a button two down from the top.

Ragged along the hem from her morning checks of the garden where she'd stoop to pinch an offending weed from her precious tomatoes. A spattering of chocolate on the sleeve. Batter from Andrew's birthday cake, baked the morning of her death? Mac jammed the sleeve against his face and inhaled. Peppermint. Andrew's favorite and, as such, a done deal.

If only they'd had the chance to celebrate that last birthday. To eat the cake and sing the birthday song around a table bathed in the glow of four candles.

But an evil man had changed their plans, entering this haven, this home, in the throes of a crazed vendetta, taking with him nothing of value except the life of his precious wife.

Mac sank to his knees and let the ache eat him alive.

CHAPTER 9

All a man's ways seem innocent to him,
but motives are weighed by the Lord.

PROVERBS 16:2

It was a fact of life: When one room was painted, suddenly every other room looked dingy. So it was with the church. Once Sarah saw the sanctuary in the daylight, she suggested the fellowship hall could use sprucing up. She only suggested, but there was no way Leon wanted to see disappointment cloud those eyes.

"Let me finish my coffee, and I'll get right to it." She'd come over to the church to make them eggs, muffins, and coffee.

The touch of her hand on his arm was ample payment. Or at least an ample down payment.

"I'll clean up these breakfast dishes, and you can have the place to yourself," she said.

"You don't have to leave on my ac—"

There was a knock on the kitchen door. Sarah answered it.

A man in a suit stood outside. He tipped his hat. *Salesman.*

" 'Morning, ma'am. My name is Charlie Winston, and I'm selling this new invention, the Suds Handle."

"I'm not interest—"

"You wash dishes, ma'am?"

"Of course."

"You use soap?"

"Of course."

Leon rolled his eyes. *Get to the point, buddy.*

"—use a sponge?"

Sarah smiled. "Instead of playing twenty questions through the door, why don't you come in?"

Sarah and Roosevelt. Easy marks.

The man removed his hat and stepped to the side. "I've got my daughter here, too. She's on break from school and is doing a little traveling with me. Helping out. Come on, darlin'. The nice lady has invited us inside."

The way he said it told Leon he wasn't used to getting this far.

A pretty teenager came in the door, her eyes skirting Sarah, then Leon, then the floor like she didn't appreciate being involved in this whole thing. Leon couldn't blame her. How many teenagers wanted to hang out with their fathers? Especially fathers who were selling Suds Handles—whatever that was.

"Would you like some coffee? A glass of milk?"

"Thank you, ma'am. That would be nice."

The duo sat at the table. Leon raised his cup to get a refill. The painting could wait.

The man dug into his bag and pulled out a funny-looking gadget with a sponge attached to a long plastic handle. He unscrewed the end. "See, you fill this here handle with dish-washing soap. And it comes out through the sponge while you're washing dishes."

Sarah took a seat, bringing with her a plate of the blueberry muffins. The girl took one and had it halfway to her mouth before she backtracked and set it on a napkin first, like by letting it sit a second, Leon and Sarah wouldn't notice how much she wanted to eat it. Needed to eat it. The man eyed the muffins, too, but he had other things to think about first. Like getting a sale.

Sarah took the gadget in hand. She studied it. "Looks interesting."

"Oh, it is, it is. Very modern."

"You say you invented it."

The man reddened. "No, not me. Not this anyway."

"Daddy's always inventing stuff." It was the first time the daughter had spoken.

The man patted her hand. "Now, now, darlin', don't go on about me. This is what I'm selling now."

"Would I have heard of any of your inventions?" Sarah asked.

He took out another Suds Handle and handed it to Leon. "You will someday. I keep trying, but the world isn't cooperating."

The girl smashed a crumb with her finger. "Grandma

always says, 'Don't cooperate with the world, change it.' That's what Daddy is trying to do."

By selling soap handles?

Sarah smacked the handle against her hand. "I like that saying. The world seems to work against us so much of the time. Telling us to be or do one thing, when the right thing might be something quite different. The world wants us to be bad, but being good takes more work. 'Don't cooperate with the world.' I like it. Jesus didn't cooperate with the world. . . ."

She looked at Leon, and he had to look away. *Right, wrong. Good, bad. . .*

"At any rate, I'd like to buy one of these doodads—depending on the price, of course."

The man beamed like he'd won the lottery. "Fifty-nine cents, ma'am."

"Reasonable enough. I'll take two."

The girl squeezed her father's arm and they exchanged a look that declared that the day had just become good. Leon was glad he wasn't in their racket. To get all excited about a buck.

"Let me get some money."

While Sarah was gone to the sanctuary, the girl ate a second muffin, and the father ate his first one. Leon refilled her milk. Same with the man's coffee.

They heard the door to the sanctuary close with Sarah coming back. The girl shoved the rest of her muffin in her mouth, chewing behind a napkin.

"Here we go. Two dollars. You got change?"

This was obviously the girl's job. She dug in the satchel

for a change bag that was slim and weightless.

"These muffins sure are tasty. My wife would love to have the recipe if you wouldn't mind sharing it."

Sarah pocketed the change. "Is your wife traveling with you?"

"Well, yes. . ." The man looked toward the door. "She is . . .back at the hotel."

Leon didn't believe him.

"I'll do better than a recipe." Sarah fetched a paper bag. She put the rest of the muffins inside. "I know how awful hotel food can be. You let her try them firsthand. And the recipe. . ." She got out a recipe box and pulled out a card. "Just give her this."

"Don't you need it?"

She waved his question away. "I've made them a hundred times."

The girl stood, holding the bag of muffins with two hands like it was precious. The man adjusted his hat. "Thanks for your business, ma'am. Sir. And thanks for the muffins. God bless you both. Come on, Phoebe, thank the nice people."

As soon as they left, Leon ran to a side window. "Just as I thought, the wife's not at any hotel. She's sitting in the car."

Sarah shrugged. "I figured as much. They've probably been sleeping in there."

"Then why did you play along?"

"You don't want to take away their dignity, Leon—especially in front of the daughter. The man's trying to earn a living. He's trying to keep his family together. I admire him for that."

"But he's a terrible salesman." He picked up the Suds Handle. "Why'd you buy two of these things?"

"Buying what he's got to sell is better than just giving him a dollar."

"Dignity again?"

Sarah got out the dish soap and began to fill a handle. "I've been around rich folk, and I've been around poor. Both sides want the same thing."

"Money?"

She gave him a look. "Dignity. You give people that, and everybody's rich."

Leon put his mug in the sink. "I'd rather have money."

"Then I feel sorry for you, Leon."

"But—"

"The girl's grandma was right. Don't cooperate with the world—change it. The world wants to bring us down. Every man for himself. That's not right."

She's pegged me good.

"Go on, Leon. Get the paint. You've got work to do. Honest work."

Good people were mighty puzzling.

Tommy showed up at Cheryl's house while she was watching TV Sunday afternoon.

"Hi," he said.

"Hi."

"Can I come in?"

"Sure."

They went into the family room and sat on the couch—

closer than friends would sit, but farther apart than a boyfriend and girlfriend.

Tommy fidgeted and looked around the room. "Your parents home?"

What did he have in mind? "No."

He nodded but didn't say any more. Cheryl focused on the TV, to a documentary about snow geese.

Suddenly, Tommy turned toward her. "I love you."

"Uh. . .that's. . .nice."

"I want to apologize for last night, Cheryl. I behaved like a jerk, taking advantage of you on the first date."

As Tommy's words started to flow, she stared at him as if he were a specimen in a museum, his monologue inducing thoughts but no audible words.

"But you are so beautiful and sexy and soft, and when you agreed to go out with me it was like a dream."

I've had a few dreams of my own.

"Then at the game when you kissed me, right there in front of everybody. . ."

My mistake.

". . .and I thought you wanted to be alone. . ."

Temporary hormonal insanity.

". . .I couldn't contain myself. You bring out the animal in me, Cheryl."

Down, boy.

"I couldn't get to sleep last night. . . ."

Me, neither.

". . .thinking about being with you again. I love you, Cheryl. I hope you don't mind me saying so."

Cheryl stared at the TV. The geese had been replaced by

a commercial for Herbal Essence shampoo. The whole thing was absurd.

"I know this comes as a shock," he said, "and I don't expect you to answer, but I had to tell you how I felt or I would burst." He took a deep breath and looked at his watch. "But now, I have to go. I have to get to Jake's to tutor him in history, plus I have a huge paper due in a few days. If Jake doesn't get a passing grade on this next test, the coach won't let him play. But I had to come over to tell—"

Cheryl found her throat dry. "Jake?"

"I hate to take the time, but I'm Mrs. Tranfield's assistant, and she's counting on me to help him."

"I'll go."

Tommy did a double take. "What?"

"I'll tutor Jake, so you can work on your paper."

His puppy love smile was classic. "You would do that for me?"

"Sure." Cheryl stood. "If I'm going to help Jake, I'd better get going. We'd both better get going."

Tommy stood, too. But his face had changed. His eyebrows dipped. "Well. . .I guess so."

Cheryl walked him to the door where he stopped, obviously expecting some token in payment for his declaration of love. Cheryl kissed his lips quickly.

Then he was gone, and Cheryl was left not quite believing how Jake Carlisle had been laid in her eager hands.

It was fate.

As soon as Tommy left, Cheryl hurried upstairs to change

for Jake's tutoring. At the moment, Jake liked Andrea. Andrea was crisp pleats and starched underwear. Cheryl's jeans, worn from dragging on the ground, wouldn't cut it. If Cheryl wanted to be Jake's girl, she had to look like Jake's *kind* of girl. She ripped the tags off an aqua and brown plaid skirt her grandma had given her a year ago Christmas. A white turtleneck and knee socks finished the look. She drew the line at pigtails.

When Cheryl pulled up to Jake's house, she was surprised it wasn't a fancier place. Wasn't Jake rich? Wasn't rich a criterion for the in-group?

It was a ranch-style house with a one-car garage that needed painting. Christmas lights were strung along the eaves even though it was February. The brass knocker on the door was tarnished and was engraved *Smythe*. The doorbell was out of order.

Mrs. Carlisle was a further shock. She looked too young to be Jake's mother. Or maybe it was just her clothes. She wore a red miniskirt that would make the pep club proud and displayed legs extending into four-inch heels. She smiled, her teeth perfect except for a dab of red lipstick.

"Aren't you cute." Cute was obviously a four-letter word.

"I'm Cheryl Nickolby. I'm here to tutor Jake."

Mrs. Carlisle took a step into the doorway and looked past Cheryl toward the street. "Where's that Tommy-fellow? Were we too much for him?"

Cheryl had the sickening feeling that the outfit was for Tommy's benefit. She wondered where Mr. Carlisle was this afternoon. "I'm taking Tommy's place."

Jake's mother shrugged and stood aside. "Too bad. But

come on in. Jake's in the den pretending to study." She pointed to a hallway. "Last door on the left."

Before Cheryl could say thank you, Mrs. Carlisle disappeared in the opposite direction.

Cheryl took a moment to look around, trying to glean as much about Jake as she could from his surroundings.

The living room was white and cotton candy pink, totally foo-foo except for the trophies sitting on a bookcase by the television. The couch was white with pink flowers and had two satin throw pillows placed at angles in each corner. A pair of yellow slippers sat on the floor by a pink velveteen chair. *Vogue, Women's Day,* and *Reader's Digest* were piled in neat succession on the glass-topped coffee table.

Jake didn't fit in this woman's paradise.

Cheryl walked down the hall that led to the den. There were four doors. She passed a bedroom that was an advertisement for French Provincial, and a bathroom that had fuzzy carpet and a fish-shaped soap holder. Through the last door on the right she spotted an unmade bed with a poster of *American Graffiti* hung above it. The door across the hall was slightly ajar, letting her peek inside.

Jake was sitting behind a desk, his feet crossed at the ankles, propped on a pile of books. He was reading a magazine which he had set inside his history book. It was a useless gesture as the magazine was inches bigger and spilled over its camouflage. He was humming a song by Three Dog Night, bouncing his head to the beat.

He looked up, as if sensing a presence. "Tommy?"

Cheryl pushed the door open, clutching a notebook against her chest. "It's me, Cheryl."

He took his feet off the desk and grinned. "And what is me-Cheryl doing here?"

She took a step closer. "Tommy couldn't come. I'm going to take his place."

"Dr. Cheryl. Ready to take on another emergency?"

"I'll do my best."

"I bet you know mouth-to-mouth, too."

Cheryl felt herself blush. What happened to goody-goody Jake? Mr. Nice Guy? The All-American boy?

Jake waved a hand in her direction. "Why the get-up?"

Cheryl tugged at her skirt. "What get up?"

"You look like you're playing dress up."

I am. I'm dressing up for you, Jake.

He got up and circled her, rubbing his hand against his chin as if making an assessment. "You look good, don't get me wrong. But something's not right. It's not *you.*"

Cheryl hated his inspection—and the truth behind his statement. "It *is* me. I'm the one wearing the clothes, aren't I?"

Jake stopped walking. "The style is wrong for you. I prefer your more earthy look. You're Carole King, not Betty and Veronica."

"You make it sound like I'm playing a role. I'm not."

"Sure you are. We both are."

"We are?"

"Of course." Jake went back to the desk. "I play the role of the jock, and you play the role of the disapproving but envious outsider who only wants—"

"Envious? Why, you egotistical, cocky. . . Who are you to think that other people envy you?"

He put his feet back on the desk, unmoved by her anger.

"It's true, isn't it?"

"No!"

"You're always looking at us, watching us."

"Because you disgust us."

"I don't think so. We are what you can't be."

"Arrogant pigs?"

He shrugged, undisturbed. "Popular."

Forget commitment. Forget having a lasting relationship. Forget Jake being a nice—

Jake pulled a chair close to his. "Have a seat, Cheryl. Next to me."

She stood where she was, calming the heave of her chest. He smiled at her, totally confident. It was unnerving. He had definitely taken control of the situation, and Cheryl didn't like it. She was the smart one. She had come there to help *him.*

He patted the chair. "Don't take everything so personally. I didn't make the rules. Neither did you."

"I don't like rules."

"Glad to hear it."

Just when she thought she knew where the conversation was going, he changed gears. She took a cleansing breath and hooked a finger in the turtleneck, trying to buy some space. He was right. These clothes were not her style. She set her notebook on the desk and picked up the magazine Jake had been reading: *Sports Illustrated.*

"Studying hard, I see?"

"All work and no play. . ."

"You're hardly a dull boy."

He gave her a long look. "You've got quite the mouth on you, haven't you?"

She stopped her first thought, then let it out. If he wanted her to be herself, fine. . . "My mouth is not my best feature."

Jake shook his head, real slow. "My, my. You are a feisty one."

She was pleased at his approving tone and felt better now that the control was shifting into familiar territory. Cheryl opened his history book and rummaged through the mess on the desk to find a notebook and two pencils. She held one out for him. He made no attempt to take it. "Come on. Take it."

"Drop it."

"What?"

"Drop the pencil on the floor like you do in class."

"What are you talking about?"

"I've seen how you purposely drop your pencil so you have to lean over real slow, showing us guys a glimpse down your blouse."

Her face grew hot. Had she been *that* obvious? "I assure you, if I drop my pencil it is by accident."

"Being brilliant is no accident."

It disturbed Cheryl that Jake knew her secrets and disturbed her more that her suggestive actions had become so much a part of what she considered a normal day that she didn't even realize she'd been doing them.

"Caught you, didn't I?"

She tried not to smile, but it was impossible with him grinning at her like that. She closed the textbook along with all thoughts of tutoring him. "Did you really like it?"

He leaned forward, resting his elbows on the arms of the chair. "If you'd done it in my direction. . ." He shrugged.

"What about Andrea?"

"Nobody drops a pencil the way you do."

Too soon. Too soon. It was going too fast. This time things were supposed to be different, more than just the physical. She was trying to start a relationship here. Maybe she should play hard to get. Unfortunately, she didn't know how.

She opened the history book a second time. "We need to get to work before we get distracted. I've got a lot to teach you."

"I'll bet you do." He sat back and laughed, raising his face to the ceiling.

The situation was veering left when it should have veered right. "You're not like I expected."

"Is that good or bad?"

"I'm not sure. I always thought you were a nice guy. . .I mean Andrea. . .you know the type."

"Clean-cut letterman dates head cheerleader. The American flag, chocolate malts, and 'love means never having to say you're sorry.' "

"Right."

"I'm deeper than that."

"Glad to hear it."

"You'll have to get to know me better to find out *how* deep."

"Why should I?"

"How else will you know what you've missed?"

His eyes met hers. He winked. Cheryl's brain and body warred. The words between them had been lobbed like a tennis ball, back and forth. Who had won the first set?

Before she could start the next serve, he lunged, grabbing her shoulders. He kissed her. Hard.

That was it. Destiny. Fate. *Déjà vu.* After only a moment's hesitation, Cheryl wrapped her arms around his neck and pulled him close. Her chair tipped over. Her hip bore the brunt of the fall. Jake shoved the chair out of the way and moved on top of her. Increased respiration. Sweat. Her own.

Cheryl didn't want to come up for air. Let him give her what air she needed through his kisses. *Closer, please get close—*

"Well, well. Guinevere and Lancelot."

They lifted their heads and saw Mrs. Carlisle standing in the doorway, her fingers spread as she blew on freshly painted nails.

Cheryl pulled her skirt down. Jake sat up.

"Just paying the tutor, Momsie."

She turned to leave. "Cute, Jake. Better you than me."

Cheryl stood and tucked in her turtleneck. Humiliation was not part of the deal. Neither was lust. If she wanted her relationship with Jake to be different—more lasting—then shouldn't it follow a different road instead of speeding her down the same one she'd been down a dozen times before? The old way was to get their interest, take control, prove who had the power, then leave. How should the new way go?

She had no idea. Maybe this was a bad plan. Maybe it wasn't in her constitution to play the commitment game. Jake was full of surprises. He left her confused. She pulled up her knee socks and gathered her school supplies.

Jake watched her from the floor. "Hey, Cheryl?"

She turned toward him, expecting some words of embarrassment or contrition.

He tossed her a pencil. "I'll get it later."

Cheryl ran.

She shut off the car radio to concentrate on the noise of her own thoughts. Things were not going according to plan. Not exactly. Cheryl had wanted Jake's interest. And after her tutoring session, she had it—oh, how she had it. But she had wanted something more. The whole boy-girl going steady thing. She'd thought Jake was different. Special. And yet he had jumped on her just like every other guy.

It had all started the other night when she'd seen Jake on the highway while she was helping that bum. The sudden yearning for commitment had come out of nowhere, a foreign idea that had slid in between other thoughts like an infiltrating traitor. *Commitment. Try commitment.*

But why? Why now, all of a sudden?

What did commitment ever get anyone except heartache? Look at her mother. She committed to a man, then got hurt. Committed, got hurt. Wasn't Cheryl's way better? *Hi, bye, nice knowing you.* No pain. No torment. Fun and games, then gone.

Cheryl stopped at an intersection and leaned her head on the steering wheel. She was wandering aimlessly as if a plan for what to do next could be found on the street. But she wasn't used to planning her life. It just happened. Impulsive and spontaneous. Maybe that was part of her problem. Commitment involved planning, thinking ahead, making promises that involved more than the here and now. She didn't want that responsibility. She wanted freedom. What had the sixties been for if not to grant her the freedom to be who she wanted to be, to do what she wanted to do, to go where she. . .like that bum she'd helped. He had true freedom. No strings, none at—

"Dr. Cheryl? You all right?"

Cheryl looked up to see the bum—Leon—standing on the curb. He was hunched over, looking in the passenger window.

"Hey, Doc. You okay? You sick or something?"

It took her a moment to understand what he was talking about. She moved back from the steering wheel and ran a hand through her hair. "I'm fine."

"You don't look fine. You look hungry."

"Huh?"

He grinned, then pointed to a burger joint down the street.

Why not? She could use the company, and obviously, Leon could use the meal. Cheryl leaned across the seat and opened the door for him.

Leon was on his second burger.

"So, girlie-girl. What got you down enough to cry on your steering wheel?"

"I wasn't crying."

"Maybe not on the outside. . ."

"What makes you so smart?"

"Mistakes."

It was a good answer. "You've made a few?"

His laugh was bitter. He extended his arms, displaying his worn clothing. "I didn't get where I am today doing right."

She didn't like him getting down on himself. "Well. . . who knows what's right anyway?"

"You do. I do."

She looked up. Her question had been hypothetical.

"And how do we know that?"

"Everybody knows."

"How?"

He shrugged. "From the time we're bitsy. It starts as a gut thing then turns real when our parents teach us stuff." He stopped with the burger halfway to his mouth. "You have a grammy?"

"Sure. Lots of them."

"They ever do the Bible stuff with you? Moses, the Ten Commandments, Jesus loves me, that sort of thing?"

"Nope." She said it too quick, like she was proud of it. She wasn't proud. She knew how grandparents *could* be. She'd met Julie's. She'd even gone to church with Julie once or twice.

"You never had any God-stuff in your life?"

This time she was slower to answer. "I've picked up the basics here and there. Don't feel much need for it, though. I've got things under control."

"Do you now?"

She felt herself redden. She took a sip of her malt. "If you know God so well, why are you out on the streets, wearing. . ."

He grinned. "Designer clothes?"

"Yeah."

"I said no to God a few times too many."

"Those mistakes you were talking about?"

"Those mistakes."

"What happened to 'Jesus loves me'?"

"Oh, He loves me all right, forgives me, too, probably. But *I* don't love me. *I* don't forgive me."

"You're pretty hard on yourself."

"It's not just me. The world's given me a few licks along the way."

She hesitated. "Have you been in jail?"

He laughed and bit a French fry in two. "Jail yanks me back like a fisherman. Even though I'd rather stay far away—and know it's best if I do everything in my power to swim in the other direction—I end up falling for the bait 'til jail hooks me and reels me in. The minute it happens, I know I'm a goner. Even before then, I know the odds of swimming in the wrong end of the pond, but I seems to do it anyway."

"Too bad they don't throw you back."

"Oh, they do. After awhile." He licked the salt off his fingers. "Sometimes I wish they would just get it over with. Fry me up for dinner."

"You don't mean that."

He looked away, and Cheryl saw his hand shake. When he looked back his eyes were shiny. "I'm tired, Dr. Cheryl. I'm a thirty-four-year-old man who feels ninety. I'm tired and alone." His shoulders slumped. "Don't ever be alone, Doc. Find somebody to love you and keep you safe. Someone who cares whether you're there or not."

Her throat was dry.

"You got a boyfriend?"

"A few."

He eyed her like he knew the truth. "Don't sell yourself short, girlie. Don't sell yourself at all. Hold out. Do it the right way. Choose better'n me. The bait that lures *you* toward wrong is different than the bait that lures me, but it's there. Don't kid yourself. The devil works that way, you know. I've met him face-to-face a few times. . . Wish I'd listened to the God side more—did more God-fearing." Leon looked up, his eyes busy with a memory. "I can't tell you how many God-fearing people I've scammed. Good people." Leon shook his head. "Bad doings, that. Bad bait. Strong bait that hooked me good. Still hooks me. . ."

"What did you do?"

He shook his head and balled up the sandwich's paper wrappings. "Too much. Not enough." He pushed away from the table. "Someone told me once, 'Don't cooperate with the world.' If only I'd followed. . ."

His words made Cheryl's mind flash back to a woman she'd met on the street. She'd been fourteen at the time, wearing a long dress. *It was San Francisco. After Mom's wedding to Oscar.* "I've heard that saying, too."

Leon blinked. "What d'you know? Small world, isn't it?"

"It's a good saying. I'd forgotten about it."

"Me, too; me, too. Remembered some. Forgot some. Like I was saying, if only I'd followed that saying and stopped doing what the world wanted me to do. I didn't think things through. I went along." He stood and looked down at her, his eyes sad. "Don't make mistakes, Dr. Cheryl. Find those right things and do them."

"I'll try." It seemed like such a feeble thing to say.

"Try hard." He turned toward the door, then back. "You got a cigarette?"

She was relieved the conversation had passed from the profound into the mundane. "No, and as your doctor, I have to warn you that cigarettes are bad for your health. They can kill you."

His smile was full of irony. "That's what I'm hoping for."

Jake answered the door to his house. "Forget your pencil?"

She thought of forgetting the whole thing.

He waited. "Yes?"

Cheryl took a huge breath, hoping the words would spill out in one cascade so he wouldn't be able to interrupt. "Things got off wrong, Jake. I don't want sex—what I mean is, I don't want a relationship based on sex. I want to play the dating game; go to movies, go out to eat, sit and talk, get to know each other."

His smile was wicked. "The dating game can include sex."

"It can. Maybe it will. But not right away. Not first." She tried to take another breath, but her lungs were deflated balloons. "I want us to be a real couple. I want a commitment. If you can't handle that then—"

"Okay."

She blinked. "Okay?"

"If you don't mind being my rebound girl. I just decided to break up with Andrea."

"I'll be your foul-shot-hook-shot-hard-court-press girl." She looked up at him, feeling a foreign uncertainty in her embarrassment. Where was the power in this? This groveling, this pleading.

"You got it."

"I do?"

"Sure. You are now my steady." He reached for her hand. I've never met anyone quite like you, Cheryl. Brains and a body. I think we might have a lot to offer each other."

"Really?"

He laughed. "Take off the pathetic puppy look. I like my woman to have confidence."

His woman?

The phone rang. Phoebe fumbled for it. The clock read 5:00 A.M.

"Honey, it's Mom. Grandma fell."

Phoebe sat up. "Is she okay?"

"Nothing broken, and she's home now. But Grandma *has* to move into the home. Soon. We have to find a way. But the money. . .it's so much."

"Don't worry, Mom. I'll think of something." She hung up. Sleep was impossible. With one phone call, her whole life had changed. Time was up.

Phoebe was deep into the third page of a letter when Colin sauntered in, reading a stack of papers. He did not look up.

" 'Morning, Colin."

"Hmm."

That was it? Phoebe got more than that from the boy in the mailroom.

For the next few hours, she watched him through the glass wall of his office. He was all business. He never looked in her direction, and he took her intercom pages with a formal air. A regular stuffed shirt. . .who happened to be part of the solution to her problems. She had to make amends. Keep her job. It was her turn to say sorry. Her future depended on it.

She couldn't wait any longer. She grabbed some papers and went into his office. He looked up. "Yes?"

"I want to thank you for the wonderful dinner last night."

He raised an eyebrow, then looked down.

"But later. . .I hope I didn't offend—"

His eyes flashed. "Offend me by leading me on and then shoving me away? Oh, no, I live for such moments."

She couldn't think of anything to say. Why did he always make her feel so small?

He flipped a hand. "Go on. If you're waiting for another apology you're going to get very old. Forgive me if I was attracted to you. I thought you were attracted to me."

"I was. I am." She shuffled the papers as if they were the focus of their discussion. "But. . .but you're my boss."

He swiveled his chair to face her. "A boss who needs you."

Her mind waved warning flags.

"I need a stone, Phoebe. A stepping-stone."

Any hint of romance died. "That's what I am: a stepping-stone to your success?"

"Yes, Phoebe. You are my stone, and I am yours."

She walked out of his office. There had to be another way.

Phoebe smelled Linda Friberg's *Jungle Gardenia* perfume. She didn't even have to look up from her typing. She'd felt Linda's eyes all morning. Her friend didn't miss much. "Quit staring at me, Linda."

"Fine. Then break for lunch. Now. Me and you. Out."

"I brought a sand—"

"I know you brought a sandwich. You always bring a

sandwich. You'll have it for dinner. Right now you're going to go out to lunch with me."

"I can't afford it."

"Your baloney's gone to your brain, Phoebe. One lunch will not break your budget. The kids in Biafra eat better than you. Besides, you need it."

"I do?"

Linda glanced toward Colin's office. "You need a boss break. Grab your purse."

It was amazing how good a simple burger tasted when one never ate burgers.

"You're supposed to chew the meat, not inhale it."

Phoebe licked some ketchup off her finger. "This was a very good idea."

Linda sipped her iced tea. "Of course it was. I am all-wise, all-knowing. Plus I feel very ignored. We've barely talked since your new boss-man showed up."

"I could use all-wise, all-knowing right now."

"I knew that."

Phoebe laughed. Although she was friendly with the other secretaries, her relationship with Linda went a step further. They could *talk*. "What do you think of Colin?"

"Beyond the obvious?"

"What's obvious?"

Linda considered this a moment. "He's handsome and has an ego the size of China. He does not walk anywhere, he struts. He thinks he's hot stuff—and unfortunately, he is." She looked to the ceiling. "He doesn't like to work but he wants to take over the company. And he is prepared—and planning—to do whatever it takes to get what he wants."

"You can tell all that by watching him?"

She shrugged. "He's your basic career climber. It's nothing complicated. We've both seen it before."

"I think Colin's perfected the process."

"Ambition fuels the world, my dear. The difference between the haves and have-nots is directly related to the degree of ambition firing up their innards."

"But he's so. . ." She tried to think of a subtle word for Colin's ways.

"Cunning? Blatant? Devious?"

So forget subtle.

"There are different roads to the same destination," Linda said. "Colin's road happens to be a little curvy. . . ."

"He makes mistakes, Linda. And his feet are on his desk more than under it."

"I know. And here's the secretary's catch-22: Her job is to help her boss. Catch what he misses. Make him look good. But if he's repeatedly not doing the work properly in the first place, then. . ."

"Then what?"

"Then you'd be a fool to take on that kind of responsibility."

Phoebe dragged a French fry through her ketchup. "What if I don't have a choice?"

"The plot thickens."

Phoebe told Linda about Grandma's situation.

"There are other jobs out there, Phoebe. And other men. Men with money, potential, and integrity."

"But I need a quick solution."

"No such thing in this life."

Phoebe shoved her plate aside. "It's hopeless."

"I didn't say that."

"But—"

"Do what you have to do, Phoebe. But remember you're the one who's going to have to live with it." Linda lifted her glass to get a tea refill. "In the meantime, help Colin when you can, tell him to buzz off when you have to, and pray for a miracle. By the way, are you going to the office Christmas party Saturday night?"

Christmas. Love, joy, laughter. And hope. Phoebe needed them all.

CHAPTER 10

Watch and pray so that you will not fall into temptation.
The spirit is willing, but the body is weak.

MATTHEW 26:41

Cheryl sat between Jake and Tommy in biology class. Tommy—who didn't know that she and Jake were now an item—pulled her attention to the right, and Jake—who didn't know Tommy had declared his love—pulled her to the left. She felt like a rubber band.

Tommy leaned over her desk and spoke to Jake. "Sorry I couldn't make it yesterday to tutor you. How'd it go with Cheryl?"

Jake grinned. "We only touched the surface." He gave Cheryl a wink which she tried to deflect by looking at her biology notes.

During class Mr. Rodgerson got after Jake. "Where is your pencil, Mr. Carlisle? It is difficult to take notes without one."

Jake turned to Cheryl. "Do you have a pencil?" He started to cackle.

Tommy looked confused.

After class Tommy took Cheryl's books and said, "I had a nice time at your house yesterday."

Now it was Jake's turn to look interested.

Two of them! Although Cheryl always had more than one boy on her reel, never had she had one who loved her and one whom she wanted to love. She grabbed her books out of Tommy's arms and elbowed her way down the hall to the restroom. She hid in a stall until the bell rang. When all was quiet, she went out in the corridor. Jake was waiting.

"You're late."

Cheryl started walking toward P.E. Mrs. Baumgart would give her a demerit for being tardy. She'd take twenty demerits to be able to go home.

Jake walked beside her. "Two guys at one time, Cheryl. I'm impressed."

"Three's my record."

"You don't seem Tommy's type."

"I'm not." She took his hand and pulled him around the corner into a deserted doorway. She kissed his cheek. "I'm your type, Jake."

"Really."

"Really."

He shook his head. "You're going to drive me crazy, aren't you?"

"I'll do my best."

He grinned. "Tonight. Seven o'clock. I'll pick you up."

"Our first official date?"

"The beginning of a beautiful relationship."

"Where are you taking me?"

"It's a surprise."

"I love surprises."

"Then you'll love tonight." He sent her on her way with a smack to her behind.

Things were going well.

Weren't they?

Being nervous was not a familiar feeling for Cheryl. But when Jake drove them out of town, the nerves spilled out. "Where are you taking us?"

"To our destiny."

Her laugh was shaky. "What street is that on?"

"Pencil-vania." He laughed at his joke, moving his right arm around her shoulders, giving them a squeeze.

"I'm never going to live that down, am I?"

"It might be a question of living *up* to it."

Cheryl took a deep breath, trying to find her old verve. She noticed the lights of the city fading behind them. Pavement turned to gravel, gravel to dirt. "Jake. . ."

"Almost there, pretty lady."

"Where?"

He turned into a driveway—a long, abandoned driveway. The car jostled right and then left as the tires played teeter-totter in the rutted dirt. The winter remnants of two-foot weeds bent beneath the front bumper of the car. The headlights finally came to rest on a farmhouse, or what had been a farmhouse when her great-grandparents were alive.

Jake stopped the car. "What do you think?" There was pride in his voice.

"I think you need glasses."

"It's mine. As much as it belongs to anybody. I found it." He opened his door and held out his hand. Cheryl scooted across the seat and got out.

"We're not going inside, are we?"

"Of course."

He grabbed a flashlight and blanket from the back seat. They stepped over melting piles of snow. Jake opened the front door and led the way in. A stairway rose to a dark oblivion. Blackened carpet was centered in each rise, with leaves and generations of dust covering hints of rose bouquets. Three layers of wallpaper vied for attention in the hall.

The dining room was to the right, a cockeyed, bulbless chandelier identifying the space reserved for the table. Jake pulled her to the left, to the parlor. His flashlight revealed gray upon gray as if, through the years, the house had suffered the same fate as a human's head of hair.

Cheryl marveled how it could be colder inside than out. "Do you take all your first dates here?"

"Nope." Jake spread the blanket on the floor in front of a stone fireplace. He tossed a beer can to the side. "You're the first one to see it."

For a brief moment Cheryl felt honored—until she realized he probably thought his in-crowd girlfriends like Andrea were too good for the dust and dankness.

He sat down and patted the space beside him. "Have a

seat. I have a proposition for you."

"Jake. . ."

"A business proposition."

She knelt beside him, stuffing her hands in the pockets of her pea-coat. "Actually, I'm disappointed. I thought you brought me here to ravish me."

He leaned over and snuggled under her hair, kissing her neck. "I did."

Cheryl shrugged his hand away and chastised herself for saying such a thing. Old habits died hard. "I'm just kidding. Commitment, Jake. Remember?"

He rolled his eyes.

Cheryl raised the collar of her coat. "So what's your proposition?"

He stood, letting the flashlight bob and dance as he paced. "You and I had a strange beginning yesterday."

Cheryl snickered. "True. I don't usually say hello by rolling around on the floor."

"That's not what I hear."

"Hey!"

"My humblest apologies for compromising your character." He executed the bow of a cavalier.

"Apology noted. Get to the point."

He came back to the blanket and dropped to his knees. "You excite me, Cheryl, and I don't just mean physically. Like I said yesterday, we've got something between us. Maybe opposites attract. Salt and pepper, fire and water."

"Bert and Ernie."

"I'm serious. Don't you feel it?"

Cheryl nodded. Her desire to be a part of his life was

disconcerting. She had thought they were so different, yet they seemed to be on the—

"We're on the same wavelength." He picked up a withered leaf and spun it between his fingers. "But it's odd that I don't know anything about you except what I've heard and seen at school."

"Which is?" Cheryl braced herself for the worst.

"You're smart. And you told me you want to be a doctor."

"I will be a doctor."

"Exactly. Both of us know what we want, and we're used to getting it—one way or the other."

"And what do you want?"

He sighed. His eyes lost their sarcastic twinkle. He looked at her straight on. "I want to try everything once. I want to make use of every single day and never be stuck in a job I don't like or a marriage that's bad or be afraid to start over when one part of my life is through." He left his knees and sat beside her. "But in order to do that, I have to make some money. I need to get a basketball scholarship to college, so I can get a decent job. And I need to pass history to keep playing basketball."

"I'll keep tutoring you. No problem."

He leaned back on his elbows. "Right. I learned so much from yesterday's session."

"You *could* learn."

"I have an easier way."

"Uh-oh."

He aimed the light at the water-spotted ceiling. "I want you to get me the history test ahead of time."

In all the directions her mind had been heading, this wasn't one of them. "Me? How?"

"Tommy."

"Tommy won't give it to you."

"He'll give it to you. If you. . .drop your pencil for him."

Cheryl hopped off the blanket as if it were a lake of fire. "You want me to prostitute myself so you can pass a test?"

"We'll trade."

"What do you have to trade?"

He smiled. "I have Andrea."

She brushed off her rear end. "I certainly don't want Andrea in my life."

"Exactly. She's not a part of your life, except to be an icon of who you aren't and what you don't have."

"I like who I am, and I don't want what she has."

"Is that why you dressed in your Andrea costume to tutor me?"

Cheryl felt herself blush. "Temporary insanity. I'm over it."

"But wouldn't you like to see her broken?"

This was going too far. Was this what guys were like when you really got to know them and became a couple? Intent on finding ways to use each other? "Take me home, Jake."

He pulled at her hand. "You didn't steal Susan Burger's earrings."

It took Cheryl a moment to change gears. "No, I didn't. What does that have—?"

"Andrea's a klepto. She took them."

Cheryl sank to her knees. "Andrea? But she accused me! She got *me* in trouble. The whole school thought I stole them."

He shrugged. "You should see her closet. She's got a box full of jewelry she can't wear because someone would recognize it."

"Why haven't you turned her in?"

"We all have our vices."

"Stealing isn't a vice; it's a crime."

"Then help me punish the criminal."

"I thought you liked her."

He shrugged. "I do. I did. But she's a prima donna. It wouldn't hurt to have her brought down a peg. Besides, wouldn't it prove my commitment to you?"

Cheryl tried to follow his reasoning.

He took her hand and kissed it. "I am yours, and you are mine, Cheryl. This will prove it."

The new information about Andrea fueled her. It was one thing for Andrea to accuse her, but even worse for Andrea to be the thief herself. And a box full of jewelry? The girl needed to be stopped.

She looked at Jake. He looked so sincere. Maybe this *was* what relationships were about: helping each other. She'd help Jake stay eligible for a scholarship, and he would avenge her name. "I may agree. . .on three conditions," she said.

"Only three?" He let go of her hand.

"Number one, Andrea gets hers first. Once my name is cleared, then, and only then, will I get you the test. And you'll still have to study, Jake. You'll have the questions, but you'll still have to find the answers."

"With your help, right?"

"I suppose."

"I need it by next week."

"Then you'll have to work fast."

"Two?"

"Andrea is humiliated in front of an audience. As many

people from school as possible." She would do this for Andrea's other victims, and for Julie and Pam and all the other unpopular kids.

"A woman scorned, huh?"

"You bet."

"I'll keep that in mind. What's number three?"

"You let me handle Tommy—in my own way."

"You are in total control."

She liked the sound of that.

Just back from lunch, Phoebe saw Matt Rogers poke his head in Colin's door. "Hey, Colin. Got a minute?"

Phoebe had known Matt for four years. He was a good associate. Hardworking, kind. . .everything Colin was not.

She tried not to eavesdrop when Matt's voice rose with enthusiasm while he told Colin about an idea concerning a very important merger of the Delbert companies. Matt wanted to incorporate Delbert's merger with Econo Brothers into their current advertising campaign. His ideas were fascinating and very innovative. He was nearly oozing with excitement. From what Phoebe could hear, he had a right to be.

After Matt left, Colin closed his door. He leaned back in his chair, his head against his hand, his brow drawn in deep thought. A half hour later, she saw him on the phone. After hanging up, he immediately put on his suit coat and straightened his tie.

"I'll be back in an hour or so, Phoebe. I'm in the building but take messages." He took two steps and turned back to her, touching his diamond tack with a finger. "Luck."

Something was up.

An hour later, he returned—a triumphant soldier. He slapped his hands on her desk. "I did it, Phoebe-girl. I did it!" He swaggered into his office and closed the door with flourish. Off came the suit coat, up went the feet, and so began a series of continuous phone calls.

A few minutes later, Phoebe received a phone call of her own from Matt Rogers' secretary. "Phoebe, it's Cindy Lewis." Her voice was intense, her words racing over the line. "Mr. Rogers is on his way over to have it out with Mr. Thurgood. He's hot, real hot. I don't know what's going on, but I wanted to warn you."

Before Phoebe's ear had cooled, Matt Rogers came tearing down the corridor, his face red, his mouth set. He bypassed Phoebe's desk and burst into Colin's office. The door cannoned off the wall. "You creep! You stealing creep!"

Colin's feet fell off the desk as he pushed his chair away from Matt. "Hold up, Matt. What's going on?" He glanced at Phoebe. She couldn't tell whether he wanted to be saved or simply didn't want her to witness what was going on.

"You stole my idea on the Delbert merger! You brought it to Mr. Hopner and passed it off as your own. You conceited, thieving—"

Her heart dropped. It couldn't be true.

"Prove it."

Matt pointed a finger. "You know I can't prove it—the idea was in my head. You befriend me, get me to trust you. . . You were the only one I'd talked to. You were the only one who knew."

Not quite the only one.

Matt was at the door. "You'd better watch your back, Colin Thurgood. I'll be behind you from now on." He stormed away.

Phoebe looked around the office. All eyes were on Colin. She couldn't be sure what they'd heard. She hoped the details of his transgressions were still between the three of them.

She looked down at her hands. They were shaking. She forced them to behave by sitting on them, leaning toward her typewriter, pretending to proofread the letter she had just typed. The words swam in front of her eyes.

She glanced up and saw that Colin had turned his chair toward the window, the back of his head motionless. She could only imagine what he was thinking. Maybe she didn't want to know. Just a few moments before, when she had expected him to be repentant, he had spit acid.

The telephone rang. Phoebe said Colin was out. Hanging up, she caught Linda's eye. Her shoulders lifted expectantly. *What was going on?* Phoebe answered with a shrug of her own before she turned to the impartiality of the typewriter.

But she couldn't type. She looked into Colin's office again and found him still facing the window, but now his arms were clasped nonchalantly behind his head. Her heart raced. How dare he act as though nothing had happened? As if the biggest event of the day was the fog rolling by outside his window? How dare he put her in such a position of knowing the truth?

She had a big decision to make.

Leon pounded a fencepost into the ground. It would have been easier to start over than work with the dilapidated pickets that edged the church. The only good thing to come out of doing the labor was that it gave him time to think about the big score. Every scam was different. The trick was to figure how much money was available and then match it to some logical repair. It didn't matter if the repair was needed. Leon would *make* it needed.

Thunder rumbled behind him. Leon turned to look at the clouds. A fall storm loomed close. It didn't matter. He'd be done with the fence soon, and he was sure he could find something interesting to do under cover. Maybe Sarah's house needed some fixing. . .

His eyes passed over the roofline of the church. Then it hit him. Roof. Storm. Rain.

He laughed. It was perfect. Roosevelt had three hundred dollars. Plenty of money to fix a leaky roof.

He gathered his tools and hurried to the church. He'd seen a ladder out back. He had to work quickly. Roosevelt and Sarah had gone off on errands. They'd be back soon. The storm would be upon them shortly.

He carried the ladder to the sanctuary end and leaned it against the side. He slid the handle of the hammer between his belt and pants. He climbed the ladder. He pulled out the hammer, ready to cause some damage. One leaky roof coming up.

He stopped. What was he doing? He liked Sarah and Roosevelt. They were keeping him plenty busy with real work—even though the money they paid him was pitiful.

And if he stuck around here, his expenses wouldn't be much. Maybe it was time to settle down. There was no real reason he had to scam them.

He looked over the churchyard to Sarah's house. It was nothing much. Pitiful, actually. Did he want to live in such a house? Was this place, this town, the extent of his dreams for the future?

I am what I am. So be it.

Without thinking about it further, he shook his head, peeled the shingles back, and used the hammer's claw to tear holes in the tarpaper. One hole, two, three—

Leon felt the first raindrops moments before he got inside. Alone in the church, he knew he should be happy. The holes were made, the ladder was put away. Things were progressing nicely. The con was set in place.

He heard the crackle of tires on gravel. Sarah and Roosevelt were driving into the parking lot. He shoved all doubts away and rushed to the sanctuary, wanting to draw them into the area that would leak. *Lift a few shingles, tear a few holes in the tarpaper. . .come on, rain!*

As if hearing his wish, the rain poured. Lightning flashed. He felt the thunder through the floor. He glanced to the ceiling. Was that a dark spot over the third pew, or was it his imagination?

He needed to be doing something. He spotted a few popped nails in the floorboards. He took the hammer and got on his knees. He waited until he heard the back door open. Then he pounded.

They took the bait, appearing at the door from the fellowship hall.

He looked up from his work. "You two get wet?"

Sarah ran a hand over her hair. "We nearly made it."

Roosevelt moved to Leon's side. "What you doing?"

Leon moved from his knees to his behind and leaned against the end of a pew. "Saw the storm coming. Had to leave the fence—though I'm nearly done with it. Thought I'd come in here and see what needed fixing. Just pounding a few popped nails."

Roosevelt scratched his chin. "That's mighty nice of you, Leon. I never even noticed—"

Ploop. Ploop.

They turned toward the sound. Water dripped from the ceiling onto a pew.

Thank You, Jesus!

Sarah ran toward the dripping as if her presence could make it stop. "Oh no! Not the roof!"

Roosevelt headed for the back. "I'll get a bucket."

The drip turned into a stream. Another drip started a few feet away. "Get two! Get towels! Oh, Lord, no!"

Oh, Lord, yes.

CHAPTER 11

Do not conform any longer to the pattern of this world,
but be transformed by the renewing of your mind.
Then you will be able to test and approve what God's will is—
his good, pleasing and perfect will.

ROMANS 12:2

Cheryl's mother called up the stairs. "Cheryl? Julie called. And Pam. And Tommy. Twice each. They want you to call them back."

Cheryl raced downstairs, brushing past her mother. She put an arm in the sleeve of her coat, wishing it were a suit of armor, a shield against guilt.

For Cheryl was guilty. She'd avoided her friends all day, afraid they would find out about her deal with Jake; afraid they would talk her out of it.

She liked how she felt when she was around him. All-powerful. Together, they ruled the world, running with passionate frenzy toward their wants and desires. All others were mere pawns. But away from him. . .doubt surrounded her, seeping between the cracks.

"Aren't you going to call them?" her mother asked.

Cheryl buttoned her armor, sealing the cracks. "Not now. Jake asked me to come early to help. I'll see everyone at the party."

Her mother adjusted the wool collar of Cheryl's coat, flipping her hair free of its grip. "You shouldn't ignore them, Cheryl. They're your best friends." She found a stray string and plucked it away. "Besides, Jake's not being very polite expecting you to come help with his last-minute party. That simply isn't done. And in the middle of the week yet."

"Semester break starts tomorrow, Mom. It's fine."

Her mother shrugged. "I do wish you'd have let me make more than my velvet cola cake. Mary Alice Giles told me the most scrumptious recipe for spicy pecan sponge cake. It gets its spice from cloves and cinnamon and uses only a half-cup of. . ."

Cheryl exchanged a kiss for her mother's silence and went out the door. A soldier did not think about food before going into battle. Tonight was the night.

Cheryl was shocked to see Julie's baby blue Volkswagen in front of Jake's house. The party wasn't due to start for a half hour. As soon as Cheryl pulled up, her friends emerged.

She tried to act nonchalant. "Hi, you two."

Pam grabbed the cake, pulled her to the car, and pushed her inside. Cheryl squeezed into the tiny backseat.

"If you guys want the cake so badly, you can—"

Her friends filled the front seats, turning around to face her. They had nasty lines between their eyes. "Why are you avoiding us?"

"I refuse to answer on the grounds it might incriminate me."

"Not acceptable."

She tried to look past them out the window. "Sorry."

Julie fiddled with the happy-face key chain that dangled from the ignition. She looked serious. "We're worried about you."

Pam took over. "Tommy's worried, too. Everything's suddenly different. You don't eat with us at lunch, you don't return our calls, and. . .and we're invited to this party. We've never been invited to be with this crowd before. And it's so sudden. Why?"

Cheryl felt a pang of doubt. Why was she doing all this? It was like she had started rolling down a hill, gaining speed, and now she couldn't stop.

"Cheryl? Why so sudden?"

Because Jake needs to get the test, and I said I wouldn't get the test until Andrea had been humiliated. . . "I thought you'd be thrilled."

"Ah, pity the lowly masses!" Pam made a channel in the frosting and licked her finger.

Julie nodded. "Every time we see you, you're nose to nose with Jake, laughing and snickering like two witches over a cauldron."

"Two evil witches."

"Thanks, guys. I appreciate the analogy."

"So? Prove us wrong."

Cheryl considered telling them about the deal, but Julie's worried eyes and Pam's firm jaw told her they'd try to talk her out of it. "Jake wanted me to help with the party. That's all."

Julie bit her lip. "You're not really dating, are you? You never went through with your commitment idea, did you? Because you've never said a thing to us and—"

"No, no, nothing like that. We've just become good friends." Another lie came to her with amazing ease. "The party's a surprise for Andrea."

"A surprise party?"

"Sort of. She knows about the party, but. . .later on she's due to be surprised." Lame, real lame.

"Cheryl. . ." Pam knew her too well.

She wanted out. She pushed Pam's seat forward an inch. "Don't worry about it. I've got everything under control."

Or so she hoped.

Jake's mother opened the door. She was wearing black velveteen hot pants and a white silky blouse unbuttoned one button more than even Cheryl would dare.

"Well, if it isn't Guinevere."

"Hello, Mrs. Carlisle."

"Can the *Missus,* dearie. I stopped being a Missus eons ago. Call me Mitzi. Are these your ladies in waiting?"

"These are my friends, Pam and Julie."

"Charmed." She moved aside and let them pass. "Jake's in the kitchen concocting punch. I expect it's close to ninety-proof by now."

They moved through the living room. Julie leaned close and whispered, "She's a mother?"

"Every other Wednesday."

Jake was pouring a bottle of vodka into a large bowl of purple liquid. "Hey, girl," he said, seeing Cheryl. "All set?" When Julie and Pam appeared behind her, his hand jerked and he poured some vodka on the counter.

Julie handed him a towel. "Hi, Jake."

"Julie."

She blushed.

"Come on, girls," Mitzi said, "make yourselves useful. Bring those bowls of chips into the dining room. And, Jake, if you or any of your little friends spill that purple punch on my carpet, I'll personally punch them where it hurts the most. *Comprenez vous*, darling?"

"Yeah, yeah." Jake carried the punch bowl into the dining room.

Mitzi followed. "As you see, I got out my best crystal for your friends, Jakey." She ripped open a package of Styrofoam cups and placed a stack next to the punch bowl. The doorbell rang. "The fun begins." She kissed her finger and pressed it to Jake's mouth. "I'll get the door, love, but then I'm out of here. Remember, if the police get called it's your behind. *Ciao."* She left.

"Your mother is. . ." Pam couldn't find the word.

"Cool. Yeah, I know."

That wasn't the word.

Jake turned to Cheryl. "You got the bracelet?"

Cheryl held up her arm, revealing a charm bracelet with a dozen jangling baubles. "I'm surprised you didn't hear it."

"Just make sure you-know-who hears it—and sees it." He went back to the kitchen.

"What was all that about?" Pam asked.

Cheryl heard new voices. She escaped to the living room. "It's a surprise."

Tommy showed up ten minutes later. He made a beeline to Cheryl's side. Cheryl wanted to brush him away but remembered that her part of the bargain with Jake would have to be consummated in the next few days. She needed Tommy. . .pliable. She took his elbow and led him to the dining room. "Have some cake—you'll love my mother's cooking." Cheryl took up a slice of chocolate goo. Cheryl noticed Jake in the doorway, motioning her over. She made an excuse and left Tommy to his eating.

"Andrea's here. Just here. Go do your stuff."

Cheryl looked past him, hunting for her prey. She found her, coming down the hallway from the den where the coats were piled. Andrea stopped and chatted with a group on her right, then floated to a group on her left. Giggling. Touching. Showing off. She was disgustingly perfect. Her straight hair flowed over her shoulders in one sleek line, making her look like Olivia Hussey from the movie *Romeo and Juliet.* Her skin was zitless and her hip-huggers balanced primly on two hip bones separated by the flattest stomach west of Omaha. She was just asking to be humanized.

Cheryl began her approach, physically pulling Pam out

of a conversation nearby.

"What—?"

"Come with me. Just play along." Cheryl kept hold of Pam's arm, not wanting her to escape. She stopped in Andrea's path and began to talk. Loudly.

"See my new charm bracelet? My stepfather was in New York last week where he saw this in a specialty shop." Cheryl looked toward Andrea to see if she was listening. Her head was tilted, just a bit. "The owner told Ralph this bracelet belonged to Carole King." Pam looked at Cheryl like she was crazy. Pam had given Cheryl the bracelet for her birthday the previous year. "See, this record charm represents her *Tapestry* album. The rest of the charms she collected growing up. Isn't it cool?"

Two seconds. Three. Andrea came over. "I couldn't help but hear about your bracelet. Can I see it?"

Cheryl held out her wrist and gave it a tempting jingle. Cheryl felt a hand on her shoulder. It was Julie. "But, Cheryl, didn't you get—?"

". . .this from my stepdad last week? Yeah, this is the one. It was Carole King's. Isn't it neat?"

Julie swallowed and retreated a step. Pam went with her. Their heads nearly touched as they walked away.

Fine. Be that way. Cheryl didn't need them anymore. She smiled her friendliest smile at Andrea. *All's fair in love and war, and this is both.* "Want to try it on?" Cheryl fiddled with the clasp.

"Well, yeah. . .sure."

Cheryl hooked it on her wrist. Andrea moved it back and forth, enjoying its music.

"I don't think it's worth a lot, but it *is* special because it was hers. Be careful, the clasp needs work. I almost lost it once already."

Andrea wasn't listening as she rolled her arm. "Carole King. Wow."

Cheryl gave her a few more seconds to fall in love. "I'd better take it back. My stepdad would kill me if I lost it. In fact, it was dumb to wear it with that faulty clasp. I'll just put it in the pocket of my coat." Cheryl headed toward the den. She could feel Andrea's eyes.

When Cheryl came out—after making sure her coat was on top of the pile—Andrea was gone. Cheryl found Jake by the kitchen. "Where is she?"

He pointed down the hall. "After you left to put it in your coat, she went into the bathroom. She's still in there."

Cheryl gripped his arm. "She's really going to do it."

"Told you. She can't resist jewelry. Even if she can't wear it in public."

"But it will be obvious who took it."

Jake shook his head. "Not really. She played this game with you once before, and you didn't catch on, remember? She hardly looks the thief type. She depends on that."

Cheryl slid her hand across his back. "Jake, this is going to be so. . ." The proper word escaped her.

He leaned toward her ear. "Cool. I know. We'll celebrate later."

Cheryl heard the bathroom door open. She saw Andrea come out. She saw her slip into the room with the coats. . .

She's actually going to do it. A part of Cheryl had hoped that Andrea wouldn't take the bracelet, that they wouldn't have to humiliate her. That Cheryl's deal with Jake could be voided. This commitment thing wasn't what she'd hoped it would be. Too much stress and sneaking around.

Tommy showed up by Cheryl's side. "What's going on? You keep looking at Andrea and Jake.

"Sorry. I don't mean to."

"I was wondering if we could go out tomorrow night. There's a good movie come to town, *Cabaret*—"

Jake gave her the nod from across the room. It was time. Cheryl turned to Tommy. "I want to go home now. Would you drive me?"

His face crinkled in confusion. "But we just got here. And don't you have your car?"

Cheryl took his arm and pushed against him. "I do, but I'd rather you take me." She smiled a Scarlett O'Hara smile.

"Well, I suppose. I'll get our coats."

"No! I'll get them." Cheryl went into the den, feeling her pulse in her throat. Her coat was still on top of the heap, but it was turned over. Cheryl felt the pocket. The bracelet was gone. She felt sick.

"Cheryl?" Tommy stood in the doorway. "I didn't know if you'd remember which coat was mine." Cheryl left her doubt behind and remembered her part. She made her face fall in what she hoped looked like shock. "It's gone!"

"What's gone?"

"My bracelet. I put it in my pocket a few minutes ago, and now it's gone. Stolen!"

Tommy dug through the pile of coats. "It can't be. No one would do that. It must have fallen out."

"It didn't. I know it. I put it deep in the pocket."

Jake's figure filled the door. "Hurry up, Cheryl. She's leaving."

Cheryl ran from the room, her coat clutched to her chest. Her words started before she reached the living room, rising above the music and the chatter. "Someone stole my bracelet!" The talking stopped. All eyes were on her. Jake turned off the music. The silence accentuated the crime.

"My charm bracelet is gone. It was in my coat pocket."

Julie came to comfort her. She took Cheryl's coat and checked the pockets for herself. "Maybe it fell out."

Cheryl shook her head, glancing toward the door. Jake leaned against it. Andrea slipped into the dining room. Cheryl thought of the kitchen door and signaled to Jake.

Jake pulled Tommy to his place by the door. "Nobody out." He moved toward the kitchen.

Cheryl returned to her recitation, wishing she could rewind the past few minutes, take the words back, get back in the car with Julie and Pam and drive away. But it was too late. She buried her face in Julie's shoulder. "That bracelet was very important to me. My stepfather bought it for me in New York. It belonged to Carole King."

That statement brought a wave of impressed "ohs" from the crowd.

She stood erect with a sniff. "I had just let Andrea try it on. It had a faulty clasp, so I decided not to risk losing it. I put it in my coat pocket, thinking it was safe."

Cheryl waited for someone to make the connection between Andrea and the bracelet. Nothing. *Come on, people.* Cheryl finished the scene, putting a hand to her mouth in a show of sudden enlightenment. "Andrea!"

The crowd murmured, passing the foreign idea around the room.

"Where is she?" Cheryl looked over the crowd, hunting for the villain.

There was a scuffling sound in the kitchen. Suddenly Jake appeared with Andrea in tow. "Here she is!"

The crowd parted, making a path for the accused. Andrea staggered as she was propelled forward by Jake's powerful grip. He wheeled her to a halt. "Show them."

Andrea looked straight ahead, her eyes at waist level as if studying everyone's belt buckle. She shook her head.

"Show her or I will."

Black tears stained Andrea's cheeks. She didn't move.

Jake yanked her purse off her shoulder and tossed it toward Cheryl. "Look inside."

Cheryl bit her lip and opened the purse. She tried to make her hand shake as she pulled out the bracelet. She opened her mouth in a show of disbelief.

Jake prodded Andrea's back. She seemed to awaken from a daze. She clasped her hands to her throat. "Admit it!"

Andrea looked up for the first time, finding Cheryl's eyes. "I'm sorry."

Her eternal springtime was trampled. It was repulsive. Cheryl wished she would turn away. She didn't want Andrea's desperate eyes locked on hers. She didn't want to see the perky fingers turned white as they clung to each other, trying to stroke away the pain.

"Wait a minute, Andrea," Jake said. "Didn't you tell me once that you'd taken things before? That's right. I'd forgotten all about that. Something about a box in your closet?"

"Enough," Cheryl said.

Jake blinked. "Oh, wait! And wasn't there something about Susan Burger's earrings? Now I re—"

"Enough, Jake!" Cheryl tossed the purse at Andrea. "Get out of here, Andrea. Go home."

Andrea's eyes showed her amazement. *What was she expecting? A firing squad?*

"And here," Cheryl said. She tossed her the bracelet, its charms clattering through the air. "It's yours."

Phoebe went into work early, even getting there before Mr. Hopner's secretary. But Mr. Hopner was already there, hard at work.

She knocked on the doorjamb. He looked up. "Good morning, Miss. . ."

"Winston."

"Miss Winston. You're in early."

"Yes, well. . ." She took a step closer. "May I talk with you a few moments, sir?"

He motioned to a chair and she sat. Her heart beat double time. "I feel very awkward coming here."

"You work on the twenty-third floor, don't you?"

"Yes, sir. I work for Colin Thurgood."

"Ah. What can I do to help, Miss Winston?"

She took a deep breath and began her story.

Mr. Hopner was very attentive.

Later that morning Matt Rogers called Phoebe into his

office. She felt odd going there, like a defector being invited to the enemy camp. He rose when she entered.

"Come in, Phoebe. Sit. Sit." He didn't return to his seat, but leaned on the ledge of his desk a few feet away. "I wanted to thank you for going to Mr. Hopner; for straightening things out."

She looked to the floor. "You're welcome."

"I'm sure it wasn't an easy decision."

She shook her head, then looked up. "What's going to happen to Colin?"

"Not enough, I'm afraid."

"He's not fired?"

Matt's laugh was full of sarcasm. "You'd think so, wouldn't you? But the guy talked them out of it. Made them focus on his potential. He got a slap on the wrist and a dock in pay."

"Amazing," Phoebe said.

"That's one word for it."

"What's going to happen to me? I can't work for him anymore. Not when he finds out what I did."

"He won't find out. Mr. Hopner assured me that your name was kept out of it. As far as Colin knows, Mr. Hopner figured things out on his own."

"But still. . ."

"Actually, I have a better idea," Matt said. "How would you like to be an associate-intern?"

Phoebe tried to take it in. "Me?"

"I'm sponsoring you. It's the least I can do to pay you back for your honesty—and guts."

"When do I start? Where do I go? What should I—?"

Matt laughed. "We're working on the details now. Just hang

tough with Colin for a few more days. We'll let you know."

Phoebe stood, grabbing his hand. "Oh, Mr. Rogers, thank you, thank you."

"You're welcome, Phoebe." He led her to the door. "But one hint. . .if I were you, I wouldn't tell Colin about your promotion just yet. He'll find out soon enough."

"Understood."

Colin returned from Mr. Hopner's office looking sullen. He didn't seem to appreciate Phoebe's good mood. "What's gotten into you?"

She tried not to smile but found it impossible. "I just had good news."

"And. . . ?"

She thought fast. "My sick mother isn't sick anymore. Isn't that wonderful?"

"Well, goodie for her."

The rain was unrelenting, falling through the night and well into the next day. And the drips—which had increased to six—didn't stop until midafternoon.

Roosevelt, Sarah, and Leon sat on the pews, looking at the ceiling, exhausted from toweling up and emptying buckets and bowls.

Sarah sighed the loudest. "What are we going to do?"

It was time. Leon stood and strolled under the leaks, peering upward, applying his most concerned look. "I know a thing or two about fixing roofs." *And damaging them.*

Roosevelt perked up. "You do?"

"I'd have to go up-top to take a look, but I could probably fix it." He looked at Roosevelt. "But roof-fixing can get kind of expensive."

"How expensive?"

Leon let his eyes stray upward again. It was best not to look them in the eye when he lied. He was good at deceiving, but it never hurt to be careful. "Oh. . .six leaks. . .that's a lot. Two hundred, two-twenty-five. Thereabouts."

"Two hundred dollars?" Sarah shook her head, back and forth, back and forth. "Might as well be two thousand."

Roosevelt shook his head. "Can't we do a quick fix? There's more pressing things need repairing. I know the furnace is on its last leg, and what with winter coming up. . ."

Leon jumped in. "I could fix the furnace, too."

"My, you *are* handy. But what would that cost?"

This was getting hairy. If he said too much, Roosevelt might decide to forget the whole thing. After all, he only had $300 in savings, and Leon had already overestimated the roof in hopes of dipping into it. "Let me take a look at the furnace, then I'll give you an amount."

Roosevelt headed for the basement. "You're a good man, Leon Burke. What would we do without you?"

Leon didn't know a thing about furnaces. But he knocked and rattled enough to make it look like he did.

"What do you think?" Roosevelt asked.

Leon rubbed his chin. "This is a little beyond me, but I have a friend in the heating business up in Nashville. I could maybe do a patch-up on the roof—to save you money—and I could stop by my friend's office while I'm getting roofing supplies and tell him what's what. Get it all set up for him to come down here."

"But what will that cost?"

Leon looked at the furnace mournfully, like it was dead. "Don't know. But I'd guess three hundred or so."

Roosevelt's face sagged. "That's all I have. Plus with the roof. . ."

Leon put a hand on his shoulder. "You know what? I'll bet I can get my friend to do it for less, especially if I show him some good faith money up front. And I'll help him—which will help bring the cost down."

"So what are we talking about? Moneywise?"

Leon scuffed the floor with his shoe. "I hate to ask you this, Roosevelt, but I think if I had the three hundred, I could get the supplies for a temporary fix of the roof *and* get my friend signed up to fix the furnace. I know that's all you've got and. . ."

"This church is all I've got." Roosevelt raised his face toward the cobwebbed ceiling and closed his eyes a moment. Then he opened them and nodded. "The Lord never gives us what we can't handle. And we can handle this. You need three hundred, you've got it."

"I'll try to do it cheap as possible. I promise." Leon put on his best con-man eyes.

"I'm sure you will, Leon. And it does need doing. We can't have our congregation sitting in puddles or shivering." They headed for the basement steps. "When can you get it done?"

Soon as I get the money. . . "It's too late today, but I could go to Nashville tomorrow. Have at least the roof part done by tomorrow night."

"In time for church on Sunday."

Sure. Why not? "In time for church.

"Let's pray it doesn't rain again," Roosevelt said.

He got that right. Leon knew that when it rained, it tended to pour.

While Sarah was gathering the wet towels to take out to the clothesline, Leon slipped into the storeroom, gathered his things, and ran them out to his truck. He had to be ready for the getaway.

Then he got the ladder and took a look-see at the roof, acting all professional like he knew what he was doing. He wrote down numbers on a piece of paper and did some scribbling. As he climbed down the ladder, Sarah appeared, a basket of wet towels in her hands. "Is it really going to cost the three hundred, Leon?"

He stepped off the last rung, then did some more scribbling. "Looks like it. Sorry, Sarah."

She nodded, then walked toward the clothesline to hang the towels.

Leon watched her go. He couldn't let himself feel guilty. No sir, a body never would make a living if he thought too much about the hows of it. He saw Sarah put the basket down. But instead of hanging a towel, she just stood there, her head bowed.

She's praying over towels? Leon was drawn toward her. He joined her at the line. "Don't be sad, Miss Sarah. These things happen." She nodded, her wistful smile making him want to forget the whole thing. He pointed to the towels.

"Need some help with these?"

"Thank you, Leon. Seems you're full of help today."

The words sounded odd, and he studied her face a moment to see if she intended to be sarcastic. But her face was purity itself. Just because he never said one thing without meaning another didn't mean others were as shifty.

They finished hoisting the last towel over the line. Water dripped from the corners onto the grass.

"There." She faced him.

"There." He faced her. Electricity passed between them, bouncing off one, only to leap back to the other.

She opened her mouth to speak. Then closed it. She looked at the grass.

"Sarah. . ." He had no idea what he wanted to say. Once again, she had him tongue-tied.

She looked up at him. "Yes?"

"I. . .I admire you greatly." His words sounded like some hoity-toity dime novel. They didn't sound real—even though he meant them.

"I admire you, too, Leon. You make me feel. . ." She looked to the sky for the word. "Special."

He extended an arm to touch her—but didn't. Somehow he couldn't. Suddenly he knew just what Roosevelt went through during those times he'd seen him almost—but never quite—touch Sarah.

She watched his hand pull away and looked regretful for it. Then she took a breath. "I'd better make us dinner. We've had a hard day."

Easy, compared to tomorrow.

CHAPTER 12

They plot injustice and say,
"We have devised a perfect plan!"
Surely the mind and heart of man are cunning.

Psalm 64:6

"His name is Leon Rodney Burke."

Mac held the phone in the crook of his neck and wrote down the name.

Bob continued. "They matched the fingerprints. He's been in and out of jail for years. A con artist. Repair scams. Repair something to get their confidence, then get a bigger job and take the money and run. Robbery, too. Couldn't keep his hands in his own pockets. A real gem. And now we have to add murder to the list."

"Poor guy," Mac said.

"I know. Winning the lottery and then being killed for it."

"Well, yeah, poor Hazen, but I was talking about the Burke guy."

"Poor Leon Burke?" Bob said.

"Yeah, him. He must have been pretty desperate to kill somebody."

"He's a criminal, Macky. He's been in jail for theft, and now he's a murderer."

"We don't know that."

"Oh yes, we do. That's the rest of my news. They found his fingerprints on a bottle in the alley next to the real Roosevelt, and some bloody prints nearby. They match the ones here, Macky. That's about as conclusive as you can get without an eyewitness."

Mac closed his eyes. "I wonder what made him cross the line."

"We may never know."

Wriggens stood in front of Mac's desk and listened but shook his head the entire time. "I don't care why he did it, I just want to know what *you're* going to do about it."

"There's not much we can do." Mac eyed his boss. "Is there?"

Wriggens ignored him. "At least this will give us a reprieve from dealing with the love life of our sex-crazed Dr. Nickolby. Your press release barely appeased the media. I just wish I'd known she was that kind of woman before we sent her back in time. I would have liked a shot at her."

Mac added this to his list of reasons-I-don't-respect-John Wriggens. "I'm sure your wife would love to hear that."

"Cut the holier-than-thou act, Mac. You're a single man."

He wondered how Wriggens could be so callous. He seemed to ignore the fact Holly had been murdered and repeatedly set it aside as being inconsequential; something comparable to losing a pet gerbil. "I happen to think that both love and marriage are essential prerequisites to sex."

"You're behind the times, Mac."

"So be it." Mac felt dirty just talking to him. "Back to the subject at hand. . . Leon Burke only has a few more days and—"

"Not good enough. We have to make sure he comes back to face charges." He jammed a finger on Mac's desk with each word: "Justice must be done."

Wriggens knew nothing about justice. If anyone should want justice for a murder, it should be Mac.

But Mac felt there was something different about Leon's case. This was a more complicated issue than Wriggens was comprehending. He took a deep breath to calm his voice. "The clincher is that Leon Burke seemed like a nice man. As you mentioned before, I was the only one who spent any time with him, who talked to him at length."

"He was acting. Conning you. Pretending to be a nice man—Roosevelt Hazen. If he was desperate enough to murder, he was desperate enough to play whatever part was necessary to get away with it."

"That's why I want to find out more about him. Find out what drove him to murder." *What drives anyone to murder? What drove Sidney Graves to murder Holly?*

"Greed."

Mac had to switch his thinking from Holly's case to Roosevelt's. "That doesn't make sense—in this case."

"Sure it does. Who can put a value on winning the Time Lottery? The chance is priceless." Wriggens continued. "But who cares about motive? The point is that he's not coming back."

"You don't know that for sure."

"But I do. If he comes back here, he faces murder charges. He knows that. He left knowing it would be for good."

Although Mac didn't want to admit it, what Wriggens said made sense. "No wonder he was nervous."

"You bet. Taking a dip into the past is one thing, but to go knowing you have no choice about coming back? I'd be nervous, too."

There was a knock, and Bob stuck his head in the door. "Macky! I've got—" He saw Wriggens. "Sorry. I didn't know you were—"

"You have news on Burke?"

Bob looked to Mac as if he wondered how he should answer. Mac waved him in. "What's your news?"

He entered, holding a file. "Leon Burke is dying."

"How do you know?"

"The police in Memphis told me it appeared Burke was homeless like Hazen. I did a little checking in the area, and I got a clinic to tell me Leon Burke is dying of lung cancer."

Wriggens plucked the file from Bob's hands and opened it while Bob continued. "That certainly explains his motive for taking Hazen's place. Imminent death will push people to do desperate things."

"He certainly had nothing to lose." Wriggens pointed to the page. "And with his criminal record. . ."

A broken record. Mac unclenched his jaw and forced himself to breathe. He held out his hand, wanting the file. "Let me—"

Wriggens ignored him. "Now this is interesting. Care to guess when he committed the first crime that earned him jail time?"

Mac sensed what the answer would be. His heart sank. "1962?"

"You got it." Wriggens waved a copy of Leon's record like bait. "Care to guess who the victim was?"

Oh, no. . . Mac sighed and said the name. "Roosevelt Hazen?"

Wriggens leered, savoring the moment. "It says here that Burke conned Roosevelt Hazen—occupation, Baptist minister—of $300 for a roof and furnace Burke never fixed." He slapped the file against his hand. "He robs Hazen in the past and murders him in the future. He needs to face as many charges as we can throw at him. "So. . .we're going to wake him up," Wriggens said. "Now. For the sake of the Lottery. We can make a big deal about parading him before the press. A killer apprehended."

"We can't," Mac said. "The serum is in his system. It wears off on its own."

"And he'll never wake up *here* on his own," Bob said. "The murder thing—and his cancer. He'll choose to stay. He's out of our reach. For good."

"This is *not* good," Wriggens said.

But they had no choice. Leon had left them to handle

his mess. Maybe he had the best idea. The past might be a very good place to hide.

Colin Thurgood tapped a pencil against his thigh, beating a frantic rhythm. He'd sold stock at a loss and cashed in a few money markets. . . . The dollar figures in front of him were a start, but hardly enough to cover his immediate needs.

He'd put the Tahoe house up for sale, but that was a long-term answer. Selling the Lexus was insignificant. If only he hadn't paid cash for both of them. But at the time he'd felt cocky about his ability to do so. And the stock tip had seemed like such a sure thing.

He looked at the numbers again. He might be able to appease the brokerage firm with this token, but he still needed a quick fix. He still needed Phoebe's insurance money. He still needed her to stay behind in her past. It was the only solution he could think of.

He had to give it another try. Before, he'd talked to some peon, Bill, Bob. . . . He'd avoided MacMillan knowing he'd get flack. But maybe if Mac knew the facts? He seemed like a reasonable man. And maybe if Colin agreed to split some of the insurance money with him. . . .

It was a long shot he would have to take. In person. He called the airlines.

Cheryl's mother put a hand to the back of her hair, checking to see if it was flipping under the way it was supposed to. For her first—and possibly last—picture in a newspaper, she didn't want her hair to appear undone. She'd practically been a celebrity at the beauty parlor that morning. Everyone had made her feel so good about being the mother of the Time Lottery winner, Cheryl Nickolby, that she'd tipped her operator an extra dollar.

The reporter and the photographer conferred in the corner of her living room. "Excuse me?" she said. They ignored her. "Yoo-hoo? Excuse me? Do I have enough lipstick on?"

"Sure, sure, lady," the reporter said. "You're gorgeous. A regular Molly Sims."

Dorothy knew they were lying. Now if they would have said Ava Gardner. . .but Ava was before their time.

She tugged her skirt an additional smidgen below her knees and ground her bottom deeper in the couch's cushions. *Come on, gentlemen, get on with it. Ted will be back from his golf game any minute, and I don't want him to—*

The men finished their discussion. It was finally happening. Her moment in the spotlight.

The photographer took the next five minutes positioning her body just so. *Chin up. . .no, no, don't smile. You need to look like you're worried about your daughter. . .yes, that's it. I like the frown lines. . . .* If this was modeling, Dorothy didn't like it much.

"That will do it." The photographer packed up his equipment.

"Now then." The reporter took a seat in the cattycorner wing chair in the condo's living room. A view of the Florida Gulf loomed before them. This place was a splurge, but as the parents of one of the Time Lottery winners, they'd decided to do their vacation up right. The reporter continued. "Let's get to the meat of this thing."

Dorothy clasped her hands in her lap. "This *thing* is my daughter's life."

"Uh, right. And I'm sure it's a terrible experience to have her away and have to deal with all of these nasty allegations."

"She is not *away*. She is roaming around in her past, facing all sorts of danger."

"Huh?" The reporter recovered. "What kind of danger?"

Dorothy put a hand to her chest. "Well, obviously I don't know exactly. But she is stuck in some time machine. That must be a terrifying experience."

The reporter opened his mouth to speak, shut it, then took a breath. "Back to the present situation. You called us with information regarding the allegations from your daughter's lovers?"

Now they were getting somewhere. Dorothy straightened her shoulders. "I just want to say that what they did was terribly rude."

"But is it the truth?"

Dorothy blinked. "Well, I'm sure I don't know. Cheryl is a grown woman. She does not confide in me regarding her love life."

The reporter closed his eyes. His head was shaking. "Then why did you call us?"

Dorothy fingered her pukka shell necklace. "Because it's. . .it's just not right. They shouldn't be able to say those things about her. If it wasn't for that nice Mr. MacMillan at the Time Lottery calling Mercy Hospital, my daughter would be out of a job."

The reporter perked up. "So the TTC intervened?"

"The TT-what?"

"The TTC, the company who created the Time Lottery."

She laughed nervously. "Oh, one of those companies with letters. . . I just hate those, especially when they don't spell anything special. Why, my fifth husband used to work for a company called JM—"

"Your *fifth* husband? How many times have you been married?"

Dorothy didn't like the glint in his eye. "My current husband is number six but—"

He was writing frantically. "Apparently commitment is an issue with both generations."

"Excuse me?"

He pointed his pen at her. "Both you and your daughter have trouble committing to one—"

"Young man, I assure you that while I was married to each of my husbands, I loved them very much. I was the essence of commitment."

Dorothy hesitated. But then the reporter smiled at her. Such a nice smile, on such a nice young man. She leaned toward him confidentially. "Well, let me tell you something. Husband number one—Cheryl's father—was a real heel. He left us when she was only six. Now if that wasn't a blow to a girl's ego, I don't know what is. . ."

It was so nice to find someone willing to listen.

CHAPTER 13

Do you want to be free from fear of
the one in authority?
Then do what is right and he will commend you.

ROMANS 13:3

The day after the party, the phone woke her. Cheryl brought the receiver into bed, sandwiching it between her ear and the pillow. "Hello?"

"Time to pay up, gorgeous."

Jake's voice brought unwanted memories. Andrea's humiliated eyes. The heads of Julie and Pam locked together in mutual disapproval. Jake's gloating grin. The awful silence.

"I'm tired. I didn't sleep much last night."

"Neither did I. I was so pumped! Finally little Miss Pris had to admit she isn't perfect. That'll teach her to tell me not. . .anyway, she deserved it. I just wish you wouldn't have stopped me. I was on a roll."

Cheryl pulled the quilt—and the guilt—over her head.

"Cheryl? Wasn't it great?"

"Sure."

A moment of silence. "You ready to do your part?"

She'd already done her part in messing up one person's life. Now there was more. Cheryl turned on her back and peeled away the quilt, forcing herself to face the morning light. "I'm ready. I guess."

"Good. When?"

Today, tomorrow, 1980? "Tomorrow."

"That long?"

She sat up so she could scream at him. "What do you want me to do? Run over to Tommy's house, throw him down on the floor, and threaten him until he promises to give me the test?"

"I don't care how you go about getting the test, but it has to be soon."

Cheryl put a hand to her chest, trying to push her heart back to its easy, morning rhythm. "I don't think I can do—"

"Mom never came home last night. I'm alone." He paused. "I want to talk."

"We are talking."

"But you're unsure. . . I want to help you make the right decision. In person."

Cheryl wasn't sure she wanted to be alone with him.

"Come over, Cheryl. We can work this out. I'll be good, I promise."

"Fine. I'll be right over."

Is this stupid?

She'd find out soon enough.

The Christmas party for Hopner, Wagner, and Greenfield was a high-class affair. It was held every year at the Greenfield mansion with plenty of champagne, eggnog, and Yuletide hors d'oeuvres. It was the one time during the year when all 224 employees of the company got together in one place, at one time, for the single purpose of having fun.

The latter was not entirely true. Although 95 percent of the employees went to the Christmas party with nothing more in mind than an evening filled with dancing, free food, and drink, 5 percent had more serious matters on their mind, such as trying to use the party to further their careers.

Colin was one of the 5 percent. He had instructed Phoebe to make him late afternoon appointments with his barber for a shave and a haircut, as well as a men's club for a massage.

While Colin had probably taken hours to primp for the party, Phoebe had managed to dress in ten minutes. In her own opinion, the effect was no less impressive. She had found the evergreen sheath dress in a secondhand store. It was simple and timeless with a boat neck and long, straight sleeves. She had hemmed it to the proper mini length and, *voilà*, she had a cocktail dress. She added a black velveteen wrap, bought for $1.95.

She immediately caught sight of Colin at the bottom of the winding stairway, laughing too hard with Mr. Wagner. The marble floor reflected hundreds of tiny lights strung among the poinsettias and pine boughs, like stars come down to earth. Phoebe handed her wrap to the butler and tried to catch her breath.

Although she'd been to three other Christmas parties at the Greenfield mansion, she was always awed by its elegance. It was a place where dreams were made, or better yet, enjoyed.

Before she hooked up with Linda, Phoebe decided to freshen up. She found the lavatory and enjoyed its opulence. She sat at the dressing table, fingering the gold boxes and crystal perfume bottles. She pulled a stopper and took a lingering whiff. Heady, sensuous, expensive. She touched it to her wrists. Life was good. In a short time, she'd be in the job of her dreams, and her need to deal with the likes of Colin Thurgood would be history. It was like waiting for a prison sentence to end.

Phoebe stood and smoothed her dress. Another coat of lipstick and she was ready. She would find Linda and enjoy herself. Tonight was for fun.

She grabbed the doorknob, ready for action. It didn't turn. She fiddled with the lock and tried again. Nothing. She pulled. She twisted. She yanked.

She was locked in.

All right. . .calm down, be logical. Try it again. Button in. Button out. There was no difference. The knob did not move.

She tapped on the door and called out discreetly, "Hello. Can anyone hear me? I'm locked in here. Can you help me?"

She put her ear to the door. The sounds of laughter and live music filtered in. Sooner or later someone would need to use the facilities. But until then. . . She sank to the carpet.

"Is somebody in there?" A man's voice.

She scrambled to her feet. "Yes, yes! The door won't

open, it won't unlock."

"I'll try it from this side. Get back."

Phoebe retreated a few steps, expecting a male body to come crashing through the door shoulder first. Instead, the door opened quietly, and two enormous blue eyes peered in at her.

"It opened just fine from out here. Are you all right?"

She tried the knob from her side. It turned easily in her hand. "It didn't turn before. Honest. It was locked."

The young man was wearing a black tuxedo. "Do you do this often?"

Phoebe retrieved her purse and what little was left of her dignity. "Only on special occasions."

"Birthdays, Christmas parties, and. . ."

"Bar mitzvahs."

"Interesting hobby. Shall we escape to the eggnog? Rescuing frightened maidens makes me thirsty."

"I wasn't frightened."

"Properly flustered then. By the way, I'm Peter, architect extraordinaire, at your service. And the lady is?"

"Phoebe Winston, idiot in training."

"You really shouldn't boast." He held out his arm. "Shall we, Miss Winston?"

She took it. "Only if you keep my secret."

"Consider it kept."

They walked down the hall and into the dining room, where the music and laughter swelled. Peter got her a glass of eggnog. Its creaminess soothed her nerves. She felt his hand at her back, leading her into the living room.

"Come with me," Peter said. "I want to show you off to

my father."

"Your father?" Phoebe saw where they were heading, but her mind wouldn't accept it. She suddenly yearned for the privacy of the bathroom.

Peter must have felt her hesitance. "Come on. He won't bite."

"Are you sure?"

Phoebe found herself face-to-face with Mr. Greenfield, the first time since the incident with the telephone bill. Peter put an arm around her waist. "Father, you know Miss Winston."

Mr. Greenfield held out a hand. "Of course, I do, Peter. She's one of our most loyal employees." He leaned forward confidentially. "And a budding intern, eh?"

Phoebe assumed she shook his hand.

"How is your mother, Miss Winston? Better, I hope?"

"Yes. Yes, sir, she's fine."

"Good, good." He looked past her; another guest beckoned. He took her hand and held it between his. "I hope you have a nice time tonight. Peter will take good care of you. Excuse me."

Peter looked concerned. "Are you all right? Your face has turned the color of the eggnog."

Phoebe gulped the rest of her drink. "I feel a little weak."

"Would you like to splash some water on your face?"

That brought her back. "No, thank you. I plan on giving up bathrooms for awhile."

"That should be interesting." He laughed and led her onto the terrace. They leaned against the railing that overlooked the formal gardens. The house was like a lantern in the night.

"Why does my father frighten you so?"

Phoebe took a deep breath, trying to capture her bearings. "He doesn't frighten me. I just feel awkward. The last time I saw him, I was being called down for some unexplained long distance phone charges. It was a difficult moment."

Peter snapped his fingers. "Phoebe Winston? I thought I'd heard your name. You work for Colin Thurgood, don't you?"

The eggnog threatened to reverse its path. "You heard about it?"

He looked at the stars, nodding. "Absolutely. Sunday night is family night. All of us come back here for dinner. Father tells us stories of his work week. You were number two on the list, I believe. Thurgood tried to blame the phone calls on you."

"You heard that?" Her legs wobbled.

"Hey, it's okay. You weren't the villain. Thurgood was." He sipped his drink. "Budding intern, eh? Tell me about it."

It was her pleasure.

Roosevelt set down his forkful of eggs and dabbed his mouth with a napkin. "You're not your usual talkative self, Leon. Something wrong?"

Leon forced a smile. "No, nothing." *Yes, everything.*

Roosevelt set his napkin on the table. He leaned to the side to get at his wallet and pulled out a wad of twenties. "Maybe this will help ease your mind about the work ahead. Here's three hundred dollars."

Sarah interrupted. "But he said two hundred."

"Leon's going to arrange to have the furnace fixed, too,

Sarah. We agreed to it."

"When—?"

Roosevelt pushed himself away from the table. "I think this situation calls for a special prayer time. Then we can let Leon get on his way. It's supposed to rain again tonight. I'd sure like to get the worst of the roof fixed before then."

"Prayer time?"

Sarah took their plates to the sink. " 'Consider it pure joy, my brothers, whenever you face trials of many kinds, because you know that the testing of your faith develops perseverance.' "

Leon wasn't sure if the words were hers or a verse, but either way, they didn't make much sense.

"Prayer helps us keep focused," Roosevelt said.

"Focused on what?"

Sarah answered for him. "On God."

The way she said it, so simply, so matter-of-factly, stunned him. Only old people getting ready to die talked as if God was sitting close. Not young people like Sarah. Vital people like Sarah and Leon—and even Roosevelt—had better things to do than spend their time praying. They had *living* to do.

But he'd go along with them. After all, a farewell prayer couldn't hurt.

They moved into the sanctuary, and Roosevelt and Sarah sat in the front pew. Leon sat one pew behind.

Sarah looked back at him, her face an invitation. "You can come up here with us, Leon."

"No, no, this is fine."

Roosevelt nodded. "Of course it is. God doesn't care where you sit to do your praying. He just cares that you *do* your praying." He glanced back. "Do you pray, Leon?"

"Now and then."

"I'm sure He's glad to hear from you." Roosevelt lifted his Bible for Leon to see. "I got this when I was confirmed, right here in this town." He ran a hand over the cover like it was velvet, and he liked the feel. "This here book has brought me through a lot of trouble. An awful lot." He looked at Leon. "It can do that for you, too, Leon."

"I'm sure it can. But I'm doing fine. I'm not going through anything." *You're going to be the one needing the Bible once I'm gone.*

Sarah angled her body, putting a hand on the back of her pew. "Roosevelt didn't mean any offense. It's just that we've both known adversity. And God's been the answer for us. He can be the answer for you, too. For everyone."

When she talked about God, she became a different Sarah. Her face practically glowed when she said it, and suddenly Leon wanted what she had, that inner *something* that seemed to calm her from the inside out.

But no. . .I can't. . .I can't go calling after God when I'm doing wrong. I can't draw His attention. Not now. Not while—

Roosevelt opened the Bible. "We've been reading from Acts. I'll continue where we left off." His finger coursed down the page, then stopped. "It's the apostle Paul talking about his work for God and His people. 'In everything I did, I showed you that by this kind of hard work we must help the weak, remembering the words the Lord Jesus Himself said: "It is more blessed to give than to receive." ' "

Sarah sighed. "I love hearing those words. It's a good reminder."

"And timely." Roosevelt smiled at Leon. "What with Leon working so hard for us, giving so much. I wish there was something we could give you, Leon—besides what little we can afford to pay you."

Leon's face was hot. The sanctuary was cool. He wiped his sleeve across his forehead. "It's nothing, Roosevelt. Really. I'm glad to—"

"It's not nothing. People helping people, that's what it's all about. There's so much bad out there. . ." His eyes drifted, seeing something in the past. "Doing good gives us hope."

Sarah began to speak—but not to them. She'd turned her face toward the cross, and Leon watched her profile. The words came in a stream, her voice soft, but firm.

" 'I lift up my eyes to the hills—where does my help come from? My help comes from the Lord, the Maker of heaven and earth. He will not let your foot slip—He who watches over you will not slumber; indeed, He who watches over Israel will neither slumber nor sleep. The Lord watches over you—the Lord is your shade at your right hand; the sun will not harm you by day, nor the moon by night. The Lord will keep you from all harm—He will watch over your life; the Lord will watch over your coming and going both now and forevermore.' "

She blinked. Then she blushed and lowered her eyes as if the words had come unbidden. She shrugged. "Psalm 121."

Roosevelt reached toward her and this time made contact. He patted her knee. "Those words comfort like God giving us a hug, don't they?"

Leon felt left out.

"Why don't we pray?" Roosevelt and Sarah bowed their heads, but Leon didn't. He looked past them to the simple wooden cross on the altar with mismatched legs. It was nothing special. Nothing grand, yet Sarah had looked at it—spoken to it—like it was pure gold.

Then suddenly he felt a churning in his innards. He had that old feeling that time was running short. He always felt it when the time to end a con was drawing near.

Relax. Relax. The scam would be done soon enough. He was what he was. He wasn't good like Roosevelt and Sarah. He was just a man who needed to do what he needed to do.

Leon heard a buzzing like a neon light gone bad. He opened his eyes, then blinked them again, not believing.

The cross on the altar was glowing.

It can't glow. . .it's made of wood!

He looked at Sarah and Roosevelt. Their heads were still bowed. Roosevelt was still praying out loud, "Help us, Lord, as we repair the roof. . . ."

The cross throbbed, making the room glow white—angel white. The pulse of the light was a heart beating, gaining force to come after him. He scooted a few inches toward the aisle, wanting to run. The cross glowed brighter with a fire inside, burning but not eating it up. He put a hand up, shielding his eyes. It was too bright. Too much.

Then he knew. It was God.

He could feel the heat now, invisible heat seeping toward him, showing its pow—

The sanctuary door burst open. "Pastor!"

They all turned around. It was Addie Whitney with Marco in tow. Roosevelt popped out of the pew and hurried down the aisle to meet her. "Did your husband hurt—?"

She shook her head no. "It's the plumbing. It broke.

Water everywhere. What am I going to do?" Roosevelt led her to a pew. Marco hesitated in the aisle. He was looking toward the front of the church.

The cross! Leon whipped his head toward the altar. The wooden cross stood dull in the shadows of the cloudy day.

God had left. More than anything, Leon wanted Him back.

Marco slid into the pew behind his mama, but he kept staring. Had he seen something?

Mrs. Whitney filled the sanctuary with her words. "I called a plumber. He came over and stopped the water from coming in. But he said it's going to cost nearly two hundred dollars!" She heaved with fresh sobs. "I don't have that kind of money." She looked at Roosevelt with soulful eyes. "Can you help me, Pastor? I'd pay you back. Somehow."

Roosevelt and Sarah exchanged a look, then they both looked to Leon. "I'm sorry, Addie, but the roof started leaking and the furnace—"

A thought fell upon Leon like a cat falling on a mouse. He discarded it as ridiculous. *O God, I don't think You realize what You're asking me to do.*

The idea returned. Leon glanced at the cross, then stood. "There's a chance I could fix things for less than we thought, Roosevelt."

Roosevelt beamed. "Well, that's a good start now, isn't it?" He pulled Mrs. Whitney to standing. "Let's go have a look. Maybe it's not as bad as you think."

They walked to the door and out. Sarah followed after them.

Marco didn't move, his eyes still pressed on the cross.

Leon slid into the pew beside him. "What you doing so quietlike, Marco?"

"I'm waiting for the cross to glow again."

Leon's heart jumped into his throat. "It glowed?"

Marco nodded, pulling his eyes away to glance at Leon. "God was here."

Leon started to laugh out loud. *What do you know?* "Want to know a secret?"

Marco nodded.

"I saw it glow, too."

"Mama, the preacher, and Miss Sarah. . .they didn't see it, did they?"

"I don't think so."

"Just you and me."

"Just you and me."

Marco smiled and reached for Leon's hand. The warm smallness shocked him. He hadn't felt a child's hand since his sister was tiny and had looked to him for protection. She'd depended on him. Looked up to him. And back then he'd been someone to look up *to.* Things had changed so much. *Too* much?

Leon looked to the cross. Although it wasn't glowing at the moment, it *had* glowed. And knowing that someone else had seen it. . .that he wasn't crazy. . .

God had been present in that glowing cross. He'd felt it. Marco had felt it. Leon looked at their hands, big holding little. Connecting. Fingers twined through fingers. He jumped up, taking Marco with him.

"What's wrong?"

Leon hugged him. "Absolutely nothing. Let's go catch

up with the others."

At that moment, the door opened, and Mrs. Whitney popped her head inside. "You coming, little boy? I turn around, and you aren't there. Come on now, we can't take up all the preacher's time."

Marco took her hand, and she pulled him out the door. Leon followed behind, taking one last look at the cross before he closed the door.

Glow or no glow, God was there. He knew it.

Roosevelt was surprised to see Leon coming with them. "Didn't you want to get going to Nashville, Leon?"

Marco took Leon's hand. "I figured I'd take a look at Mrs. Whitney's troubles. Maybe I can help."

Roosevelt's face lit up.

"Why, Mr. Burke, that would be mighty nice."

Sarah nodded. "Very nice, Leon."

He was just going to look. He couldn't think any further than that.

They walked toward town. The Whitney house was on the edge of the business district. It was a box with a door. Weeds threatened to capture the yard. Mrs. Whitney started apologizing, as if she hadn't noticed how bad it looked until just that moment.

"I've been working at the diner such long hours. . . I shoulda trimmed back the summer flowers by now and weeded but—"

"You've had a hard time of it, Addie," Roosevelt said. "We know that. That's why we're here to help."

"And don't you know I appreciate it." She opened the door and led them in.

The carpet in the front room squished as they walked, sucking at their shoes. Mrs. Whitney made a beeline for the kitchen. The cupboard doors under the sink were swung wide. Wet towels sat in soggy globs.

"Must be the week for mopping up," Sarah said.

Mrs. Whitney nudged a wet towel with her toe, making room for Leon. He knelt at the sink, looking at the pipes. One had busted through, but it was fixable. A few lengths of pipe, a new gooseneck, and some elbow grease. It wasn't two hundred dollars' worth. The plumber was ripping her off.

As if he should talk.

Roosevelt leaned beside him, peering at the pipes. "Can you fix it, Leon?"

Leon thought of himself on the road heading north—in the opposite direction of Nashville. Away from Roosevelt and Sarah and the law they would inevitably call. He could feel the three hundred in his pocket. It was a done deal. He didn't need to complicate things by helping—

He felt a presence to his right. He looked up to see Marco standing beside him. "Can you fix it, Leon? I'll help." As if the little boy knew the power of his touch, he put a hand on Leon's shoulder.

Ah, criminy. . . "Sure. I can do it. I'll pick up the supplies I need while I'm in Nashville getting the roofing."

Before he saw it coming, Mrs. Whitney had leaned over, grabbed his face, and planted a kiss on his forehead. "You are a godsend, Leon. A real godsend!"

He wished people would quit saying that.

The screen door slammed behind them, and everyone gathered on the Whitney porch to see him off.

"Sarah and I will stay here and help Addie sop up the water. Hurry back, Leon."

Marco piped up. "Can I go with him, Mama?"

Leon swung around. "Go? With me?"

"What do you think, Pastor Hazen?" asked Mrs. Whitney.

"I think that would be nice. For both of them."

"All right. You can go."

"I can go! I can go!"

Leon was stunned. *What just happened?*

The woman called after them. "You be good for Leon, little boy. We owe him big-time for saying he'll fix our plumbing. Good men like him are hard to find. I don't want him regretting taking you along on his errands."

"Yes'm."

"You got the money safe, Leon?" Roosevelt called out.

Leon slapped his hip pocket. "Got it right here." *But with this boy along I don't know how I'm going to turn it from your money into my money. My plan is shot.*

Marco climbed into the truck. "Can I really help you fix Mama's sink? I want to use a tool. A real tool."

Leon shut the boy's door and went around to the driver's side. "Maybe. But I got a roof to fix, too."

He started the engine, then took a moment to just sit while the truck rumbled beneath him. The sky to the west was dark. He sighed deeply and pulled onto the street.

"It looks like rain. The roof leaks when it rains. Gets all over the pews, splashing on the hymnals. It's going to ruin 'em if it's not fixed real soon."

"You're a good fix-it man," Marco said.

"Nah, not at all. Not really."

"I want to be a fix-it man when I grow up, just like you."

Leon's voice hardened, and he pointed a finger at him. "No, you don't. You can do better'n me—be better'n me. No matter what your mama says, I'm not that good a man, Marco. Now, Roosevelt. . .he's a good man. You be like him, okay?" Talking good versus bad made him nervous. "You want a peppermint?"

"Sure."

Leon pulled two from his shirt pocket.

"We saw a cross glow, didn't we, Leon?"

Leon changed gears. "You shush about that, Marco. You don't just say that to anybody."

"I won't. But it happened. God came."

It all sounded dumb now. "We. . .I felt something, that's for sure. But I don't know if it was God. Why would God be bothering with me? And you?"

"I dunno. But I liked it. It made me feel special."

He looked at the gathering storm. "Yeah. . .me, too, me, too."

"Mama says you're a traveling repair man, that you won't be staying long. But I want you to stay, Leon. Preacher's church has tons of stuff needs fixin', and our house, too. We could keep you busy."

You got that right.

"We need you."

Leon's throat pulled, and he let the peppermint clatter against his teeth. "You're a good boy, Marco. You stay that way, you hear? No matter what."

"I will. . .if you stay."

"And if I don't you'll suddenly turn into a bad boy?"

A pause. "If I say yes will it make you stay?"

He shook his head. "Staying put's not in my blood, kid."

"Don't you like us?"

" 'Course I like you. In fact, I probably like you too much."

"Huh?"

He slapped a hand on the steering wheel. "Enough of this talk. Let's just say I'll consider it."

"I'll ask God to make you stay."

"You don't need to do—"

"But I want to. If I can't make you do it, maybe He can."

CHAPTER 14

Learn to do right! Seek justice,
encourage the oppressed.

ISAIAH 1:17

It was five in the morning. Mac sat on the edge of Andrew's bed and watched him sleep by the glow of the bedside table. Andrew insisted on sleeping with a light on. Mac wondered how many years it would be before his son would be free of fear, free of the memories.

Mac adjusted the covers. Andrew's limbs sprawled across the single bed in the heedless way children slept. In sleep his son was without worry, but in his waking hours. . .that's when the fear came back.

He watched Andrew's chest rise and fall and thought of his own upcoming chance to travel back in time. And yet. . .

Andrew was in the here and now. How could Mac go back to protect and save Holly when his little boy needed protecting and saving here? If only he could let go of the desire to go back.

Mac prayed Leon was doing some good with his second chance. He knew the desperation of life and death situations. He understood the panic Leon must have experienced when he found out about the cancer. He imagined Leon contemplating his past life, his past deeds, and having regrets. *If only*. . .

Mac had to believe that Leon had killed Roosevelt Hazen out of a desire to do better, to make up for wrongs in the past. Mac did not excuse him, but he thought he understood. A little bit.

He didn't agree with Wriggens's philosophy that Leon should be punished, no matter what. If Leon was trying to lead a righteous life, Mac wanted him to stay in the past and live it through. What good would it do for him to come back to face a lifetime of jail—especially if that lifetime was destined to be short because of cancer? There had to be some purpose to all this happening, something beyond their comprehension. God was the ultimate judge.

Yet prison *was* the place some people belonged. . .like Holly's murderer. Sidney Graves should not get out. Ever.

With an intake of breath, Mac realized he could forgive Roosevelt's murderer, but never forgive Holly's. He was a hypocrite.

He stroked Andrew's head, being careful to avoid the scar now hidden beneath his hair. He was still waiting to fathom some reason for their family's tragedy. If God was in control, if God had a perfect plan, then how did Holly's death fit in? He realized he might never get an answer—at least not in this life. Only heaven would supply such insight. Of course, in heaven he would be with her again. He smiled at the thought.

"Daddy?"

He hadn't noticed Andrew coming awake. "Hi, buddy."

"Is it morning?"

"It's still time to sleep; I have to go to work early. Amy will be here any minute."

"Why are you here with me?"

Mac kissed his forehead. "Because I like to look at you."

Andrew's face was serious. "Are you going away, Daddy?"

Mac sat upright. "No, no. . ." *Not yet.* "Whatever made you think that?"

Andrew did not smile. "You want to be with Mommy real bad, don't you?"

Mac let out a breath.

Suddenly Andrew wrapped his arms around his father. "You're never going to leave me, are you, Daddy? You're never going to go away like Mommy did, are you?"

"Oh, buddy. . ."

"I don't want to be alone."

Mac held him tight and let the tears come. "Do you think I'd leave you alone here?"

"I see you cry when you think I'm not looking. You hug Mommy every night real hard."

Mac created a space between them. "I hug her?"

Andrew grabbed his pillow and smothered it just like Mac did every night alone in his bed. He imagined his son standing in the doorway in need of a drink of water or comfort after a bad dream. Looking at his dad. . .seeing his dad clutching the pillow as if getting it close enough, holding it tight enough, could conjure up his wife. His son had heard his tears. Witnessed his pain.

Andrew released the pillow. "I do that sometimes, but not too much. I have you to hug."

His words were like a dagger slicing him in two. He was the father. He was supposed to be helping his son deal with his mother's death. Obviously, he hadn't done a very good job.

Mac took Andrew's face in his hands. He wanted to tell him he would never leave him, never go back to change the past, but he couldn't. Not yet. The desire was still too strong.

"Tell you what, bud, tonight we'll have a special dinner together, just the two of us. Hot dogs, lime Jell-O, and grape Kool-Aid. They're still your favorites, aren't they?"

He nodded. "You'll be here for dinner? You're really not leaving me?"

The hope in Andrew's eyes wrenched his heart. He kissed his head. "I'll see you tonight. I promise."

Mac wished he could make a better promise, but at the moment, it was the best he could do.

At the Kansas City airport, Colin Thurgood hailed a cab. He threw his carry-on in the backseat and got in. "Take me to the TTC building."

"The what?"

He wasn't in the mood. "The Sphere? The Time Lottery—"

"Oh, right."

They sped into traffic.

Colin did not have a plan—which didn't bother him too much. He was a seat-of-your-pants kind of guy. For years Phoebe had nagged him about his lack of preparation, his total reliance on instinct. But when success followed in spite of her criticism, Phoebe stopped nagging. How could she argue about a character trait that brought her diamond bracelets and cruises with personal porters named Philippe?

The key to Colin's philosophy of life was confidence. It didn't matter whether it was genuine or implied, Colin found that if he *acted* as if he knew what he was doing, people believed it. And once they believed it, the real confidence followed, and he could not be denied—*would* not be denied.

As the cabby zoomed down the interstate toward downtown Kansas City, Colin took inventory. He patted the breast of his suit coat, reassuring himself that the cash was there. Fifty one-hundred-dollar bills were stacked in a neat wallet, ready to hand out to whoever needed a little encouragement to help him get what he wanted.

He'd borrowed the five thousand from his mistress, Rosie. She was reluctant, but he pointed out that she owed him big time. It wasn't unusual for him to drop that much during a single weekend with her. Now it was her turn to pay up. However, because of her vested interest in his plan, she'd wanted to come along to Kansas City. Only the promise of a cruise once this whole thing was over kept his trip solo. Women. He couldn't seem to live without them, nor easily live with them.

Whatever. He was here. He had the money and the confidence to make this thing go.

He *had* to make it go. It was his last chance.

As he walked through the front doors of the TTC headquarters, a part of Colin wanted to be recognized. But at the same moment he sought notoriety, he panicked at the thought of receiving it. It might be easier to get what he wanted if he remained anonymous until he hooked up with Mac and—

"Mr. Thurgood? What are you doing here?"

So much for anonymity. Colin turned on his stricken face. He put a hand to his mouth as if hiding a quiver.

The man came to his side. "Are you all right?"

Colin managed a nod. He snuck a look from under his lashes and saw the man's ID badge: Bob. The flunky on the phone. A follower, not a leader. Followers were easier to buy. Maybe he still didn't need to talk to Mac. Who would be more open to some extra cash—a peon or a hotshot celebrity?

Bob led Colin to a bench on the perimeter of the lobby. "Sit down. I'll get you a glass of water."

While he was gone, Colin raised his face as if searching for the sight of God. He clasped his hands and bounced them on his lap a few times. Such an anguished man. He looked around to see the extent of his audience. The receptionist poured a glass of water, looking at him with sympathetic eyes. But the people coming and going gave him only a passing glance as if they didn't want to get involved.

That was fine with him. It was none of their business.

Bob returned with the water, and Colin held the paper

cup in both hands. He took a sip. "Thanks."

"Sure. Any time." Bob sat beside him. "We didn't expect you so soon. Your wife's not due back for two and a half days."

Colin moaned. He brought a hand to his head. "I can't wait. It's killing me."

Bob leaned away. There was silence, and Colin feared he had gone too far.

"I hope you're not asking me again to go back and see her, because that's not possible."

I'm losing him. Colin angled his body toward Bob's. He put a hand on his arm. His desperation was real. "You have to help me. I have to talk to her. Now."

Bob pulled his arm free and shook his head. "This doesn't make sense. She'll be back soon. Certainly, you can wait—"

"I can't!"

He'd shouted the words. They both looked around the lobby. The receptionist's sympathy had changed to wary concern. Her hand inched toward the phone.

Colin was running out of time—in more ways than one. No more bull. He pulled the wallet from his inner pocket. He opened it. Fifty Ben Franklins stared back at them.

Bob sucked in a breath.

"This is all yours if you'll help me—and there's more where this came from. But I have to talk to my—"

"Bob? What's going on here?"

Colin snapped the wallet shut. A stuffy-looking man came close. Colin recalled seeing him before but couldn't remember his name. The man's eyes didn't miss much. He looked at Bob, the wallet, then Colin.

"Mr. Thurgood. What *are* you doing here?"

Bob popped off the bench. "Nice seeing you again." He hurried away like an ant escaping a shoe.

Coward.

"Is there something I can help you with, Mr. Thurgood?"

Colin looked at the wallet. Should he make an offer to *this* man? What did he have to lose? He put on his business face. He looked at the man's ID badge. "Chief Administrator John Wriggens, just the man I wanted to see."

"Is that so?"

"Is there someplace we could talk privately?" Colin said.

Wriggens hesitated the slightest moment. "Certainly. Right down here."

He led them to a small conference room. He closed the door. Colin did not take the seat that was offered. He needed to stand. Standing was the power position. Wriggens also stood. A battle of the titans.

"What do you want, Mr. Thurgood?"

"I want—I *need*—to go back to the past and see my wife before she comes home. And I'm willing to pay for it." He opened his wallet. The stack of hundred-dollar bills fanned and fell still. Waiting.

Colin watched Wriggens watch the money.

"There's more of this. Plenty more."

Wriggens swallowed and lifted his eyes to meet Colin's. "Why?"

Colin considered lying but dismissed the idea. Good, bad, or ugly, it was time for truth. "I need Phoebe's insurance money."

A crease appeared between Wriggens's eyes. "But the only way you can get the insurance money is for her to—"

"Stay in the past. I know. That's why you have to send me back there, to convince her to stay. For my sake." A slight pause. "And for the sake of our children."

Wriggens's lifted eyebrow told Colin that he didn't accept that last statement. Colin made a mental note to can any sentimental references. Wriggens was a facts-man.

"What about your wife's sake?"

Colin cleared his throat. "Let's cut to it. I'm a heel. I'm not a good husband. I don't love my wife, and she doesn't love me. There's not much here to love. What I do love is business and money and making the deal. I've worked hard to build myself a good life, and I don't aim to lose it."

"Lose it?"

Colin waved the question away. "To win big you have to risk big. I lost. Temporarily. I will recover. But I need that insurance money. And this waiting and not knowing is driving me crazy. Every hour counts."

Wriggens looked at the pile of hundreds, and Colin pinched the corner of the stack to make it neat in the wallet.

"But I'm afraid sending you back is not possible. Every person's time travel experience is unique. She's in an Alternity of her own creation. You can't enter it."

Colin let out his air. "Then why are you leading me on?"

"Sending you back to her Alternity isn't possible, and neither is contacting your wife."

Colin snapped the wallet closed. "Our dialogue is over."

Wriggens touched the wallet.

This is getting interesting. . . Colin opened the wallet again, exposing the bribe. "Do you have a proposal for me, Mr. Wriggens?"

"Your wife's choice to stay in her past or return is hers alone; however, if I had my way, chances to use our technology would be sold to those who—"

"Pay the highest dollar?"

"Who are the most. . .deserving."

Colin grinned. He'd have to hope for the best regarding the insurance money. But to get his own chance. . . "Oh, I'm deserving. I'm extremely deserving." He picked up the money and fanned it again. "I want to go right away. When can I—?"

Wriggens snatched the wallet away. "I'll take this—as a first installment."

Colin had to admire his guts. "I'm so glad we can work something out. It appears we're soul mates, Chief Administrator John Wriggens."

Wriggens tucked the wallet into the inside pocket of his suit.

Suddenly the door to the conference room opened, and Mac appeared. He looked from one to the other. "What's going on, John? And what is he doing here?"

Mac entered the room. Bob followed and shut the door, standing with his back against it. "Well?" Mac said. "I ask again: What are you doing here?"

Colin and Wriggens exchanged a glance, and instantly Mac knew that all Bob had told him was true. The last of his respect for Wriggens dissipated like fog in the sunlight.

Colin crooked a thumb to his chest. "I belong here. My wife is coming back in two days."

"You belong here then. Not now."

Wriggens flipped a dismissive hand at Bob. "Bob, you can go now. We've got this handled."

Bob shook his head. Mac wished his cousin wasn't smiling with such smug self-satisfaction—though Mac understood the feeling. "I'm staying."

Mac was about to agree, when he realized that he was the master of how this situation would be played out. He could choose the high road, or the—

"Actually, Bob, I think it would be best if you left the chief and me alone to handle this. Perhaps you can escort Mr. Thurgood out?"

Colin face flashed. "Out? I'm not going out." He smacked Wriggens with the back of his hand. "You and I have a deal. We have things to do. Now."

Mac purposely raised an eyebrow. "Would you care to explain?"

"No, I wouldn't care to—"

Wriggens spoke. "Perhaps it *would* be best if you leave, Mr. Thurgood. Bob can show you to the—"

"I don't need Bob to show me anything. I need you to stop being so gutless and stick to our agreement."

Wriggens looked to the floor. "I don't know what you're talking about."

Colin grabbed the front of Wriggens' suit coat, pulled it open, and snatched out a wallet. He spread it, revealing a pile of hundreds.

Mac felt his control leaving him. "Bob, now that Mr. Thurgood has regained his property, please show him out of the building. Immediately."

Colin glared at Mac, then at Wriggens. He jabbed a

finger at each of them. "This is *not* over. You told me I could go back, and I'm going to hold you to it." He threw open the door and stormed away. Bob ran after him.

Mac closed the door with a controlled click.

Wriggens spoke first. "Okay, you got me, Mac. I had a moment of weakness. He snowed me. You know Thurgood. He's slick; he's a shark."

"You make a good match."

His eyes flashed. "Watch it."

Mac felt a surge of strength. "I don't need to watch it. You may have been the one to hire me, but my ultimate loyalty is to the reputation of the Time Lottery. And you telling him he could go back—selling a chance—goes against everything the Lottery stands for."

Wriggens sat down as if he hadn't a care in the world. He checked his manicure in a movement that reminded Mac of the first time they'd met. "You can cut the high and mighty attitude. You have no idea what you would have done in the same situation."

"Oh yes, I do."

"It's a good idea, selling trips. We talked about it."

"But it's not final. You can't implement your own pet projects without authorization."

Wriggens shrugged. "Perhaps I let my enthusiasm for a good idea take over. I suppose you wouldn't understand, having never done anything you regret."

"Of course I have."

Wriggens spread his hands. "Well, I have, too. There you have it."

Mac was amazed at how easily Wriggens dismissed his

own wrongdoing. He'd expected *some* contriteness, but this. . . this deserved. . . Mac moved closer so he stood above his boss. "You took a bribe."

"But I *didn't* take it. Not really."

"Only because I caught you."

Wriggens curled his manicured nails under. "Like I say, you got me. What are you going to do now? Dangle me by my thumbs? Take over my job?"

Mac smiled. "That depends on you."

Wriggens smile faded. "Continue."

Mac put his hands in his pockets. What *did* he want from Wriggens? What would give him the ultimate satisfaction? Suddenly, some words escaped. "I want my contract to be extended. I want this job to be permanent."

Wriggens's face revealed his shock. "What about your Image-Maker status? You'd give up your celebrity hobnobbing to become a corporate employee?"

He made "employee" sound like a dirty word. "I like what I'm doing here. I like giving people a second chance. And at the risk of sounding trite, I like helping them."

Wriggens shook his head. "My, my, my. . .what will Hollywood do without you?"

"Go on as they always have." He shifted his weight. "So? Is it a deal? We exchange my silence for a job?"

"Is blackmail truly the way you want to get employment?"

"Is bribery truly the way you want to get income?"

Mac heard Wriggens's breath go in. Then out.

Wriggens stood. "Consider it done."

Mac was left in the room alone. Only then did it hit him. *What have I done?*

Mac had *never* been so glad to leave work. Catching a colleague in unethical conduct made him exhausted and sad—even if he didn't like the man. It was bad for the company.

Mac had to laugh at his surge of loyalty. He'd taken the TTC job as a temporary assignment. He thought he'd do his stuff and move on. And yet, there was something magical about this project that had made him think about staying on indefinitely.

He drove through his neighborhood, shucking off all thoughts of work. He'd had enough of time travel—for now. He pulled into his driveway. Andrew appeared at the kitchen door before he got out of the car.

"You're home! You're home! You really came home!"

The boy's relief pulled at Mac's heart. Obviously, Andrew had not fully believed his father's morning promises. "Of course I'm home." He took a grocery sack from the backseat.

The babysitter appeared at the door. " 'Evening, Mr. MacMillan. Do you want me to make something for your dinner? Andrew said something about Jell-O and Kool-Aid but—"

"Not tonight, Amy. We have special plans tonight."

Andrew peeked in the sack. "Ice cream!"

"Oh, not just any ice cream, young man. I was thinking that it's time you were introduced to one of my favorite delicacies. You put two scoops in a tall glass and pour in some root beer. . . ."

Pam Pentola tossed the tabloid into the fireplace. A blue

flame seared through the face of Dorothy Nickolby. *Serves you right.*

She couldn't believe the stupidity of Cheryl's mother. Hadn't Cheryl gotten enough bad press without Dorothy compounding it by giving an interview?

Not that Pam hadn't thought of doing the same thing. It burned her to see Cheryl's reputation slogged through the mud. Yet Pam had not called any reporters to restore her best friend's reputation. For two reasons. One, as far as she knew, the ex-lovers were just that. Although they had proved themselves men of dishonor and sleaziness, they weren't lying. What could she refute? *Stop that! You're not being nice telling the truth about Cheryl!*

The second reason Pam didn't want to get involved was that she didn't want the press to do any research on her own love life. Although she was single—and would most likely always remain single—she preferred to keep her private life as private as possible. Dorothy Nickolby was embarrassing proof of the consequences of letting the media in the front door of your life. Pam was working things out. Slowly. Recently, she'd met a very nice man. . . .

If only Cheryl were here, *she'd* give the press what-for. Cheryl had gotten where she was because she didn't take guff from anybody. Cheryl could take care of herself. At least in the present she could. But what about in the past? What was she thinking going back to hook up with Jake Carlisle? Forget Jake, what was Cheryl doing going back to high school in general? Except for Julie and Cheryl's friendship, Pam would have preferred to forget those four dubious years.

The phone rang. Pam answered it.

"Did you see the article?" It was Julie.

Julie waved good-bye to her son as he went out the kitchen door to go to work. She stuck the phone between ear and shoulder and pushed Control-P on her computer. The manuscript for her latest children's book came out. "I can't believe Dorothy would do such a thing. She didn't help Cheryl one bit."

"Now the entire world thinks Cheryl comes from a long line of nympho women."

"At least Dorothy married her lovers."

Julie expected Pam's response to be harsh. And it was. "So that's better? Marrying six or seven times? Divorcing over and over?"

Julie had no answer. Although her religious convictions said that sex outside of marriage was wrong, it also said that marriage was for a lifetime. Neither Nickolby female was doing it right.

She adjusted the chain on her cross necklace. "So what should we do?"

"Nothing."

Julie stopped rocking. "Nothing?"

"If we do a counter interview to counter Dorothy's counter interview, we'll just make things worse."

"I'm not sure things can get any worse."

"At least Cheryl's still got her job."

"Barely."

Julie moved away from the noise of the printer and began pacing the room. "I cringe when I think of her coming back from her adventure and running headlong into a messed-up life."

"She might not be coming back, Julie."

Julie stopped pacing. Although she understood the possibility, she had never seriously considered it. High school had been okay, but adulthood was much, much better. And as far as Jake went. . .Julie had been successful in keeping that memory locked away until Cheryl had brought him up again. Jake had stolen her virginity. Long ago she'd forgiven him—and herself—but it was still a wound that smarted when memories and regrets brushed too close.

"She's coming back, Pam. Jake wasn't that good a catch."

"How would you know?"

"I just do." It was the one secret she'd kept from her friends. They'd never known she had been so stupid. They would never know. She was the good one. The chaste one. The moral one. She wasn't going to let them know she had fallen. Ever.

Pam sighed. "I feel so helpless. I want to be like a bodyguard, walking in front of her, keeping the sick gawkers away."

"You always were our protector."

"And you always were our mother."

Suddenly, it became important to have the three of them together again. "Let's go to Kansas City and be there when she gets back."

"*If* she gets back."

"Don't talk that way. Let's just go. Let our faces be the first ones she sees."

"She made us promise not to—"

"To see her *off.* She never asked us not to be there when she got back."

"A convenient technicality."

"Exactly."

"Can you get away?"

"My youngest is nearly grown. I've got plenty of time," Julie said. "I'll be there. Cheryl will be so happy to see us."

"*If* she comes back."

"Pam. . ."

"Sorry. I'm coming."

CHAPTER 15

The Lord is my light and my salvation—
whom shall I fear?
The Lord is the stronghold of my life—
of whom shall I be afraid?

PSALM 27:1

Cheryl thought Jake was dressed oddly. He'd told her to come over and they'd talk about the test, yet he answered the door wearing a pair of gray sweat-shorts and a Dallas Cowboys T-shirt.

Cheryl took off her coat and looked around at the party debris that littered the house. There were cups, right-side up and otherwise on every horizontal surface. There were plates, napkins, and a few purple stains on the carpet. It was lucky Jake's mom hadn't stayed to chaperon. It saved a few kids some bodily damage. But even then, Cheryl couldn't imagine Mitzi picking up garbage and washing dishes in a vision of domestic busyness. Maybe Jake did it?

Her image of Jake washing dishes was interrupted by the reality of Jake hauling her over his shoulder, caveman style. He headed down the hallway toward the bedrooms.

"Jake!" She found it hard to breathe when she was bent like a pretzel. "I'm here to talk, remember?"

He ducked under the doorway to his bedroom, making Cheryl cling to his back to prevent being beaned. He tossed her down on his unmade bed like a sack of dirty laundry. He pulled his T-shirt off by clawing at a spot between his shoulder blades until the shirt had no choice but to fall over his head.

He shut the door with his foot. "We can talk later. I feel like celebrating."

There was not an ounce of celebration in her heart. Everything had changed. It was as if someone had come into the room and kicked over the gameboard, scattering all the pieces, forcing her out of her stupor. *This isn't a game. This is life.*

Cheryl scooted back on the bed until she leaned against the headboard. As Jake moved closer, her heart pounded—with fear. She swung her legs over the side of the bed. "Can't a girl get some breakfast around here?" She headed toward the door.

He blocked the way and grabbed her arms, lifting her body off the floor until she stood on tiptoes, her face even with his. His smile was reptilian, slithering on and off his face in a frenzied dance of uncontrolled emotion. "Duty comes first, little lady." He rammed his lips onto hers. His breath was stale and held the memory of Cheerios and milk.

"Jake, wait!" Cheryl squeezed the words out the side of her mouth.

He let her feet find the ground but kept hold of her arms. His eyes were black, his voice low. "Don't get coy with me, Cheryl. You owe me."

Something had gone wrong. Her control was gone, transferred to another. She struggled against his hands. "Jake, no. I want to go home."

He edged back, just enough to see her face. "Don't you want to do it?"

"No. No, I don't."

"Then why'd you even come over?"

"To discuss my second thoughts about getting the test for you."

His grin was wicked. He pushed her back on the bed. "Wrong answer."

Cheryl heard water running in the bathroom. A flush. Gargling.

The phone rang. She almost answered it. *Help! I've just been raped!* But she didn't want anyone to know she was there, had ever *been* there. She didn't *want* to be there. She wasn't there.

Jake came out of the bathroom and picked it up. "Yeah?"

He turned his back, hunching over the receiver protectively. "Oh, hi. . . . Thanks. . . . Sure, I suppose. Now? . . . Yeah, okay. See ya in a minute." He hung up. He tossed her blouse at her face. "You gotta go."

Gladly.

Although Cheryl desperately wanted a long hot shower and the comfort of her pillow, her curiosity took over. Who was coming over to Jake's?

She parked her car around the corner and cut through yards to get back to his house. She snuck behind the bushes that guarded the front door. The ground was mushy from the melting snow, so she sat on her haunches. The jutting branches poked in rude places, but she had a good view of the front porch and a limited view of the driveway. It would have to do.

She stuffed her hands in her pockets. The tears began as she remembered Jake's rough hands. Did going steady mean he could take her whenever he wanted? It wasn't right. She felt dirty. She rubbed her tears and nose against her sleeve. She sat on the damp ground, easing her legs, but freezing her behind. Misery wrapped around her like a damp shroud.

She heard a car. Two cars. They drove by. Three more minutes. *Go home. Forget this. Forget Jake. Forget—*

The putt-putt of another car. It pulled into the driveway. Cheryl could see a streak of color: baby blue.

Footsteps on the sidewalk. A girl's footsteps. Cheryl ducked so she wouldn't be seen. One, two, three, up the front steps. Knock, knock, knock.

Cheryl saw who it was and heard Jake say her name at the same moment.

"Hi, Julie."

Cheryl eased herself from behind the bushes up to the stoop. She stood to the side of the door and peeked into the entry. She pulled back an inch as she saw Jake and Julie standing in the space where the entry became the living room. He took her coat and tossed it on one of the pink velvet chairs. Cheryl strained to hear, finding if she didn't breathe, she could make out their words. She chose knowledge over breath.

". . .now that you're not interested in Andrea anymore. . ."

Jake stuffed his hands in his pockets. "What makes you say that?"

Cheryl watched as Julie's mouth opened. "Well. . .last night you helped trap her, you told everyone about the jewelry in her closet."

He shrugged. "Sometimes the truth hurts."

Julie's fingers played nervous games with each other. "You're still interested in her?"

He shrugged again. "Why do you ask?"

She took a deep breath and let it out. "I thought we could get back. . .be together again."

Cheryl took her own deep breath, needing a second and a third. Julie? And Jake?

Jake leaned against the wall, his hands in his pockets. "I don't know, Julie. You didn't seem that interested."

Julie looked at the floor. "I was nervous, Jake. You're so. . .so. . ."

"Great. I know." He moved into the living room. Cheryl watched his eyes brighten. "I suppose dating is a possibility."

What?

Julie moved beside him again. "Really, Jake?" She was like an innocent in a soap opera—the girl who gets hurt over and over because she's inescapably attracted to the rogue.

Jake turned away from Julie a second time, and Cheryl could see a smirk forming. "But. . .I need something from you, Julie. A favor."

She hesitated and took a step back.

He laughed. "I need you to help me pass my history test. If I don't pass I'll be dropped from the team, and I won't get a scholarship to college. I'll end up digging ditches or working as a busboy my whole life."

You two-faced. . .

"I'll help you study, Jake."

He jerked his head back and cackled. "Study? Me, study?"

"Then how?"

"Get me the test." He wasn't laughing.

She hesitated. "I took that class last year. I'm sure I still have the tests. You can study from them."

He shook his head. "Not good enough. You work in the mimeo room. Get me the real test."

Julie's head shook in negative jerks. "That would be cheating. I don't think—"

In one sleek movement Jake wrapped an arm around her waist and pulled her tight against him. Instinctively, her arms barricaded themselves on his chest, trying to push herself free. Jake used the space to his advantage.

Cheryl ran all the way to her car.

As she slammed the car door, Cheryl suddenly realized that the vision she'd had on the highway, the one of Jake and a blond girl kissing in a foyer, had not been Cheryl and Jake, but Julie and Jake.

What did it mean?

She shivered. She shook the thought away. She didn't care what it meant. She was mad. At both of them.

But after rejecting two dozen possible ways to murder Julie and Jake, Cheryl realized it didn't need to be a double hanging. Only one perpetrator needed to take the blame for her hurt ego and her violated body. Only one person needed to feel her wrath.

It was no contest.

After meeting Peter at the Christmas party, Phoebe didn't attempt to talk to Colin—or even Linda Friberg. The two women exchanged a wave across the Greenfield's living room, and Linda had winked, giving her approval for Phoebe's companion. As for Colin? He hadn't noticed her. Each time she saw him, he was talking to someone high in the corporate food chain.

Near midnight, her energy gave out. She asked Peter to call her a cab.

"Nonsense. I'll take you home."

"Rescuing me twice in one night. . .don't use up your whole supply of gallantry on me."

"Why not?"

She felt herself blush. It was so nice to have someone treat her special.

Peter took her home, and she asked him up for coffee. They had a wonderful conversation spanning subjects from Gothic architecture to the best recipe for Mexican salsa. He seemed eager to listen to her opinions.

Unlike Colin, Peter did not make a single rude comment about the size of her apartment. In fact, he seemed impressed with her combination of antiques and early-garage-sale treasures.

She laughed. "It's not done by design. Necessity is the mother of eclectic."

He ran a hand along a walnut dresser. "Don't sell yourself short, Phoebe. You have an eye for making it work. And the way you've hung that paisley curtain to separate your kitchen area from the rest of the room. . .that shows talent."

"Talent for what?"

"Interior design." He turned to face her, his eyes bright. "Have you had any experience?"

She thought of the decorating influences of her life. Her parents' slip-covered couch and the legless doll that covered the extra roll of toilet paper with its crocheted dress. "None."

"No college?"

"It wasn't possible. Still isn't. My parents need my help and. . ." She hesitated. Should she tell him about her grandmother? Would he react like Colin had reacted—telling her it was not her responsibility?

"And what?"

His eyes were understanding. "And my grandma needs to go into a nursing home that's expensive. I'll be paying the bills, so I'm stuck being a working girl."

"What a wonderful granddaughter you are."

She blinked. It was the first time anyone had commended her sacrifice—or even acknowledged it.

"In fact. . ." He looked around the room. "Do you

have a Bible handy?"

She'd never heard that line before. "Why?"

"Just this morning, in my reading, I came across a verse I'd like to share with you."

Her eyes widened. Peter Greenfield was definitely one of a kind. She pulled a Bible from the shelf. Its cover was stiff. Peter sat on the couch and flipped the pages like he was searching for treasure. His finger ran down a page. "Here, here it is: 'If anyone does not provide for his relatives, and especially for his immediate family, he has denied the faith and is worse than an unbeliever.' " He held the page for her to see.

She nodded and sat beside him. "So I am doing the right thing?"

He closed the book with a *thwap*. "Of course you are." His brow furrowed. "But you knew that, didn't you?"

"I guess so. But common wisdom says I should worry about me. The world says it's not my responsibility."

"The world is wrong."

So bluntly said. So right. *Do not cooperate with the world.* Hadn't she spewed that bit of wisdom to Cheryl, the girl on the street? But had Phoebe shared it without living it herself?

Phoebe pulled a throw pillow to her chest. "Why does life have to be so difficult?"

"So we turn to God."

She blinked. "What?"

He moved toward the door, picking up his coat along the way. "It's late. Keep the Bible off the shelf awhile, Phoebe. What's inside can help you more than I can."

"Don't leave."

He paused with one hand on the doorknob. "Don't worry, I'll be back. In the meantime, read Job 36:15–16."

He left. The room lost its energy.

Phoebe opened the Bible. She had no idea where she'd find the book of Job. She used the index and looked up the verse. *"Hard times and trouble are God's way of getting our attention. And at this very moment, God deeply desires to lead you from trouble."*

He had her attention all right. And in a moment full of hope and longing, Phoebe realized she desperately wanted to be led.

That night Phoebe read the Bible for two hours. Peter was right. What was inside helped. A lot.

I can't believe I'm doing this.

Leon held a wad of money toward Roosevelt. "Here's your change."

Roosevelt stared at the bills. "This is a lot of money. I didn't expect—"

"It's $273.85."

"Two hundred seventy— But I gave you three hundred. That's less than thirty dollars. Didn't you get the supplies for the roof—and Addie's sink? And didn't you give your furnace-man friend some money up front?"

Leon took the lengths of pipe and fittings out of his truck. "I got the supplies." He wished Roosevelt would drop it. "I got a good deal, that's all. But my friend. . .he doesn't work there anymore. Sorry."

"But you said fixing the roof alone would cost over two hundred."

Leon slammed the door of the truck and headed up the walk to the Whitney house. He stopped and turned. "I guessed wrong, okay? Now if you want to help me fix the sink, you can hold a wrench or something. If not, go write a sermon and thank God for a miracle."

Roosevelt raised an eyebrow. A smile lifted the corner of his mouth. "A miracle?"

"Let's just say the Lord works in mysterious ways."

Leon hated working under sinks. There was never enough room to move around properly, and he kept hitting his head. But if the cabinet offered close quarters, the presence of Roosevelt Hazen and Marco was stifling.

Marco sat on the floor nearby, holding a flashlight on the pipes so Leon could see. Roosevelt sat behind him, grinning the stupidest grin. Every time Leon glanced over, he found Roosevelt grinning and shaking his head like he'd just witnessed a waterfall flowing *up* or seen it snow in July.

And though it was annoying, a part of Leon didn't mind. Having Roosevelt think highly of him made him stop thinking about what a stupid chump he'd been. Glowing cross or no glowing cross, little boy with big brown eyes or no little boy, a fella had to make a living, didn't he? Yet Leon had just given up $273.85.

"Mm-mm, praise the Lord," Roosevelt said.

Okay. That's it. Leon pulled his head out from under the sink and sat up. He tossed a wrench on the floor. "You're bursting to ask me something, say something. . . I can't stand you sitting over there like you know this mighty secret. Out with it."

Roosevelt dug some coins from his pocket. "Marco, why don't you go to the gas station and get us some Nehis."

Marco gladly relinquished the flashlight to Roosevelt. "I'll be right back!"

"Don't drop 'em now."

Roosevelt turned the flashlight off. "You're a con man, aren't you?"

Leon glanced under the sink. If only he could shove his head under there permanently, like an ostrich hiding his head in the ground. But he was tired of hiding. "Maybe."

"You were going to take the money and keep driving, right?"

"I had Marco with me. I couldn't have—"

Roosevelt raised a finger like he was Sherlock Holmes making a point. "But you weren't planning on having Marco go with you."

Leon shrugged. "That don't prove nothing."

"But you took him."

"So?"

"By taking him you made it impossible to run with the money. Marco was your insurance policy against yourself."

Leon liked the sound of that but wouldn't admit it. He grabbed another wrench and ducked under the sink. "You're talking crazy."

"No, I'm not."

"Suit yourself. Hey, can I have some light here?" Nothing happened. "Roosevelt. I need some light."

"You certainly do."

Leon sat up. "What do you mean by that?"

"Leon Burke, you're a good man, and you don't even know it."

"Don't overestimate—"

"But God knows it. God knows it and gave you a chance to prove it to yourself. It truly is a miracle. I had faith in you, Leon. From the first moment I met you, I had faith."

Roosevelt's words were like balm on an old wound. Someone believed in him. Someone trusted him. Leon disguised his pleasure with busyness. "I'll leave the miracle business to you, Preach. At the moment, I got plumbing to attend to." He waved a hand toward the pipes. "Do you mind? I'd like a little light here."

"Certainly. 'Though I have fallen, I will rise. Though I sit in darkness, the Lord will be my light.' Praise the Lord!"

Roosevelt looked downright smug. Leon couldn't blame him.

Leon turned the faucet on. He sat on his haunches next to Marco. They watched the pipes.

"It's not leaking!"

"You look surprised, little man."

Marco stood. "You really are a fix-it man. I gotta show Mama." He ran off.

Leon gathered his tools. Marco came back, pulling his mother by the hand. "See, Mama? Leon fixed it."

Addie Whitney leaned over to look at the pipes. "Indeed he did." She straightened. "What do I owe you, Leon?"

Here was his chance to get something out of the whole affair. But before he could mesh a number in his head, his mouth said, "Nothing."

"Nothing?"

Nothing? Was he crazy? "Let's call it a favor."

"That's very nice of you, Leon, but I can't allow it. A man deserves honest pay for an honest day's work." She pointed to a cookie jar shaped like a cow that sat on top of the refrigerator. "Can you reach that for me?"

He took it down and set it on the counter. The tail formed a handle she used to lift off part of its back. She dipped her hand inside and pulled out a crisp twenty-dollar bill. "This is for you."

Leon backed away like the money was hot. "No, I can't take your cookie money."

She laughed. "It's not cookie money, it's emergency money, and you *will* take it."

"But what if Mr. Whitney finds out?"

She put a hand to her eye, which was now turning a sickly shade of yellow. "I think he's gone for good. I told him I'd call the police next time—and I will." She pulled Marco under her arm. "Marco needs good men around him, not the likes of a bully father. Good men like you and Pastor Hazen."

Me, good? He liked the sound of it. He liked it a lot.

She held out the money a second time. "An honest day's work, Leon."

Honest. He took the bill and stared at it. It felt heavy in his hands. Yet in that moment, it felt right. It felt *good.*

It was a glowing gift from God.

CHAPTER 16

So do not fear, for I am with you;
do not be dismayed, for I am your God.
I will strengthen you and help you;
I will uphold you with my righteous right hand.

ISAIAH 41:10

The day after the rape and her revelation about Jake and Julie, Cheryl had trouble getting out of bed. She'd slept badly for two nights. Stupid party. If only it hadn't happened.

She lay back amidst the pillows, adjusting her stuffed gorilla so it wouldn't poke her in the ribs. She couldn't lie here forever. She had to do something. Get things back to normal—or make them better than normal. But she couldn't do it alone.

She picked up the phone and called Pam. It was good to

hear her voice. A friendly voice? Maybe not. But a friend's voice? Certainly. "I need your help," Cheryl said.

"It's my day off."

"There are no days off in friendship."

A pause. "I don't like being your pawn."

"You're not."

"Wanna bet? I was at the party the other night."

Touché. "Sorry."

"Andrea's the one you should apologize to."

"You want the victim to apologize to the thief?"

Pam snickered. "You? A victim?"

Cheryl shuddered. If this is what her best friend thought of her, what did the rest of the school think? "You're not being fair, Pam."

"Spoken from the queen of fighting dirty."

"She accused me of stealing from Susan. She stole from me at the party."

"You set her up."

"She deserved to be stopped."

"So do you."

Pam's breathing was a syncopation of Cheryl's. A minute passed. Cheryl expected to hear a click on the line. But she didn't. So much had happened since the party. "Pam?"

"Yeah?"

"Help me. Please."

A huge sigh. "I'll be right over."

Somehow, Pam sitting cross-legged on the end of the bed with a bottle of Squirt in one hand and an Oreo in the other made a discussion of rape seem way out of place. Maybe Cheryl would have to ease into it.

"Julie's got the hots for Jake."

Pam shook her head. "Impossible."

"Fact. I saw them. She practically begged Jake to be her boyfriend. He agreed, on the condition she get him a copy of the history test he needs to take next week."

"Get?"

"Steal."

"Julie? Steal? Surely you jest."

Cheryl raised an eyebrow. "And Julie, attracted to Jake?"

Pam shrugged. "A day of surprises."

You have no idea. . . . "Remember last week's sleepover when Julie acted all weird, talking about love?"

"No, no, no, no. . .not Jake."

Cheryl nodded. "She's smitten."

"Do you think she'll get him the test?"

"She's not thinking clearly." It was a common malady. "Actually, neither am I. Neither was I."

Pam stopped eating. "Uh-oh. What else did you do?"

"I promised Jake *I'd* get him the test."

"Then why did he ask Julie for it?"

Cheryl shrugged. "Insurance."

"How are you supposed to get it?"

"Lure it out of Tommy. He's the history teacher's assistant."

"And how were you supposed to do that?"

Cheryl looked to the carpet.

Pam stuffed a cookie in her mouth without licking out the middle. "You two are terrible. What does Jake have that can make two normally sane females act like fools?" She raised a hand. "Don't answer that."

"If Jake doesn't get the test from one of us. . ."

"What can he do?"

Whatever he wants.

"Cheryl?"

She pulled herself out of the memory. "The point is, we can't let Julie give him the test. We can't let her even be tempted to give it to him. It's against her character. She'd never forgive herself."

"So what do we do?"

"I'll get Jake the test. *A* test."

"Through Tommy?"

"No. . .I don't want to involve him anymore. I've used him enough. We'll make up a test. We'll give Jake the wrong test."

"He'll flunk."

"Yeah."

"He'll be kicked off the team."

"Yeah."

"And why are we doing this? It sounds as though Julie went to him willingly."

Cheryl evaded the question. "Jake needs to get a test, or he'll keep bugging us. But I will *not* get him the real test. I will not!"

Pam raised her hands to fend off Cheryl's zeal. "I believe you. But have you thought of the consequences? He'll be furious. More than furious."

"I can handle whatever he dishes out. But Julie can't. That's why I have to be the one to do this. We need to get Julie out of the picture."

"But if she really loves—"

"No!"

The clock ticked twice.

"Cheryl. . .what aren't you telling me?"

Cheryl shook the question away. "You were in Mrs. Tranfield's class last semester, weren't you? You have your old tests?"

"Sure. But she changes them. And you haven't answered my—"

"Jake doesn't know that. And we'll even supply him with the answers—the wrong answers. He'll never do the studying to make sure they're right. And *voilà.* We'll have our revenge for Julie." She finally let it out. "And me."

"You? What do you want revenge for? I thought you liked him. At the sleepover you wanted him. Beyond wanting him: You wanted a commitment, remember? You wanted to be together and—"

Together. . .oh yeah, we've been together all right. Cheryl pulled a teddy bear to her chest.

Pam put her hand on Cheryl's knee. "Cheryl? What's wrong?"

She bit the bear's ear. Then the words escaped. "He raped me."

"Jake? Raped you?"

Cheryl didn't like the tone of unbelief in her voice. "Yesterday, at his house."

A pause. "Are you all right?"

The wonder of best friends. Cheryl began to cry.

Pam rocked her and told her everything would be all right. But Cheryl wasn't sure feeling right was an option. Not anymore.

Cheryl told Pam everything: about the deal she'd made with Jake and her confusion about what real commitment involved. She hadn't meant to tell, but the thought of letting one forgiving soul know her sins seemed to promise a kind of redemption. And more than anything, Cheryl wanted to feel redeemed.

And her first act as a redeemed person was to make amends and stop using people. Like Tommy. She called him up. "I'm sorry, Tommy. I'm really not interested right now. . . sorry. . .yeah, me, too. . .well, maybe someday. . .bye." Cheryl hung up the phone and fell onto the bed. "I feel like a heel."

Pam looked up from the typewriter. "You're not a heel. You're being honest. You're not leading him on. That's the right thing to do."

"But Tommy's a nice guy." She looked up. "You want him?"

"I don't take leftovers."

Cheryl reached over and grabbed the second page of the fake test, letting the thoughts of revenge swallow her guilt. "What do you think would be a good answer to number fifteen: 'Name two provinces of Canada'?"

Pam bit her lip. "How about California and New York?"

"Jake's not that dumb." Cheryl scribbled on the page. "Vancouver and Winnipeg ought to work. If he was listening at all, they'll sound familiar." She glanced at Pam's test from the previous year. "For the last question, 'Name the woman who was empress of India in 1876.' "

"The queen of Sheba."

"Perfect."

The phone rang. "Hey, gorgeous."

Her heart flipped. "I'm busy, Jake."

Pam made a cutting motion across her throat.

"Just checking on the test."

"I'm working on it."

"Working on Tommy, you mean."

"Working real hard." *You sickening, sleazy, disgusting. . .* "Gotta go now, Jake. Duty calls." Cheryl hung up, and Pam threw a wad of paper at her.

"You're wicked."

Cheryl forced a smile. "Only when provoked."

There was a tap on the bedroom door. "Cheryl?"

Pam and Cheryl looked at each other. It was Julie.

They sat Julie on the bed and stood before her.

"What's going on?" she asked.

"We need to talk to you."

"And I need to talk to you, but why am I sitting here alone? It's like you're ganging up on me."

"We are. We're ganging up on you to save you."

"From yourself."

Julie traced the stitching on the bedspread. "Why do you say that?"

"We know about you and Jake."

Julie's face was a billboard of her guilt. "I have sinned" could be read between her chin and eyes. "How—?"

"It doesn't matter how. The point is, he's bad news."

She looked up at Cheryl. "But *you* like him."

"I did." *Before I saw his true nature.*

"So I'm not good enough for him?"

"You're too good."

She bit her lower lip. "But he's so popular. . .and. . .and I'm not."

"Popular is not the same as good."

Julie's eyes moved between them. "Do you two know something I don't?"

Cheryl hesitated. Oh, to be innocent like Julie again. But to do that she'd have to go back a long, long time. "Jake shouldn't have asked you to take the test."

She swallowed hard. "How did you know about that?"

"He asked me, too."

"But why—?"

"Two patsies are better than one."

Pam sat beside her. "You can't do it, Julie."

"I know."

"You know?"

Her jaw lifted. "I'm not as naïve as you think. I saw Jake yesterday. I went over to his house to ask him to. . ." She looked at the carpet. Her toe made a figure eight. "After the party, when I saw he wasn't with Andrea anymore, and you said you two were just friends. . ." She shook her head at her own stupidity. "Sometimes more than anything, I want to belong. I want to walk down the halls at school with a boy's arm around my shoulders and laugh at his jokes and have him sneak a kiss at our lockers." A tear slid down her cheek, but she didn't do anything to stop it. "Jake has been the only boy who's shown any interest in me."

"He'll use you."

She shrugged as if that was okay. "When I went over to his house yesterday, I'd decided that could be enough. To be used by a handsome, popular guy like Jake was better than being alone."

Cheryl remembered her conversation with Leon. "Remember that bum we picked up on the highway?"

"Leon?"

"I had lunch with him the other day and—"

"You had lunch with him?"

She waved Pam's question away. "He said something about being alone. He said I should find somebody to love me. Someone who cares whether I'm around or not."

"That's what we all want."

Julie's tears started afresh. "I want to feel special. Feel as if I belong. It seems like everyone in the whole world has a boyfriend. And they're doing. . .you know. . ."

Cheryl sat on Julie's other side. "Leon said something else: 'Don't cooperate with the world.' "

They sat in silence a moment, taking it in.

"Smart bum."

Julie blew her nose. "You do what the world says, Cheryl. You have sex all the time. Don't you think it's wrong?"

Cheryl escaped to the anonymity of the window. "I don't have the background people like you have, Julie. The church stuff. The parents who've been married a thousand years."

"But you know it's wrong anyway, don't you?"

She faced them. "It's right for me."

"Liar."

Cheryl was shocked by the conviction in Julie's voice. Julie joined her at the window. "You know what you're doing isn't right. You don't need family and church to tell you that. You know it in your gut. So don't blame your lack of those things for your actions. You play life with the cards you're dealt. You had choices to make, Cheryl. You still have choices."

"Is that why you slept with Jake yesterday?"

Julie took a step back. "That's why I did *not* sleep with Jake yesterday."

"You didn't sleep with him?"

Julie aligned Cheryl's ballerina jewelry box with the edge of the dresser. "I. . .I went over there with every intention of . . .But then he asked for the test and everything became clear. It's like moments, both past and possible, flashed before me. And I knew—I knew—the whole thing was bad news." She shook her head, her hair rasping against her shoulders. "I've been so stupid." She looked up, her face determined. "But there *is* someone out there for me. Someone God has chosen just for *me.* And Jake is not him. I will always regret going after him, but I know I'm forgiven, and I'll not make the same mistake again."

To be forgiven. . .how wonderful that would feel. "How do you know you're forgiven?"

"Jesus."

The answer had come from Pam, not Julie.

Julie went back to the bed. "Pam, you believe, too?"

Pam shrugged. "Sure. I'm not the heathen you think I am. Not quite."

Cheryl put her hands on her hips. "So I'm the only heathen here?"

Pam and Julie looked at each other and laughed. "Apparently."

Although it seemed ridiculous, Cheryl felt left out. "Two against one. Not fair."

"Then join us."

Suddenly, there was a gulf between them. A chasm between Cheryl and her friends sitting on the bed. They had something she didn't. But how could she have what they had? She had done so many things wrong.

When Julie stood to move toward her, Cheryl feared her friend might fall into the abyss. Yet Julie walked across the floor without incident. She unhooked her necklace. Cheryl knew what it was. Julie never took it off. Julie took Cheryl's hand and dropped the cross necklace inside. She closed Cheryl's hand over it.

"God forgives you, Cheryl. All you have to do is say you're sorry and ask for forgiveness. You can start over. Do things differently. We don't hold your past against you. We love you. So does He."

Cheryl fell into her arms. She felt safe. And cleansed.

Julie looked at the test. "We can't give this to Jake."

"Why not?"

"It would affect too much. He'd flunk. He'd get kicked off the team. It might prevent him from going to college." She set the test on the bed.

"Cheryl needs revenge."

Cheryl flashed Pam a dirty look. She didn't want Julie to know about the rape. She was starting over. She wanted to feel good about things.

"What are you talking about?"

"Jake raped her."

Julie's eyes widened. "Are you all right?"

"I'm fine. Pam had no right—"

"I had every right. We're friends. We care about you."

"Have you called the police?"

"No! No police."

"But you should. Rape is a crime. You need to turn him—"

"No." Cheryl grabbed the test off the bed, needing something to hold. "They won't be able to do anything anyway."

"Why not?"

She looked at them straight on. "Because of my reputation."

Julie stared at the air, then looked to Cheryl. "He doesn't have the right to force you. No one does."

"Julie's right. This is 1973. Women have rights. We can say no—to anyone."

Cheryl began to pace. "Just drop it. I never want to think of it again."

"But you will."

I will.

Pam turned to Julie. "That's why Cheryl wants to get back at him. And the test is the best way."

"You're lowering yourself to his level."

Pam raised a fist in the air. "Revenge is sweet, saith the Lord!"

"He never said that."

Pam shrugged. "It sounds good."

"We're supposed to forgive our enemies."

"Sounds like a raw deal."

"Not really. Revenge eats us up. Forgiveness gives us peace. Isn't that right, Cheryl? After you asked for forgiveness, didn't you feel peace?"

"Yeah, but that's because I was *getting* it. It's different *giving* it."

Julie shook her head adamantly. "No, it isn't. In fact, it's better, because it takes more effort. It's the challenge to do the right thing—even though it's hard."

Cheryl snickered. "Hard ain't the word."

Julie took the test away from her. She tore the sheets in two, then four.

"Hey!"

She put them in the wastebasket. "You won't give Jake the bogus test."

"Then what do we do?"

"You won't give him any test at all."

"But we made a deal."

"A devil's deal. Bad for bad. There's no need to follow through with it. In fact, it's your responsibility to stop it before it goes any further."

"So what are we going to tell him?"

"No."

Cheryl waved her hands. "It won't be that easy. He will be mad."

"And do what?"

" 'If God is for us, who can be against us?' " Pam said.

"Jake Carlisle for one."

Julie smiled as if she knew a wonderful secret. "We've got to do the right thing. Things will work out perfectly. I know they will."

Perfect was in the eye of the beholder.

When Phoebe got out of the elevator the Monday after the Christmas party, she walked with a new bounce to her step. Peter Greenfield and God. What an evening.

But her happy mood did not spring entirely from pure motives. She had come to work hoping that Colin would make some comment about seeing her at the party. Her chance came right before noon.

She happened to be in Colin's office when Peter came to pick her up for lunch. She waved at him through the glass and held up a finger. Returning to her discussion with Colin, she noticed him staring at her date. His jaw tightened.

Phoebe cleared her throat. He looked up. "Have you ever met Peter?"

"He looks familiar. Where did you meet him?"

"At the Christmas party."

"I don't remember seeing him."

"You were busy."

"What's his name?"

"Peter. Peter Greenfield." Phoebe held back a smile.

It only took him a moment. "Greenfield? He's Greenfield's son? You're going out with a Greenfield?"

"Yes on all accounts." *Now* she smiled.

Colin closed his mouth. "So. . .I get it. I see you found a better offer. Sleeping with the boss's son certainly can't hurt."

Phoebe ignored him. His comments solidified her previous decision. "He's here to pick me up for lunch. Would it be all right if we went over the rest of these figures later?"

Colin's eyes did not leave Peter. "Sure. Go on. Have a nice lunch. But, Phoebe?"

"Yes?"

"Don't slip off *your* stepping-stone. It's easy to drown."

Her thoughts exactly.

Midafternoon, Phoebe knocked on the door to Colin's office.

He was on the phone but put a hand over the receiver. "What's up?"

She placed the Atchison report in front of him. "On the second page it looks as if a figure might be—"

He flipped her away. "That's the final draft. I'm not putting another minute into it—it's taken far too long already. Type it up and be done with it."

"But I think there's an error with your number. Shouldn't it be sixteen million? You have one-point-six."

Colin glanced quickly at the figures but was drawn back to the phone. "Hey, Jason. . .right. . .Tahoe is all set for next weekend. . .you'd never believe her. I mean, she's incredible." He glanced at Phoebe, cradling the phone. "Do whatever you have to, Phoebe."

He went back to his call, and she went back to her desk. A weekend in Tahoe with a woman. It certainly didn't take him many days to get over her rejection.

She reinserted the merger report in the typewriter and stared at the numbers. Colin's words echoed: *Do what you have to, Phoebe.*

She pulled the paper from the typewriter and set it aside.

Addie Whitney's pipes were fixed; the church's roof leaks were history. It was Sunday. A day to give thanks.

Leon sat in the back row. He hadn't been to church since he'd squirmed his way through two services every Sunday sitting next to his grammy.

He noticed there was a squirmer one row up. It was Marco sitting next to his mama. Lucky for Marco, she was listening hard to Pastor Hazen and didn't notice. Leon wished he'd had it so easy. His own mama and grammy had surrounded him every Sunday, peppering him with pinches and jabs to make him sit still "as became the house of the Lord."

Church was a woman thing. Though men did the talking up front, it seemed to Leon women were the ones who listened the hardest. They'd nod their heads like they understood. Men nodded their heads, too, but only because they were asleep. Leon's father had never gone to church with them. He couldn't remember why exactly. Maybe he hadn't wanted to, or maybe it had been because he was gone a lot on weekends. Not working. Just gone—Leon never knew where. Mama, Grammy, and Leon's little sister went every Sunday, and Leon went with them, acting like the man of the family. He wished they would've let him sleep like the other men.

He had to admit Roosevelt gave a mighty sermon. Not that he listened too hard, but what Leon did let in was kind of interesting. Roosevelt wasn't a scream-at-you preacher, scaring you into following the straight and narrow. His style was like him; quiet and soothing; talking about love and being nice and believing in God, no matter what.

Leon had come to his own sort of believing since God had made the cross glow and nudged him to do the right thing. Leon hadn't told anybody about that miracle, and he didn't plan to. Only Marco knew, and his knowing was enough. He'd had trouble sleeping the night before thinking about the money he could've had. But they were the regrets of an honest man.

Leon's mind wandered. He looked around the church. The ladies' colored hats were like flowers, bobbing and dancing in a field of angel white. People sat in groups, shoulders touching family with spaces in between. Nobody had taken off their coats. He could hear the furnace chunk and spur as it tried, but failed, to take away the chill of the morning. The ceiling showed brown marks where wet had been and left. A lot to do.

The offering hymn started, the piano missing a note as Sarah played.

Beneath the cross of Jesus
I fain would take my stand.
The shadow of a mighty Rock
Within a weary land;
A home within the wilderness
A rest upon the way,
From the burning of the noontide heat,
And the burden of the day.

When the offering dish got to Marco's row, it slowed a bit.

Leon leaned forward and saw the boy snatch a handful of change and push it in his pocket. His mama was singing hard, her head back and her eyes closed. She hadn't seen a thing.

Leon thought of grabbing him and whispering a threat of kiddie-jail in his ear, but he didn't. Shoot, he'd stolen plenty in his lifetime. So he waited, boring his eyes into the back of Marco's head until he looked around and *knew* that Leon had seen.

After the service, Leon corralled Marco at the back of the church before he could run outside. "Put it back."

Marco's eyes got bigger than usual.

"Put the money back. I saw you take it."

His chin got hard, then crumpled. "I'm sorry. You can have it. I didn't mean it." He fished into his pocket. Out came ninety-three cents.

"Don't give it to me. Go put it there." Leon pointed to the dish on the altar.

"Way up there?" Marco looked at the dish like it was miles away.

Leon touched his back. "Go on."

Marco held back, like he was giving himself one last chance to change his mind. Then he trudged down the aisle, his feet dragging. People standing nearby moved out of the way when the serious little boy walked by. By the time Marco got to the altar, he had everybody's eyes.

Sarah came over to Leon. "What's going on?"

"Penance."

Marco lifted his hand above the collection dish and opened it, letting the ninety-three cents fall with a rattle.

When he turned around and saw everybody looking, he winced like he was waiting to be yelled at. He did not expect them to clap.

He ran to Leon and wrapped his arms around his waist. "Did the cross glow?"

Leon stroked his head. "You bet it did."

At the evening church service, Leon was in his usual place—it was kind of nice to have a usual place. This time, Marco sat next to him. His mama was singing with the choir, so Leon had offered to watch the boy.

The Sunday evening service was different from the one in the morning. With the morning came the sermon, with the evening came a bevy of songs.

Sarah was the choir director. She'd even asked Leon to join, but he had declined seeing as how he had the voice of a frog needing cold medicine. He liked listening to her sing. She had a thick alto that filled the room like a warm quilt on a rainy day.

Other than a few readings of Scripture, the service was hers. Sarah never stood still. She walked in and out of the rows, urging people to join in; teasing, getting them to sing louder. "Put your hearts into it! Wake up the Lord, Mr. Stevens, and it'll wake you up, too!"

During every song, Sarah brought the people to their feet where they sang, clapped, and swayed to the music of their souls.

Though Leon kept his frog to myself, he did his share of clapping. Marco joined in, too, singing the songs he knew from memory and clapping to the rest.

During the Scripture reading, Leon felt Marco looking at him instead of listening to Roosevelt, up front. He leaned over and whispered, "My face green?"

Marco shook his head. "You love her, don't you?"

Leon's mouth went dry.

"You love Miss Sarah, don't you?"

Leon poked his finger into the boy's thigh and then pointed toward the reverend. "Pay attention."

Marco did as he was told.

CHAPTER 17

The Lord *appeared to us in the past, saying:*
"I have loved you with an everlasting love;
I have drawn you with loving-kindness."

Jeremiah 31:3

Julie and Pam had slept over, waiting for Jake's phone call, waiting for him to ask for the test. The call never came—which didn't help the state of their stomachs. Midafternoon, the next day, her friends went home. Life must go on.

Waiting alone only made things worse.

Fact #1: Jake needed the test. That need would not go away.

Fact #2: Though it would have made things simpler, she couldn't bring herself to call him. One did not hand the executioner the pistol.

Although Cheryl usually avoided her parents' company, after dinner she felt the need to have friendly bodies nearby. Ralph was stretched out on the recliner, his bifocals balanced on his nose so he could look past his feet to watch *Baretta.* Cheryl's mother looked through recipe books.

Cheryl sat on the couch with a pillow clutched to her chest, watching cop cars and bad guys flash before her eyes. When the phone rang, she jerked the air out of both the pillow and her lungs.

Her mother answered it. "Hello, Jake. How nice of. . . why yes, she's sitting right here. She rarely sits with us, so this is rather. . .well, all right." She covered the receiver. "Cheryl, it's for—"

Cheryl grabbed the phone away, making a line appear between her mother's eyes. She prayed for a tornado, an earthquake, a tsunami to intervene. "Hello?"

"Did you get the test?"

The question of the year.

"Cheryl?"

"No."

"No?"

She considered saying something righteous, like she couldn't do that to poor Tommy. Mention how she wasn't as low as some people; she didn't use people up and then throw them out with the trash. But she couldn't say any of that. She was as low, and she did use, and she did throw. At least she had in the past.

"I couldn't get it." She smiled, trying to ease her mother's frown. She wished she were alone, but if she moved to the extension, there was a chance her mother would listen in.

"Tommy wouldn't fall for your charms?"

She wanted to tell Jake that Tommy would have begged for her charms, but she hadn't given him the chance. She couldn't say such a thing with her mother's antennae fully extended.

"I don't need you, you know. I have other ways to get the test."

"Julie won't give it to you either."

There was silence on the line.

"Oh, I get it now. The two wannabes have banded together, trying to make themselves feel important."

"Actually, the two *don't*-wannabes have banded together knowing that the never-bes like you have to be stopped." She smiled at her mother's puzzled look.

"But I won't be stopped. You know that, don't you? We had a deal."

"Which is now officially null and void."

"I gave you Andrea's dignity."

"And took mine in the process."

"What are you talking about?"

"The other day."

A pause. "What about it?"

"No is no, Jake."

"Oh please. . ."

"The answer's no, Jake. On all accounts."

Jake shared three new cuss words, or actually two new words and one Cheryl had heard before but had forgotten until that moment.

"I knew you'd bug out on me. I'll pass without your help."

"Don't get too cocky, Jake."

"I'll do what I please, traitor."

"I'm sure you will."

Cheryl hung up and fled from the family room before her mother could ask too many questions.

"Ralph! Cheryl!"

Cheryl followed her mother's voice. She and her stepfather reached the front door at the same time. Together, they went outside where her mother was in the process of putting out the garbage for the morning pickup. Her mother pointed at the house.

WHORE. Illuminated by the porch light, the blood red spray paint slashed across the white siding.

"Who would do this?" Ralph turned to Cheryl. "What do you know about this?"

Although it was the logical conclusion to think that the whore-word was related to his stepdaughter, the deduction hurt.

"I am a whore. Didn't you know that, Daddy-dear?"

The slap was unexpected. Especially since it came from her mother.

Cheryl ran. Away from her mother. Away from the word on the wall. Away from the truth.

Cheryl stopped in the middle of the street and stared. She couldn't believe what she was seeing.

"No!"

She ran up the sidewalk to Julie's house where the same

word shouted to the world. *How dare he? I deserved it, but Julie—*

Julie came out the front door carrying a bucket and a brush. She waved a yellow-gloved hand. "Welcome to Jake's wrath. Did you get the same treatment?"

"Yes, but—" Cheryl tried to catch her breath. "Aren't you furious?"

Julie shrugged. "There are always consequences. Even to doing the right thing."

Cheryl fell onto the porch swing, making it gyrate wildly. "What did your parents say?"

Julie dipped the brush in the water and held it there a moment. She did not look up. "That was the hard part. I had to tell them."

"Tell them what?"

She started scrubbing the wall. The soap and water had no effect on the paint. "I told them how I practically threw myself at Jake. And about the test."

"You don't deserve this."

Julie put her entire weight against the brush, a certain frenzy suddenly fueling her motions. It still did nothing. "Consequences, Cheryl. Like I said, there are always consequen—"

"Is it working, honey?" Mrs. Norman popped her head outside. "Oh, hello, Cheryl." She nodded toward the graffiti. "There are nasty people in the world, aren't there?"

"Yes, ma'am."

She took the brush from her daughter and tried a few strokes. She set it in the bucket and sighed. "So much for that. I think we've got some leftover paint in the garage. I'll take care of this."

"No, Mom. I'll do it."

"I'll help, Mrs. Norman. And we'll call Pam."

Mrs. Norman nodded. Then she took Julie's hands and peered into her eyes. "The house can be made fresh again, honey. Everyone who matters knows that word is a lie. You were tempted, but you made the right choice. I'm very, very proud of you."

Julie nodded and Cheryl saw tears in her eyes.

She had a few of her own.

Cheryl dipped the brush in the paint can, then pulled it across the graffiti. "How can your mom be so nice, so supportive?"

Julie shrugged. "What did your mother say?"

"She slapped me."

Pam made a face. "Whoa. That's harsh."

"But she didn't really think you were—?"

"Face it, Julie, in my case, the graffiti wasn't that far off. If I confessed all my sins to my mother and Ted, we'd all die of old age."

"Ted? Who's Ted?"

Cheryl stopped painting. Her stepfather's name was Ralph. Where did the name Ted come from? Odd.

Julie smoothed the edges of her brush stroke. "Like my mom said, everything is fresh and new now. You and I both need to start over."

Pam wiped a drip. "Jake won't stop with this, you know. He'll say stuff, spread rumors. . ."

Julie froze, paintbrush in hand. "I never thought of that.

The whole school will know what a fool I was."

"A fool for love."

"No love involved. Just a fool."

Cheryl raised her brush. "Make that two fools."

Pam raised hers, too. "Might as well make it three. I do hate to be left out."

"Then three it—"

Cheryl saw a flash. Her eyes were drawn to the porch light. The glow wavered and pulsed like the hypnotic pin-wheel in a B-movie. When she looked at Julie, the afterglow created a halo around her head.

Julie? She looks so young.

"Cheryl? Are you all right?"

Cheryl turned toward the voice. "Pam! Where did you come from?"

"Well, the mama bird gets with the papa bird. . .paint fumes affecting your brain, Cher?"

Then she knew. Like a revelation from heaven, Cheryl knew who she was. Where she was. When she was.

She walked to the edge of the porch and looked over the neighborhood—her childhood neighborhood. Were the trees really this tiny while she was in high school? The cars parked in the driveways were boats. They made her Lexus back home look like a toy.

Home. Cheryl tossed the paintbrush onto the grass and put her hands to her face, trying to rub away the flood of images that were colliding. Her hands. They were soft and supple—but strong. Their talent was yet to be realized in the operating room.

"Cheryl? What's wrong?"

She heard the concern of her friends, but did not react. Not yet.

She looked to the moon. Could this be the same moon that watched over her in the future? The moon that left an angled slice of light across her bed every night? That lit the way for two deer as they strolled in front of her cabin?

With a jolt, she remembered that this clarity of both times—this Dual Consciousness—meant it was time to make a choice to stay in 1973 or go back to her life in the future.

A quick thought became a decision. "I want to go back."

"Go back where?"

Cheryl turned to see her best friends staring at her as if she were an alien in their beloved *Creature Feature.* She sank to the step as a sudden fear chilled her from within. It was a fear born from the awesome weight of seeing both lives—the way it was and the way it could have been.

She was so close to home, her high school home. Her mother was currently on husband number four. Ralph would last six more years before succumbing to cancer. Then would come Gerald, and finally, Ted. Six fathers, yet not a daddy in the bunch.

A cloud slid in front of the moon. This wasn't right. Knowing both times was too much knowledge. Cheryl closed her eyes, remembering her sins. What kind of person had she been during this second chance? Manipulative, obsessive, selfish. Variations of these traits had stayed with her in the future.

But Jake had been the catalyst that had changed her vices from tolerable to excessive. They were too much alike. Two wills without a conscience.

Julie sat beside her and put an arm around her shoulders. She didn't say anything, probably thinking that Cheryl needed silent time to work through Jake's graffiti revenge. If she only knew how complicated things had just become.

Julie was her conscience. Julie, who had shared her faith in a time of crisis. How special that had been. Cheryl had witnessed Julie's faith their entire lives. But there had never been a time—before this time in the past—where she had shared it so openly. Because of it, the young Cheryl Nickolby had changed. And thanks to the Time Lottery, the older—and now wiser—Dr. Nickolby had also changed.

She had come to the past to find a companion. She had failed. And yet. . .she *had* found a companion, more loyal, more loving, more compassionate than any man could ever be. She had found Jesus.

Pam moved in front of her and kicked her toe. "You're acting wacky on us, friend. Let's go inside and pig out on popcorn and Oreos. That will get you right again."

Cheryl laughed. Some things never changed.

But she didn't have time for eating. They'd told her the Dual Consciousness wouldn't last long. It would fade and the thoughts she had in this life—in this timeline—would take over.

Pam held out her hand, offering to pull Cheryl to standing. "Inside, O weird one."

Cheryl let herself be pulled up. But she didn't want to go inside and eat or watch *Creature Feature.* She didn't even want to talk with these old friends anymore. These same friends—in their older versions—were waiting for her in the future. She liked the fact the three of them had such a long history. It wasn't necessary to live that history anymore.

Cheryl wanted to be a doctor again. She wanted her cushy bed with the faded pink quilt back in Boulder. She wanted the sleep mask.

It was time to go back—forward—into her rightful time. But first, she had to say good-bye. She pulled Pam into her arms. "I love you, Pam."

Pam resisted. "Now you're really acting wacko."

Cheryl looked into her friend's eyes. "You are going to be the neatest lady. You're going to conquer the business world. Or at least New Jersey."

"New Jersey? Give me a break."

Cheryl turned to Julie. Just a month ago—in the future—she had seen these same eyes during Christmas, framed by fine lines, but still full of a special innocence that remained in spite of the passage of years. "And you, my dear Julie, are going to be such a mother. Have you ever considered writing children's books?"

Julie blinked. "Well, actually, I've been working on—"

"It's about a panda, isn't it?"

"How did you know?"

Cheryl hugged her fiercely. *"Panda's Progress* will be a huge success."

Julie pulled away to look at Cheryl's eyes. *"Panda's Progress?"* Her face lit up. "I like that title."

"You should."

Pam put her hands on her hips. "Okay. What's going on? Who declared it to be Cheryl's crystal ball night?"

Cheryl realized she'd said enough. "I have to go home."

"What about our sleepover?"

"Another time."

"But we were going to paint your house next."

"Don't worry about it. Jake's graffiti means nothing." *And it will be gone very, very soon.*

She walked down the steps, turning to look one last time at her friends. "I love you both. See you soon."

She ran down the street toward her childhood house. She felt the need to see it one more time. For what more appropriate place could she spend her last moments of childhood?

Cheryl's mother turned out the porch light, hiding the graffiti. Morning would declare her sin soon enough. Cheryl saw something on the floor of the porch, near the door. She picked it up. It was a pencil. A #2 pencil. It was broken in half. Another of Jake's calling cards. *You're right, Jake. There will be no more dropped pencils for either of us.*

Cheryl sat sideways on the top step, looking back at her home with the avocado refrigerator and the gold shag carpet. Her room with the *new* pink quilt and the poster of the Monkees above her bed. Her 8-track tape player that would soon be obsolete. The seventies. The age of polyester knit and clunky shoes. Watergate trials, two Germanys, and the end of the Vietnam war.

She didn't want to live her life over again. Once was enough. Her life wasn't perfect in the future, but it was of her own making. Good and bad.

She had lived her years free and easy. No commitment. Lots of men. How wrong it all seemed now. How fruitless.

She had always thought that being aggressive was proof she was in control. It was exactly the opposite. By forcing a physical connection with men, she had lost the control that comes with a slow and easy, calm and measured path to knowing one person better than oneself.

By forcing control, Cheryl knew no one. Not even herself. Commitment was not possession and obsession; it was something more. . .something she had not yet experienced—perhaps never *would* experience.

Her hand strayed to the cross necklace Julie had given her. The cross. The symbol of her new faith. How would her life have been different if God had been a part of it the first time around? She would never know.

It was time.

Should I do something? Say something?

She laughed when the answer came to her. She closed her eyes. She bowed her head. She prayed, thanking God for friends, past and future. She asked Him to watch over them after she'd gone. And she thanked Him for second chances.

Then Cheryl focused her thoughts on the future and went home.

Phoebe pushed the intercom button. "Colin? Mr. Hopner and Mr. Greenfield have been calling for us. They're waiting in the west conference room."

"I know, I know! I'll be there in a minute."

She watched as Colin tried to scrape together the papers on his desk. It was pitiful. It was his D-Day, and he didn't even know it. Only Phoebe knew.

If he ever got to the meeting at all. . . She finally showed mercy and helped him collect the papers and the charts he needed. He rushed out the door; she after him.

The meeting had already started by the time they got there. Colin burst through the door, dropping his charts at the feet of Mr. Hopner. Matt Rogers helped pick them up. Colin's face was flushed, his tie askew.

Mr. Hopner waited until they had taken a seat at the long table. Phoebe got out her notepad and proceeded to fade into the background.

Mr. Hopner acknowledged her presence with a nod. Then, "Mr. Thurgood. Nice of you to join us."

Colin straightened his tie and fingered his diamond stud. "Sorry we're late, sir. I was getting these charts together."

"We've already seen your charts." The others chuckled softly. "Mr. Thurgood, why don't you distribute the report and lead us through it."

"Certainly." Colin regained his composure and handed out the reports without further incident. He stood at his place. He looked so handsome in his crisp white shirt, red tie, and double-breasted jacket. Phoebe actually crossed her fingers, knowing it would do as much good as his lucky tie tack.

"If you'll turn to page two, I would like to point out the earnings of Atchison Industries for the last three fiscal years has averaged over sixteen million dollars. With that kind of sales, we can—"

Mr. Greenfield raised a finger. "Excuse me, Mr. Thurgood. You say the sales of Atchison Industries averaged sixteen million? Your report says one-point-six million. Which number is correct?"

Colin's face pulled convulsively. He glanced in Phoebe's direction, his eyes widening. Phoebe looked at the table. He scanned page two of the report, putting a finger on the number. He cleared his throat. "I see there has been a typographical error in the report. The correct figure is sixteen million."

Phoebe cringed at his excuse. When his next words entered the room, she nearly gasped.

"I wish to apologize for my secretary." He spoke as if she were not seated next to him. "She obviously made an error when she typed the original."

Before Phoebe could jump to her own defense, Matt spoke, his voice confident. "But, Colin, there seems to be another error on page fourteen. You state that the *gross* profit of Atchison Industries is two-point-five percent. If that's so, we should have nothing to do with such a company."

Colin fumbled to the page in question. There it was again, another mistake. Phoebe knew he had meant to say "net" profit. . . . He shook his head and shrugged. "I must apologize again for the typo. Atchison Industries' average *net* profit—after taxes—for those three fiscal years was two-point-five percent as the report indicates. If you check the math on my figures, you will see—"

Mr. Hopner stood, stealing a look in Phoebe's direction. "Mr. Thurgood, perhaps you do not understand the purpose of these meetings. At this point in our negotiations we expect *you* to have done your math so you're able to give us the necessary statistics in order to make a sound business decision. Surely you understand that?"

Colin fiddled with his tie. "Of course I do, sir. But I don't always have time to check Miss Winston's typing. I just assumed she had proofread the reports before she had them printed. I can hardly be held accountable for her mistakes."

Phoebe found herself mouthing silent words of defense. Her hands gripped the arms of the chair, and her head jerked in tiny negative movements. She had never expected this.

Mr. Greenfield came to her rescue. "Miss Winston, do you still have the final draft copy of Mr. Thurgood's report?"

She nodded mutely, not trusting her voice.

He smiled a fatherly smile. "Will you please get it for us? We'll wait."

Phoebe hurried back to her desk to retrieve the original. This was it. She would be vindicated, and Colin would be damned. She was exhilarated and shamed at the same time.

She knocked quietly before letting herself back into the conference room. From the carefree looks on everyone's faces—except Colin's—you would have thought a celebration was in progress. Cups of coffee had been added. But there was no coffee in front of Colin. The space was bare except for his copy of the report. The pages were closed, and his hands were clasped tightly on top of them, the knuckles white.

Mr. Greenfield rose and escorted her back to her chair. "You have heard the accusations made by Mr. Thurgood regarding your typing proficiency. Do you have any words to say in your defense?" He was the essence of courtesy.

Phoebe drew upon every ounce of control, feeling as if she were scraping the innermost layer of her being. She lifted her chin slightly. "Yes, I do. The report I typed was exactly as it appeared in the final draft copy."

"She's lying!" Colin said.

"May I take a look at the draft, please?" Mr. Greenfield asked.

"Certainly." She handed it to him.

Colin's head drooped like a candle in the sun. He stared at his hands.

After leafing through the draft, Mr. Greenfield handed it to Mr. Hopner. He, in turn, quickly checked the two pages. They nodded to each other in agreement. Mr. Greenfield rose to his feet.

"Mr. Thurgood. We at Hopner, Wagner, and Greenfield find it deplorable that you have attempted to tarnish the good name of your secretary, Miss Winston, in order to cover your own incompetence. Your draft copy of the Atchison report—in your own writing—has the errors that we discovered on pages two and fourteen. Miss Winston typed the information you had given her. You were the one who processed the information, and you were the one who transferred the numbers into the report. It is therefore your error, and yours alone, that confronts us this afternoon."

He began to pace at the head of the table, buttoning his suit coat with a steady hand. "Mind you, we all make mistakes—some of them minor and some. . . However, one thing we will not condone at Hopner, Wagner, and Greenfield is cowardice, Mr. Thurgood, cowardice and downright deceit. Every desk in this office should have a plaque that says, 'The buck stops here.' When an error is made, it is the obligation and duty of the guilty party to admit and take full responsibility for its consequences. That is the honorable way. That is *our* way, Mr. Thurgood." He paused and looked at each face around the table. "We've given you multiple chances. But now, I am afraid your services are no longer needed at our company."

Colin burst out of his chair. "But that's not fair. I can explain—"

Mr. Greenfield turned and walked from the room. The rest of the employees followed, with Mr. Hopner giving Phoebe her own personal escort. Colin was left alone.

As she looked back, Phoebe saw him sink into his chair. His face crumbled and fell into his hands. She felt sorry for him.

Yet also triumphant.

Phoebe stared into Colin's darkened office. She struggled with blaming herself, yet she knew that kind of thinking was absurd. Colin had killed his own career. She had merely watched. It was not a pleasant memory.

And knowing Colin, he would charm his way into another corporation and would sit with his shoes on some other desk. Suddenly a different image of Colin with his feet up formed in her mind. But the office was different. Gone were the orange vinyl chairs and the view of downtown. In their place were maroon leather, mahogany, and a view of the Transamerica Pyramid.

Transamerica Pyramid? What's that?

A mental image took shape, that of a skyscraper with a pyramidal top. . . .

Phoebe walked to Colin's office and flipped on the light, needing to reinforce that it was as she had left it.

It was.

She sighed. Her mind was playing tricks on her. The morning had been long and hard. So hard, the company had given her the afternoon off.

She walked to the elevator and forced her thoughts back to Colin. Had he learned a lesson from his blunder? Phoebe hoped so, but doubted that hope. Most likely he was merely upset that he'd gotten caught. She did not worry for his career. She worried for his character. What would it take to blast through his arrogance?

She punched the down button. It was none of her business. Not anymore.

Peter was her focus right now. Through Peter's eyes she was seeing a better world where people cared and laughed and made plans that benefited others as well as themselves. Through Peter's eyes she was beginning to see God.

God had never been important to her. When Peter had made her take her Bible off the shelf, it was the first time she had opened it since receiving it as a present for her confirmation. God was for old people. God was for weak people. God was for people who had nothing better to do than sit and ponder the universe. She was too young, independent, and busy for God.

The way Peter talked so openly about his faith. . .it made Phoebe yearn to know his God as much as it made her yearn to know him. She found herself desperately wanting to be a part of what he had. Of what he was.

Phoebe exited the building and grabbed a newspaper from a stand. On the front page was a picture of Peter and a story about a new school he had designed. He hadn't told her he was going to be in the paper. But that was like him. Humble.

She had an idea. Instead of heading to the bus stop, Phoebe stopped in front of a cable car stop. She wasn't going home right away. She had a mission: to buy Peter a Christmas gift that would show him just how special he was to her.

The bell of the cable car announced its arrival. It was full of shoppers, and Phoebe had to stand on the outside, holding onto the railing. She liked the feel of the wind against her face. She liked looking to the tops of the buildings as they filed past. She liked the give and sway as the cable car climbed up a hill and then rushed—

Phoebe saw a flash. She sucked in a breath. She blinked, trying to focus. The bell of the cable car clanged.

Cable car? I haven't been on a cable car in years. Not since I—

Phoebe looked at the traffic. The pedestrians. The lady seated next to her was holding a *Glamour* magazine with Cheryl Tiegs on the cover. Within seconds, her thoughts were purged. She looked at the world with new understanding. She hesitated a moment, concentrating. Each color and sound was vivid and sharp as if combining the process of watching an old movie and actually being there. She put a hand to her temple to try to keep the images in line.

I'm in 1969! But I'm really a middle-aged woman. I'm married. I have two grown children who are nearly the age I am now—or was a moment ago. She looked up. *Hey, I remember that store! I used to buy used furniture there. And that Chinese restaurant had great kung pao. . . .*

Phoebe gawked as her memories collided with her reality. So many sights and sounds that she'd forgotten were now familiar, yet new.

"Miss? Excuse me. Do you have the time?"

Time! Soon the Dual Consciousness would fade and she'd be stuck in the past. She had to make the decision of her life. Now.

She tore her eyes away from the world that encircled her. The cable car slowed, and she stepped down. Her shopping trip was of no importance. *I've got to be alone. I've got to think.*

As if in direct answer to her need, she saw a neighborhood park. She ran toward the solitude of the trees. She ignored the suspicious looks people gave her as she staggered past. She sank beneath an old oak, rubbing her unlined face, trying to calm down. Her thoughts were jumbled. She needed to find a starting point.

"Colin." She said his name out loud. He was at the core of her decision. He was the only person who was a part of her present *and* her future.

But was he?

He had been fired from his job because she had not covered for him.

In seeing both lives, she was amazed how everything had changed with the weight of one decision. The first time through this situation, she had continued covering up for him until his dependence on her had led to marriage. He had offered many apology dinners during that time—and more. She had found an absurd pleasure in taking his increasingly expensive gifts. In truth, she had used him as much as he had used her.

The first time through 1969, she'd slept with him. That had changed everything—at least for her. Although Colin would have had no trouble loving her and leaving her, once she had crossed over the line into sex, she was committed. She suddenly had a horrid thought. Had she married him as a response to her own shame *and* for his money? Had she married him to prove to herself that she wasn't the kind of woman who slept around? It was disconcerting to realize her marriage might have been based on an attempt to recover self-esteem.

Colin was her husband in the future, but here in the past he was. . .what? When she had decided not to cover for him, it had changed everything. He'd lost his job, lost her respect, and lost the possibility of a future together. Because of that, Phoebe knew if she stayed in the past, Colin would not, could not, be a part of her life.

She looked down at the newspaper photo of Peter. Peter and Phoebe were like two colors, blending together to become a third. Comparing the two men. . .there was no comparison. Although Colin was a great provider, he had never given himself to her. Their two had never truly become one. They had never sat and talked about their dreams. He had his dreams and his career, and Phoebe was only necessary as long as she did her part to further his plans. As far as any dreams she might have had? They were never mentioned. Perhaps Colin didn't think she had any.

In all their years together, Colin had given her two things: material possessions and children. One was inconsequential and the other, her life.

Thomas and Suzanne. She began to cry, the tears dropping on the blade of grass she dissected. If she stayed in 1969, she would never see them again. She would never see them graduate, fall in love, get married, and have children.

Grandchildren. . .her grandchildren.

She wouldn't remember them, and yet they would remember her as they lived out their lives in the future. She would be gone to them—it would be as if she were dead. In fact, her body in the future would die. They would mourn her and look at her picture and remember the mother they'd had and wonder how she could have abandoned them. They would be forced to depend on their father for everything. Would Colin be enough for them? Could he be?

But here, in 1969. . .what if Peter and Phoebe got married? She looked down at her young body, ripe for motherhood. To be twenty-two again, starting fresh. She thought of the kind of children she might have with Peter. What could they accomplish with a father like him—a loving, godly man who was kind and generous with his time?

And what about her? Phoebe stared blankly at the trees. What about her?

In the future with Colin, she had every *thing* she could ever want. She had everything except love and satisfaction in herself.

But in 1969? How would things turn out? That was the unknown.

At least that was the type of decision Phoebe was used to making—the type where the future was in question. Knowing the future was the problem. Knowing the future made it harder.

She felt sorry for Colin. In the future he was unhappy—he may not have admitted it, but he was. He was so engrossed in making the deal that he didn't give himself or his family time to enjoy his riches. In 1969, Phoebe had witnessed his lust for power. But this time around, he had been caught and disgraced. Would that cure him of his obsession? Or would he become embittered and turn to even more devious methods?

Another unknown.

Yet by staying in this timeline, she would also be giving Colin another chance. He'd hit bottom. How he came out of it would determine his future. Maybe, if she stayed behind, she could stay in touch with him and help him—not as a wife, but as a friend. Maybe she could lead him toward a life full of success and compassion. It would be interesting to witness.

The count was three votes to stay: herself, Peter, and Colin; and two to go back: Thomas and Suzanne.

All she had to do was continue on with her day, and she would remain where she was. Her knowledge of the future would fade. She could get back on the cable car and go shopping for a Christmas present for Peter. They would have dinner tonight and take a walk by the docks. They would watch the lights of the Golden Gate come on and see the fog settle in. She would snuggle under his arm and they would talk of life and hope and God.

Forgive me, Suzanne. Forgive me, Thomas. I love you, but I've got to stay behind and start over. I hate to leave you, but you're good kids and you're on the threshold of your own lives. I hope you make good decisions, and I'm sorry I'm not going to be around to help you. Take care of yourself and take care of your—

No.

Lord, help me. . .

She stared straight ahead and suddenly knew. She couldn't

do it. She thought of the first verse that Peter had shared with her: *If anyone does not provide for his relatives, and especially for his immediate family, he has denied the faith and is worse than an unbeliever.*

She could not deny her family in order to indulge her own pleasure and happiness. Hadn't her time with Peter made her see that doing the right thing was always the right thing to do? The God thing?

The right thing was to go back. God would be there for her. He would help her through it.

She carefully folded the newspaper with Peter's picture in it and placed it in her purse. Then she walked out of the park and caught the first cable car that came by. This is how she wanted to spend a few last moments in the past. Even though there was an available seat, she hung onto the side. She liked the feel of the wind against her face. She liked looking to the tops of the buildings as they filed past. She liked the give and sway as the cable car climbed up a hill and then. . .

Rushed home.

The day after Marco guessed that Leon loved Sarah, Leon avoided her as much as possible. Pretending he had errands, he returned to Harvey's Bar. It was the only place he was sure they wouldn't be.

He was one confused man.

Leon ordered his second draw and lit up his sixth smoke. The bartender, Milt, scratched at a sticky spot on the counter. "Why am I seeing you here again? I thought you were a traveling man."

"I'm thinking."

"What's her name?"

"Sarah."

"Ah. Miss Hudson. You in love with her?"

Did everyone know? Leon looked to his beer, not finding many answers in the froth disappearing on top. "I think about her all the time."

Milt chuckled. "You sure you ain't just after a romp in the hay?"

Leon raised an eyebrow. "I think it's more than that."

"Then what's the problem?"

"I think she loves somebody else." *And He was put in a manger on Christmas.* "You think so? You *think* so?" His voice got louder as he made fun. "You don't know much, do you? You don't know if you love her, you don't know if you're just after a tumble, and you don't even know if the lady loves somebody else. You're a stitch, Leon." He folded his towel, shaking his head.

Leon hesitated. "It's not a man she loves. Not exactly."

Milt raised an eyebrow. "You're going to have to explain that one."

"She loves Jesus. You know. . .God."

"Yeah, I know God. Even know 'bout Jesus. I can 'Amen, brother' with the best of them. Just don't get 'round to it much." He dunked some glasses in sudsy water. "But just 'cause a woman loves the Lord don't mean she can't love a man."

"It don't?"

" 'Course not. God likes marriage."

Leon hadn't been thinking of marriage.

"You *were* thinking of marrying her, weren't you?"

Leon took a sip of beer. "Sure. Maybe."

Milt rinsed the glasses clean. "Don't go messing with a good woman, hoping to enjoy some fireworks you ain't willing to pay for—and no discounts allowed. God don't take to cheaters. He might snuff out that kind of spark—or make it blow up in your face."

If Leon thought he loved Sarah, he had to do things right. He had to be willing to pay the price. "So, what do I do?"

Milt leaned on the bar. "I ain't no psychoantagonist, Leon. I ain't even very bright, but I do know that you'll never know nothin' if you sit in here. You got to make a move. Find out where you stand."

"How do I do that?"

Milt thwacked Leon's head with the towel. "You go after her—in a nice way, of course. You take her someplace romantic. Show her what's what. Make her do something, say something."

"What if she gets mad?"

"Go on with your life." He poured a draw for another customer. "Take a chance, and maybe I won't have to look at your poutin' mug no more." He laughed and moved to the other end of the bar.

Leon downed the rest of his beer. Then he wandered up the street, his head down to hide his puzzlement. Other than the one try on the ladder and a few words under the clothesline, he'd left Sarah alone. He'd done his share of thinking about her, but like a kid whose innards were just waking up, he hadn't gone through with anything.

Part of it was, Leon didn't feel he was good enough for her—nor that he had much to offer compared to the Father,

Son, and Holy Ghost. Sarah was a lady. She was strong and had ideas of her own. She didn't need no slouch like him—it was the other way around. He needed a lady like her.

And he'd changed. Some. Since sticking around and not running off with Roosevelt's money, people treated him differently. Yesterday, a lady from church had kissed his cheek, telling him how proud she was of him for fixing Addie Whitney's sink.

He wished it had been Sarah kissing his cheek.

She hadn't said much about the other day's events, and he wondered if Roosevelt had told her what Leon had nearly done. Leon had caught her looking at him sideways, like she was trying to catch his thoughts, but she hadn't said a thing, good or bad. Like Milt said, he'd have to do something about that.

Leon pulled his hands out of his pockets and walked faster. He'd get Sarah alone somewhere, somehow. He'd let her know his heart. He'd show her what a flesh and blood man had to offer.

As he reached the edge of town near the church, he felt downright cocky. He would show her the man of her dreams. He'd show her that loving him wouldn't mean she couldn't love Jesus, too. He'd take care of her on earth, and Jesus could have her for all eternity.

If that wasn't a good deal, what was?

All he had to do was do a bit of heavy romancing.

Setting up the romancing of Sarah was no easy matter. For one thing, the Hillside Baptist Church was not exactly his first choice for flirtation. Secondly, the times Leon and Sarah were alone in the church were few. At first, that had been fine. Now, it was a hardship. Leon knew he had to get her away from the church. He didn't want any cross glowing right in the middle of things.

He finally figured it out. His plan mixed two problems to one: getting Sarah alone and spending his money.

Ever since he'd come to work at the church, he'd been bothered by the oak table pretending to be the altar. The top was battered and carved with initials. That was easy enough taken care of with the cloth over it. But the legs couldn't be hidden. It had two legs that matched and two others that were different. Leon could only guess at the whys and the wheres of it. It leaned toward the shorter leg, looking like a mutt you'd shoot out of kindness to end its misery.

Having such a stray in the place of honor did not speak well for the generosity of the congregation. Of course, Leon realized there were more pressing problems tapping into the church funds—the needy furnace, the needy neighbors. . .so he decided he would be the one to replace the altar table. And Sarah was going to help pick it out.

Although he could've used more time thinking about it, Leon had the funny feeling time was running out. Made no sense really. After all, he'd only been staying at the church a few days. Was it time enough to fall in love? It certainly had been time enough to change his life in other ways. From a con man to an ordinary fix-it man; from a man who spent time running from the law to a man who went to church twice on Sundays to hear about the laws of God. From a man who stole other people's money to one who was going to spend his own money on an altar. Yup. He'd had plenty of time for plenty of things to happen.

Today was the day. If Sarah had known how much Leon planned the excursion, she would never have gone with him. She didn't notice that after coming back from Harvey's Bar he spent a half hour cleaning out his truck, or that he packed a picnic complete with a checkered blanket he'd found in the storeroom. It was just as well. She'd find out soon enough what he had in mind.

He invited her to come with him, and miraculously, she said yes. They left at two to visit the furniture store in town, looking at new tables—and used ones. Once Sarah discovered how Leon was spending his money, she had very serious ideas about what kind of table it should be. And the store in Hendersonville didn't have it.

They pulled away from the curb. "Let's drive to Nashville."

"I don't know, Leon. Truth is, I'm getting hungry, and we really should get—"

"We can stop for a snack on the way."

Sarah checked her watch. "I told Roosevelt we wouldn't be gone long."

"We'll stop by and tell him, so he won't worry. We've come this far, we shouldn't stop now."

She didn't argue.

After telling Roosevelt, they drove out of town and Leon's spirits flew with the dust behind them. He tried not to think about the hint of jealousy he'd seen in Roosevelt's eyes. After a few miles, he turned off the highway onto a dirt road. Sarah's spine straightened like a schoolteacher seeing something fishy at the back of the room.

"Where are you going? Nashville is straight ahead."

"I'm hungry."

Her lips got tight, but she kept quiet—until he stopped the truck.

"Where are we? I don't see a place to eat around here."

Leon got out and rummaged behind the seat. "I brought a snack with us." He pulled out the basket of food and the blanket.

She made a face as if she was torn between being pleasured and mad. He led the way down a narrow path to a much trampled place beneath an ash tree. He smoothed the blanket, fixing the corners. "Here we are. Have a seat."

Sarah stood at the edge of the blanket and eyed it like it would jump at her. "When did you plan all this?"

"This morning, in case we couldn't find a table right away. Don't you like it?"

"It surprised me, that's all." She knelt down on the blanket like she was going to pray.

Leon unpacked the food: apples, leftover carrot cake, and a thermos of coffee.

"You thought of everything, didn't you?" She took a napkin.

He leaned back on one elbow and bit into an apple. The hills stretched for miles, dotted with green, gold, and orange. "Pretty here, ain't it?"

Her shoulders relaxed a bit, and she looked around. He could see she agreed with him. The breeze made the branches bow and sway. She buttoned her jacket.

When they were nearly done eating, Leon decided it was

time to make his move. He got up fast. "Oww!" He pretended to hurt his shoulder. "I must have twisted something." He sat back down, acting like it was aching bad.

"Oh, dear. Let me rub it for you." She moved behind him and began kneading his shoulders like bread dough. Then it hit him: *This is just like my vision.* He closed his eyes and moaned with the pleasure of it. She mistook it for a sign of pain.

"Does it hurt bad?"

"Yeah, but it's getting better." Move number two. "It'd be easier if I lie down." He didn't wait for her to say no. He stretched out on his stomach, putting his arms under his head.

She didn't touch him, and he nearly panicked, thinking he'd gone too far. But then her fingers started in again, and he relaxed. Now he knew why rich folks paid somebody to push their muscles around. It was heaven.

He let himself enjoy it for a minute before moving on. Then he reached back and took one of her hands. Without letting go, he rolled over, pulling her close.

She tried to push away, but Leon held her tight against him. With his free hand he cradled the back of her head and pulled her lips toward his. She resisted, whimpering like a hurt puppy. But then the whimpering stopped, and she kissed him back. It was hot and hard and held the promise of more to come.

But there was no more. Sarah pulled away and stood up, smoothing her dress. "What are we doing?"

Leon sat up. "I'm kissing the woman I love."

Her hands stopped smoothing. "Love?"

"I love you, Sarah."

She fingered the buttons of her jacket. "You can't love me."

"Why not?" He wanted to stand, to go close to her, but he didn't.

She took a step away. "I can't love any man."

He stood and pulled her into his arms, but she pushed herself away and looked out over the waving grass.

"That's not fair, Leon. We're talking about two different kinds of love."

He shook his head. "Loving is all that and more."

"Oh, I know," she said, glancing at him. "I truly know. I was married once."

Leon felt his knees buckle.

She walked out of the shade of the tree, lifting her face toward the sun. "It was two years ago. I got married after I was in a family way." She turned to face him. "You see, I've experienced the lust you're after."

It's more than lust. Isn't it? "So where is he?"

"Gone." There was no sadness. "He never wanted to be married. He couldn't handle the responsibility of a wife and new baby on the way. It lasted three months."

Leon swallowed hard. He had to ask. "Where's the baby?"

She crossed her arms, hugging herself. Her voice was small. "She died. She was born too early and died." Tears dropped on the grass. "I was all alone. Don't you see? I was all alone."

Leon looked into the branches. "That's when Roosevelt took you in, isn't it?"

She nodded and wiped her cheeks with her hand. "My life was a mess, and he gave me a place to stay, a place to work. And he showed me a reason to live. Jesus."

Leon wished he didn't understand. He made one last try.

"You feel grateful. Is that enough?"

She nodded strongly, the old Sarah come back. "Yes, it is. And it's more than gratitude. My faith has changed my life. I used to think of *me* all the time. Now, I think of others. I like that. And I even like the struggle to keep it that way. It makes me stronger." She smiled at him. "You make me struggle, Leon."

"I do?"

"If I would let myself be interested in any man, you'd be the one, Leon. There's good in you, just bursting to get out."

"I'd marry you. You could change me. Make me better."

She shook her head.

Leon knew he was licked. He held out his hand. She hesitated but took it. He pulled her close. Her head fit perfectly against his shoulder.

It would have to be enough.

The new altar table found in Nashville was a beauty. It was walnut with—what Sarah called—Queen Anne legs. The white tablecloth with the torn lace could be tossed away. The curving of the wood grain was pretty by itself.

Leon was left alone to admire it while Sarah went off to make supper. He ran a hand over the smooth surface. It felt as good as it looked. He picked up the wooden cross and placed it in the center, eyeing it from two directions to make sure it was just so.

"Um-um-um, now that is truly an altar fit for a King." Roosevelt had slipped in without Leon knowing.

Leon stepped back so Roosevelt could see it better. "I'm

glad you like it."

"I like that it came from you. But you didn't have to spend your money that way."

Leon shrugged. They both sat in the front pew. Leon's hands kept each other company. He looked away from the cross. "You've guessed everything about me, haven't you? About my past?"

"We all have a past."

"But mine. . .I've been weak."

Roosevelt put a hand on his shoulder. "We all should be stronger. Point is, you *were* strong—in the end. When it counts. We all get tempted now and again."

Like this afternoon with Sarah. . .

Roosevelt sighed loudly. "I get weary sometimes, fighting it."

"You? Fight temptation?"

He snickered. "Oh, yeah."

Leon faced him. "Tell me how."

"This isn't a confession time, Leon."

"But it'll help me."

"Entertain you."

Leon shook his head. "It'll help me feel. . .feel like I'm not alone in fighting it."

Roosevelt looked at him closely. "I suppose you're right about that one. Sometimes a fellow gets discouraged when everybody else runs by, and he's stopped on the track tying his shoe. It helps to know that those others, they've had to stop and tie their shoes a few times, too. Maybe they've even tripped and fell down."

"Have you tripped?"

Roosevelt looked front again. "Tripped hard."

"But you're a preacher."

"Preachers trip, Leon. But this was before. . ."

Leon looked forward, too, hoping to give Roosevelt room. "What did you do?"

"I killed a man."

Leon's head whipped toward him. "What? When?"

"Ten years ago. They say it was self-defense, but. . ." He shook his head.

"Was it?"

"A fight's a fight. I wish I'd done things different."

"Did you go to jail?"

"Not the bars and doors kind."

Leon understood. Even though he'd yet to be in the real kind of jail, he'd done enough wrong that he hadn't been caught for, that he knew the kind of jail Roosevelt was talking about. "Sometimes that kind is worse. No end of sentence. No getting out."

"Not true, Leon. That last part, anyways."

"What do you mean?"

"Jesus gets you out. He's the only one can do it. Died to do it for us."

Leon shook his head. "Not for me."

"Why not?"

" 'Cause I haven't been living right for a long time. I try, but I mess up. Over and over."

Roosevelt faced him. "You think Leon Burke is so special, so bad, that Jesus can't handle you and what you've done?"

"Well, no but—"

"I guarantee you, Jesus did not hang on that cross and

say, 'I'm doing this for everybody else in the world except for Leon Burke.' "

"When you put it that way—"

"There is only one way, Leon." Roosevelt pointed to the cross.

Leon saw a flash. *Oh, no. . .was the cross going to glow again?* He heard Roosevelt talking, but he sounded far away. Then his voice came closer like they were moving together from opposite sides of the room.

". . .can live forever, Leon. Here for awhile, then in etern—" He stopped talking and stared at Leon. "What's wrong?"

Roosevelt. He was sitting beside Roosevelt Hazen. But that's not possible. He's dead. I killed—

Leon whipped his head, looking around the room. The angel-white walls of the Hillside Baptist Church looked back at him. He put his hands to his face. Hands that had killed Roosevelt Hazen. Where was the glowing cross when he'd picked up that concrete block and thrown it at Roosevelt's face? Why didn't God stop him? Why did he ever think he deserved a second chance?

Roosevelt started to get up. "You look sick. Let me get you a drink of—"

Leon pulled him back down. "No. I'm fine. Sit with me, Roosevelt."

"I didn't mean to make you uncomfortable with all my talk about Jesus, Leon. But when you love Him as much as I do, He just splashes out in ordinary conversation. Can't help myself."

Leon shook his head. He didn't need Roosevelt apologizing. He'd wanted to hear. It helped to hear. But now. . .

The Dual Consciousness had taken over. He had to make his decision. He—

"I'm staying."

"What?" Roosevelt blinked twice.

There was nothing for Leon in the future. He'd known this was a one-way trip. He repeated himself, his voice stronger. "I'm staying." It meant so much more than Roosevelt could ever imagine.

"Glad to hear it. We can use you long as you care to stay, Leon. Besides, I'd like to take more time getting to know you."

Time. They would have plenty of time. But for the moment, Leon needed a few moments alone. "I could use that glass of water, if you don't mind."

"Don't mind a bit. I'll be right back." Roosevelt left for the kitchen.

He let himself think for one last time of the future, a future that promised death—Roosevelt's and his own, from the cancer or from jail for Roosevelt's murder. It was a future that was inhabited by a different Leon Burke, a man who'd lived a lifetime of cons, who'd shoved the good part of himself deeper and deeper until he couldn't find it anymore.

The past was fresh and new. And special now that he'd made the choice to be a part of Roosevelt's and Sarah's lives. It was amazing how good people had affected him so strongly. They'd made the difference in his life. Them. . .and God.

Leon still wasn't sure about this Jesus they talked about. But it seemed with every word a part of him woke up. Like it had been there all along, but Leon had been too busy choosing the bad part of life to let it free. And now, more than ever, he needed some of that forgiving Roosevelt had talked about. Now, while the memories of the future were strong and clear.

Leon slipped to his knees, facing the cross on the new altar table. He clasped his hands and held them against his chin. "I don't know the words, Lord, but I want to tell You I'm sorry. I was an evil man. . .but now. . .thank You for giving me this second chance. I promise I'll do better. I promise I'll take time to get to know You. I promise—"

Roosevelt came back, carrying a glass of water. "Here we go. . ."

Leon slipped back on the pew. Roosevelt did a double take but didn't mention what he'd seen. Leon took the water. "Thanks."

Roosevelt sat back down. "Anytime. You look better already." He nodded to the cross. "He has that effect on people."

"I'm counting on it."

Roosevelt's smile touched his eyes that were still dark as olives—and very much alive. "Sarah says supper will be ready in ten minutes."

Leon took a deep breath, tasting the aroma. "Pot roast."

"She knows my favorite—she'll get to know yours, too." He settled into the chair. "Meanwhile, we can just relax and enjoy some time together."

"That sounds perfect."

And it was.

CHAPTER 18

For everything that was written in the past
was written to teach us,
so that through endurance and the encouragement of
the Scriptures we might have hope.

ROMANS 15:4

Cheryl heard whispering. She opened her eyes.

"She's back!"

Before she had time to let her brain log in the familiar voice, Julie rushed toward her. And Pam. Dr. Rodriguez extended his arms, protecting her from their hugs.

"Ladies! Just a moment, please."

The doctor and nurse checked her vitals, removed the IV and other tubes, and lifted off the MRI machine. With help, Cheryl sat up and turned toward Alexander MacMillan.

Somehow his face, more than anyone's, proved she was back.

"Hi, Mac."

"I'm glad you're with us again, Dr. Nickolby."

"Me, too." She meant it.

Julie gave her the once-over. "You feel okay?"

"A little groggy, but not bad. What are you guys doing here?"

Julie took her hand, taking possession. She looked to Mac. "Can we take her somewhere to talk? We're just dying to know what happened."

Wriggens stepped forward. "She has a press conference scheduled, and we need to talk to—"

"But it's not until tomorrow, and we can talk to her later." Mac pointed to the door leading to the hall with its waiting rooms. "Help yourself, ladies."

Pam, Julie, and Cheryl exited the Sphere. Cheryl interrupted her friends' animated questions to turn back to Mac. "Thank you. I appreciate the trip. It was quite. . . enlightening."

"I can hardly wait to hear about it."

Mac had the most marvelous smile. "Oh, you will. You will."

Julie placed Cheryl on the couch between them. Cheryl wriggled, trying to gain some space. "Give me room to breathe, Jules."

She laughed and moved an inch to the side. "I guess I don't want to risk losing you again. Life is not the same without our Cheryl."

Pam put it all in perspective. "Yeah, yeah. But she's back. And I, for one, want to hear all the gory details. How was Jake?"

Cheryl had not had any time to figure out how much to say, and what to keep to herself. These were her best friends. Should she tell them everything?

She began her story.

When Cheryl was nearly finished, Pam fell back into the cushions like she was exhausted. "I can't believe Jake turned out to be such a sleaze. I remember looking up to him. And you said Julie was involved with him? No way."

"I know. When I first saw them together in the entryway of his house, and he kissed—" Cheryl noticed that Julie was looking to the floor, her fingers creasing the hem of her dress. "Jules? Are you all right?"

First she shrugged. Then she shook her head. When she raised her face, she was crying. "I can't believe I did that. I *did* sleep with Jake Carlisle."

"No, you didn't," Pam said.

"But I did."

"You only said you liked him. You asked him to be your boyfriend. You—"

Pam was still incredulous. "You never told us."

Julie's eyes were tragic. "How could I? I was the good one. The forever-virgin. I was the one who kept you guys in line—as much as I could. How could I ever admit *I'd* blown it?"

Pam stood and began to pace. "But we were your best friends."

"I wanted you to love me. I didn't want you to be disappointed in me."

Cheryl pulled Julie close. "We could never be disappointed in you."

"We could have helped you."

Julie sniffed and retrieved a tissue from under the edge of her sleeve. "I got through it. I told my mom, and we prayed about it and—"

Cheryl had to interrupt. "I pray now—because of you."

"What?"

"You told me about God."

"I did?"

Cheryl put a hand on her knee. "When everything was falling apart, after Jake raped me and I saw him with you, I went into a depression. You and Pam came over and. . .and you told me how God was there for me, that He would forgive me and give me strength. And then you gave me your cross necklace because—"

Julie's hand flew to her neck, her fingers touching the gold cross. "What?"

Cheryl pointed. "That cross necklace that you never take off. You gave it to me because I said yes. Yes to you and yes to God."

Julie's forehead dipped, and instant tears formed. "You said yes?"

"Your words changed me, Julie. They changed me then, and they've changed me now. I brought that back with me."

Julie unhooked the necklace and handed it to Cheryl.

"No, no. I didn't tell you that story so you'd give me your neck—"

Julie closed Cheryl's hand over it. "I want you to have it. I should have given it to you long ago."

"You did. This time."

Julie shrugged. "Maybe going back to find God is why you were chosen to win the Time Lottery. You were supposed to get another chance to hear God's message."

Pam shook her head. "It's a lottery, Julie. A game of chance. God doesn't—"

She clasped her hands together. "But He does. He has control of everything. Don't kid yourself. He did the choosing. And look at the result. He finally got Cheryl's attention."

"That He did."

Julie tucked the tissue back into her sleeve. "For years I've thought about talking to you about Him, but the time never seemed right. I put it off and off—" Her face was stricken. "You had to go back in the past to hear about Him because I was too chicken and lazy to do it here."

"It wasn't your responsibility to tell me about God."

"Then whose responsibility was it?"

Cheryl had no answer.

Pam interrupted the silence. "So, was going back worth it?"

"Absolutely. The main thing I learned is that choices count. They all have consequences—good or bad. But one choice doesn't necessarily have to determine our whole life. People can change—even now."

"How do you want to change?"

Cheryl stood and faced them. Their faces were decades older, but their hearts were the same—if not larger with the continued friendship of many years. "I went into my past looking for commitment. Instead I found that commitment for the sake of commitment is just as wrong as living a loose life. If the motives aren't right, then both alternatives are wrong." She ran her hands through her hair, which was chin length once again. "I've given up men."

"What?"

"You?"

She raised a hand to stop their questions. "Let me put it another way. I'm not going to sleep around anymore. Am I so needy for love that I have to hunt for it with every Tom, Dick, and Harry? Am I so sexually desperate that I can't control myself?" She laughed. "Control, maybe too much control? Somehow that's the key. I need to stop trying to control other people and situations. I need to learn to relinquish control."

Julie smiled. "To God?"

Cheryl shrugged. "I'm still new at this, but yes, I think I'm supposed to relinquish control to Him. I've done it my way for the first half of my life, I figure it's only fair to give Him a shot at the second half."

"He'll be happy to hear that."

Cheryl sighed. "I hope so. Because this isn't easy for me."

Pam shook her head. "Cheryl Nickolby, giving up men. I'll believe it when I see it."

"I'm giving up *using* men, Pam. But I'm still open, if the right one came—"

There was a tap on the door. Mac came in, carrying Cheryl's clothes. "I thought you might like these."

Cheryl laughed with the memories of her seventies garb still fresh in her mind. She made a peace sign. "Peace, flower power, love baby." She took her clothes. "Did you need to talk to me?"

"Not yet. Enjoy yourselves. We expect to know about Phoebe Thurgood's decision shortly, and then soon after, we'll know about Leon."

"Leon?"

Pam explained. "Leon Burke killed Roosevelt Hazen and took his place. He was a bum—"

Cheryl sucked in a breath. "Leon Burke?"

"You act like you know him."

"I met him! In the past. He was a bum—a transient." She turned to her friends. "Remember that one night when we nearly ran over the man lying on the side of the road?"

Julie put a hand to her mouth, thinking. "The guy we drove to the shelter?"

"That's him." Cheryl turned to Mac. "Could your Leon be our Leon?"

"Perhaps."

Cheryl thought back to the lottery winner in the cheap blue suit. He had been so quiet. She tried to remember his face. It was much older, more haggard, but. . . "It was him. The Roosevelt I met looked like the Leon in my past."

"How odd to have your lives intersect like that."

"Sounds like a miracle," Julie said.

Cheryl couldn't disagree.

Colin Thurgood had tried to avoid the eyes of Mac and Wriggens. He was not going to tolerate any abuse from these *administrators* who thought they were better than he was. If Wriggens hadn't been such a coward, none of this would be happening.

He sat on the chair at the perimeter of the Sphere and crossed his legs, trying to look nonchalant. His foot gyrated wildly, and he forced it to stop. He had things to do. He really hadn't had the time to waste two days here, yet actually, staying over to meet his celebrity wife as she stepped off the Time Lottery adventure had been a good excuse to avoid those who were beating down his door demanding money. *Give me time. Everything will be taken care of as soon as I get back from Kansas City.*

He'd even been approached by two tabloids wanting to buy the story—his, if she stayed behind, and hers, if she came back. The offers had not been enough to cover his debts, but if he let them dangle a bit longer, the price would go up.

So he *did* have options, but the best scenario was still if Phoebe didn't come back. He just hoped he wouldn't have trouble collecting the insurance money from the Time Lottery's ethics police.

He looked at his watch. Mac had said they expected her back—or not back—soon. There was no exact amount of time that the Dual Consciousness would stay in effect. They said it would fade gradually in the past. It could be as long as two days before they'd know for sure whether she was staying in her—

There was a flurry of activity from the technicians who were manning the console. "She's waking up!" Colin moved toward the bed holding Phoebe's sleeping body. His stomach grabbed. He closed his eyes, but only for a moment. He had to see. His whole future depended on the next few moments. *No, no. . .don't wake up, don't—*

Suddenly, Phoebe was awake. She sucked in a breath and

opened her eyes.

There was clapping all around. Except from him. No clapping from Colin. He said a cuss word under his breath. The doctor and nurses rushed to her side. Colin stood back, unsure what he should do.

"Welcome back, Mrs. Thurgood," said Mac as the medical people fiddled with some tubes and removed the machine around her head so she could move.

She blinked a few times. She looked around the room, and Colin could tell she was remembering where she should be. Their eyes met. He smiled in the way he always smiled to disarm her. He expected her to smile, to hold out a hand and tell him how glad she was to be home.

She didn't do that. She kept her eyes locked on his. With help, she sat up. She eased her legs off the side of the bed. He looked away, then realized he should return her gaze. But he didn't like the look of determination in her eyes. There was no longing there, no relief.

She stood on wobbly legs before him. "Hello, Colin."

Wasn't she going to hug him? He had never been a hugger, but Phoebe always hugged. Hugged too much. It was his turn to say something. "Glad you're back, Phoebe."

She sighed and nodded. "It was not an easy decision."

Colin couldn't believe his ears. Although he'd wanted her to stay in the past, to think that she'd *wanted* to stay. . . that she liked it better. . . "That's a rude thing to say."

She considered this a moment then looked at Mac. "Hello, Mr. MacMillan."

"How are you feeling?"

"Okay, I think." She glanced at Colin. "Is there someplace

my husband and I can talk?"

Wriggens stepped forward. "We need to talk to you, too, Mrs. Thurgood. Debrief—"

Mac motioned toward the door. "Follow me."

Once they were settled in a waiting room, Phoebe insisted on sitting. You'd think she would want to stand after lying around so long. Colin did *not* sit. Instead, he paced. "What do you mean saying—in front of all those people—that it wasn't an easy decision. That was beyond rude, Phoebe. That was uncalled for."

She looked up at him. "Perhaps. But I don't think you can expect eloquence the moment I come out of a coma."

Good point. "Why *did* you come back?"

"Speaking of rude."

"You know what I mean."

She started to speak, then stopped. She patted the chair beside her. Reluctantly, he sat. She took his hand. "I learned so much in the past."

"Like what?"

She looked down. She seemed fascinated with her hands, turning them over and over. "It was nice being young again." She glanced around the room. "Where are the children?"

"At their homes."

She nodded, once. "That's probably best."

"What's that supposed to mean?"

She folded her arms. "We have some talking to do, Colin. Things aren't going to be the same."

"Why not?"

"Because I'm not the same."

"No, apparently you're not. And I'm not sure I like it."

"Tough."

Colin blinked. His wife, Phoebe Winston Thurgood, saying *tough*? He had no idea what Phoebe was up to, but it couldn't be good. He stood, taking her hand. "Let's go. We can talk about it later."

She sighed and allowed him to move her toward the door. He opened it. Wriggens met them in the hall. "You can't just leave."

Colin scarred him with a look. "And why not?"

Mac joined them and answered. "We need to have a short debriefing and then tomorrow there will be a press conference. We are understandably curious about your experience."

"Did the others come back?" Phoebe asked.

"Dr. Nickolby did, but we still haven't heard from Leon."

"Leon?"

Mac waved the question away. "Roosevelt Hazen. . .it's a long story."

Colin wasn't going to let them wriggle out of this one. "Some guy murdered Hazen and took his place."

"Mr. Thurgood, that is none of your affair."

Colin pointed a finger at Wriggens. "You guys run a shoddy operation. And I, for one, am going to tell the world—"

In one quick movement, Wriggens was in his face, his voice low. "I gave you the money back and you *will* be qu—"

"What's this about money?" Phoebe asked.

Colin tried to pull her past them. "Nothing, Phoebe. Let's—"

Mac stepped forward. "Your husband wanted to collect your insurance money, and he also tried to buy his own trip into his past."

Colin snarled. "Quiet!" He changed to a smile. "You don't need to bring that up. . ."

Mac crossed his arms and bounced on his heels, looking like a smug know-it-all. "I think there is every need to bring it up."

"You guys are despicable. I could sue."

"Try it."

Phoebe faced Colin. "What are you up to this time?"

She made it sound like he was a little boy who'd gotten caught snitching a cookie. "A lot has happened while you were gone, Phoebe."

"Such as?"

"I've had a few financial losses that need to be covered and—"

"And you wanted my insurance money to do it?"

She made it sound so cold. "We're in deep trouble."

"*We* are not in trouble; you are. That's one of the things we have to talk about. The issue of *we*. There never was a marriage partnership from your point of view. I went through life thinking *we*, while you only thought of *me*—meaning you, Colin. You only thought of yourself. You're still only thinking of yourself."

Colin couldn't grasp what she was saying. He and she. They had a partnership. He needed—

He didn't let himself complete the thought. He didn't need anybody.

Phoebe turned to the others. "How was he going to

get my insurance money?"

Mac spoke for the group, looking way too pleased with himself. "He wanted to go back into 1969 to convince you to stay. But since that's impossible. . ."

Phoebe stared at Colin. A tear ran down her cheek. "You wanted to leave me in the past? You were willing to sacrifice me for money? To pay a few bills?"

"I wasn't going to *leave* you." *I was going to get you to leave me.* "And it's not just a few bills, Phoebe. There were—" He stopped before he dug himself any deeper. He fingered his diamond tie tack. He needed some luck right now.

"I came back for the family, Colin. For the children." She flipped away a tear. "But you aren't going to change a whit, are you?"

Colin didn't see the point.

She sighed. "Part of this is my fault. I went along, I allowed you to relinquish your integrity for success. I didn't tell you no."

"You've always been a big help to me."

She shook her head. "No. I didn't help you, and I didn't help me. By letting you cheat I cheated both of us. I cheated you out of becoming a decent man, and I cheated myself out of being married to someone who loved me for me, not for what I could do to help his career."

Suddenly, Colin understood. "You found someone else in the past! You had an affair."

"Yes, I found someone, but no, I did not have an affair. I had something you cannot fathom. I had a relationship."

He rolled his eyes. "A touchy-feely term."

Her breathing was heavy. She turned toward Mac. "Can

we go have our debriefing now?"

"Very soon. I'll take you to a room." He took her arm and led her down the hall.

"Phoebe?" Colin said. "What are you doing?"

She turned to face him. Her smile was as cunning and deadly as the ones he had perfected. "I'm going on, Colin. I'm going on."

Wriggens checked his watch and then looked back at Leon Burke's body. "He's not coming back."

Mac nodded.

Dr. Rodriguez spoke up. "We can't be certain for another twenty-four hours when the serum fully wears off and the Dual Consciousness disappears."

"Then he can't come back," Mac said.

Wriggens glared at him. "Thank you for that bit of good cheer to brighten our day."

"Sorry." Mac wanted to add, *I'm glad he's staying in the past,* but didn't feel like riling Wriggens right now. "I *do* think it's time I get the others debriefed. They're eager to have a chance to wind down so they can be fresh for the press tomorrow."

"Speaking of which, what do you plan on revealing about Leon Burke?"

"The truth."

"You can't do that."

"What do you suggest?" Mac asked.

"This is your mess to deal with, Mac. This is where you earn your big bucks. Make us sound good."

Your support is overwhelming.

Mac turned toward the Sphere's exit, then had a thought. "Someone should stay here with Leon in case. . ."

"He graces us with his presence?" Wriggens snickered. "Fat chance. But the medical people will be here, won't you, Doctor?"

Dr. Rodriguez nodded. "I'll stay as long as I'm needed."

Mac spoke up. "What about tomorrow? If he doesn't come back, his body is going to die. He has no family, no one to—"

"Hold his hand?" Wriggens said.

Mac wanted to punch him. No way should this man be head of the Time Lottery—and if Mac had his way, he would not be for much longer. "I'll come back and stay with him."

"Me, too," Dr. Rodriguez said. The nurses nodded.

"Well then," Wriggens said. "You won't need me."

I couldn't have said it better myself.

Cheryl and Phoebe sat in the room that would be used for the debriefing. They waited for Mac to join them—with or without Leon.

Cheryl wanted to go home. She knew debriefing and meeting the press was necessary—and there would be the inevitable interview shows, but right now, all she really wanted was home. She squirmed in her chair.

"You, too?" Phoebe asked.

"Home-itis. It's been fun but. . ." She looked to the socialite. She looked different somehow. Less like a doormat. "Where's your lovely hubby?"

"Probably pouting somewhere."

"Why?"

"He wanted me to stay in the past. He wanted the insurance money to pay off some debts."

Cheryl gawked. "You're not kidding, are you?"

"Unfortunately, no."

Cheryl clapped her hands once. "I'd leave the guy. Pronto. He obviously doesn't want to be with you."

Phoebe sighed. "I know. And I must say that's a prevalent thought right now."

"What's stopping you?"

Phoebe searched the ceiling for her answer. "He's quite the pitiful soul. I want to do the right thing."

"And you don't know if that right thing means divorcing him?"

"I've made so many mistakes. . .I don't want to make another one." Her smile was wistful. "I went back to my past and found the integrity and backbone I'd misplaced the first time around. But even those things can get used badly. Like just a few moments ago, I *really* wanted to tell Colin I was leaving him." She grinned. "And oh, it would have felt so good saying it—even if I don't go through with it."

Cheryl laughed. "So are you leaving your husband?"

Phoebe sighed and looked to the ceiling. "He's a bad influence."

Cheryl laughed. "I was involved with that kind of man, too."

"I can't blame it all on Colin. But when I did things his way. . .my grandma had a saying, 'Don't cooperate with—' "

"—the world!" Cheryl turned to face Phoebe. "I know that line!"

"Really?"

Cheryl turned forward again. "Actually, I heard it ages ago, but I'd forgotten about it until my little dip into the past. Then it popped up again. In fact, Leon—the other winner who's an imposter—was the one who told me about it."

"I heard about him. He took Roosevelt's place somehow?"

"I don't know all the details. I'm sure we'll hear. But the amazing thing is that I met Leon Burke in *my* past. And he repeated that quote."

"Good wisdom spreads, I guess. Actually, I've shared that quote with a lot of people over the years. It always seems to come to me at just the right moment."

"Well, it was given to me—twice. The first time was right after my mom married her third or fourth husband. I was upset and wandering the streets of San Francisco. I came across this lady who—"

Phoebe's eyes turned wild. "Were you wearing a long granny-style dress? Pink?"

Cheryl looked hard at Phoebe. "Was that you?"

"Haight-Ashbury? We had a discussion about love—"

"—and commitment."

"This is too strange."

Cheryl's mind raced. "No! It's marvelous. Miraculous. You didn't happen to share this bit of wisdom with Leon prior to 1973, did you?"

"I don't know. I could have."

"I think he was from Tennessee."

Phoebe tapped her lower lip. "My dad traveled through Tennessee once. Selling stuff. Mom and I went with him for awhile. I guess it's possible."

"We'll have to ask him when he gets back. Wouldn't that be fantastic, if the three of us somehow intersected in each other's lives and heard the same bit of wisdom?"

Phoebe shivered. "It's too strange."

Cheryl shook her head. "Nah. It's perfect. And I, for one, don't think it's a coincidence."

Phoebe bit her lip as if she wanted to say something but wasn't sure if she should.

"What?"

"Did you have an encounter with. . . Did you find yourself thinking about. . ."

"Phoebe, spill it."

"Did you find God in your past?"

Cheryl's memory flipped to her conversation with Julie. "As a matter of fact. . ."

"Me, too. I met a man. . ." She looked to the floor. "A godly man. Not at all like you know who."

Suddenly, Cheryl's thoughts merged into one salient point. "Do you think God had anything to do with us winning this thing? Going back? Meeting? With us finding *Him?*"

Phoebe shook her head no, but Cheryl could tell by her face that she was thinking yes. "But we're just ordinary. . .at least I'm ordinary. I certainly haven't done anything special to gain God's interest. In fact, most of my life, I've pretty much ignored Him."

"Then maybe He wanted to get your attention. My attention."

"Sending us back in time is kind of drastic."

"And I'm kind of stubborn."

"Yeah. Me, too."

Cheryl sighed. Her experience had been powerful in its own right, but to think that God had set it up so that Julie would tell her about God—and she would listen. . . To think that a scientific discovery like the Time Lottery might fit into God's purposes. . . Another thought flashed. "I've got an addendum to your grandma's wisdom."

"What is it?"

Cheryl smiled with complete confidence. "Don't cooperate with the world—cooperate with God."

"That pretty much sums it up, doesn't it?"

"You betcha. It's per—" She saw Mac coming toward them. "There's Mac. He's alone."

"Leon stayed behind?"

"It appears so."

"So we'll never know for sure if we're all linked."

"We know."

Phoebe hesitated, then nodded. "You're right. We know."

Mac and Dr. Rodriguez sat in chairs around the comatose body of Leon Burke. The doctor checked Leon's pulse. "It's slowing. I'd say he has only a few more minutes."

They turned their heads as Bob and a few other technicians came into the Sphere, changing shifts. Mac turned his attention back to Leon. "He did the logical thing—he stayed in his new, better life."

"Either way, Roosevelt Hazen is dead," Dr. Rodriguez said.

Mac nodded.

Bob came close, his voice lowered respectfully. "Don't be so down. I have some good news."

"We could use some."

Bob cleared his throat and pulled a paper out of his lab coat pocket. "Last night I couldn't sleep, so I decided to do some more research about Leon Burke. I found out some new stuff about his life—the first time around."

"What kind of *stuff?*"

Bob nodded. "The first time around, Leon stole Roosevelt's savings, but he was eventually caught and sent to jail."

"We knew that."

"But what you may not know is that soon after the crime, the Hillside Baptist Church blew up, killing Sarah Hudson and six others."

"How did it blow up?"

"A faulty furnace. I read some article that quoted Roosevelt as saying that a lot of things around the church needed fixing, but that he wasn't very good at that sort of thing. One of the bigger to-dos was fixing the furnace. But by the time the police caught Leon, most of Roosevelt's stolen savings had been spent. Roosevelt was going to use that money to fix the furnace."

Mac was beginning to follow the gist of it. "Maybe that's what drove Roosevelt to the streets."

"Could be."

Mac thought a moment more. "But if Leon's doing better in the past. If he's changed the kind of person he was. . ."

"Maybe he isn't conning them out of the money," Bob said. "Maybe the furnace is getting fixed. Maybe—"

Mac sighed. "We'll never know. That's the hardest part in having a winner stay behind. We'll never know what happened."

Bob shrugged. "I heard they're working on that. They've got a prototype of some kind of surveillance device that can watch. . ."

"Maybe. Someday. But until then, we can only use conjecture, and hope for the—"

Suddenly, Leon sucked in a breath. They all stood. He let it out. They held their breaths, waiting, but Leon breathed no more.

Dr. Rodriguez checked the vital signs. "He's gone."

Mac looked around the Sphere. Everyone was hushed. He wanted to say a few words to mark Leon's passing, but in this corporate setting he knew it wouldn't be appropriate.

But it wouldn't be appropriate not to. He raised his voice so all could hear. "I'm going to say a prayer now. If you'd like, you can bow your heads." He lowered his own. "Lord, the body of Leon Burke has passed on in this time, but due to Your miracles, it lives on in another time. Help Leon come to know You so that he can spend eternity with You in heaven."

There was a sprinkling of amens.

EPILOGUE

Be joyful always; pray continually;
give thanks in all circumstances,
for this is God's will for you in Christ Jesus.

1 THESSALONIANS 5:16–18

Sarah Hudson held her hand in front of the heating register. "Leon, feel this."

Leon put his hand near hers. "It's cold air."

"Exactly." She turned to Roosevelt. "The furnace isn't working again, Roosevelt. We really need to get it fixed."

Roosevelt scratched his chin. "I was wondering whether we should hold off and use some of the money to help folks get through Thanksgiving. Maybe have a big Thanksgiving dinner for all the congregation—invite the whole neighborhood and—"

"No," Leon said. The word had come bursting out. "It's important we replace the furnace. Now." He was as surprised as Sarah and Roosevelt by the power behind his words.

Roosevelt stopped with one arm still in his jacket. "Mercy, Leon. What's got into you?"

Leon didn't know. But he couldn't shake an odd sense that this was important. He took hold of Roosevelt's arm. "We have to replace it right away. Don't ask me how I know, just trust me. This one time in your life, trust me."

"I'm sure the furnace can wait, Leon. Maybe we'll get enough in the collection plate to help out at Thanksgiving *and* fix the—"

Leon grabbed Roosevelt's wrist, squeezing hard enough for the preacher to wince. He felt as if a time bomb were ticking away inside him. "Listen to me, Roosevelt. It's important we replace the furnace. It's dangerous. It might blow up."

"How do you know that?" Sarah looked at him funny. He'd told her about his past life. She'd said it didn't matter as long as he was doing good now, but he could tell it would take awhile for her to feel easy about him.

"I just know. Remember, *I* checked it out. I told you it's in bad shape. You don't want it to blow and have people get hurt, do you? People like Sarah. . .and Marco?"

The lines in Roosevelt's forehead deepened. "Of course I don't want anyone to get hurt." Roosevelt stared at him, as if trying to figure what he'd been drinking. Then he nodded. "I've never seen you like this before, Leon. If you feel so strongly about the furnace, I'm not the one to tell you different."

Leon shook Roosevelt's hand and kissed Sarah on the

cheek. "Thank you, thank you. You won't be sorry."

Leon felt better. He didn't know why, but he felt much better.

Phoebe set a moving box on the dining room table. Things had not worked out as planned. Although her resolve to stick with her marriage had not waned, in the end, Colin had been the one to do the leaving.

Oh, she'd wanted to leave him, and according to her friends, she had every reason to do so. But Grandma's saying kept creeping back into her thoughts, so she'd sought the godly counsel of the pastor of her new church. Surely God had an opinion about all this.

It turned out He did. God hated divorce, and as a believer she was supposed to make an effort to stick with her marriage. She could be a light to Colin. Maybe even help him turn to God by her example.

She'd had every intention to try, but when she found out about the mistress he'd been keeping for three years (the woman—Rosie—had left a message on their answering machine asking if the cruise was still on even though Phoebe had come back), she'd felt the fight go out of her. Phoebe had confronted Colin about it, but then, surprisingly, *he* had been the one to leave *her*, citing how he didn't like the change that had come over her. "This God stuff is very unappealing, Phoebe. You never minded my flings before. . ."

Minded? How could she mind what she hadn't let herself see? Sigh and double sigh.

So, the divorce was moving forward. She took solace in

a verse Pastor Bill had told her. First Corinthians 7:15—"But if the unbeliever leaves, let him do so. A believing man or woman is not bound in such circumstances; God has called us to live in peace."

Peace sounded good. Real good. And having second thoughts did her *no* good.

Phoebe rolled a crystal goblet along the strip of bubble wrap, taped it tight, and tucked the ends into the top of the glass. She set it in the box. Packing to move was tedious work she usually left to professionals. But not this time. This time she needed to touch every possession and say good-bye.

Although she was getting the house in the divorce settlement, she didn't want it. All the carefully decorated rooms screamed of a time when their creation had been her only solace. She had hidden in this luxury, and she was not going to hide anymore, nor simply move the elements from one location to another. She needed to be cleansed. Purged. It was the only way she could truly start over.

She had vowed to take with her only those possessions that meant something to her history, instead of those items bought to impress. The crystal she was wrapping *would* go with her. It was not her best set, but it had been Grandma Winston's. It had been Phoebe's since they'd moved Grandma into the nursing home so many decades ago. . . .

Phoebe was moving into a two-bedroom bungalow across the bay in Sausalito. Her new house, though small, had been expensive—as was the fate of all bay-view properties—but it was modest compared to the opulence she had lived with before. The same couple had lived in the house for fifty-two years. It needed remodeling. Although she didn't require luxuries, she did want an updated kitchen and a bathtub with a shower. Her main request was going to be a bigger balcony. She planned on spending a lot of time out there. Otherwise there were only two bedrooms. One bedroom for her, and one guest room for the kids when they came to visit.

The kids. . .she'd given up happiness in the past with Peter in order to be here for them. Had they appreciated her sacrifice?

Nope.

When Phoebe had confided in Suzanne that she'd met someone special in 1969 but had returned for *her* sake, Suzanne had said, "Gee, Mom. That was dumb. I would've stayed."

Suzanne would have stayed. Thomas would have stayed. Colin *certainly* would have stayed. But they were not like her. Although she was often wistful about her decision, it was a wistfulness brought on by satisfaction. She'd done the right thing. There was comfort in that—even if it wasn't the comfort of Peter Greenfield's arms.

At least the Phoebe in that timeline had gotten to marry Peter. Lucky dog. She wondered what that Phoebe was doing now.

She realized that, in many ways, her children did not deserve her sacrifice. They were selfish, egotistical, and consumed with being consumers. They took after their parents.

But one of their parents had changed and wasn't going to allow such behavior anymore. Phoebe would give them love, support, and advice, but the bottomless checkbook was out of business. At least on her part. But she wouldn't be able to control Colin, and she was sure he would distribute plenty of cash in lieu of love. However, with his financial setbacks, that might not be an option.

She held a goblet up to the light. There was a chip in the foot. Phoebe ran her finger across it. The piece was still beautiful. The chip was proof it had been used for many years. Just like Phoebe. She laughed at the thought. She, too, had a few chips, proof that she had been used many years. It had been nice to be young again, chipless. Oh well. . .

The doorbell rang. She checked her watch. It was time for her appointment. She ran a hand through her hair and answered the door.

"You must be Mrs. Thurgood?"

Phoebe's heart raced to her throat. No words were possible.

"Ma'am? Are you all right?"

She nodded but wasn't sure.

The man looked to the ground, then up again. "I'm here to talk about the remodeling?"

She laughed, not caring if he understood why. That would come. That would definitely come.

She held out her hand. "Nice to meet you. I'm Phoebe Thurgood."

His blue eyes were just like she remembered. "Nice to meet you, too. My name is Peter. Peter Greenfield."

Cheryl tossed her keys on the entry table and lunged for the phone before the answering machine picked up.

"Hello! I'm here!"

"Glad to hear it."

She smiled at the voice. "Well, well, well. Alexander

MacMillan? Is that you?"

"Yes, it is, Dr. Nickolby."

"Are you checking up on us winners?"

"Yes, I am."

She sank into a chair, enjoying herself. "I'm flattered."

"I've seen you on television. You give a mighty interview."

"People love a woman of scandal. By the way, thanks for trying to take care of my job while I was gone. I should have known my past indiscretions would rise up to haunt me one day. A man scorned, you know."

"I heard you say you've begged off men."

She sat up straighter in the chair. "I want the lessons of my past to steep awhile. But I'm not sure it's a permanent condition."

"That's good to hear."

"What are you implying, Mac?"

There was a moment of silence between them. She hoped she hadn't offended him.

"As far as I can tell, you still have not had a relationship with a man of integrity. You belittle yourself by settling for less."

"I don't like to settle."

"You don't have to. I'd like to be your friend."

"Are you offering this service to Phoebe, too?"

A pause.

"I'd love to be your friend, Mac. I've rarely had a male friend. It will be a new experience."

"Glad to be of service."

"But you live in Kansas City. I live in Boulder."

"Mere logistics."

"We're both busy people."

"Indeed we are. And I have a son."

"What's his name?"

"Andrew. He's five."

A nice man with integrity. A man with a son. A friend. What a novel idea. "Let's do this thing, Mac. Let's be friends."

"I'm glad you agree."

"How could I not? I have the feeling that everything will work out—given time."

The call from Wriggens came unexpectedly.

"It's time, Mac."

Mac looked across the den at Andrew, who was holding up two bedtime storybooks for Mac to choose from. Mac pointed to the one on the left. "Time for what, John?"

"What else? Time for you to go back in time."

Mac nearly dropped the phone. He clenched it between chin and shoulder as Andrew climbed onto his lap, carrying the book.

"Mac? Did you hear me?"

"I heard you."

One moment grew to two. "You don't sound thrilled," Wriggens said. "This is what you've hoped for. Right?"

Mac couldn't lie. "Yes."

"Look, Mac, though you and I don't always agree, I still pay my debts. A new five-year contract is on your desk, awaiting your signature. And your chance to use the technology is waiting for you, too."

The words flew out. "I don't want it."

"What? Oh, you mean you don't want it now? I suppose we can wait a little while. But we *are* getting ready for the next lottery, so time's tight."

Mac looked at the opening page of the book: *The Tale of Three Trees.* It had been Holly's favorite.

Andrew put his finger on the words and recited the first line from memory, as if he were actually reading: "Once upon a mountaintop, three little trees stood and dreamed of what they wanted to be when they grew up. . . ."

"No, John," Mac said into the phone. "I don't want it at all. Ever."

"Don't be ridiculous. It was in our original agreement. You did the work. You're due."

Andrew looked up at him. "Read it, Daddy. Read!"

Mac was amazed at how simple the decision was.

"If you'll excuse me, John, I need to hang up now. It appears I'm needed right here."

The time has come," he said.
"The kingdom of God is near.
Repent and believe the good news!"

MARK 1:15

TIME LOTTERY BIBLE VERSES

PROLOGUE:	Time/Ecclesiastes 3:1
ONE:	Hope/Job 33:28
TWO:	Time/Ecclesiastes 9:11; Wisdom/Proverbs 2:10
THREE:	Hope/Proverbs 13:12
FOUR:	Worry/Matthew 6:34; Sin/John 8:7
FIVE:	Hope/Job 11:17–18
SIX:	Chosen/John 15:16
SEVEN:	Temptation/1 Corinthians 10:13
EIGHT:	Hardship/Job 2:10; Help/Psalm 70:1
NINE:	Motives/Proverbs 16:2
TEN:	Temptation/Matthew 26:41
ELEVEN:	Conformity/Romans 12:2
TWELVE:	Cunning/Psalm 64:6
THIRTEEN:	Authority/Romans 13:3; Trials/James 1:2–3; Work/Acts 20:35; Hope/Psalm 121:all
FOURTEEN:	Justice/Isaiah 1:17
FIFTEEN:	Protection/Psalm 27:1; Relatives/1 Timothy 5:8 Troubles/Job 36:15–16 (CEV); God's Light/Micah 7:8
SIXTEEN:	God's support/Isaiah 41:10 God's support/Romans 8:31
SEVENTEEN:	Love/Jeremiah 31:3 Relatives/1 Timothy 5:8
EIGHTEEN:	Fate/Romans 15:4
EPILOGUE:	Gratitude/I Thessalonians 5:16–18; Divorce/1 Corinthians 7:15; Good News/Mark 1:15

ACKNOWLEDGMENTS

This is the most complicated book I've ever written. I'm no science fiction aficionado, and I have to admit the technology of this book was often beyond me (I'm glad my characters understood it). Ordinary people, that's what I write about. Add a few extraordinary circumstances, and I'm set. But time travel? Now *that* was a challenge. Luckily, I had some wonderful people to help me.

A big thank-you to Mike Nappa, the editor who had the guts to say, "Let's do it." This book has been in my head, heart, and computer for ten years. Thank you, Mike, for setting it free. And a very special thank-you to Jeff Gerke (a.k.a. Jefferson Scott: *Operation Firebrand),* who spent hours helping me with the final edit. The amazing way your mind works is a thing to behold! I truly could not have done it without you. Thanks also to Liz Duckworth for her keen insights during the preliminary phases of editing.

Then there are those writer friends and normal friends (ha!) who let me pick their brains as I tried to figure out how time travel could work. First the authors: Randy Ingermanson *(The Fifth Man),* Kathy Tyers *(The Firebird Trilogy),* Colleen Coble *(Wyoming),* and Clay Jacobsen *(Interview with the Devil).* Your encouragement and imaginations are much appreciated. Any scientific impossibilities and inconsistencies are my own.

Then the normal people (I use that term loosely). . . I will never forget coming to rehearsal for my octet, "Seeds of Faith," where we ended up brainstorming how time travel might work. Who knew you people had such warped minds? So to Dallas, Liz, Kathryn, Linda, Nancy, Marilyn, Jill, Debbie, and Sue, thanks for letting your imaginations run wild. It helped. And thanks to everyone who listened to me ramble about *what if. . . ?*

A special acknowledgment to my husband, Mark. I first started writing this book in 1992 when being published was only a dream. My office was a corner in our unfinished basement. There I was, down in that dusty, cobweb dungeon, typing away, while you handled our kids (ages 14, 11, and 7). For that time, and for all the times since when you hung in there while I escaped to the worlds in my head, I thank you. And love you.

Above all, I thank God for not letting this story die. While other manuscripts were set aside and deemed practice, this one held on and would not go away. It's been through more metamorphoses than a butterfly, and it often made me want to scream, yet I wouldn't change a moment. As always, You know best.

ALSO FROM BARBOUR PUBLISHING

Operation: Firebrand
by Jefferson Scott
ISBN 1-58660-586-0

Former Navy SEAL Jason Kromer is appointed leader of Operation: Firebrand, a covert operations team specializing in nonlethal missions of mercy. Its first challenge: a winter rescue of orphaned children made homeless by Russian rebels.

The Silence
by Jim Kraus
ISBN 1-59310-162-7

Global catastropes throw the world into mass panic. . .and virtual silence. A solar storm burns communication satellites and computers. Earthquakes shake North America. Is it the end of the world?

Chayatocha
by Shane Johnson
ISBN 1-59310-051-5

One hundred forty years ago, pioneers traveling to the American West faced a rugged and dangerous journey. But when Daniel Paradine, his family, and a small band of fellow travelers guide their wagons onto a treacherous mountain detour, no one is prepared for the evil that awaits them.

Gideon's Dawn
by Michael D. Warden
ISBN 1-58660-725-1

Two thousand years after High Lord Gideon unleashed a corrupting perversion in the Inherited Lands, another Gideon has appeared—though no one knows his origin.

Available wherever books are sold.